The Cinderella Pact

**Center Point
Large Print**

**This Large Print Book carries the
Seal of Approval of N.A.V.H.**

For Lisa, of course

For Lisa, of course

The Fabulous Belinda Apple's
Guide to Indulging
Your Inner Cinderella

- Take that photo of you as a little girl off your mother's refrigerator. Tape it to your bathroom mirror. Admire how happy she is, how sparkling. Be her, again.
- Buy a tiara. Admit that it looks good on you. Fantastic, in fact. Wear it whenever.
- Take a personal assessment test. Do you have what it takes to be a fairy princess? Do you feel peas? Prick your fingers? Kiss talking frogs? On second thought . . .
- Believe it. Be it. Maybe that means more exercise, fewer calories, Swedish skin care. Or maybe it just means realizing that you're worth being treated like royalty.
- Remember that you don't need a prince to be Cinderella, and that Prince Charming was nothing but an icky foot fetishist.
- Find your fairy godmother. Or godsister. Or godgirlfriend. You know who she is. Thank her. Buy her a special gift—some perfume, flowers, tickets to Hunk-O-Mania.
- Stick with the program! We know it's hard treating yourself like royalty. Keep in mind that eventually

you will rise to meet your destiny. It'll be worth it. If you don't think so, ask that little girl taped to your bathroom mirror. Remember, you're changing for her.

- Act like Cinderella. Trill while you do the dishes. Invite birds to sit on your fingers, chipmunks to nestle in the folds of your skirts. Do not mind that the neighbors have called your relatives, expressing concern. Pity them, for they know not that you are a woman of noble birth kept captive among commoners.

- Look like Cinderella. Start with your hair and your feet while your body catches up. Become a stunning blonde or a sultry brunette. Get your brows done. Your pores minimized. Your wrinkles eliminated. Treat yourself to the most fabulous shoes you can afford.

- Unveil your inner Cinderella. Step into your new, glittering, body-hugging dress with the plunging neckline. Put up your hair. Slip on great shoes and, finally, add your tiara. Smile to the girl in the mirror, who will be smiling back. Tell her you did it! Feel the joy of accomplishment, the thrill of being glamorous. And now, let the whole world see the Cinderella you've kept hidden. Her pumpkin carriage has been waiting for far too long.

Chapter One

We are all Cinderellas, no matter what our size. This is what I, Nola Devlin, fervently believe.

I believe that within every one of us is a woman of undiscovered beauty, a woman who is charming and talented and light of heart. I believe that all we need is a fairy godmother to dust us off and bring out our potential and, while she's at it, turn the rats in our lives into coachmen.

I don't know about the glass slipper, though. That seems to me to be a design flaw.

Perhaps it was my fascination with Cinderella that brought me to a town named Princeton. Princeton is, in fact, a magical kingdom with shady, tree-lined streets and, at its center, a big castle of a university complete with Tudor turrets and courtyards of lush green lawns.

There are even a few genuine princes who have come to study here, honing diplomatic skills they will later use to seduce buxom snow bunnies on the Italian Alps. Unfortunately, these princes tend to wear leather jeans and snap their fingers at the local waitstaff before racing off in their $100,000 Maserati Spyders. Honestly, they're enough to put you off princes entirely.

That's the annoying thing about Princeton— everyone's rich, everyone's perfect. Well, most people are, especially the students. Walk down Nassau Street on a sunny Saturday in spring and you're surrounded by lithe, taut, vigorous youth. Bronzed men in bicycle shorts whose biceps bulge as they carry their front wheels. Blond women with flawless skin and zilch upper-arm flab, their flat stomachs bared above skintight jeans.

This is why Nancy, Deb, and I are best friends—because we're far from perfect. Well, that's not entirely true. Nancy, who's a passionate lawyer and smarter than Perry Mason, has the perfect career, and Deb, who married her childhood sweetheart and has two lively kids, has the perfect family.

Me? I've got the perfect imagination, I suppose. Then again, my imagination tends to get me in a lot of trouble, so maybe it's not so perfect after all.

What we don't have are perfect bodies.

In Princeton, where appearance is 99.9 percent of success, not having a perfect body is a definite handicap. Wait, you say. No one has the perfect body. We all have flaws. Too big on the bottom or too thin on top. Frankly, we would give anything to be too thin anywhere.

Thin. A word so unattainable, so revered and denied to us, that we never speak it. Thin makes us cry. Thin makes us angry. Thin conjures up memories of years of starvation on high protein, cabbage soup, hot-dog-and-banana, two-day fasting, and all-liquid diets only to see our weight drop and then—*poof*—rise again, more determined to stick around than before.

Thin is why guests at our tenth birthdays got cake and we got frozen yogurt. Thin is what we weren't in high school. Thin is what *other* people are. Not us.

This morning I don't have time to worry about thin. Something big is brewing at *Sass!*, the magazine where I am a far too undervalued editor. Something bad. Lawyers at our parent company in Manhattan are driving down to Princeton to meet with our ailing, eighty-five-year-old publisher, David Stanton, who has ordered up additional nurses and oxygen for the occasion. That's how we know it's really serious, when the nurses and oxygen are called in.

The truth is we don't know exactly what's going on, though I'm sure we'll find out during the sure-to-be-a-thrill-a-minute "Reemphasis of Ethical Standards Mandatory Staff Meeting" this afternoon. If we don't show, don't bother coming to work, the memo from our managing editor (aka, prison camp overseer), Lori DiGrigio, threatened. She'll be happy to put our severance check in the mail.

My fellow editor Joel and I are discussing what the big scandal might be and whether it has to do with rumors of fashion writer Donatella Mark embezzling Christian Louboutins in her coat, when Lori pops up in Features, Palm Pilot in hand.

Joel turns to his desk and pretends to edit, though really he's reading the local newspaper's sports scores, while I quickly call up a copy of Belinda Apple's latest column and stare at my computer screen intently, tapping on the keyboard every now and then to add authenticity. Seeing Belinda Apple's byline, Lori sneers, makes a tic on her Palm Pilot, and cruises past me to Fashion. In *Sass!* land, Lori's evil has no power over the good witch that is Belinda Apple.

Belinda Apple is *Sass!*'s most cherished columnist, partially because she is British and chic, along with being *très* au courant and other cheap French adjectives. Everyone praises her as being a wonderful writer with wry wit and sharp observations, though I think the real reason she's famous is because of her footwear—pink cowboy boots with silver studs.

That's what she's wearing in her column photo, along with a mauve gossamer shirt open to reveal the rack of ribs that passes for a chest, her red hair falling over half her face and her long legs in skinny jeans tucked into those boots. All across the country, women are wearing pink leather cowboy boots, thanks to Belinda Apple. She is fast becoming the Sally Starr of our generation.

As if being thin, gorgeous, witty, British, and the owner of hand-stenciled pink cowboy boots wasn't enough, it is also rumored that Belinda is dating *Sass!*'s other high-profile columnist, Nigel Barnes.

Like Belinda, Nigel's British and hot, with a twist. He's intellectual enough to be a pop-culture professor (with tenure) at Princeton and groovy enough to appear regularly on CNN's *90-Second Pop* as the slightly irreverent Popper. He's also written scripts for several movies featuring Hugh Grant and is supposedly the genius behind Hugh's famous stutter—or so Nigel claims.

Vanity Fair has been dying to do a cover story on

Sass!'s dream couple, only they haven't been able to get a hold of Belinda. Belinda's very reclusive. Some say mysterious, despite tabloid accounts of her partying in SoHo with her fabulous model friends and zipping off in limousines stocked with champagne.

But of course these stories of her wild behavior aren't true. They couldn't be. Belinda's too hardworking and dedicated to be out socializing at all hours.

Plus, Belinda Apple doesn't really exist.

This I alone know, and it is a secret that must never, ever be revealed. Because if it gets out that frumpy Nola Devlin from Manville, New Jersey, is the real Belinda Apple, my readers will hate me, my publisher will fire me, and my mother—who has openly proclaimed Belinda a "smart-mouthed slut who is single-handedly destroying the morals of our society"—will never speak to me again.

Then again, the markdown on pink studded cowboy boots will be phenomenal.

Shortly before noon I skip out to meet Nancy and Deb for our standing first-Friday-of-the-month lunch date. You might think, with the "Reemphasis of Ethical Standards Mandatory Staff Meeting" hanging over my head, not to mention possible immediate employment termination if I miss it, that I might reconsider the crab salad croissant with homemade sweet potato chips at the Willoughby Café. But it's the Willoughby Café. Princeton's best restaurant, smack on Nassau Street. Are you kidding?

Also, Deb's having a crisis of her own. She is refusing to go to her son's sixth-grade graduation tomorrow supposedly because she doesn't want to publicly embarrass him with her fatness. Therefore, this is not so much a meal as a therapy session. And Rule #1 is that a friend's mental health takes precedence over a regular paycheck, especially if her mental health requires the consumption of crab salad on a fresh, flaky, buttery croissant at the Willoughby Café.

But something's off at the Willoughby. Nancy and Deb are not sitting at our usual table by the plate glass window overlooking the street. They appear to have been relegated to the back near the swinging kitchen door, and they look none too happy.

"New management," Nancy says as I squeeze into a tight booth. "They claim they didn't know we wanted the table by the window. If you ask me, it's discrimination."

"Fat discrimination," Deb whispers, taking a furtive sip of her ice water. "Nancy says they don't want to turn off potential clientele by having us displayed at the window. She's asked to speak with the manager."

I try to be balanced about this. You have to watch out for Nancy. Great kid. Big heart. Card-carrying member of the ASPCA and all that. But as a razor-sharp litigator, instinctively on the hunt for a possible federal lawsuit.

"They probably didn't know our routine. Just an innocent mistake." I scan the menu for something new, now that there's new management.

14

"Is there a problem?" The manager is a bony man with a mustache and a name tag that reads CHESTER. He shifts his feet impatiently and eyes the table one over, as though dealing with us one more minute will be sheer torture.

"I wonder if we could move to the table by the window. That's our favorite spot," Nancy says, pointing to "our" table, which sits empty and set, ready for patrons.

"I'm sorry," Chester says. "But that table is reserved."

"Really? I didn't know you could reserve tables."

"Oh, yes," says Chester. "You can now."

Nancy is undaunted. "Well, oddly enough, I've been here twenty minutes and no one's sat there the entire time."

"I suppose they're late. Or maybe they've had a change of plans."

"Then we'll be happy to take it."

Chester frowns. "I'm afraid not. It's still reserved, even if the reservers aren't coming."

There's no doubt about it, we've been dissed.

Deb, who is a mass of blond curls and has the backbone of mashed potatoes, blushes as pink as the shirt under her flowered jumper. I just wish Nancy would drop it. I have to get back to that meeting and I don't have time to debate the nuances of civil rights with a restaurant manager.

But Nancy won't drop it. Her eyes flash and her expertly polished red lips twitch like leaves before a storm. I brace myself against the table for the oncoming torrent. When you've known Nancy as long as I have, you know it's risky to confront her without comprehensive insurance coverage.

"You wouldn't, by any chance, not be giving us that table because we're . . . on the heavy side, would you?" She keeps her gaze on Chester, level and determined.

I tense up, riveted by this interchange between my friend, who, though, yes, *on the heavy side,* is rather glorious in a subdued fawn silk duster adorned with Russian amber, and Chester, who is definitely a reincarnated squirrel. What I can't get over is how Nancy has the guts to call herself "on the heavy side" in public. I mean, I don't even use those kinds of words with my own doctor.

"I have no idea what you mean," he says, lifting his pencil. "Shall I take your order?"

"Yes," Nancy says, "we'd like the window table."

Chester blanches and then recovers. "If you're unhappy with our service, ma'am, there are other restaurants in the neighborhood. This isn't the only place to eat. Hoagie Haven is right up the block."

"Yesss," Deb murmurs under her breath. "Let's get out of here. Please."

"I don't think so," Nancy counters. "That's exactly what he wants. Chester is trying to appeal to the upscale lunch crowd and he fears three fat broads in the window is bad for business."

Interestingly, Chester doesn't dispute this.

Nancy flips open the menu. "We will have one side salad and three waters. Oh, and three forks. We'll split it." It is the cheapest order possible.

Chester snatches our menus and storms off. The rubbernecking patrons in the restaurant sheepishly turn away from us, the car wreck of feminine destruction in their midst.

I don't dislike many people, but I think I dislike Chester. And so, being the mature, stable woman I am, I immediately imagine a way to get revenge.

"I wish I had a magic wand that could make us instantly thin," I say. "And then we could walk in the door and he would rush to seat us at the table by the window and we could bust him and his fat-phobic ways on the spot."

"Like Cinderella," Deb says, "only instead of new clothes we get new bodies."

"Maybe it's time," Nancy says.

"Sorry, Nancy," I say. "My magic wand's at the shop under repair."

"I'm not talking about magic. I'm talking about finally taking off the weight once and for all."

Deb groans. "Not this again. I hate when you get on your we-need-to-lose-weight soapbox."

Me too. "Besides," I say, "we are who we are. Isn't that our mantra?"

Nancy begins rummaging around in her purse. "Lookit. I've been carrying around this clip for a month, waiting for the perfect opportunity." She spreads out a copy of Belinda Apple's April column. I

17

flinch upon spying the headline:

IF I CAN DO IT, SO CAN YOU!

Dear Fabulous Belinda!
I am so tired of being overweight. I have dieted and exercised all my life and now I'm in my midthirties and still 265 pounds. I fear I will only get fatter as I get older and my doctor has warned me that I risk heart disease and diabetes if I don't take drastic action.

The thing is, I've already been on every diet known to man and I understand that after years of yo-yo dieting it's even harder to lose weight. Plus, I'm no spring chicken. I fear it's too late for me.

Should I resign myself to my fate and just give up? Or do I have an obligation to my husband and children to lose the weight I can't seem to lose? Help!

Signed, SEXY UNDERNEATH IT ALL

I move on to the answer that I can recite by heart:

Dear SEXY UNDERNEATH IT ALL,
If you read my column regularly, then you know that my philosophy is that the women of our generation have to stop worrying and start living! We spend sixteen hours out of every day—and even more, if you count the sleepless hours in the

middle of the night—fretting about other people: our kids, our bosses, our husbands. No wonder we're suffering from record rates of depression, cancer, and heart disease. Not to mention obesity.

With this in mind, I will let you in on my deepest secret. *I used to be* desperately *overweight*. My excess weight held me back in so many ways. It kept me from developing normal relationships with men, it nearly lost me a job and, worse, it completely curtailed my activity. I didn't ski. I didn't ride. I didn't even shop. Eventually, I found myself becoming a hermit.

The turning point was the day I was to interview a famous actor, of whose work I am a total fan. I can't say who he was, except that I was unable to interview him at his Italian villa. Instead, I had to settle for a VIP lounge at Heathrow, in a cramped space with barely enough room for two folding chairs.

If you're as overweight as I was, you know what happened next. I was accompanied by said famous actor to the tiny room where I sat and promptly broke the chair, falling—*smash!*—to the floor. I was so embarrassed, I had to flee, unable to ask him even one question.

That's when I decided: enough! From that moment on I would consciously monitor my caloric intake, I would increase my activity and I would STOP WORRYING how long it would take me to lose the weight. I would just do it. My way.

It was a simple equation, really. Nothing more than high school thermodynamics. If it takes the burning of 3,500 calories to lose a pound in a week, then I should burn 250 calories through exercise and eat 250 calories less each day. I figured out how many calories I needed to eat to be a healthy weight and worked from there. (There are plenty of free calorie calculators on the Internet.)

By walking a mere five miles a day (to work, shopping, etc.); later kickboxing, which I love; and simply changing what foods I ate (no white flour or sugar, minimal fat), I was down to ten stone (140 lbs.) after a year and I've continued to lose without ever feeling deprived. I've never felt better or been happier.

So, my fellow fat friend, my opinion is that it's not too late if you still have the will and determination to do it. It's only too late when they put you in the coffin, which they might very well do soon if you don't take a few simple, painless steps now.

Best of luck,
Belinda

I stare at the article. Total fiction. One hundred percent whopping lies. *A few simple, painless steps? Without ever feeling deprived?* Puhleeze. What kind of ditz would buy that?

"I totally buy that," Deb says. "I've heard that walking five miles a day and cutting out a couple hundred calories can take off the weight."

I slap my forehead. OK. So Deb's a pea brain, but not Nancy. Surely she's too smart to agree.

"I completely agree. Don't you, Nola?" Nancy says, folding up the article.

My jaw drops. "No. I don't think you can lose a ton of weight by walking and cutting out two hundred and fifty calories a day. I think that's more Belinda spin."

"Then why did you print it if it's spin?" Nancy asks.

Have to admit, she has me there. "Because it was saleable spin?"

Nancy gives me a look. "Anyway, what I propose is that we follow Belinda's example and just do it."

"Diet?" Deb asks. "But I hate diets. I've been on so many diets I've given up. They don't work. You just gain the weight right back. And now that we're in our thirties, it'll be doubly impossible to lose."

Deb's right. I despise diets too, especially any diet involving gelatin. As for exercise, I just don't have the time, not with my commute. That's another problem, sitting. I do a lot of it. Forty-five minutes in the car to work. Then at my desk all day. Forty-five minutes back. By the time I get home, I've been sitting so much that I'm exhausted.

"I don't know," I say unenthusiastically. "I can't summon the energy for another weight-loss thing."

Nancy regards us with disappointment. "Look at us. Are we dead yet? No. We're in our thirties. We're young. I, for one, have plenty of living to do." She takes a deep breath. "My goal is to get down to what

I was in college. I'd like to be able to wear anything I want and do anything I want without worrying about my size. Especially now that I'm about to get a divorce. I need a better body if I ever hope to have sex again."

Aha, so that's her motivation. Now I get it. Last year Nancy's super husband, Ron—at least, I always thought of him as super—ran off to Cozumel with a fresh, young law clerk for a long weekend. Though he begged and pleaded for Nancy's forgiveness, she refused to take him back. A mistake, in my opinion. They don't get much better than Ron—er, when he's not running off to Cozumel with twenty-five-year-old law clerks, that is.

"It'll be easy," Nancy says. "Two hundred and fifty calories a day. Let's try it. For six months. And if it doesn't work, we scrap everything and go back to our old ways."

I study Deb. Nancy's preaching is wearing her down. I can tell she's seriously considering this ridiculous diet business.

"Actually," Deb ventures, "I've been looking into weight-loss surgery . . ."

"Weight-loss surgery!" Nancy snaps. "Are you kidding? Do you know that mortality rate? Weight-loss surgery is obscene."

"It was just a thought," says Deb, who is easily cowed. "Anyway, Paul's not keen on it either. He says he likes me fat and happy, so I guess I don't have a real reason to lose."

"Except your son, whose graduation you're not going to tomorrow because you don't want to embarrass him."

Deb bristles. "OK. I'll do it. But only for six months."

Nancy pats her hand. "That's a good girl. How about you, Nola? Are you ready to get down to the weight your driver's license says you are?"

"Is this some kind of legal threat?" I ask.

"I do happen to be on a first-name basis with several state police, and lying to the Department of Motor Vehicles is a punishable offense."

Unfortunately, I am not up to speed on New Jersey motor vehicle code, so I'm not sure if claiming that I am one hundred and twenty-eight pounds will get me thrown in the slammer. But I do know that Nancy will give me no peace unless I concur.

"All right. Count me in. On one condition."

Nancy raises an eyebrow.

"That in December we come back here and get the table by the window and shame Chester until he grovels at our feet."

"It's a deal. And now a toast." Nancy lifts her glass of water. "To the Cinderella Pact. If we don't lose it now, we never will. So here's to one last try."

"To one last try," we chime. And clink our waters enthusiastically.

I give us exactly forty-eight hours to cave.

Chapter Two

Being overweight hasn't been all bad. Being overweight has made me more tolerant of other people's foibles because I know that as humans we can't help who we are or what we do one hundred percent of the time.

And if I hadn't been overweight, I'd never have become thin and famous—as Belinda Apple.

Last year Managing Editor Lori DiGrigio decided what *Sass!* needed to distinguish itself from other gossip sheets was an ethics columnist. Not any ethics columnist. One who "could answer the personal, occasionally embarrassing, and always unique ethical issues facing women today. Someone edgy and biting."

At the time I had been editing columns at *Sass!* for four years, so I had a pretty good handle on what worked and what didn't when it came to biting ethics columnists. Wait. That doesn't sound right. . . .

Anyway, I walked into Lori's office with my application in hand, her "sample questions" answered with a fresh and original voice (mine), at which point Lori looked up at me and—I am not making this up—laughed out loud. She even snorted.

"You?" she said.

Seriously. That's what she said. *"You?"*

I was still naive, so I didn't quite catch what she was implying. Stupid, silly me. I assumed she was referring to the fact that I was an editor, not a writer.

"Actually," I remember saying, "I've always wanted to be a writer here. If you look at my résumé, it says that my five-year goal is to become a columnist and, well, this is my fourth year so here I am."

Lori didn't know how to respond. In retrospect, I realize her top concern was probably a legal one: How can I tell this frump that I'd no more have her writing ethics columns than resurrect John Candy to critique fashion?

To that end, she shoved my application into a file and said with as straight a face as she could muster, "I'll give it a thoughtful review."

"She's not going to give it a thoughtful review," Joel scoffed when I returned to my desk, blue and confused.

"That's what she said." I tried not to sound defensive. But, really, she did say that.

"Lori is a ruthlessly ambitious shrew who doesn't give a gnat's ass about you or anyone except herself. She wants to present Stanton with a new columnist who's candy for the eye, because that's what we turn out here at *Sass!* Readable eye candy." Joel bit into his turkey sandwich and licked mustard from the corner of his mouth. "And, besides, she doesn't like nice girls."

"Are you calling me nice? Take it back."

"Nice. Nice. Nice."

I punched him on the shoulder. If Joel and I were in grade school, they'd have to separate us even though

25

he's old enough to be my father and has the fashion sense of a high school janitor.

Underneath the jokes, I knew the harsh reality of what he was saying. Lori didn't want the picture of a fat chick accompanying a column that was supposed to appeal to hip, trendy twentysomethings with "personal, occasionally embarrassing, and always unique" ethical questions. She wanted Carrie Bradshaw.

So I decided to test his theory. I dug out an old photo of me sans glasses taken for my college yearbook. In it I am leaning against a building on the Rutgers main campus, one cowboy-footed boot against the wall, my brown hair hanging across half my face (to hide my chin—fat-girl trick). I was at my thinnest then—relatively speaking—and, to be honest, I didn't look bad at all.

I scanned the photo into my home computer and then dug in.

Three hours with Photoshop (O, that we could Photoshop our real lives) and Belinda was born—a much slimmer, redheaded version of me. For fun, I colored my brown cowboy boots pink and superimposed a bony chest on mine, but otherwise kept everything the same. I am still waiting for the day when a bored student in the Rutgers yearbook room comes across my picture and puts two and two together.

Belinda's résumé was trickier. I had hoped that, being foreign, Belinda's background would be harder to check. I made sure that she had written for British publications that couldn't be traced, because they

26

were invented. For example, Belinda enjoyed an immensely popular stint as an advice columnist at the short-lived and totally fictional *Go Fab!* (The more British-sounding, the better, I figured.) As for her personal reference? None other than *moi,* followed by my home phone number.

In a last-minute stroke of brilliance, I printed out the original answers from my application, photocopied them on cheap paper to look grainy, and included them in the package as Belinda's. Surely this would set off bells in personnel when they saw my same answers and my name as a reference.

But no one from *Sass!* ever called.

Not even after Belinda's application made it through the first round of cuts. Not even after Lori cruised by my desk one day and said casually, "Nola, I wonder if you could find a number for that applicant you recommended, Belinda Apple. The one on her résumé seems to be out of service."

Finally, I thought, Lori is going to call Belinda and offer her the job. At which point I would come clean and we'd have a little discussion about judging people according to their qualifications, not their jeans size.

On my lunch hour I ran out and signed up for a new cell phone. I registered it under the name Belinda Apple.

"Apparently, Belinda has an American cell," I said, handing Lori a slip of paper on which the number was written. "You wouldn't believe what I had to go through to find it."

Lori snatched the number out of my hand.

Ten minutes later "Belinda's" phone rang "Rule Britannia."

"New ring tone?" Joel asked casually.

Yipes! How could I talk to Lori in a British accent with Joel sitting right next to me overhearing every word? Grabbing the phone, I found a vacant, dark conference room, shut the door, and locked it. Then I tried to channel my best Brit—I thought of teatime at Harrods and the Ministry of Silly Walks, and the entire cast of *Love Actually*. What the hell? If Renée Zellweger could pull it off as Bridget Jones, why couldn't I?

" 'Ellooo?"

Lori seemed confused. "Oh, I'm looking for a Belinda Apple. Is this she?"

Editors are so mindful of using the right pronoun. "This is she."

After a few niceties Lori got right down to business. "We've read your columns and reviewed your application thoroughly, Belinda. And, well, let me just say that we found your answers to be exceptional. Such an original voice."

"Brilliant," I cooed. Though I was thinking, *original?* Are you blind? Those answers were photocopied!

"I especially liked what you said in your cover letter, that the women of today are faced with more thorny ethical issues than their mothers ever were. Whether or not to put the children in day care, if it's OK to lie to your boss and say you're sick when really your children are, if you should pretend that your husband makes more than you do, just to bolster his ego . . . Fantastic stuff!"

"Yes. It's no wonder we are worrying ourselves into eating disorders, isn't it?"

"So true, so true," Lori agreed. "And I think your idea of teaching women how to stop worrying and to 'be fab' is fantastic. I mean what woman doesn't want to learn how to, what was it again? . . ."

" 'Treasure every ordinary day while reaching for every extraordinary treasure.' "

"I *love* it."

I have to say. It was rather a good idea. Now if only I could apply it to my own life.

"We were wondering if you could come in for an interview. I realize this might be difficult considering the distance . . ."

"Oooh, sorry," I interrupted. "I'd love to but me mum's sick." I blushed. *Me mum.*

"Oh." Lori paused. "Well, then, it's a good thing our sales rep in London's available to meet you in person."

Eeep! Total and utter panic. London? *Sass!* has a sales rep in London?

"The thing is," I said, trying to act quick on my feet, "is that I'm not in London, actually. I'm in . . . Ireland."

"Ireland? But I thought you were . . ."

"British. I am, very. But me mum's Irish and, you

29

know, being on death's door and all, she wanted to . . ."
OK. What did she want to do? What would a dying Irish woman's last wish be? To boil corned beef? Knock back a Guinness? Catch a leprechaun? "She wanted to visit the coast to look out on the Cliffs of Moher one last . . ."

"Say no more," Lori cut in. "Listen, I feel confident, Belinda, in extending our offer anyway. Sight unseen."

I waited. Sight unseen? Could it be that Lori was really attracted to the content of my application and not the appearance of Belinda?

"I've received approval from our publisher, David Stanton, to formally offer you employment as the author of an advice column we'd like to call 'On Being Fab!: How to Do the Right Thing.' I do hope you'll accept."

OK, that was it. That was my cue to declare dramatically, "Aha! So it was my size after all that made you dismiss me. Those answers were identical to the ones I, Nola Devlin, your very own Columns editor, had written, but you didn't even bother to read them, did you, Lori DiGrigio?"

Yes. I had it all planned. My mouth was even open, my index finger lifted accusatorily and the "Ah" was already out when Lori said, "And I'll be honest. One of the features that made you so attractive was your photo. I hope you won't find this, ahem, *unethical* when I say you are simply stunning."

My breath caught in the back of my throat. Stunning? No one in my life, not even my mother—and she's not stingy with the compliments—had ever used the word stunning.

"Oh," I said, so befuddled that I forgot to add the British accent.

"I mean, you must have done some professional modeling. David Stanton described you as 'devastating,' which, if you've read anything about Stanton, is very flattering."

I found myself staggered. Suddenly, I was dizzy and delirious. I was *devastating*. I had no idea that being called devastating, stunning, whatever, could have such a loopy effect.

So this is why pretty women defy age at any cost. This is why they spend thousands of dollars on plastic surgery and starve themselves to itty-bitty dolls—because this being pretty shtick is better than being on drugs. Not that I take drugs. But if I did, I just think that going around every day being stunning would be better.

I wasn't making any sense. Not even to myself. If I were behind the wheel, the cops could have arrested me for driving under the influence of feeling beautiful (DUIFB).

"Belinda?" Lori's voice broke through my hallucinations. "Are you there? Is the connection all right? This call's not going to Ireland, is it?"

"Yes, quite," I managed to say, Brit accent and all. "I have an American mobile." *Mobile?* From what Anglophilic portion of my brain had that come from?

31

"How odd. I didn't know that was possible, to use an American cell overseas."

Shit. Maybe it wasn't possible. Quick. Fudge it, Nola. "Cuts down on long-distance charges to the States, doesn't it?" Alone in the dark conference room, I was getting in the groove. The gorgeous Belinda groove. And like anyone on a high, the last thing I wanted to do was come down. No way was I giving this up—ever.

"Oh, I forgot the salary." Lori coughed nervously. "We're thinking of a graduated scale. Perhaps three thousand for each weekly column the first three months, increased to four thousand per column the next quarter and five thousand for the following two quarters. Does that seem . . . right?"

"Uh?" I was still doing the math. Geesh. That was more than two hundred thousand. Four times what I made in a year.

"Though you must have a literary agent. How stupid of me to approach you with this."

"Ab—absolutely," I stammered. "An agent."

"Then just give me her name and we'll work out the details."

Agent? I didn't have a freaking agent. The only agent I had was Tod Starett at Getaway Now! Travel in Piscataway. "Actually, I'm between agents. My one in London isn't licensed to work in the States."

"I see." Lori sounded skeptical. "Interesting that your agents require licenses. That must be a British law."

Literary agents didn't require licenses?

"Well, as soon as you settle on one, give me the agency's address and I'll messenger the contracts over. Would starting next month be too soon? We'll need to promo it for a while first. To build reader interest."

"Next month? Brilliant."

"*Brilliant.* I love the way you speak, I have to confess. I'm a sucker for British accents."

"Me too."

"Pardon?"

I flushed. "Nothing." There was a knock at the conference room door, and the knob was twisting. Outside, someone was complaining about having reserved it for three o'clock. "I'm so sorry, but I have to rush off."

"I totally understand. I'm late for a meeting as it is too. So glad to have you on board, Belinda. I'm positive you'll be a definite asset to our publication."

She hung up and I sat for a few minutes in the darkness, ignoring the banging on the door and the shouts for a key as rambling questions seared through my muddled brain. What had I done? How could I pull this off? Where does one find an agent? What if David Stanton insists on meeting me in person? How *do* you boil corned beef anyway?

Then it occurred to me that in the course of my "interview" to be an ethics columnist, I had committed no fewer than a dozen ethical violations, including lying about who I was, about my supposed

Irish-born mother dying, and even her last wish on Earth. Surely I would burn in hell for if not eternity, then a damn long time.

When I did get around to opening the door, I found my worries vanish. I was face-to-face with none other than Lori herself, hands on hips, as sharp as ever. In fact, everything about Lori, from the bob of her jet-black hair, to the points of her silk collars, was angled viciously.

"Honestly, Devlin, if you need to make a personal call, go outside. It's incredibly inconsiderate of you to tie up a reserved conference room." She marched right past me, never giving me a second glance.

That, right there, sums up the difference between Belinda Apple and me. Belinda is a woman who doesn't exist but whom people can't help but notice, while I, who do exist, am almost always invisible.

Chapter Three

By the end of lunch—if you can call one-third of a salad lunch—I begin to get into this diet business. I could stick with it this time, I think. I could really, really, once and for all reveal my inner Cinderella. What I need is just a bit of motivation. Literary motivation.

What I need is a good, uplifting story from an overweight housewife who went from being a fuzzy blob in bad shorts on a green couch to a digitally clear busty babe in a bikini. Or perhaps a diet doctor who can relate case study after case study about patients who were too fat to walk through his door and after six months on his program—*voilà!*—were entering the Ironman Competition and throwing out all their medications and using their old jeans as leaf bags.

Yes. That's what I must do, acquire some motivation immediately, before I lose momentum and drop out of the Cinderella Pact.

But I draw the line at gelatin.

Also, any recipe having to do with frozen butter-milk. I've been on too many eating programs where the dieticians try to "turn your favorite foods" into "healthy choices" with the ingenious but simple use of unflavored gelatin and frozen buttermilk.

Let's be honest. Chocolate mousse made with dark Swiss chocolate, Grand Marnier, and heavy double cream is a delight to savor and should never be compared to the concoction made from unsweetened cocoa, Splenda, orange flavoring, and gelatin. Nor can frozen buttermilk ever be transformed into anything approaching ice cream. This is what drives veteran dieters like me back to the Toll House.

After Nancy, Deb, and I part outside the awful, new-management Willoughby Café, I detour down the street into a local bookstore, figuring I can afford a few minutes to check out the diet books before getting back to work.

I feel excited and rejuvenated as I march myself to the self-help section. This will be the moment I'll look back on years from now when I am thin. I will be able to say, "I owe it all to Dr. _____ and his/her book on weight loss/exercise/self-esteem, which put me on the road to wellness/thinness/being a hot, sexy babe."

There are so many subsections, it's hard to figure out what I want. Am I diabetic? No. High cholesterol? Nope. Am I a sugar buster? A carb-o-holic? The adult child of a compulsive eater? Uh, yes. Perhaps I should eat according to my blood type. I can't do that, though, since I can never remember if I'm an A or an O, and I'm too squeamish to take a test to find out.

Atkins I've done already—three times. With each Atkins diet I lost exactly twelve pounds, all of which immediately came back—like overnight—with one slice of pizza. Plus, testing my urine for ketosis got a bit stale.

South Beach takes too much work. Jane Brody means beans, and I hate beans. Dean Ornish is no fun. Ditto for the Zone. Then again, none of them is exactly a trip to the circus.

And then I see it—*Who Moved My Fat?: Making the Weight-Loss Journey Fun!* by Anne Renée Krugenheim, Ph.D. Hmm. She's German and she has three names, so she must be a scientific expert.

I scan the index, searching for any disturbing signs of gelatin usage. Finding none, I venture to the back cover.

Congratulations! If you're reading this right now, then you are taking the first step toward controlling your weight. You should be proud.

I smile. I am proud. Good for me.

And probably you've been on many diets before.

It's like she knows me!

That's because you've been taught to think of diets as a torturous means to a desired end.

They're not?

No! Diet comes from the Greek word diata, *which means "prescribed way of living."*

That makes me feel much better.

In Who Moved My Fat?: Making the Weight-Loss Journey Fun! *Dr. Anne Renée Krugenheim will teach you to love your diet and yourself. Most importantly, you'll learn how to lose weight without once feeling deprived or denied. She will map out a journey that you'll want to take over and over for the rest of your life!*

Ugh. I hate that, the rest-of-your-life part.

So what are you waiting for? Why not start your journey now?

Yes. Why not? I think, flinching at the cost—$34.00. Well, it's money well spent and, besides, imagine all I'll be saving by not buying ice cream and Doritos and cheese and crackers and chocolate.

I buy the book and rush back to my car, having taken much longer in the bookstore than I'd expected. I'll have to hoof it if I want to make that mandatory ethics meeting on time and not lose my job.

The day has heated quickly and traffic is creeping up Route 1 to East Brunswick, home to the Princeton North Corporate Office Park that, in turn, houses

Sass!'s editorial offices. Most readers assume we're posh, writing from brick-walled lofts in Greenwich Village when, really, all the "magic" takes place in gray cubicles on gray, soundproof carpet in a concrete fortress of dental offices and insurance agencies.

As we stop and start up the crowded highway in an inexplicable traffic jam, I fear for my ancient Audi Fox, which is buckling and making odd sounds in its front. I've had to turn on the heater to cool off the engine, which means it is now a sweltering 100 degrees behind the wheel. I can't tell you the wondrous miracles this heat is doing for my hair and general body odor.

I flip through *Who Moved My Fat?* and pick a chapter at random entitled "Go Tell It on the Mountain." In it Dr. Anne Renée Krugenheim discusses the importance of informing everyone you know that you are embarking on "an exciting weight-loss journey that is guaranteed to change your life forever."

The theory behind this is similar to the Alcoholics Anonymous step where you have to apologize to people for trashing their lampshades or puking on their carpet along with telling them that you've stopped drinking. That's the thing about being fat. There aren't many opportunities to trash lampshades. Still, Dr. Anne Renée Krugenheim is confident that making these phone calls will ensure that I won't be "sidetracked" or "lost in the woods."

I get the impression there will be no shortage of travel metaphors in *Who Moved My Fat?*

Call your loved ones now, Dr. Anne Renée Krugenheim admonishes us. *Any delay postpones the journey.*

Gee. I wouldn't want to do that. I look up and discover the traffic has moved approximately one inch.

Before I hesitate a minute longer, I take out my cell and dial Mom's number at work.

Mom is a secretary in the Princeton municipal clerk's office. She's the rectangular one in the sexless, hand-sewn denim jumpers and booster pins that say Go Tigers!, who puts homemade oatmeal raisin cookies on the counter to appease the locals coming in to pay their property taxes or buy dog tags. I am convinced that she has outlasted eight administrations, both Republican and Democrat, solely because of her secret recipe for Swedish meatballs in tangy sour cream sauce—a dish that could melt the hardest heart of any conniving politician.

Like me, Mom is not small, though she was thin—allegedly—when she married Dad. Somewhere after the honeymoon she got it into her head that being a wife meant serving up meat smothered in sauce, buttered vegetables (one grown above ground/one grown below), and a starch for every dinner, followed by a dessert to rival the ones on the cover of *Woman's Day.*

Butterscotch brownies topped by vanilla ice cream (honestly, did we need the ice cream?). Banana pudding made with Nilla wafers. Blueberry pie and "lite" Cool Whip . . .

This was the house I grew up in. Meatloaf and twice-baked potatoes with sour cream. Short ribs and poppyseed noodles. Chicken potpie in a flaky crust. Pot roast cooked with dark beer. Lasagna with sausage and three kinds of cheese, accompanied by garlic bread. Knockwurst and sauerkraut in a crockpot. (Crockpots are very big with my mother. She reveres them as miracles akin to the NASA space station.)

For dessert there was homemade thick hot-fudge sauce over mint-chip ice cream. Ginger cookies with unsulfured molasses for a snack every day after school along with a tall glass of cold whole milk. Even our Friday night fish was battered and fried. Plus, just in case we hadn't been satisfied, a big basket of sliced white bread at every table at every meal, accompanied by a stick of butter.

And the doctor was confused as to why I topped 150 in seventh grade.

Mom answers the phone like she's at home. "It's Betty!"

"Hi, Mom."

"Nola! I was just going to call you."

"First hear me out. I have big news," I begin dramatically, already feeling teary at the thought of what I'm about to declare. "I am going on an exciting weight-loss journey that is guaranteed to change my life forever."

"A spa? Caroline Spivak went to a spa and lost ten pounds of sweat."

"No." I clear my throat and try again. "I'm going on a diet, or *diata*—which, I don't know if you know this, means 'prescribed way of living' in Greek."

40

"I'll have to tell Nicky Spanadopolous. He's Greek, you know."

"It's Greek to me!" someone in the background yells, spawning an uproarious round of laughter at the Princeton muni clerk's office.

"Are you coming to Eileen's birthday party?" Mom asks.

Clearly, she does not appreciate the gravity of what I have just announced, that I am embarking on an exciting weight-loss journey that is guaranteed to change my life forever.

"It's on the twentieth," she reminds me. "At her house. Your father and I are buying her a new set of tires."

My parents cannot do enough for Eileen, the baby in the family. And I say this without one ounce of sibling rivalry. My sister is thirty-two, works full-time as a hairdresser, drives a leased late-model Camaro, and has a serious boyfriend named Jim Russell, whom we've secretly nicknamed *Jack* Russell because he is as wiry and hyperactive as a terrier. Despite this adult lifestyle, she somehow gets our mother to wash and iron all her clothes and our dad to help pay her Visa bill, on which she once charged a spontaneous trip to Hawaii.

Don't even talk to me about Eileen.

"Of course," I say, though it had completely slipped my mind.

"If you haven't gotten her a gift yet, I have the perfect one in mind."

41

Here it comes. The diamond ring my grandmother gave me. My left kidney. My favorite spleen.

"See, Eileen was over for dinner and *E!* came on. There was a brief segment about Belinda Apple and Nigel Barnes and how they're an item and all. Now Eileen wants to talk to Belinda about something personal," Mom is saying. "I told her to write Belinda a letter like everyone else, but apparently whatever is bugging her can't wait. I thought maybe, for her birthday, you could have Belinda give Eileen a call at the party. She can put her on speakerphone!"

Nooo!! I give my head a slight bang against the steering wheel. I can see it now. Me as Belinda on speakerphone. Eileen, Mom, Dad, and Jack Russell all listening in, commenting that her voice sounds so familiar. Why, you could swear she's Nola.

"Eileen will be forever grateful to you. It'll be a hoot!"

It'll be hooting impossible. How am I supposed to pull off Belinda on the telephone if I have to be at the same party at the same time? Ventriloquism is not one of my talents. Not yet.

I really want to dissuade Mom of this brainstorm except for some reason my windshield is fogging up. No. It's not really fogging up, it's . . . smoke. Smoke rising from the hood of my car, which has been idling in the traffic jam. A mere twenty feet from my exit ramp to the Princeton North Corporate Office Park.

"Gotta go, Mom," I say, waving the smoke out of my eyes.

"Wait! What about Belinda Apple calling on Sunday? Is that a yes?"

I quickly shout "Whatever!" and then click off because the smell inside my car is worse than the perpetually burning trash fires down in Perth Amboy and I have started coughing uncontrollably. I careen my ancient and now exploding Audi Fox off the highway, past the breakdown lane, and onto the grass before I wiggle out, remembering at the very last minute to grab Belinda's cell phone from the seat next to me.

Which means I am standing at the edge of the highway in a black pantsuit on a ninety-degree June day. Of course I am wearing black. I always wear black to work, no matter what the temperature. I also always wear long sleeves and, if I'm in a skirt, hose. Queen size. I'd do well in Afghanistan.

Something goes poof under the hood of my Fox, and the front of my car explodes in flames. I'd rush around and do something except that I am already five minutes late to the "Mandatory Staff Meeting" on which hangs my entire career. I freeze, uncertain what to do.

"This your car?"

An East Brunswick cop who is equally sweaty and hot is standing next to me with a red fire extinguisher. "Don't go near it, OK? Back off."

He lifts the extinguisher and sprays the hood. The flames disappear as white steam rises along with a sickening acrid smell. "Thank you," I say, coughing. "I'll move her off the berm."

"There's nothing you can do with this heap now," he

43

says cruelly. "She's history."

"But it can't be a heap. It's my car."

"Trust me. It's a heap. I'd lose my badge if I let you get behind the wheel." He pulls out a walkie-talkie and radios for a tow truck.

I regard my forlorn Audi. My first car, ever. This is the car that drove me to college and the Jersey Shore and, once, to Boston to see the Rolling Stones. This is the car in which I made out with Robbie Spillman in twelfth grade. This car defines me.

"You need a ride somewhere?" the cop is asking nicely.

"Actually, I work right up there." I point behind me to the fortress. I am reluctant to leave my car but here's the tow truck, its yellow lights flashing, coming to take my Audi to the Big Scrap Heap in the sky.

I can't bear to see the Audi treated like a piece of junk. I turn my attention to the hillside littered with McDonald's bags and dirty socks and various bits of garbage. Climb the hill and I'll be at the Princeton North parking lot. Climb the hill and I just might make the meeting in time.

I thank the cop again, give him my address so the tow truck can bill me, and start the climb.

The hill turns out to be much steeper than it seems from the highway and I can feel rivulets of sweat running down my arms. There's a mirror in my purse, but I don't dare check my reflection lest I turn myself into stone. My black pants are snagged and covered with burrs. Good thing I've got twenty more pairs at home.

I pause halfway up to catch my breath. Over to the right I can see the cause of the traffic jam: a car with a front crumpled end at the top of the exit ramp. People are standing around uninjured, so that's a relief.

I plow onward, finally reaching the parking lot, sweat popping out of places I didn't even know sweat could pop out of. To think that Mom's friend Caroline Spivak paid good money to do this. Hah! Bet I've lost five pounds of sweat already.

All I have to do is step over this rather high, rather rusty line of barbed wire, and then I'm safely on the macadam, two steps from the side entrance, a half a stairwell from the conference room, and—*bing!*—I'm home free.

I lift my leg and safely step over. I lift my other and feel a tug on my ass. Wait. Was that a rip? It couldn't be a rip. I pat my behind, cautiously searching for a hole. Nothing. Whew! And then I feel a slight breeze.

Damn. It *is* a rip and not on the seam, either.

I can't see it, though. Maybe if it's not too big I can get by. Hold on. What color underwear am I wearing? No biggie if it's black. I can just slide into the conference room and sit down and no one will be the wiser. Then, after the meeting, I'll slide out and down the stairs, get my friend Lisa or someone to drive me home and change my pants.

Oh shoot, it's pink. All-cotton baby pink Hanes. Perhaps it doesn't show. If I check underneath. I'll just bend over and . . .

45

" 'Ello, luv."

I stop dead in my tracks. My head is between my knees looking up.

"Have you lost something?" The voice is British. Genuine British. Not my fake Monty Python/Posh Spice/Mr. Bean/Belinda Apple British.

I snap up and, in so doing, my hair falls out of its clip and over my face like Cousin Itt. I feel a bit dizzy and I must be dizzy because in front of me is standing Mick Jagger, only thirty years younger. But what would Mick Jagger only thirty years younger (Son of Mick?) be doing near the Route 18 overpass in East Brunswick in the Princeton North Corporate Center?

He grins, and that's when it comes into focus. This isn't Son of Mick. This is Nigel Barnes. *The* Nigel Barnes. Belinda's Nigel Barnes, whom I last saw in the flesh at the annual *Sass!* Christmas party.

That's where he said to me, and I quote, "Did you make these meatballs? They're rather good."

And I wittily retorted, "Uh-huh."

And he said, "Family recipe?"

And I grunted, "Mother's."

At which point he smiled politely and chirped, "Jolly good." Then some tart from Personnel threw her arms around his neck and dragged him to a group of giggling fellow Personnel tarts tipsy on punch.

He is taller than I remembered. Confident in a classic white shirt, a rather preppy striped tie, and worn jeans and somewhat unshaven face. His hands are large with long, almost graceful fingers. Artistic, I

46

think. And other things that I wouldn't say unless I were Belinda. But I'm not Belinda. I'm Nola. If I were Belinda, I wouldn't be as eloquent as I am now.

"Um." I start searching my database for a lie that might explain why I, literally, had my head up my ass. "You see . . ."

Forget it. There simply is no easy way to recover from being caught checking the state of your underwear.

Chapter Four

"My car exploded," I say by way of idiotic explanation as Nigel, probably suspecting that I am a runaway mental patient, insists on escorting me to *Sass!* Much to his obvious surprise, I declare that we are both late for the same meeting.

"You work . . . here?" He turns to me on the stairs where I am keeping a careful distance to fall behind. As a general rule, I try to never end up walking ahead of someone up the stairs so that my rear end is in their face. But today this rule has a codicil. The pink underwear codicil. Today no one will see my ass, not as long as there are walls against which to slink.

"I'm Belinda Apple's editor. We met once at a Christmas party two years ago." I raise my eyebrows alluringly. "Swedish meatballs."

"Oh, yes, right. Of course," he flubs, not remembering me or my meatballs one bit.

Which means I have to gracefully bring up my name so that he won't have to stumble around it. "Yessirree," I say, as we reach the corridor leading to the conference room. "It's hard to forget *Nola* Devlin's Swedish meatballs."

"Right. Nola." He smiles weakly and opens the door to the hallway, though I demur because of the pink-undie codicil. "Apparently Belinda and I are an item. You know, I should sue since I've never even laid eyes on the woman."

"You've never met her?" I ask innocently.

"Never. I have to say I am a closet fan of her columns. Though don't tell my students that I read such trash."

We both laugh conspiratorially about my trashy prose.

"Seriously. I think her message of encouraging women to relax and enjoy life is simply brilliant. I can't tell you how many uptight women I've met at Princeton who drive me up the wall with their insecurities, their 'How come you didn't call me's' and 'Will I get tenure's' and 'Do I look . . .' Well, you get the idea. Really, most men are sick of it."

I should be listening to his rant, but I stopped at the word brilliant. Brilliant! Nigel Barnes, *the* Nigel Barnes, said I was brilliant! I try to appear unflustered by this and reply with a classic non sequitur. "Yes, she's not bad."

We have arrived at the closed conference room, but Nigel shows no signs of eagerness to make the meeting. Perhaps he is such a star here that his job is assured, whereas I, like any editor, can be replaced with a phone call.

"So what's she like in person?" he asks. "Belinda, I mean."

"Well, she's very tall," I begin, uncertain whether it's her physical beauty he's interested in.

"Oh?" He makes a curious face. "Freakish *Guinness Book of World Records* tall or model tall?"

"Model tall," I say quickly. "Definitely not freakish. And she has long red hair . . ."

"Yes, yes," he says, with a dismissive wave of his hand. "I can tell all that from her photo. I mean, what's she *really* like. Is she as laid back as she claims? Or is she actually a witch? Does she sleep around? Or is she perhaps a lesbian?"

"Lesbian!" I scream as if I've just seen a centipede.

"You have something against lesbians?"

"No. No I'm perfectly fine with lesbians. It's just that I never thought of her in *that* way."

"So she sleeps around, then? Lots of men, is it?"

"No!"

"You mean she's a virgin?"

"What?" I have to slap my hands to my ears. This is nuts. Belinda Apple doesn't even exist and now she's a lesbian whore with a Madonna complex.

"I'm sorry," he says, smiling. "I suppose what I'm trying to find out is whether it would be acceptable for me to, you know, look her up. I do travel to London quite a bit."

Look her up. My heart skips a few beats.

"I mean," he hesitates, stumbling, "I'm asking if . . . if she's seeing anyone."

And then the sweetness wears off and the truth hits me. This pompous Princeton half-professor is talking to me like I'm an automated gatekeeper to the fantasyland that is Belinda Apple. Oooh, I so hate that. This has been my role since high school when my close friend Constance Maxwell—the concert pianist, the blond-wavy-haired, could've-been-a-cheerleader-but-was-too-smart Constance Maxwell—drew boys to me like dogs to roadkill.

Was Connie seeing anyone? Did she like so and so? Did I think she'd go out with him? Could I put in a good word for him?

"We don't delve into her personal life much," I snap, a mischievous scheme popping into my head. "Besides, she's quite preoccupied these days, what with Wills and all that. Royalty can be *sooo* demanding."

"By Wills, you mean Prince William?" Nigel looks as though he's swallowed an egg.

"Whoops! I shouldn't have said that. Then again, I suppose it's obvious, with her living at Balmoral . . ."

"Balmoral!" This elicits an even more satisfactory reaction. Nigel is practically salivating. "I've always wanted to go to Balmoral. I have quite a bit of Scottish blood in me, you know. My father was a MacLeod."

"Really?" What the hell is a MacLeod?

"I'd give anything for a chance to stay at Balmoral.

50

I've already been to Deeside. Lovely area, absolutely lovely. Um"—the wheels in Nigel's brain are clicking—"I do wonder if there's a chance she might fancy a visit from the likes of me."

"You?"

"Well, I am rather famous, aren't I? I mean dozens of women write to me every day. They even send me their knickers."

"That's nasty."

"And I am a professor at Princeton. There's some cachet in that. What do you think? Do you think I would pass? I mean, not to your American standards, rather to Belinda's higher—er, British ones."

I grip my purse. *Not my standards, Belinda's higher British ones?* Listen, I'm tired of being the nun from *Romeo and Juliet,* I want to tell him. Look at my chin. Do you see hairs? Is there a cowl around my head and a cross dangling from my neck?

And then it hits me. OK, Princeton's Gift to Women, let's have some real fun.

"I'll tell you what." I reach into in my purse, pulling out the tiny black "food diary" I picked up at the bookstore along with *Who Moved My Fat?* I rip off a blank page. "I'll give you Belinda's e-mail, her personal e-mail, not the one her columns go to, and you can write her yourself." I scribble it and hand it to him.

Nigel takes the paper with gleaming eyes. "You won't regret it."

"Oh, I'm sure I won't."

Boom! The conference door flings open and there stands Lori DiGrigio looking nothing short of insane.

"I can hear you two all the way in there." She waves to the conference room where I spy my friend Lisa from Books, her eyes wide. "Why weren't you at the meeting? You're so late, it's over."

"There was a meeting? Fancy that." Nigel, calm as crystal ice, checks inside where everyone is standing, pushing in their chairs and mumbling somberly. Joel, Lisa, and Dawn, Lori's former secretary who was replaced by a dimwitted Valley Girl from Swarthmore, file past us.

"Sorry, Lori," I begin, feeling the familiar panic rise again, "I didn't know if . . . ."

"You." She points a finger straight at me. "I need to see *you* now. Alone."

I flash Nigel a wave of my fingertips, wishing that I were as lucky as he to be spared a private conference with this rabid pit bull, and slide against the wall into the room. Lori slams the doors behind me. It is just the two of us, and her bloodred nails are digging into the flesh of her elbows.

"I have a question for you," she says. "Just who in the hell is the real Belinda Apple?"

Chapter Five

Five Things You Couldn't Pay Me to Wear (Even If I Were Thin):

1) Cropped tops
2) Flimsy T-shirts that say things in sparkly lettering
3) Polyester bicycle shorts
4) White pants
5) Thongs

Thong! is the first word that pops into my mind when Lori DiGrigio demands to know who the real Belinda Apple is. No matter what she is saying, all my attention has turned to the very faint straps of her red thong peeking above the waist of her Tahari black pants. Accident? I'll venture not.

After all, David Stanton is out of his deathbed.

It is common knowledge that Lori is plotting and planning to become the last Mrs. David Stanton so she can cash in à la Anna Nicole Smith. Seeing her thong, I realize she has taken a hint from Monica Lewinsky and decided that the first step in finding billion-dollar love is to reveal one's underwear the way baboons flash their crimson bums to show they are in heat.

Lisa heard a rumor from someone in Food that a few years back, when Lori was in Manhattan to meet with Corporate she and Mr. Stanton stayed out past his bedtime of eight p.m. to take in a Big Band swingathon and that later she unzipped his pants in an alley and . . . . Well, I'm sure it's not true. I can't imagine Lori doing that. Correction, I *don't want* to imagine Lori doing that, especially in an alleyway with an octogenarian.

"Don't you know?" Lori is saying.

"I . . ." I don't know what to say.

"That Belinda Apple doesn't exist?"

I freeze. Simply freeze when Lori says this. She is staring at me, but I am unable to stare back because my entire life is flashing before my eyes.

Somehow I find inner strength, possibly hidden in the criminal core of my id, to ask with an eerily calm voice, "What do you mean Belinda Apple doesn't exist?"

"I mean that everything about her is made up. She's a fraud. We, *Sass!* magazine, have as our ethics columnist a woman who is a total, complete, one-hundred-percent hoax." Lori sighs deeply, and not even her regular Botox injections can prevent the wrinkles creasing her face. "Can you imagine what the flak's going to be when this gets out? *Star* is going to have a freaking orgy. Nola, this is the absolute worst. You have to help us find out who she is."

Oh my God, Lori doesn't know, I realize, trying to maintain a straight face. Relief is washing me like a cool breeze so that my body temperature drops and instead of feeling sweaty I feel clammy. *She doesn't know that I am the real Belinda Apple.*

And then a new concern. "Is this what the meeting was about?"

"Of course. Though it's been hanging over my head for over a week. You don't know the stress this so-called Belinda Apple has caused. I've had to triple my Zoloft." Lori is actually confiding in me as though we're buddies, and I don't know whether to play along or keep her at arm's length.

"How did you find out?" I ask boldly.

"Due diligence. After the Jayson Blair scandal at the *New York Times*, Mr. Stanton demanded an internal investigation into our employees. We were doing fine until we discovered that there never was a British magazine called *Go Fab!* That's where Belinda allegedly worked before coming here."

"I see. Well, maybe there was a *Go Fab!* once but it's now defunct," I say optimistically. "You know how that happens."

"No, no. We have ways of checking these things. Personally, I think these frauds are all over the publishing world thanks to laptops and cell phones. They should be abolished."

"Good point," I say, lying through my teeth. If it weren't for my cell phone and laptop, I would have no secret identity as Belinda Apple. Then again, that kind of proves Lori's point, doesn't it?

"So . . ." I venture delicately, "do you have any other evidence that Belinda doesn't exist?"

Lori begins pacing back and forth in front of a blackboard on which the word MISREPRESENTATION is scrawled with a line through it. "Not much, aside from the fact that there's no listing for a Belinda Apple anywhere in London. I just can't believe it. I just can't believe I was so . . . careless. I know I'm going to get fired over this, I just know it." With this, Lori buries her head in her hands as though she is about to cry. I begin to feel sorry for her, which is ridiculous, as everyone knows Lori is a vampire.

It is my first experience seeing Lori in some other state besides cracking the whip, and I am conflicted. Here she is, vulnerable, weak, and scared, and it is all I can do to pat her on the shoulder. Anyone else I would throw my arms around and hug.

"Don't worry, Lori," I say, trying my best. "Maybe Belinda is legit. Have you asked her?"

Lori lifts her head. As I expected, her eyes are dry. "No! Mr. Stanton and the lawyers don't want us to contact her until we've built our case. They want to handle this delicately. If she wasn't the biggest draw at this magazine, she would have been canned already, I can tell you that."

Her hands work into tiny balls. "I don't care if she's our precious columnist. If I ever find who's behind this, I will have her head on a stick. Make a chump of Lori DiGrigio? I think not. She'll wish she never heard my name when I'm done with her."

Did I mention that my knees were shaking?

Lori emerges from her seething rant and focuses her beady eyes on me. "You've got to spy on Belinda, Devlin. Find out if she's working for another publication. Or if she's in jail. Or that there's some other reason why she's not using her real name. I want to know everything."

"Uh-huh," I manage.

"After all, this scandal wouldn't have happened if it hadn't been for you," she says, craftily turning the blame onto me. "One might say you were the catalyst."

I am not about to let her get away with that. I must

stand up to her, or she will trample me with her size-five El Vaquero python boots. "In what way was I the catalyst?"

"Well, you were on her résumé as a recommendation, weren't you?"

Heat is rising up my neck remembering how Lori essentially threw my application in the trash, thereby leading me to this farce in the first place. "Was it? You never called me."

"Don't be stupid. I certainly did call you and, as I recall, you raved about her. You even got me Belinda's new phone number when the one on her résumé turned out to be defective."

"Lori," I say firmly, "that is a total lie, and you know it."

"You didn't get me her phone number?"

"I did that, yes . . . ."

"Then let's not bicker over details. By the way, it doesn't matter what I think. Mr. Stanton already knows you were the one who recommended her. If I were you I'd think very seriously about how you're going to explain that. Mr. Stanton is not going to let this matter go by the wayside. He's outraged."

Chapter Six

I spend the rest of the afternoon in a daze. Mostly my brain mulls over the cornucopia of punishments for my deception—whether I'll be sued and then fired or fired and then sued. Or criminally prosecuted. The possibilities are endless, though I resolve to take whatever punishment I have coming in brave, Martha Stewart style. I, too, will crochet a shawl in prison.

In the *Sass!* women's room, I Scotch tape the rip in my pants. Then I turn on Belinda's cell phone and find there are thirty messages, including a bunch from the Charlotte Dawson Agency (CDA), the agent I finally found to represent Belinda. I am particularly alarmed because Charlotte never, ever calls.

I am so shocked to see CDA over and over that I nearly drop the phone into the toilet. Though I don't, because then the toilet would get backed up and the plumbers would pull out Belinda's cell, Lori would call Verizon and find I've been paying the phone's bills, and that would be the end of that.

It is much worse in the editorial department, where every five minutes someone is stopping by my desk to gossip.

"Did you have any idea? It's the most shocking thing that's ever happened here. I bet this bogus Belinda Apple is getting paid a pretty penny, too," Lisa says.

Though she's my best friend at the magazine, Lisa is a bit sheltered, seeing as how she works in Books and rarely pays attention to the outside world. She is easily titillated and, therefore, great to take to any movie starring Vince Vaughn.

"Who do you think Belinda really is?" she asks.

"Probably a mole from *Star*," suggests Joel.

Lisa gapes. "That's awful. What kind of fellow reporter would run such a scam? I'll tell you who, a person who has no respect for other people, that's who. Not to mention a person without an ounce of ethics."

"I don't know," I pipe up. "Maybe she couldn't get hired elsewhere and she had to fake her résumé."

"Ridiculous." Lisa folds her arms. "Unless she's a felon or something."

My only wish is to go home, to pull the covers over my head, and not come out until everyone has forgotten Belinda Apple. And I'd do that, too, if I only had a car.

Which I don't. It has been towed upon order of the East Brunswick police to hell, otherwise known as a junkyard in South River. My brand-new copy of *Who Moved My Fat?* lying on the front seat, destroyed before I traveled one leg of the "exciting weight-loss journey that is"—was—"guaranteed to change my life forever."

"That's sad," says Lisa, as we stand in the parking lot and survey the patch of brown grass below us where my car once lay, albeit in flames. "Although, you know, maybe it's a good thing. How old was that heap?"

"Twenty-five years. It was my dad's."

"Aww, so it had sentimental value."

"Has," I correct. "Has. It's still alive. Somewhere in South River."

"Though it's probably crushed by now. I think they

59

do that right away. You know, scrunch it down really small."

I start to cry, the image of my Audi Fox holding all my coming-of-age memories squished into a tuna can.

"I know," Lisa says, snapping her fingers. "That new guy in Tech Assistance could give you a lift home. He lives in Princeton. Chip."

I put this together. "Would that be Computer Chip?"

"Know him?"

"No."

"Oh." Lisa frowns, not getting the joke. "Anyway, I do. He unfroze my computer last week. He's a real sweetheart. Let me see if he's still around. You stay here." And she runs off.

When she's gone I'm left with nothing to do besides stare at the burned patch of grass on which I wish were my fantasy car, a Capri blue Mercedes SLK convertible. At $185,000 this is a luxury item I will never own, but that I crave nonetheless, in the same way that diabetics must crave Milky Ways, I think. Or that teenage boys crave Pamela Anderson.

My Mercedes SLK dream is one of my few fantasies that does not require me to become Cinderella. No man is involved, or adorable tow-headed children. There is no party to attend looking smashing in a sequined gown where I am heralded for my runaway success debut novel or a wedding with an aisle where I will walk dressed in white, a long train with the letter A embossed on it. (That Sarah Ferguson divorce really messed with my head.)

No, it's just me, my long brown hair flowing in the breeze as I shift into fifth, cruising down the Jersey Shore. I run my hands over the buttery leather—color: sand. I have no problems, no fears. No one to answer to but perhaps the collection agents on my tail, angry that I have not made one payment on the $185,000 I owe on this Mercedes SLK in Capri blue. And because it is a fantasy, for once I don't care.

Daydreaming is something I do regularly and, may I say, I do well. I have daydreamed all my life. I can't remember not daydreaming. In fourth grade I could tell you the names I had given the leaves on the tree outside our classroom window. Or the fairies and elves that lived in its roots. My grade point average hovered at a C- in fourth grade.

It is the refuge of worrywarts, daydreaming. That and mindless eating. Best done in combination for full effect.

It would be nice if Computer Chip drove a Capri blue Mercedes SLK convertible, but he doesn't. He drives a black Toyota pickup and is wearing a denim shirt rolled up to the elbows when he pulls up next to me and leans out his window.

"Need a ride?" He is not bad-looking for a geek. He has blond tousled hair and tanned skin and looks more like a surfer than a nerd who likes to hole up in his room, drooling over the latest issue of *MacWorld*. I find it refreshing to meet people who are not their stereotypes, like coming across a professional cheerleader who's a feminist. Though, to be honest, I've never met one of those. I really don't think they exist.

"You must be Computer Chip," I say.

"Is that a joke?"

"Not a very good one, I guess." I pull open the door and climb in, astutely observing that he is without a wedding ring and that this could be the start of a whirlwind romance thanks to my exploded car, but I have no expectations. Expectations hurt.

We go through the usual introductions and he asks me where to. I say Park Place in Princeton, if that's not too far.

"Tough day?"

"Do I look that bad?"

"Well, you're standing in the parking lot in a hot black suit on a humid June evening, kind of dazed and daydreaming and you don't seem to have a car. You tell me." Chip talks in a slow drawl, somewhere between Texan cowboy and Californian dude, that puts a person immediately at ease.

"You wanna know the truth?" I begin. "I'm in hot water."

"Yeah?" He leans back, revealing a pair of strong thighs under faded jeans. Friday is dress-down day in the office, but I've never dressed down that far. "So, how hot is this water?"

"Boiling. For one thing, my car caught on fire and blew up."

"That's too bad. What was the car?"

"Audi. Fox."

"Must be ancient." He shifts and I take in that his

62

arm is extremely muscled for a man who spends his hours hunched over a keyboard. Again, not that I'm judging on stereotypes or anything.

"It's twenty-five years old. It was my dad's."

"What are you going to get to replace it?"

"I don't know." I shrug, having not thought about it. "A Honda, I guess."

"Sounds nice and boring."

"There's the pot calling the kettle black. You're driving a Toyota."

"They make good trucks."

"Honda makes good cars."

He squints. "I see you in something more sporty. Like maybe a BMW 325i."

I gasp because the BMW 325i is in fact my backup fantasy car. "Yes, that would be nice, except that I'm an editor at *Sass!*, which means I can't afford a BMW 325i. I can't even afford to rotate its tires."

"Really?" He seems confused by this.

"Besides. My dream car is a Mercedes SLK convertible in Capri blue. If I'm going to break the bank, that's my sledgehammer."

He nods approvingly. "Now you're talking."

"Correction. Now I'm hallucinating."

"Come on. You only live once. What if you die tomorrow? What if your last thought as you're falling over a cliff is, I should have driven a Mercedes SLK convertible in Capri blue? By then it will be too late. Shame." He shakes his head at the pity of it all.

This Computer Chip is dangerous. Financially dangerous. He is echoing the same voice in the back of my head that has sent me into overdraft too many times. Do you know how many overpriced lamps and stereo components and pieces of jewelry I have bought because I might die tomorrow?

"Anyway, it's beside the point," I say, trying to be frugal. "I'm about to be canned and I can't be going out dropping two hundred grand on a car."

"You're not going to be fired."

"Yes, I am. I can't tell you why, but I have done something—with the best intentions, mind you—that is going to get me and my desk cleaned out faster than you can say 'ethical standards.'"

"Hmm." Chip is silent for a few minutes. "Then you might want to buy that Mercedes now, while the credit agency can confirm you still have a job."

This, I decide, is an excellent point. I like Chip. I especially like his thighs, which I chalk up as two more good reasons to stick with the Cinderella Pact.

Chapter Seven

Suze the nutritionist holds up a poster of the human gastrointestinal system colored in a nonthreatening peachy pink.

"Gastric bypass reduces caloric intake in two ways. First, the stomach, which is normally the size of a fist, is divided and separated so that the space utilized is the size of a thumb. This limits the amount of food mass that it can hold. If a gastric bypass patient over-fills the 'pouch,' as it is called, the patient runs the risk of vomiting, or even bursting the pouch."

Delightful, I think, scrawling the words *Pouch Bursting* and *Vomit* on the notebook Suze has provided as part of an introductory seminar: "Gastric Bypass: Miracle Answer or Helpful Tool?"

This is Deb's idea. Listening to tales of pouch bursting and vomit was the last thing Nancy and I wanted to do on a beautiful Saturday morning. But Deb practically begged us. Then she said she tried to get Paul, her husband, to come but he had to stay home with the kids, which meant she'd have to go alone and that scared her too much. When she started crying, her shoulders heaving in sobs, we agreed. Deb can get anything she wants by crying. She could be a professional tearjerker.

What surprised Nancy and me was how quickly Deb seems to have made friends with the staff of the gastric bypass center. They know her by name and even know her kids' names. Plus, it's really weird. When we checked in for the seminar, the receptionist said, "Ready for next week, Deb?" and Deb gave her a meaningful look that caused the receptionist to bow her head over the keyboard.

Something's up. Maybe Deb is throwing a surprise party for us at the gastric bypass center. Hey. You never know.

Nancy completely ignores Suze's lecture, scrolling through her BlackBerry and answering old e-mails instead. Deb, on the other hand, is riveted, her posture straight, her face beaming like a repentant prostitute at a tent revival.

"Secondly," Suze continues, "the surgeon cuts the small intestine eighteen inches below the stomach and divides it. One branch of this surgically divided intestine is hooked up to the new pouch. This is called the gastrojejunostomy."

"That's called butchering," Nancy quips out of the side of her mouth.

"The other branch is attached into the intestine to complete the circuit. This is known as distal anastomosis. The lower stomach, by the way, is retained to produce enzymes. This Y formation of the intestines is why the procedure, developed by a Doctor Roux, is called Roux-en-Y. It reduces calorie consumption by delaying when bile and enzymes mix with newly consumed food. The miracle of this is that the food enters the lower bowel only ten minutes after eating begins."

A chorus of "oh's," rises from the audience, which is clearly impressed by the fast-moving, nonbilious food. Deb raises her eyebrows in wonder.

"Isn't that amazing?" she whispers. "Ten minutes."

"Yes," Nancy replies flatly.

Suze flips her ponytail. She looks exactly like every other nutritionist I've ever met. Trim, but not super thin. Neat. Tidy in white pants and funky blue clogs. I bet none of her sweaters pill. I bet her refrigerator coils are vacuumed dustless. She moves the pointer to a thoroughly grotesque slide of a splayed-open abdomen and doesn't even flinch at the enlarged photo of pink, squishy, slimy insides. Someone in the audience coughs. I have to look away.

"Using miniature instruments, the surgeon makes five to six slits in the abdomen to do all this. The entire procedure takes about an hour and a half to two hours. The surgeon monitors the entire procedure through a tiny video camera attached to the laparoscope, which has been inserted in one of the incisions. The image he sees is magnified one thousand times."

A laparoscopic picture of a bloodred and pink intestinal something magnified one thousand times flashes on the screen and instead of going "ooh," we go "ick."

Nancy scribbles on a piece of paper and slides it to me:

GET ME OUT OF HERE BEFORE I BARF!

"However, the procedure is not without complications. One in two hundred patients dies from it, though those stats are improving every day," says Suze, passing out a photocopied sheet that I scan with one eye closed. "Here are some warning signs to look for. Excessive bleeding or drainage from the incisions. Redness. Unusual pain or swelling in the lower intestines. Fever. Chills. Black stools. Diarrhea that is pure water."

My stomach is turning, but I try to be mature and look interested. I try not to think about how I could be walking my cat, Otis, in the park instead, or reading a book on my back porch.

"It will be normal," she informs us, "for patients to

experience some shoulder pain and gas, which, by the way, will more odiferous than before surgery."

This is pleasant. Why am I here again?

"I know it sounds gross." Suze patrols the room in which we all sit studiously, trying to act if odiferous farting is part of normal conversation. "But in the beginning it may be difficult for the patient to clean him- or herself. Therefore, after a bowel movement . . ."

No. Don't say it. I cover my ears and think maybe Paul had the right idea in staying home. Because as much as I love Deb, friendship has its limits.

Nancy dashes off another note: LOOK AROUND THE ROOM. PARTNERS.

I look around the room. She's right. Fat person is paired up with not-so-fat person. Plus, the not-so-fat people are patting and hugging the fat people. Deb is scrutinizing the sheet of warning signs as though her life depends upon them.

Which is when reality clicks. Lead falls into my unstapled stomach. I have been so stupid. Why didn't I realize it before?

I dash off a note to Nancy: DEB'S DOING THIS, ISN'T SHE?

Nancy reads it and her eyes go wide in alarm. We both glare at Deb, who has tricked us into attending this so-called introductory seminar to break it to us that she is actually undergoing gastric bypass. And to think that only a few days ago she innocently claimed she was just "looking into it."

I lean over to Nancy. "I bet she's already gone

68

through counseling and insurance approval. Maybe when the receptionist said 'Ready for next week?' she was talking about surgery?"

"No!" Nancy says, a bit too loudly.

"What?" Deb mouths.

Nancy begins to jot another note when Suze approaches us and clears her throat meaningfully. "Is there a question?" she asks.

I feel hotly embarrassed, like I used to in junior high school when our American Studies teacher caught us passing notes.

"Uh, not right now," Nancy says slinking slightly under her desk.

Suze smiles thinly and goes on. "The good news is that gastric bypass patients can expect to lose seventy to eighty percent of their excess weight in the first year after surgery, with much of it lost in the first six months. As long as the patient adheres to a program of sensible eating and daily exercise, that weight loss should be permanent and the patient can look forward to lowering his or her risk of diabetes, heart disease, and many other life-threatening conditions caused by excess weight."

Deb is back to glowing. She grins at us broadly and flashes two thumbs up.

"The most important fact to remember is that gastric bypass is a tool, not the miracle answer," Suze says. "In the end, it's up to the patient to restrict his or her diet. It takes discipline and hard, hard work. Most people don't realize that."

I can't wait for the lecture to end so we can corner Deb. Finally, Suze hands out leaflets on what diet to follow the first two weeks, the third week, and so on. LIQUIDS ARE TO BE CONSUMED BETWEEN MEALS, NOT DURING! Bold print proclaims across the bottom of each flier.

On the back of a leaflet is a model of a patient's dinner plate. There is one tiny circle for meat. A tinier circle for vegetables. And a teeny weenie circle for fruit. As a kid I had dolls who ate more.

"Well," exclaims Deb, getting up. "Wasn't *that* interesting?"

Nancy yanks her down. "Not so fast. How come you were so desperate to get us here? How come everyone knows your name?"

"Uh." Deb shoots a glance at Suze who seems to know what's going on by the way she winks at her encouragingly. "You want to know the real reason?"

"No," Nancy says. "Tell us the made-up version."

Deb seems temporarily confused. She bites her lip and then says, "About six months ago I started looking into this because, like I've said, no diet works for me."

Nancy throws up her hands. "I can't believe it!"

"Wait," Deb says, clutching her arm. "Look. It's true. You and Nola have already lost, what, six pounds since we formed the pact?"

Actually, after my slip-up on pizza last night, the ice-cream sandwich the night before, not to mention those amazing piña coladas at Caribe's on Thursday, I haven't lost one ounce. But really getting into a diet takes time. I don't want to shock my body, after all.

"Do you know how much weight I've lost? None. I've gained." Deb is near tears, her perpetual state these days. "It's like my body is working against me. But I know that if I have this surgery, I'll be able to get my weight under control. I thought that maybe if you went to Suze's seminar you might get enlightened."

"Enlightened?" Nancy says.

"Because you're always so quick to dismiss it. I mean, even after I got insurance approval and was ready to go I didn't tell you because I was sure you'd either laugh at me or try to talk me out of it or . . ." She's crying so hard now, she can't go on.

Nancy holds out her arms and Deb collapses into them. I pat her shoulder and tell her that of course we understand, of course this is right for her, though I'm thinking that this changes everything. With a stomach the size of a thumb, Deb is going to zip right past us on the weight-loss front. I mean, what are Nancy and I supposed to do, walking around with these stomach fists that need to be filled?

"I'm so glad you came," Suze says, having concluded that we are now safe to approach. "Deborah's told me so much about you during her counseling sessions."

Nancy and I smile politely, both of us silently wondering what, exactly, *Deborah* has said. I hope she didn't mention anything about me ripping my pants and exposing my pink granny underwear in front of Nigel Barnes.

"Deb's lucky to have such support when she comes in for surgery Monday."

Monday? So soon. That's just two and a half days away. Only two more days of normal eating for her—ever!

"Right," Nancy bluffs. "Monday. We're looking forward to it."

"And Paul?" Suze asks tentatively. "Has he changed his mind?"

Deb fiddles with the ring of her notebook. "He's coming around. Slowly."

Suze reaches out and squeezes Deb's hand. "I'm sure he will. It's not uncommon for a partner to have doubts. After all, this surgery is not without its risks."

"And he says he likes me the way I am."

"He'll like you even better," Suze says confidently, "alive and healthy."

Chapter Eight

"OK," says Nancy when we emerge like blinking moles into the light of day. "This calls for champagne."

"I can't have champagne. It's two days before surgery," Deb says. "I'm supposed to drink only clear liquids."

"And what do you call champagne?" Nancy opens the door of her Saab and practically pushes Deb into the backseat, giving me a *we-need-to-talk* look over the roof of her car.

I still haven't completely comprehended Deb's undertaking. Gastric bypass. She's really going to do it. No more popcorn. No more margaritas. No eighteen inches of intestines. Now I wished I'd paid more attention to Suze's lecture instead of covering my ears and eyes at all the gross parts.

Nancy insists on treating us to lunch at the Princeton Arms on Nassau Street. She parks several blocks away, part of her plan, she observes, to be like Belinda who lost tons and tons of weight simply by adding up five miles every day here and there.

"Really," I say again, "you shouldn't take Belinda too seriously. She's just a ditzy *Sass!* columnist, kind of loosey goosey with the truth." I laugh as if loosey goosey with the truth is all fun and games.

"She better not be loosey goosey with the truth, or she'll be looking at a hefty libel suit someday."

That does it. I resolve to keep my mouth shut whenever Nancy mentions Belinda's column.

We stop at the Ann Taylor window to comment on the slim pencil skirts and strapless sundresses. In the good old days we cursed Ann Taylor as an evil bitch who designed the kind of clothes that made us miserable. But now we are drawn to Ann Taylor's altar of anorexia like religious converts. Visions of us finally being allowed into stores like this are what keep us going, and override Deb's concern about pouch splitting.

At the Princeton Arms, Nancy leads us to the club level with her special key that comes from being a partner in her swanky law firm. The lounge is gorgeous. Deep walnut paneling, discreet lighting, and breathtaking panoramic views of Princeton University. It's very quiet, except for the occasional shuffling of newspapers.

A beefcake waiter named Brian pours out our glasses, plunks the bottle back in the chilled silver bucket, bows, and leaves. All three of us watch him go, his rearview almost as good as his front. Then Nancy raises her glass and we do the same.

"To Deb. For having the guts to lose her guts."

"Hear, hear," we chime, clinking glasses.

"Soooo," Nancy begins, getting right down to business. "What's this about Paul not being on board?"

Deb pushes back her blond curls. I try to imagine her sixty pounds thinner, dimple-free. Will she be the same old Deb? It's hard to envision her as something besides the Earth mother to Anna and Dylan. She's such a homebody, always doing crafts, covering her windows with children's glass paint, knitting, tatting—whatever that is. Deb hardly ever leaves the house if she can help it.

"It's not so much that he's not on board, as that he still has to get used to the idea," she says. "You know, he's so accustomed to me being *this way.* Then there are the risks of surgery. He's not exactly thrilled about that."

"Understandable." Nancy puts on her courtroom frown. "But of course he's going to take care of you when you get back from the hospital."

74

"Uhhh . . . More like Anna. She's on school vacation."

"Anna's fifteen. She has her own life. What about Paul?"

I tense up for Deb's sake. Sometimes Nancy's well-meaning grilling can be a bit hard to take.

"He has work." Deb says this in such a way that it's obvious work means something other than work.

Nancy slaps her thighs. "Alrighty. Then I'll arrange for a nurse."

"No, don't . . ." Deb starts, but Nancy won't hear of it.

"Listen. I am happy to. It'll put my mind at ease knowing that you've got professional care. I don't want you oozing and dripping all over the place with only a teenager at the helm. You can even stay with me for the first week, if you want. Lord knows I have the room now that Ron has, um, moved in with his Latina lover."

At this Nancy takes a large gulp of champagne, an overboard attempt at trying to appear carefree, in my opinion. Since Ron walked out, she's consistently maintained that his leaving was for the best. But anyone who knows Nancy and Ron knows otherwise.

I've always liked Ron. For one thing, he's incredibly tall and blocklike in a Herman Munster way. I'm a sucker for really tall, blocklike Herman Munster guys.

For another, he loves Nancy—still. Exotic Latina girlfriend or no.

Ron and Nancy fell in love at Seton Hall in South

Orange where she was a nursing student and he was a center on the school's basketball team. The first time I met him was when Nancy brought him home to meet her family and friends over Thanksgiving vacation when we were sophomores. I remember being struck by how softspoken Ron was, how he'd bend down to catch Nancy's every word, his eyes twinkling merrily as she rested her head against his upper arm.

Back then Nancy was a bubbly butterball with dimples in her cheeks, wavy brown hair, and the kind of chest that made Victoria's Secret stuff look like training bras. Boys were nuts for her, though there were signs even then—her full face, her lust for cheeseburgers and french fries—that Nancy teetered on the precipice of obesity. No one seemed to care. She was fun and light and "bursting with love," as she gushed to me shortly before saying her wedding vows, "for my Big Ron."

What changed only Nancy and Ron know, but I personally think it had more to do with Nancy than Ron. Their early marriage was textbook perfect. She worked at Hahnemann Hospital in Philadelphia to put Ron through Temple Law, spending her free hours helping him study. Then she discovered, much to Ron's delight, her own quick mind for case law and legal reasoning. When he passed the bar, she enrolled in Temple and trumped Ron's own academic performance, editing the *Bar Review* and graduating magna cum laude.

Some men might have found her successes castrating, but not Ron. He threw a surprise party when she passed the New Jersey bar, was thrilled by her clerkship in Trenton. He adjusted his work schedule to be home for her and took cooking classes. He did the food shopping and paid the bills. All of which Nancy took for granted.

The constant griping about Ron started shortly after she became an associate at Barlow, Cafferty and Kline—New Jersey's top criminal defense firm in Trenton. Suddenly, according to Nancy, Ron wasn't making enough money in the Philadelphia public defender's office. He was too laid back. Not ambitious enough. Plus, he was hinting about starting a family, an idea that she proclaimed "completely unrealistic."

It was as though her Big Ron had started to shrink.

While she had started to explode.

Each year she added an extra layer of fat the way a bear prepares for hibernation. Her cute dimples disappeared and her once pinup, Playboy-bunny chest was swallowed by the folds of fat around her middle. Her blood pressure rose and her breathing became more labored. The day Ron suggested she take an exercise class, she tossed a copy of the *New Jersey Statutes Annotated Volume 23* at his head.

Two months later, Nancy got a phone call from American Express verifying that a hotel in Cozumel was not fraud. Ron had told her he was off to the Poconos for a fishing vacation at a family cabin. He didn't mention that he'd left a few days early to join Gina, his twenty-seven-year-old Guatemalan law clerk, on a Mexican beach.

His bags were packed and on the doorstep when he got home. Nancy refused to listen to one word of explanation.

That was about a year ago, and here we are in the Princeton Arms and I, for one, am frustrated that a couple meant to be together for eternity is splitting up for no good reason.

"He wants to get remarried, you know. That's why he's been so nice to me lately. Don't cross your legs, Deb, remember? Blood clots."

Deb uncrosses her legs. I am impressed that Nancy picked this up from Suze's lecture.

"He's getting married? To Gina?" I ask.

Nancy finishes off her champagne and helps herself to a refill. "Who else? Guess it was true love all along, despite what he claimed when I caught them in Cozumel."

I don't believe it. "He's bluffing," I say. "There's only one woman he loves, and that's you."

"Really?" Nancy leans forward as if she were driving home a point to the jury. "Then tell me why he asked me if I'd be up for a legal annulment."

I am speechless, partly because I've never been sure what an annulment really entails.

"He wants an annulment," Nancy finishes, her eyes slightly glazed from the champagne, "because he wants to marry Gina in the Catholic Church so they can raise up the dozen Catholic babies he wanted me to spit out as soon as I was done putting him through law school."

With this, Nancy plunks her champagne glass on the table so hard that the stem shatters and the three of us scream. Brian the beefcake waiter rushes over, followed by a busboy carrying a heavy white cloth. We are ordered to sit still as they clean up the mess, Nancy apologizing profusely.

"Don't be sorry. No big deal," he says, leaning over and revealing a large broad back. "Looked like you girls were having fun."

"It's our last party before I undergo weight-loss surgery," Deb blurts, displaying her knack for saying odd things in awkward social situations.

"Weight-loss surgery, huh?" Brian tosses the glass in a bag. "All of you?"

"Just me." Deb raises her hand. "Nola and Nancy are going about it the old-fashioned way. Diet and exercise. Apparently if you walk five miles a day and cut back two hundred and fifty calories a day you can lose, like, a hundred pounds in a year. Did you know that?"

Brian frowns doubtfully. "Surely you ladies don't need to lose a hundred pounds."

Right then, I wish I could wrap him up and take him home. I bet he's a Princeton student, too. Smart *and* adorable.

"I don't know much about diet, but I do know a ton about exercise," he says. "And you need to ramp up the program pretty progressively. Walking around the block won't do much good for long."

"I don't like the sound of that," I say. "Ramping up."

"No. Really. Sounds worse than it is. In fact, I put my sister on a program at the gym and she lost so much, she was buying a smaller size every other week. She says I should make an infomercial or something."

"You should!" I exclaim, having no idea what he's talking about.

"I'll tell you what." He wipes the last of the champagne. "I'll let you in on my secret and if it works for you then—*booyah*—I'm going cable."

And before we can say *booyah* back, Brian outlines his infomercial-worthy regimen on a paper napkin, which I carefully tuck in my purse as though it were the map to the most valuable treasure ever hidden.

Nancy, however, declares that she'd prefer to go with a personal trainer. That's what you can buy with all the money she has, a personal trainer.

But, like the Beatles trilled, can't buy her love.

Chapter Nine

Exercise. That's what I've been missing. *This* is the genuine ticket for weight loss, ask anyone.

How many stories have I heard about people who just start, for example, jogging and before they know it they're in marathons and have stopped menstruating, they've lost so much fat. And if you ask them what diet they were on they say with surprise, "I ate just like I always did and the weight came off."

It's true!

Of course, if you're overweight like I am, you're caught in a kind of Catch-22 where you need to lose weight first before you feel comfortable going to a gym but you can't really lose the weight unless you're working out five days a week. And then there's that fear of being among the gym rats who look at you askance, as if you're a pretender to the throne of being fit and you have no right to be on the machines.

Well, I will simply have to put all that neurotic worrying behind me and take the plunge. As I drive in my Dodge Shadow rental car to the Princeton Gym and Racquet Center, I envision myself months from now in tight black yoga pants and a sports bra, my abs tanned and flat. And people will say, "Do you know she used to be extremely overweight?" To which the reaction will be, "No! She's got such a great body now."

Maybe the gym will pin up before and after photos. Or put me in one of their newspaper ads.

AS SEEN ON BRIAN THE HUNK WAITER'S INFOMERCIAL: NOLA DEVLIN!

I'll be like an in-house Princeton Gym and Racquet Club celebrity.

Armed with Brian's Fast Fitness Plan, as I suggested he call it, I boldly walk into Princeton Gym and Racquet Club, humming an old Helen Reddy song. Years from now I will be able to recall this as a moment that changed my life, much like when I read the back page of *Who Moved My Fat?* I will think of myself as walking in plump and walking out thin. Just like on that Lifetime movie.

Actually, I have had a membership to the Princeton Gym and Racquet Center for three years. It comes with my job at *Sass!* which pays for half of the membership, just like *Sass!* will pay for me to go to Weight Watchers or, if I were a smoker, SmokeEnders.

The logic here is that attending these organizations will reduce health insurance rates. Though, to be honest, it's so Big Brother that most smokers in our office refuse to go. Once you declare you're a smoker, forget it. Your insurance rates are doomed forever.

At the gym, I drink in the invigorating smells of chlorine and sweat as I swipe my card and head for the locker room.

"Excuse me," says a gum-chewing girl at the front desk. "It didn't go through. Try again."

No problem. I rub my card and give it another go.

"Still nothing." She looks me up and down. "When was the last time you were here?"

"Ohhh." I study the ceiling, trying to pinpoint a date that sounds as if I've been temporarily detained, not permanently slacking off. "I think a few, uh, weeks ago."

I give her my name which she types into the computer. "Try January."

"That long?" I feign shock. "Can't be."

"January second. Just like everyone else in town. OK. I'll have to reset your card."

I hand her my card guiltily.

"Do you need a locker key or anything?"

"Absolutely not!" I declare. "I rent a locker."

"Uh-huh." She hands me back the card. "I hope you still remember your combination."

Of course I do. It's 36-16-6. Verrry easy.

I take my reset card and towel down to the women's locker room and brace myself. It's not as though I'm a prude as much as it is that I'm . . . modest. I have never been the type to prance about in the buff slapping on lotion and yapping about some movie I've seen. Then again, I might be the type if I had a body that didn't jiggle and fold in odd places.

The locker room is filled with steam and lots of naked women slapping on lotion as I'd feared. I carefully leave my shoes by the door in ultimate gym etiquette and make my way to the rear by the sauna where I see my locker #38 and my trusty combination lock. Excellent.

Except 36-16-6 doesn't work. Neither does 16-6-36 or any combination thereafter.

"We were wondering who had that locker," says a woman wrapping a white towel around her chest. "I've been going here for years, and I've never seen anyone use it."

"IS SOMEONE USING NUMBER THIRTY-EIGHT?" screeches her friend, pulling on a pair of jeans.

"Yeah. Her."

"DOES SHE KNOW WHAT THAT SMELL WAS?"

Smell? My locker smelled? How mortifying is that?

"Bet you forgot," observes the toweled woman who shows no signs of leaving until the locker is opened. "I'll call Tricia at the front desk."

Twenty minutes, one Tricia, and one sawed-off combination lock later and I am in a pair of wrinkled black sweats and a loose white T-shirt and running shoes, which happen to reek of moldy sponges and an odor that reminds me of Super 8 Motel shower curtains.

That's OK, I assure myself, I'm in a gym. You're *supposed* to stink in a gym. I pull out Brian's Fast Fitness Plan and try to concentrate on what I'm here for. Losing weight. Feeling fit. Living longer.

Brian's plan is quite simple, though it involves a lot of running around and perfect timing, two qualities I'm not famous for. The idea is to mix an aerobic workout with an anaerobic workout so that your body is fooled into burning more fat than it normally would.

Fooling the body. I like that.

The first thing I must do is a ten-minute workout on an aerobic machine like a treadmill or elliptical trainer. Then I must immediately run to the weight room (Nautilus, Brian informs me, is for wimps and old ladies) and lift barbells for five minutes. Then it's back to the treadmill for another ten, over to the weight room for dead lifts, back to the elliptical trainer, and finally, push-ups.

I feel firmer already.

The elliptical trainer is fun, almost like a video game with digital pictures of courses and statistics. I plug in

84

my weight, which I lie and say is 150 since the guy next to me is looking over my shoulder. Course? I choose Random since Weight Loss would give me away.

And I'm off. This is very easy. Not even hard on the knees because the foot pads are actually lifting my feet! I smile at the man next to me who is wiping sweat off his brow and wincing. He must really be out of shape if he's having such a hard time on a machine that does all the work for you.

Beep! A light is blinking indicating we are going up to a harder level. See what I mean about it being like a video game? Fun, fun, fun. Well, this is slightly harder. Then again, as Brian said, they wouldn't call it a "workout" if it didn't involve "work." I would say hello to Tricia passing by except, oddly, I'm out of breath.

Beeeep! Uh-oh. Now what are we doing? PREPARE FOR REVERSE, the screen says.

Reverse?

Shit.

REVERSE! It's screaming at me. REVERSE!

I can't REVERSE! I'll fall off, I think, as I start running backward, my calves sending out messages to the brain to cease and desist with this nonsense right now. Where did I get the big idea, running backward? That's not how the human body is designed. If we were meant to run backward, we'd have toes on our heels.

And then it's over. My ten minutes are up.

I leap off, wipe down the machine, and dash to the weight room, which is populated by big, unappealing men with blue pads around their middles, grunting at their reflections. The smell here is even worse than in locker #38.

One guy in a Rider University T-shirt rolls an eyeball toward me and cocks his chin to his steroid-addicted friend. They are sending a signal loud and clear that women like me are not allowed. This is testosterone country.

We'll just see about that.

Summoning all my esteem, I confidently walk over to the barbells, settling on a ten-pounder since the threes and fives seem so puny. I need to establish a reputation, like prisoners do on their first night behind bars.

With expert skill I pick up a barbell in each hand, raise my arms, then lower them, careful to concentrate on my breathing. I may be big, but I am strong. Even the steroid junkies are checking me out with admiration as I go for—yes—a second rep.

"You gonna be done with those soon?" Rider appears in my mirror and points to the barbells.

"I've got three more sets," I say, though I can't remember how many lifts are in a set.

"OK. I'll wait." He sits himself down on a bench, folds his arms, and waits. I'd like to point out that there are plenty of other ten-pound barbells there, but I can't speak. In fact, I am having trouble controlling my bladder.

"That's two," he counts helpfully. "You got thirteen more to go."

"No," I correct, my face turning red as I lift again. "I'm doing three."

"Three sets. There should be fifteen reps in each set."

Cripes. Who is this guy? Len Barkowski, my high school gym teacher?

"Getting tired?" he taunts. "Are your muscles burning?"

"No. They're fine. It's just that I'm on a program. I have to be back to the machines." I drop both weights, narrowly missing my pinky toes. "Now."

"Yeah," he says, smiling knowingly. "I thought so."

Fuming, I run back to the machines and hop on a treadmill, setting everything for ten minutes at level 18, the highest. How dare he intimidate me out of the weight room? Am I going to stand for that? Heck no. I pay dues here. I have just as much a right to lift weights there as he does.

I'm so mad, I don't even notice that I am running up hill and that my heart is racing. When my ten minutes are up, I hop off and make a beeline straight to where the big boys are.

"Look who's back," Rider says.

I smile, feeling curiously lightheaded, and choose my weapon. A long bar lying on a mat. That should be easy enough.

Sauntering over, I dip my hands in chalk, rubbing my palms as Rider and company look on. "Dead lifts," I say. "Twenty-five."

Rider smirks. "I'll bet ten bucks you can't do ten."

"You're on."

"As is?"

I eye the plain, rather light-looking bar, which couldn't weigh more than a curtain rod. "As is."

"Shit," says his buddy. "She can't do that."

"Then she's out ten bucks."

I walk over, stretch, bend, grasp the bar firmly, and lift.

For some reason it doesn't move. Is it tied down? I check the ends. No. They seem to be free. Rider is shaking his head. "She can't even do one."

Locking my knees, setting my jaw, I try again. This time I have more success as I slowly lift the bar, the muscles in the part of my arm that prevent me from ever wearing a strapless dress fraying as I do so.

"That's one," counts Rider. "Nine more to go."

Carefully I lower the bar, the thought of raising it again, not to mention nine more times, making me vaguely ill.

My arms cry out again as I go for two. A small crowd has gathered behind me. I grit my teeth and do it again.

"Three," Rider says.

I can't. I cannot do it for ten. I had no idea this thing was so heavy.

"Just keep your legs straight, Nola. Bend from the hips."

Nola? Someone said my name. I check the mirror and see that in the middle of the crowd is the heart-stopping reflection of a tall surfer type in a ripped gray T-shirt and unbelievably sexy shorts. Chip.

"That's it," he says. "You can do it."

This is both good and bad. On the one hand he's cheering on my dead lifts. On the other hand . . . my fat ass is sticking out like a full moon over the Chesapeake. Please, I pray, please may I not be wearing my pink underwear. (Really, I should toss it all.) Then a crisis thought—*Do I have plumber's crack?*

"Whatsa matter? Give up?" taunts Rider.

OK, this is it. Are you gonna wimp, or are you gonna fight?

Number four is the hardest yet. I realize that pausing between lifts is a mistake. Maybe I can get away with not dropping the bar to the floor.

I try this strategy when I go from five to six, but Rider catches me. "Nuh-uh. You got to completely drop the bar, not just lower it. Those are the rules."

"How many does she have to do?" I hear Chip ask.

"Four more," someone says.

"Four. That's easy. You can do it, Nola." Chip moves next to me, so close I can hear him whisper. "Bend slightly at the knees. They'll never see."

I take his advice and am surprised. No wonder they tell you not to bend at the knees when doing dead lifts. It's much easier.

"Eight!" everyone shouts.

"Two more, Nola. Two more." Chip pumps his fists.

Honestly, I wish he'd go away so I could give up. I'd much rather humiliate myself among strangers.

I lick salty sweat off my lips and will what's left of my arms to function.

"Nine!"

"This is it!" Chip is shouting. "You're going to do it. Use your thighs."

I am. I am going to do it. One more. Just one more. I squeeze my eyes shut. The bar wavers from side to side. Chip steadies one end and I do it.

"Yeah!"

I drop the bar with a *clank* and slowly straighten my aching back. Through blurry vision I see that the small crowd has broken into applause.

"No fair. She cheated. You helped her," Rider claims.

"Be a man," Chip says, "and pay her the ten bucks."

"Keep it," I say, as black dots dance before my eyes.

"No way. You earned it."

"That's all right."

Chip is going in and out of focus. My sweatpants, I remember, stink. Stink famously. "I have to, I have to go."

"Wait." He follows me out the door as I stagger through the machine room to the exit. "That was awesome. I can't believe you took him on like that."

"Uh-huh." I am in no shape for conversation. I need to lie down and rest, preferably on a hospital bed with IV fluids.

He stops me at the women's room. "You know, I'd really like to see you again. Can I call you?"

Whatever, I think, unable to grasp how amazing this

90

is that a cute guy, albeit a computer geek, like Chip is writing down my number. I mumble it off and then spin into the locker room where I head for the sauna and promptly collapse.

Chapter Ten

My apartment is a total find.

The walls are painted a very faint peach with white trim and the floors are dark maple throughout. There are two bedrooms; one living room with, yes, a wood-burning fireplace and a pair of built-in bookshelves; a formal dining room separated from a small kitchen by a white Georgian post; and a bathroom with marble floors and a window, which is where Otis reigns, meowing warnings to oblivious male passersby below.

I would never have been able to afford the $2,000 a month rent if it hadn't been for Belinda's extra income. Belinda made the one bright spot in my life possible. And for that I am indebted to her.

Otis scrambles off the windowsill to meet me as I enter carrying two bags of groceries, so sore that I can barely climb the stairs. He's a slick gray cat. Untrustworthy and possibly criminally insane. I'm not sure of this, as I don't know many kitty psychologists who would be willing to be alone with him in a room to perform a diagnosis.

What I do know is that in three instances he has

leaped from the slate windowsill of the bathroom onto men wearing white T-shirts below. It's the puma in him. Or the psychopath. Either way, his claws must be deadly, judging from the howls of his victims.

I open a can of 9Lives and dump it into a dish as he wraps himself around my legs. Fat woman in her thirties with a cat in a pastel apartment. Could I be any more of a stereotype?

Ouch. My arms. My arms.

I shower off the gym sweat, the warm water doing wonders for my aching body, smear Bengay everywhere, and change into fresh gray sweats. Then I put water on to boil for whole wheat spaghetti and give myself five minutes to empty my cupboard of all unhealthy food.

This is Brian the hunk waiter's idea, one he will highlight in the infomercial. While he's not a big advocate of diets, he said he helped his sister by eliminating all junk food from her pantry. I think I can do that—though I'm not sure about returning to the gym to face Rider. I figure I'll quit while I'm ahead.

After four minutes I have filled several brown-paper grocery bags with: half a bag of Chips Ahoy! cookies; a jar of peanut butter; half a jar of Nutella; three half-full, somewhat stale bags of Nacho Cheese Doritos; three Snickers bars; movie butter microwave popcorn; a box of good old-fashioned, high-fat granola; and a six-pack of Hires root beer.

That, I decide, is enough for one night.

As the water heats, I take a bottle of Evian (spelled

backward—naive—did you know that?) down the hallway to where my laptop is hidden in the guest bedroom, what I like to think of as my own version of the mad scientist's laboratory. It would be cool if I could access it through a revolving door operated by moving a bust of Shakespeare. Better yet, if I had a fire pole.

I quickly check Belinda's personal e-mail—belinda.apple@sassmag.com—and find it is overflowing with messages from the likes of Lori DiGrigio and Belinda's agent Charlotte Barnes and even David Stanton. There is also one from lennonlives@ princeton.edu. The subject: **Met your editor recently.**

Nigel Barnes.

I am tempted to open it. However, I don't because Belinda's column was due yesterday and I have yet to write it. Not really a problem since I also edit it, which puts me in the weird position of being both anxious and mad at myself at the same time.

Anyway, enough dithering. I must get to work.

Opening Belinda's official e-mail—befab@ sassmag.com—I find there are ten pages of letters, only three of which I choose to answer. The rest I will reply to semipersonally, in that I thank them for writing and advise them to find a real counselor to help them solve their problems. OK, so I'm a bit cautious these days. Perfectly understandable, considering how I went a bit over the top, you might say, with that business about losing massive amounts of weight by walking five miles and holding off on that extra chocolate-chip cookie.

In preparation for writing my responses, I put on the Beatles' "Across the Universe" and focus on being beautiful and fabulously serene. I become Belinda, even rereading the first letter out loud in a British accent.

Dear Belinda:
My sister is forty years old and still lives off my parents even though she's married with two children, doesn't work, and her husband is a corporate executive. She gets them to water her plants, clean out her garage, drive her kids to after-school activities, and even "loan" her gobs of money. It's making me crazy, especially since I work and have never so much as asked them for a cup of sugar.

Aren't I ethically obligated to tell my parents she is fleecing them? Or should I stay out of it? I keep thinking that if I don't say anything, someday they'll wake up and find themselves bilked of all money and their golden years.

Signed,
GREEN-EYED SIBLING IN DES MOINES

I'd like to tell her that as a sister of Eileen Devlin I can relate—big-time—but I don't. Instead I answer with this:

Dear GREEN-EYED:
Let's face it; you're pissed—a state that can wreak

94

havoc on a girl's complexion. Remember that the key to being fab is to be blissfully free of the major bugaboos that torment us women—anxiety, greed, envy and lack of self-worth. Tell yourself that you are fabulous. That it is a gift being so independent and free of parental reliance.

Then reverse the karma by doing something for your parents instead of expecting them to do something for you. You might want to mow their lawn (or, better yet, hire an adorable young man to do so) or cook them a four-course meal (or, if I were you, take them to a smashing restaurant). Soon the envy will stop gnawing away at your psyche and everyone will decide you are simply the most fab person in the world and isn't it too bad your sister can't be more like you.

As for the ethical question of whether to tell your parents, you and I both know that this "dilemma" is just a ruse for your jealousy. What you're really asking is if it's OK to tattle on your sister. And it's never OK to tattle, unless not doing so somehow hurts an innocent party. Besides, I'm positive your parents are very well aware of the score that may, one expects, show up in the reading of their final will and testament.

—Belinda

I get chills seeing Belinda's name, knowing that each month 500,000 readers believe she is real and strolling through London in pink cowboy boots when, actually, she's reeking of Bengay in sweats on a Saturday night in Central New Jersey. Which reminds me—the lid on the spaghetti pot is banging in the kitchen. I rush in, dump half the box of whole-wheat spaghetti into the boiling water, and give it a quick stir before running back to the next letter.

Dear Belinda:
My boyfriend and I have been living together for seven years and he has yet to bring up the M word. My family used to tease him about it until he told my father on Christmas Eve that "there are some women you marry and some women you f*&k and guess which one your daughter is," which prompted my father to dump eggnog over his head.

Unfortunately, we—along with my father—have been invited to my cousin's wedding. My cousin is the one who introduced my boyfriend to me and she really wants us to attend as a couple. Plus, I love him and I think he does want to marry me, eventually. He's just commitment phobic.

Is it wrong for me to bring my boyfriend after the way he treated my father? Or, should I forget my family and bring him anyway?

—Signed, DOORMAT GIRLFRIEND, I KNOW

Oh, brother. Dear Shoot Yourself Now Whydontcha is what I want to say.

96

Dear DOORMAT:

I suppose the real question is why you are still living with the jerk. I mean, if one of your girl-friends confided that you were a perfectly fine mate to lie about with in the flat, eating crisps and watching *Big Brother*, but that you were not fit to be seen with in public, how long would you wait to ditch her? A minute?

Being a doormat is not fab. This prince has no intention of asking you to marry him, now or ever. And if he did, I shouldn't think you'd agree. Not if you aren't a card-carrying masochist.

The "ethical" thing to do in this case is to attend the wedding sans designated other and to wear a low-cut dress and very high, very sexy, ridicu-lously expensive shoes. Ask your cousin to seat you at the singles table and if she objects, tell her she's lucky you don't sue her for inflicting mental cruelty by setting you up with this prize. Remember to hold your head high and relax. You are desirable. You are wonderful. You are fab.

—Belinda

I check my watch. Two more minutes until the spaghetti is done. I take a swig of bottled water and scan the next one quickly.

Dear Belinda:
My husband is a great guy. Kind. Hard working.

Super with the kids. However, he has this one habit that's driving me up the wall. He snorts every five minutes. *Snort.* Pause. *Snort.* It used to be seasonal with allergies, but now as he gets older I notice it's all the time. Living with him is definitely not fab. If I bring it up, he acts like I'm the problem. I'm on the verge of divorce.

As a wife and cohabitant of this home, I feel I have the right to demand a snort-free environment. Am I wrong? No kidding. Help me!

—Signed, READY TO BLOW IN KENTUCKY

OK, this is one of the more repulsive letters I've had. I'll need to check with my doctor sources—the local clinic around the corner—before answering it. For all I know, snorting every five minutes could be the sign of some serious disease at which point, as Belinda would say, Ready to Blow in Kentucky needs to make sure hubby has left her enough in life insurance.

I should dump the spaghetti in the colander, but I don't. Instead, brimming with curiosity, I go into Belinda's personal messages and click on **Met your editor recently** from lennonlives@princeton.edu.

Dear Belinda:
Nigel Barnes here. Thought it fitting for me to properly introduce myself, considering I have been designated by the Tinseltown tabloids as

your latest paramour and all that. (I do hope you spare yourself the misery of watching CNN, but if by any chance you have been in an airport in the past forty-eight hours, it was likely impossible for you to miss seeing yours truly providing commentary on my close friend Eric Clapton and Soledad's frequent references to you and me as the latest posh couple.)

Oh, brother.

As luck would have it, I ran into your charming and delightful editor, a Nola Devlin (Irish, is she?) who was kind enough to provide me with your personal e-mail. I do believe she was coming on to me.

What? I was so not coming on to him.

Nola's very pretty, though, unfortunately, she's somewhat large-boned, if you get my drift. It's too bad, as otherwise I could see myself asking her out because she's obviously very bright and has lovely eyes.

But I can't help it. I so dislike fat people in general and fat women in particular. It's in my genes. Perhaps you could let her down gently for me, make up something about you lusting after me. I'm sure you understand.

By the way, it so happens that I'll be traveling up

to Deeside for Christmas. I'm a MacLeod, you know, so Scotland is my second home. I'd love to stop by for a visit at Balmoral.

Cheers,
Nigel

Big-boned? So dislikes fat women? Talk about a bloody twit. Livid, I change my computer clock to reflect the London five hour difference and rip off a quick note.

From: belinda.apple@sassmag.com
To: lennonlives@princeton.edu
Re: Met your editor recently

Hello, Nigel! How brilliant of you to write. I believe I've heard your name before. Is it that you work at some finishing school, Princeton School for Girls, is it? In the buildings and grounds department, I think.

Unfortunately, as you know, the Windsors have quite a hair across their arse about the MacLeod clan. Can't stand them, I'm afraid. So while I would love to entertain you at Balmoral where the hunting and riding are absolutely divine (as are our seven-course meals and fine French champagne) a visit from one of your "types" is simply out of the question.

I'm sure you understand.

It's too bad you are dead set against asking out Nola. If you'd made a favorable impression, I might have been persuaded to bend Cousin Charlie's ear or, at the very least, that of Camilla. We do go back years, even further than the infamous MacLeod/Windsor feud.

Cheers!
Belinda

Ha! I press Send and shout with glee. The rub is in. Let's see how Princeton's gift to women responds to that one.

Finally, though I don't want to, I click on Lori's e-mail, which is warmly entitled: **Record Keeping**

Belinda:
Pursuant to our Ethical Standards Policy, please fax to our offices a copy of your résumé. It seems the original one you sent us, including the entire packet of application materials, is missing.

All best,
Lori DiGrigio

Managing Editor
Sass! Magazine
Princeton North
Corporate Center, 5th Floor
East Brunswick,

New Jersey 08816
"We're *Not* Your
Mother's Magazine."

Now *that's* interesting. How lucky is that? Or . . .
wait. Maybe it's not lucky but devious. Perhaps this is
a trap set up by Lori to check whether the résumé
Belinda sends her now is the same as the one she sent
her a year ago. That would be just like her.
I respond.

Dear Ms. DiGrigio:
As I do not have a facsimile machine, I will ask
my agent, Charlotte Dawson, to send you a copy
of my vita. So sorry you are having trouble
keeping your records together. Was it the new girl
who lost them? Dawn was such an efficient secretary. Too bad you had to let her go.

Cheers,
Belinda

I sit back and reread the e-mail before sending it,
priding myself on the new-girl crack. Lori's new pam-
pered assistant Alicia needs to be sent back to Swarthmore where she came from. It was completely catty
the way she stole Dawn's job.
    There are all sorts of menacing sounds coming from
the stove. Hisses and snaps. But I just have to take a
peek first at David Stanton's e-mail—**Inquiry**—and

then I swear to myself I will run back to the kitchen.

Dear Ms. Apple:
I apologize for using this medium to correspond, but my secretary cannot seem to find your London address, as your records have inexplicably disappeared.

My main purpose in writing you is to let you know what a fine asset you have been to *Sass!* I have thoroughly enjoyed your columns, though I take issue with the way you advise our readers that "sometimes, white lies are preferable to the truth." It is my opinion, Miss Apple, that lying in any degree is never preferable, but punishable.

Oh, lighten up.

My question pertains to a problem with one of our employees. During a routine company audit, we discovered that the résumé she submitted is completely fraudulent. In fact, our lawyers are having a horrible time verifying one aspect of its truthfulness.

Tell me—should she be fired on the spot? Or should we proceed with legal proceedings to recover all the $150,000 we've paid her over the year?

I am so grateful for a "modern ethics expert" on our staff to handle this thorny issue.

Mr. David Stanton

David A. Stanton, publisher and president
Sass! Fit! and *Fix Up!* Magazines
Stanton Media, Inc.
West 57th Street
New York, New York 10019

Holy crap!

I stare at the e-mail, unable to breathe. Could it be that this is also a test? That perhaps he is poking me to see if I'm cooked?

In a flash of panic, I calculate the possibility of packing up my computer and my apartment and heading out of town, across the plains of the Far West, never to return to Jersey again. Recover the $150,000! But that's my entire savings. I must fight back.

Dear Mr. Stanton:

Thank you so much for your lovely words regarding my column and the opportunity to write for your delightful magazine. In answer to your inquiry, I'm afraid I would need more details in order to provide you with a full and complete answer. As my beloved mother—

Dang. She's Irish, right? Or was, rather. I type in the first female Irish name that comes to mind.

—Rosie O'Grady used to say, "Never be a judge and jury without sitting through the whole trial."

Looking forward to your response,
Belinda Apple

Done. That should buy me some time. Now I can get the spaghetti . . .

Just as soon as I click on Charlotte Dawson's message written in usual literary agent shorthand.

B—

where r u? Left mesgs on cell. need to discuss before mon. re: film offer. ASAP

Chapter Eleven

This is what my mother means when she says God always sends an angel to soften the sting of the devil. Here I am, reeling from David Stanton's "gotcha" e-mail and lo and behold, Charlotte drops the bomb that there's a film offer on the table.

Never have Charlotte and I spoken of film. Doing a book, yes, but it would be a book of columns. What is she talking about? I jump out of my chair and begin pacing, thoughts whirring around my head like dried peas in a blender.

It must have something to do with that article the *New York Intelligentsia* wrote about me last month—*Tempting Apple*—about how I grew up poor on the outskirts of London and was beaten by my cruel father until my Irish mother ran away with me and I changed my name to Belinda Apple so my father couldn't find me and how that's why I keep myself hidden to this day.

Damn me and my overactive imagination. I wish sometimes I could put a cork in it to keep the genie in the bottle.

If only it weren't Saturday night, then I could call Charlotte at her office and find out what all this is about. Now I'll be tormented until Monday. I wish there were some way I could . . .

Belinda's cell phone! Of course. Surely Charlotte left a more detailed message on that. I find Belinda's phone buried in the bottom of my purse. Turning it on, I dial my mailbox and enter the password. I'm so impatient, I can't stand still. Forty-two messages. Shoot. Most are hang-ups and then my agent's clipped voice comes on.

"Belinda, Charlotte." Charlotte talks as if her mouth has been wired shut. "Listen, we've had a very generous offer for the film rights to your life story from a producer with a fairly impressive track record. *Ship of Fools, Death's Door, Finesse* . . . that kind of thing. Anyway, he claims to have an in with Paramount, which has been looking for a *Sex and the City* meets *Bridget Jones* and he's convinced your biography is it. *Loves* the story of you being on the run. So *Silkwood*. Don't want to leave any more info on a message. By the way, you might need to be in California by the end of next week to brainstorm. Call me." *Click.*

Oh, my word! There really is a film deal! *Eeeeek!*

And then it all comes together. The repeat phone calls. The numerous messages from CDA. Here I thought Charlotte was calling because of the trouble Belinda's in at *Sass!* when all along it had to do with the film rights to my life story. Me. On the big screen. Who'd have ever thought that frumpy ol' Nola Devlin, who drives—drove—an Audi Fox and lives with a cat and goes to church with her parents would be the subject of a major Hollywood production?

Hold on. I survey my guest bedroom, the windows fogging from the steam wafting in from the kitchen, and reassess the situation. This biography isn't about me, Nola Devlin of Princeton, New Jersey. It's about Belinda Apple of Chelsea, London. The only problem here is there is no Belinda Apple on the run from her cruel father. How can there be a biographical film about her life when there's been no life?

More importantly, how can I go to California by the end of the week when I don't exist?

OK. I must not panic. Chances are, knowing Hollywood, the film deal will never come through. But what if it does? What if Mr. Bigshot pays for me to fly to L.A. and "brainstorm" and sees that I'm nothing but an overweight, low-level editor at a third-rate women's magazine slash tabloid? Then what?

No choice but to call Charlotte. I retrieve her cell number, press Send, and leave a convoluted message made even more convoluted by the fact that I am slipping in and out of an English accent.

"Hello, Charlotte. Belinda. Well, I don't know what

to say, honestly. Talk about fab. Is this really a film offer? What does that mean? Who's the producer?"

Beep. Beep. Beep!

I have no idea who's leaning on the horn outside my window, but they really need to cut it out. I focus on my message. "Please call me as soon as you can. I'm sorry I didn't pick up your message until now. You can call me at any hour tonight or tomorrow. Bye!"

Beep. Beep. Beep!

"Nola! Nola! Open up!"

Oh, great. It's Bitsy, my landlady, at the door. Shouting, no less. Probably coming up to complain about my pacing the floors. Hey . . . I sniff the air, which smells odd, like . . .

Burning cardboard.

I click off the phone, dash out of the bedroom, and find the hallway filled with smoke and that my kitchen stove is, in fact, about to burst into flames. I must have left the half-empty box of spaghetti by the burner.

Screaming, "Fire! Fire!" like an idiot, I run back into the bedroom to get the patchwork quilt from the guest bed. Never mind that it was the one my grand-mother sewed and gave to me on my sixteenth birthday. I can't think about that as I throw it on top of the fire just as Bitsy bursts in with an extinguisher.

Billows and billows of smoke rise up and both of us are bent over coughing. My eyes are burning. I rush to open the windows and, in the process, accidentally push off Otis, who lets out a frightened *"Yeoowww!"* as he falls two stories into the bushes below.

All I can think is: my second fire in the same month. Something is very wrong.

"You nearly burned us all down," Bitsy barks between gasps and coughs. She is a vision of bright pink and green in the smoke, a fireman in Lily Pulitzer. Bitsy is quintessentially Princetonian, right down to her espadrilles and her "tireless efforts"—the phrase she always uses—for the Princeton Historical Society.

"I was writing," I say by way of lame explanation. The top of the stove is charred black, as black as the spaghetti pot. My grandmother's quilt is a soggy heap of burned, smoldering memories and my apartment reeks of the acrid smell of fire extinguisher and fire.

We are standing there, the two of us, gaping at the damage, dumbstruck by the mess, when the phone on the wall rings.

"Fire department," Bitsy says, taking the phone of the wall and handing it to me. "I called them."

Fire department? I hesitatingly put it to my ear. "Hello?"

"Hey, Nola. How's it shakin'?" It's a man's voice. A bit laid back, one would think, for the Princeton Fire Department.

"And this is?"

"Aww, I'm sorry about that. Should have introduced myself. Chip. From the gym."

Oh, brother. Chip. What's he calling for? Then I hear in the background the unmistakable cacophony, the rise and fall of shouts peculiar to a liquor-serving establishment, and I imagine the worst.

"Are you at a bar?"

"As a matter of fact, the Annex. Listen, I wonder if you wouldn't mind doing me a little favor. It seems as if I've gotten myself into kind of a scrape . . ."

From the hallway comes the staccato ring of something more ominous. The familiar, stirring refrain of "Rule Britannia." Damn! I must have dropped the phone in the confusion of the fire. *Please don't answer it, Bitsy,* I pray, as Bitsy wanders down the hall in her flowered wrap skirt like a baby toddling toward a cliff.

"I'll get it," she chortles.

"See, there's this woman here," Chip is saying. "She's all over me. I'd be indebted to you if you could stop on by and save me from her."

Is he crazy? My apartment's been on fire and now Bitsy's answering Belinda's phone. I don't have time to rush to the Annex and save a man I hardly know. Plus, after my dead-lift experience, I'm not sure my legs can make it.

"I don't know, Chip, I'm kind of . . ."

"It'll take no more than ten minutes, honest, and then you can get back to your Saturday night. All you have to do is walk in and declare you're my girlfriend or something, throw your arms around me, and insist I go home. Oh, hell. Here she comes."

In the hallway I hear Bitsy saying "Hello" and then, "Belinda? Belinda who?"

Charlotte! Charlotte calling to tell me all the amazing news about this film offer. Wait. I can't let

110

her chitchat with Bitsy. Bitsy is the Mrs. Kravitz of Princeton proper and the greater Princeton area. She can gossip faster than a teenage girl with a party line. What if . . . ?

A surge of anxiety shoots through me. I must put an end to this right now.

"Hold on, Chip."

I put down the phone and run to where Bitsy is standing, her bright coral lips smiling broadly. "It's actually eight o'clock here, not one a.m." she says checking her watch. "Yes. No. No." She frowns. "We're not in London. Why would we be . . ."

I snatch the phone out of her hand. "Charlotte?"

"Belinda?" Charlotte coos. "For a while there I thought I had the wrong number, but it couldn't be the wrong number because right there on my teeny tiny phone screen it said Belinda Apple. Bright as day. Belinda Apple. And my cell is never wrong. You are Belinda Apple, aren't you?"

Lucky for me, Charlotte is three sheets to the wind, which is rather a refreshing change of pace, really.

"Of course, I'm Belinda. Who else would I be?" I give a nervous laugh and notice too late that Bitsy's eyes are wider than saucers.

She has overheard *everything*.

"Would you mind," I say, covering the mouthpiece of Belinda's cell phone, "taking care of my other call for me? This is business." I point to the kitchen where Chip is dangling in the air on my landline.

"Sure." Though I can tell Bitsy would much prefer

hanging around me and eavesdropping.

"So what's this about the film deal?" I say, slipping into the guest bedroom.

"Oh, darling, it's all so . . . big. Or bullshit. You never can tell with this madcap business. Hey there, boy. Not so fast with that tray." There are a few seconds where Charlotte is munching and then she gets back on. "Shitake ravioli. Delicious. At a gawdawful opening on Long Island. Wouldn't be here if my husband hadn't . . . Listen, Belinda. Let's talk Monday. There's someone here I absolutely have to meet and I can't wait a minute longer."

And that's it. She's off. Two minutes of tipsy conversation. Not enough for me to learn anything of significance, long enough for my web of lies to be destroyed by Bitsy the one-woman telegraph office.

Steeling myself with a deep breath, I sign off from my e-mail and close down the computer, shoving it under the guest bed. Maybe if I stall long enough, Bitsy will be gone.

She's not. She's on the other side of the door with my phone to her ear.

"Uh-huh. Sure," she's saying. "No problem."

I stand there, hands on hips, expecting Bitsy to hand me the phone. Instead, she hangs up and says, "Boy, does he sound sexy. Men with slow drawls. Oh, man."

"Who are we talking about, Bitsy?"

"Your boyfriend at the bar."

"He's not my boyfriend."

"I know that." Bitsy walks past me to my bedroom,

112

right to my closet, as bold as all get out. "He's pretending to be your boyfriend. I picked that up on the first bounce. That woman who's after him apparently showed up while he was on the phone and he had to pretend he was talking to you. You know, there's something about him that's very familiar. Do you know if he went to Princeton Day? Or maybe Lawrenceville?"

I have no truck with Bitsy's obsession with prep schools. "Why couldn't he pretend he was talking to you?"

"Because I'm not his girlfriend." She holds up one of my 2,064 pairs of black pants and my low-cut white silk blouse that Eileen gave me for my birthday and which I've never worn. It still has tags. "This looks nice. I have a darling necklace I picked up in Captiva that would go well with your eyes. Do you want to borrow it for tonight?"

"He's not my boyfriend!" I exclaim again.

"Not with that attitude."

"And by that you mean?"

"Boys like girls who are upbeat. Perky. Now stop standing there in those ugly sweats and get dressed. Unless you're planning to blow him off. We can always hang out together instead. I would so love to hear why that woman kept calling you Belinda Apple."

I am dressed in five minutes.

113

Bitsy, who should sell used cars she's so persuasive, has done my hair into a rather alluring twist, smeared on some makeup, and doused me in Estée Lauder. I am wearing Donna Karan heels and a funky lapis lazuli necklace. I have to admit I look relatively hot—almost as hot as my burning deltoids.

What I am doing tottering on these heels to meet a man I know briefly from a car ride and a dare at the gym, a man who wants me to pretend to be his girl-friend, is something else entirely.

What's even more disturbing is how much fun it is. God, I love pretending.

The Annex is a historic, subterranean restaurant off Nassau Street that serves a great grilled cheese and bacon sandwich and beer late at night to college students. In my mind, Chip's a bit too old to be picking up women at the Annex, but who am I to judge? I mean, besides being his girlfriend and all.

On a Saturday night it is hopping. As I descend into the dimly lit, wood-paneled bar I can barely make out the faces. I feel a bit nervous and more than a little self-conscious standing by the doorway, surveying the room. Men are assessing me quickly and, just as quickly, rejecting me, while women are giving me looks that indicate I am both overdressed and over-weight.

I hate bars. Hate them. Hate them. Hate them.

"Hey there, good-looking!" I hear as the crowd parts and Chip emerges. He has cleaned up from the gym, though still casual, wearing a white T-shirt that hangs off rather broad, well-rounded shoulders, and those jeans. His bleach-blond hair is an alluring combination with his heavy-lidded baby blues.

"'Good-looking'?" I say, just to make sure I heard right.

"You're late." He leans over and kisses me on the cheek, just like that. There's not enough time for me to react, so I stand there with all the acuity of a transfixed deer, my brain trying to catch up to what just happened. He smells terrific. Dial soap. Yup, that's it. Newly showered with Dial soap.

"You OK?" There's a slight smile at the corner of his lips. "I didn't mean to startle you." He leans toward me again and I flinch, anticipating another kiss. "Relax. I'm not going to bite," he whispers in my ear. "I'm really very gentle."

"Uh-huh." Geesh. I'm thirty-five years old. Why am I such a girl still?

"Let's get away from this bunch." As easy as one, two, three, he leads me by the hand to a wooden table where there is a sweating glass of ice water and a nearly full glass of white wine. The other woman's, I suppose.

He pulls out a chair. "Sit next to me and I'll have my arm around you or . . ." He pauses and thoughtfully taps his chin, which happens to sport an appealing dimple. "It might be better if you're standing. You

115

know, as though you just walked in and caught me."

"Standing. Yes." I don't think I'm ready to have Chip's arm around me quite yet. I'm still recovering from the kiss.

"Excellent." He sits and gives me a wink.

"Where is this other woman, by the way?"

"Angie? She's in the bathroom. She's only had a dozen glasses of wine. I'm amazed she's still vertical. Have you recovered from your dead-lift contest?"

I don't get a chance to answer, because behind me I hear, "Excuse me!"

I do believe it is the unmistakable call of a Northeastern Native Bitch. I will have to check my Peterson's field guide.

"Hello," I say graciously. "You must be Angie."

Angie is a little slip of a thing in a brown tank top, skintight white jeans, and long, chestnut hair. Her eyebrows are plucked to neat arcs and her lips are outlined in plum with the degree of exactitude I've never quite mastered sober, much less schnockered, as this woman seems to be.

"Who the hell are you?" she barks.

I've never known what to do with this question. Should I reply that I'm a sensitive, caring woman in my mid-thirties who enjoys the odd rerun of the *Dick Van Dyke Show*, felted slippers with cushy soles, the complete works of Jane Austen, as well as knitting socks? Or should I simply hand her my résumé?

I give it my best shot. "I'm . . ."

"This is Nola," Chip says, coming to my side protectively. "My girlfriend. The one I was telling you about."

OK, I know it's wrong to be thrilled by hearing those words pronounced out loud to the kind of woman who has made my life hell since seventh grade, but I'll admit it: I swooned.

"Your girlfriend." Angie surveys me from head to toe. "Get out. *She* is your girlfriend."

As if to drive home the inconceivable girlfriend angle, Chip reinforces the point by giving me an affectionate squeeze and another kiss on the cheek.

I could get used to this role. I really could.

Angie remains the true skeptic. "I don't believe it. This is the one you were talking to on the phone?"

"Yup. I told you I had a girlfriend, but you wouldn't believe me."

"A girlfriend I'll buy, but not a tractor trailer."

Ouch! Such nastiness. I reflexively lunge toward her, but Chip holds me back.

"Come on, Angie," he says, trying the mature, calm approach. "You're better than that. Why don't we call it a night?"

"Bullshit. You don't seriously think I believe this is your girlfriend. This cow?"

Five minutes, that's all I ask. Five minutes with Angie's head in a toilet and we'll be even. Is that so much?

"I'm sorry," Chip whispers. "I had no idea she'd be this bad. I thought—"

"You thought I'd go away, right?" Angie is so loud now that the Annex has quieted down. "Sleep with me

117

and then dump me, is that the way it is?"

Whoops!

"That was almost twenty years ago," he says patiently, "in high school. And if I recall, you dumped me for Mark Shrewsbury. The same night."

Angie flashes him a dirty look.

"Why don't we go outside and I'll get you a cab?" he says, letting go of me to take her hand.

"Who needs a cab when *she's* here?" Angie sneers. "Looks like she's used to carrying around plenty of wide loads."

That's it. My blue-collar Manville, New Jersey, upbringing can't take a minute more. "You want a lift? I'll give you a lift."

And before Angie can close her stupid, gaping jaw and her perfectly outlined plum lips, I deliver the neatest uppercut I've ever thrown, complete with a satisfying *crack!* Angie totters back and Chip grabs her so she doesn't fall down on the chairs.

For the second time that day, I am applauded roundly by a group of strange men.

"Sorry," I say. "I couldn't take it anymore." I push past them, past the clapping waitress who tells me that Angie is "an idiot who had it coming, the barfly" and out to the fresh air.

Thank heaven that's over with. I teeter in the fresh air, getting my bearings before attempting to walk home, though I am shaking slightly and feel ill. Listen, I may have been raised in Manville, a town known for its bars, churches, and lethal asbestos snow in July, but I'm a lover, not a fighter. It's not like I make a habit of slugging women I don't know.

"Nola! Wait!"

It's Chip. Super. The Typhoid Mary of mortification. I resolve to keep on walking.

"Listen, I never expected that to happen," he says breathlessly, catching up to me. "I figured she'd see us together and leave us alone and then we could, you know, go out."

I stop to stare at him in disbelief. "Go out? This is how you ask women for a date, invite them to a cat-fight and then escort the winner home?"

He holds up his hands in protest. "No, no. That wasn't my idea at all. I figured—"

"Or maybe that's how you get your kicks, seeing two women go at it." I am about to make a fat comment, but in a moment of rare prudence, demur and return to trudging homeward.

"What? No. It was a stupid idea because I am a stupid man."

"Though very popular. Angie was ready to claw my eyes out for you."

"Angie was too blind drunk to see anything."

"Except you." I pick up the pace.

"At least let me walk you home. You can't go by yourself. You might get mugged by a Princeton preppie. I understand those Burberry plaids can leave awful welts."

Despite my fury, I have to smile.

Chip sees his opening and tries to wedge his way

in further. "The thing is, I've lived around alcoholics all my life. Dramatic, goblet-smashing, Rolls Royce–crashing lushes."

I take mental notes. Something here is not jibing with my image of the computer geek slacker who gave me a lift in his beatup Toyota.

"And what I've learned is that the worst thing you can do when they're in one of their 'moods,' as my mother used to call it, is confront them. Better to try to extricate yourself."

We get to my apartment, where Otis is silhouetted menacingly against the second-floor window. I have no idea how he climbed up there after falling off the ledge during the fire. One of those cat things. "So you called me," I say. "The Extricator. Makes me sound like a cross between Arnold Schwarzenegger and a toilet plunger."

Chip laughs. "Well, after seeing your performance in the gym this afternoon I figured you were up to the job."

"Don't get so cocky," I warn him. "You're still on my naughty list."

"Meoow!" We both look up. I discern the telltale signs of an imminent pounce, assess Chip in his white T-shirt, and decide to do nothing. If Otis attacks, it'll serve Chip right.

"Is that yours?" he inquires.

"I'm afraid so."

"Interesting security system. It's like a meowing gargoyle."

I have second thoughts about the Otis plan simply because Chip is pretty cute in that shirt and I'd hate to see him bloodied. Though maybe a little bloodied wouldn't be too bad. "You better move. Otis tends to pounce on men in white T-shirts."

Completely ignoring my warning, Chip holds out his hands. "Jump, kitty-kitty."

"I wouldn't do that if I were you."

"Don't be afraid, kitty-kitty."

I have to cover my eyes. It's always so brutal when it happens. The jump. The thud. The sound of claws digging into skin. The howls of horror.

That's when I hear *thump* and find Otis in Chip's arms, purring in a way I have never heard him purr before. How incredibly annoying.

"He really does pounce on people and attack them," I say, holding up my fingers as claws in demonstration.

Chip is scratching Otis under the chin. Otis's eyes are closed in ecstasy. "Oh, I have no doubt this is a killer feline. So, what's your apartment like?"

Is he asking for an invitation? "Messy."

"What do I care? I'm a guy. We like messy things."

"I don't think so. I have the feeling you're trouble, Chip, and besides, I've had a fire in the kitchen tonight."

Chip puts Otis down. "Another fire? Is this the kind of disorder that's going to require professional help?"

"I swear I never had even one before this month."

"Sure. And then the arson squad finds the gasoline

121

in your basement. I know all about you firebugs. Well, I better take a look. You might have electrical damage." With this, Chip opens the front door—thanks, Bitsy—and takes the stairs two at a time as though it's his second home, his new best friend Otis at his heels.

How did this happen?

Bitsy has left my apartment door unlocked, so Chip is already inside when I arrive. A clever fellow; he must have assumed I lived on the second floor because of Otis.

Meanwhile, my apartment is miraculously neat as a pin. All my groceries have been put away. The quilt is gone and there is a faint mist of Lysol Fresh Linen Scent hanging in the air. It's an oversight on Bitsy's part that she has not put out two chilled glasses for champagne and a six-pack of Trojans. I will have to speak to her about that.

"You call this messy?"

"My landlady must have cleaned up." I peer down the hall and spy that my bedroom is tidy as well. I'm not sure that I like Bitsy cleaning up my bedroom.

"Some landlady." Chip examines the stove. "How did this happen?"

"I wasn't paying attention, and a spaghetti box caught on fire." Which reminds me. I am really, really hungry.

Grabbing a spatula, Chip gently pokes at the charred metal. "Got any baking soda?"

I go to the refrigerator and in the back find an old

box of Arm & Hammer. Somewhere along the way I have become a robot, under Chip's command. This, I think, is how serial killers murder women. You read about the circumstances and ask yourself, why did she let a strange man into her apartment? Why was she clutching a box of baking soda when they found her with her throat slit? And now I know.

"How old is this?" Chip asks, sprinkling the baking soda over the stove with abandon.

"Old."

"Might not work." He douses the mess with a wet sponge. "Should sit for an hour and then you can wipe it off."

"Thanks."

"It's the least I can do after that disaster at the Annex."

"Yes," I agree. "The least."

Chip puts his hands on his hips and takes in my apartment. There is a slight slouch in his posture, which I assume is part of the California shtick, though with his slim hips and those tanned forearms, he is definitely all male. His testosterone levels are wilting my dried flower arrangements.

"Nice place. You shouldn't keep setting it on fire."

"I don't mean to. Like I said . . ."

He waves this off. "Yeah, yeah. Well, I've got an hour to kill before I can start scrubbing. Let's see if you've got anything to eat." With this, he opens my refrigerator and peers in.

Who *is* this guy? Who is this man who invites me to

a catfight and then helps himself to my victuals?

"What's going on here?" He pulls out a package of precut broccoli. "This doesn't look like much fun. Broccoli? Carrots? Nonfat yogurt dip? Where's the beer and Cheez Whiz?"

I can feel my face turning red from embarrassment. But it's nothing compared to when Chip pulls his head out of the refrigerator, takes one look at me, and says, "You're not on a diet, are you?"

I contemplate sawing a circle in the floor and falling through à la Wile E. Coyote.

"Now, hold on. That was wrong of me." He slams the door. "Good for you for cutting the calories. I mean, you're a pretty girl. You'd look even better with a few pounds off."

OK. On paper, this is the most insulting thing that's ever been said to me before by a semiacquaintance of the male persuasion. Angie the Northeastern Native Bitch and her ilk do not count. They are in their own class. Yet, strangely, I'm not offended. I'm, in a way, appreciative. It's as though Chip has just shot the elephant in the room and has even taken the extra trouble to have the carcass bagged and stuffed.

"There's this pact," I hear myself saying as Chip moves on to the bags of discarded junk food lining the counter. "My two friends and I are going to lose weight once and for all. Today I found out that one of my friends has been secretly pursuing gastric bypass. She's going under the knife on Monday."

Chip pulls a bag of blue corn chips from my junk

food discards. "I love these! Can I have them?"

"They might be stale. I cleaned all the old junk food out of my cupboards."

"More for me. Come on." He directs me to my own couch and even boldly plunks himself in a chair and props his sneakered feet up on my coffee table. "OK, go on. What is gastric bypass, anyway?"

"It's when they slit open your stomach and . . ."

"Oh, shit. This isn't going to make me throw up, is it?"

"Might."

"Go on." Oddly enough, we continue talking for two hours, during which time I manage to polish off an entire head of broccoli and nonfat yogurt dip while Chip, who through his T-shirt is all muscle and bones, I see, grazes through most of my leftover junk food, including all my Doritos and a can of Hires, and then finishes removing the charred stuff from my stove.

It's as though my mouth is operating on autopilot. I tell him about Nancy's botched marriage. I tell him about Deb and how she was too embarrassed to attend her son's graduation, not to mention Paul's weird reaction to her gastric bypass decision. I even touch on the Belinda investigation, though I don't go so far as to reveal my key role.

Through it all, Chip keeps asking follow-up questions, never giving his opinion except to say things like, "That's a shame," when I mention how Ron and Nancy grew apart. It's not until I see that it is past eleven and note the time that Chip moves toward the door.

"What're you doing later this week?" he asks.

A fresh sweat breaks out on my palms, which is what always happens when I think men are about to ask me out for a tête-à-tête. This lifelong tendency to avoid socializing with men romantically has nothing to do with Chip being the kind of guy you think about being in bed with. It has to do with me assuming that the only reason a man would offer to take me out is because he feels obligated or guilty or, worse, sorry for me. And I want no part in any of that.

"I really should be on call for that friend of mine who's going into surgery on Monday. Who knows what kind of care her husband's going to give her."

"Great. So we have lots of time until she comes back from the hospital." Chip tosses the sponge to the sink. "Let's make it Monday night. How about if I stop by to pick you up around six?"

"Actually on Monday nights . . ." I start to say reflexively.

"You're going out with me." He taps me on the nose with his finger. "And you know it. Don't stall. I like you, Nola. You're a real person. And you're pretty, too, even if you refuse to admit it to yourself."

Chapter Thirteen

For Eileen's birthday I have bought her a book. This is a risky gift, like giving a pig farmer a bottle of eau de cologne or an AAA membership to a person who has lost her driver's license. Eileen doesn't read. OK, that's not entirely true. She reads *People* and *Sass!* and the occasional Danielle Steel. But in Eileen's mind, reading is something people were forced to do in olden days until TV was invented.

I think I'm pretty safe, since the book is *Jon Bon Jovi*, a biography written by Laura Jackson. Eileen loves Bon Jovi. She is a rock 'n' roll chick. So rock 'n' roll that she searched the Tri-State area for the ultimate town where she could live her life's dream of doing hair by day and listening to classic rock by night.

She found her El Dorado (not the ELO album) when she went to the Allentown Fair in Allentown, Pennsylvania, to see Motley Crüe. Next we knew, she'd taken up residence in Lehigh, one city over, and was working as a hairdresser in a neighborhood salon. In Lehigh, Eileen's in her element.

It takes me a little over an hour to reach Eileen's home, which is half of a brick walkup. Camaros, Corvettes, and pickup trucks line her block. These belong to Eileen's many friends who, if they're not fellow hairdressers or gum-snapping clients, are gym-rat pals of Jim's, Eileen's boyfriend who divides his time between fitness training and guessing the weight of other shoppers in the mall.

I steel myself as I hear the rough laughter emanating from her backyard over which hangs a white haze of barbecue smoke. This is not really my crowd. But it is my sister and it is her thirty-third birthday, so I suck it up.

No one notices as I enter through the back gate, carrying my gift-wrapped book and a tray of cookies I picked up at ShopRite. No one offers to help as the cookie tray tips and four or five cookies fall onto the grass. If I were like the other women in skintight, low-riding jeans with boob jobs and big, teased hair, these men would drop their foam beer coolers and come rushing to my aid. Instead they give me the same look I got at the Annex—passing curiosity and then, just as quickly, rejection.

"Let me help you with this." One of Eileen's friends teeters over to me in heels that would give an orthopedist fits. She is wearing a leopard-print, off-the-shoulder top and a black leather skirt. It crosses my mind that she has escaped from the circus. Or, perhaps, from the cast of *Shampoo*.

"That's too bad you dropped some," she says, her long red acrylic nails pinching the cookies. "And you went through all the trouble baking them."

They're on a tray that says in bold black letters SHOPRITE BAKERY DEPARTMENT.

"Bubbles!" A slim woman in dark blue jeans and a red cotton sweater runs over. "Get up. Bending over like that, everyone can see up your skirt."

Bubbles seems confused as to how this could be a problem. "Only if they're looking, Sandy," she says.

"Trust me. They're looking," says Sandy.

I retrieve the last cookie and put it on the plate (that ol' ten-second rule). Then I make a point of thanking Bubbles, who squints at me as she brushes off her knees. "Wow. You must be Eileen's sister. You're the spitting image. Isn't she the spitting image, Sandy?"

"The spitting image," says Sandy, who seems not so sure. "Are you the one who knows Belinda Apple?"

This is destined to be my role in life, I see now. In my obituary they will write: *Nola Ann Devlin, who knew Belinda Apple, died yesterday. Belinda Apple was not by her bed.* Perhaps it will be carved on my tombstone.

"I'm her editor at *Sass!*" I say.

"I *love* that magazine," Bubbles squeals. "You know what article I liked the best?"

"Which Nail Polish Makes You Lucky?"

"No. Though that was a good one, even if no way does Purple Passion help you win the Lotto. Trust me. I've been wearing it for years and all I've ever won is a Megabucks fiver. Anyway, it was that piece about that *New York Times* reporter's eighty-five days in prison."

I must admit I am taken aback like this. "Bubbles used to be a hairdresser," Sandy offers. "But now she's a journalist."

"Where?" I ask, thinking, *The Playboy Channel*?

"The *News-Times*, our local paper," Bubbles says. "Mr. Salvo, he's my editor there, he wants me to read more articles on newspaper reporting. Usually, they're as dull as overprocessed hair unless they involve some celebrity who's suing the *National Enquirer*. Anyway, that article gave me chills because what happened to her almost happened to me. A judge threatened to put me in jail for not turning over my notes."

Wow! I am impressed. And humbled. Shows you should never judge a book by its cover or, in this case, a floozy by her lumpy mascara.

"I mean, in prison you're only allowed a five-minute shower every other day. It takes me ten minutes just to get a good lather. Isn't that like a violation of the Geneva Convention or something, Sandy?"

Sandy gives me a knowing look.

"There you are, Nola." My mother in her trademark denim jumper and booster pins is coming across the lawn. "Oh, good, you brought the cookies I ordered."

"She must have been baking all morning," Bubbles says.

Mom stares at her.

"Mom," I say, "this is Bubbles."

"Yes. Everyone knows Bubbles." Mom takes the tray out of my hand and does the old grip on my elbow. It is the grip that she has used since I was in kindergarten to get across that I am in deep dirt. "Can I talk to you privately?"

Mom doesn't wait for me to say good-bye as she drags me over to the garbage cans. "Where is Belinda?"

"In England."

"I know that." Mom heaves her shoulders. "I mean, it's Eileen's birthday."

Still not getting it. "And . . ."

"And, you promised Belinda would call."

Oh, crap. I completely forgot. With all the craziness

going on, my exploded car and Deb's weight-loss surgery, the investigation and the lusciousness of Chip, making a fake phone call to my sister has moved to the bottom of my to-do list.

"It's supposed to be her birthday present, a personal phone call from a big important celebrity like Belinda."

"I'm sorry, Mom. I forgot to ask her."

"You forgot!" Mom lifts the tray as though she's about to hurl the cookies at me. "How could you forget?"

"I was . . . busy."

"Geesh, Nola. You can be so self-centered sometimes. You're hitting middle age. You have to learn to start putting other people first, or you're going to grow into one of those selfish old spinsters who frets over every little thing. Like Aunt Gerta who used to throw a fit if the label of her tea bag fell in the cup."

What she's saying is wrong on so many levels, I can't even respond.

"Eileen's going to be heartbroken. She told everyone that Belinda would call. She's counting on it."

It's a moment like this when I'm glad I bring Belinda's cell phone wherever I go. "All right, Mom. I will try Belinda in London and ask her to call Eileen. I'll need to, um"—I glance at my rental—"drive up the block to the hill because there's better reception there."

My mother nods in agreement. I love telling her

bullshit technical stuff like this because she has no clue, though she pretends to be hip. "That's a good idea, Nola. Yes, the hill. Better reception. Try it. I'll tell Eileen to stand by the phone just in case."

No pressure there.

Chapter Fourteen

I hand my mother the book, slip out the gate, grab Belinda's phone, and run smack into Jim. Eileen's Jim—aka the Jack Russell terrier.

Here's the thing about Jim. Besides being a reincarnated wire terrier—which in itself makes you want to put him on a leash and tie him up outside—he has a shtick. A stupid human trick. You know how some grown men pull pennies from behind children's ears or can turn their eyelids inside out? Jim's shtick is that he can guess people's weight—to the ounce.

I kid you not. It's freaky. It also makes you want to strangle him.

"Two hundred and . . ." He puts his finger to his temple like his brain is a calculator.

I can't let him go on. I can't bear to hear the number spoken out loud. "Nope. Not today, Jim," I say, cutting him off.

I try to move past him, but Jim blocks me on the sidewalk. He is a good two inches shorter than I am and is wearing a navy blue-and-white Adidas tracksuit. I don't think I've seen him in anything else. "Not so fast, Nola. Now that we're alone, tell me, how's that diet I gave you working out?"

"Uh . . ." I have no idea, because I threw it in a trash can in a rest area off I-78.

"Have you been staying off the carbs like I told you?"

"You see . . ."

" 'Cause it's the carbs that will kill you. That and the hidden fructose in everything that's processed. God-damn corn lobby." He smacks a fist into the palm of his hand.

Jim is obsessed with the corn lobby triumph of 1980, which he claims was able to successfully remove fructose as a sugar from nutrition labels. That's why Americans have been fat ever since, according to him. I don't dare tell him that I was fat long before 1980.

"You've got to keep drinking your water. Sixty-four ounces, minimum. That and walking five miles a day, though picking it up to a jog wouldn't hurt. And don't eat anything white except boiled egg whites. Those you can have until the cows come home." He nudges me. "No puns intended."

Jim's plan, I am ashamed to admit, was the inspiration behind Belinda's miraculous weight loss. I stole it and then I didn't follow it and then I wrote that a fictitious person lost tons of weight on it "painlessly." After all that, I tossed it in the I-78 rest area trash bin.

I am not proud.

"I've really got to go, Jim. It's a bit of an emergency."

"No sweat," and he shoots me with his finger. "Then again, no sweat means no muscle. Anytime you want to get serious about fitness, you call me. I got a program that will trim you down in six weeks."

You and everyone else I know. "Will do."

"Yeah?"

"Yeah."

He sizes me up. "Man. You could be so pretty if you dropped the weight."

"Thanks," I say, though between you and me if I never hear that line again it will be too soon.

I pull into the crowded parking lot of the St. Nicholas Greek Orthodox Church at the top of the hill and run through my usual pre-Belinda preparations, taking deep breaths and being British. *Love Actually*. Hugh Grant. *Bridget Jones*. *Monty Python*. Tea at Harrods. When I'm ready, I take a deep breath, imagine a pickle up my ass, and dial my younger sister.

"Hello?" Eileen answers on the first ring.

"Hello. I'm looking for an Eileen Devlin. Have I rung the right number?"

"This is her!" Eileen lets out an *eeek*. "Is this who I think it is?"

"If you think it is Belinda Apple, then you are correct."

"Oh my God!" Eileen does a lousy job of covering the mouthpiece. "Ohmigod, guys, it's her." There is a chorus of questions—many having to do with Belinda's trademark pink cowboy boots and if she and

Nigel are getting it on. "I'm going to take this in the other room. Sorry."

I hear what I assume to be the bedroom door slam behind her and Eileen breathing heavily. "I can't believe you called. When Mom said you would, I was so excited but then hours passed and—"

"Yes, so sorry about that. Had a bit of a *shh*edule mix-up, you see. Anyway, happy birthday and all that."

"Uh-huh. Well, to tell you the truth, that's not why I wanted you to call. I have a big problem."

Immediately a million possibilities flood my thoughts, most having to do with Camaro repair and nail-polish removal. "Oh?"

"It's pretty personal and I don't want anyone to overhear." Eileen lowers her voice. "My boyfriend and I have been dating for three years . . ."

I stifle a groan. Please, please tell me that Eileen is not going to confide some serious sexual problem. Wait. What if it's a performance issue? What if Jim the terrier can't get it up after all those eons on steroids? Or maybe he'll only do it doggy-style.

". . . and it's been great."

"Great?"

"Yeah. I mean, we are so in love. Jim's like the best. I wish you could meet him. I'm sure you'd love him right off like everyone does."

"Yes, I'm sure I would."

"He's very kind. Very smart in a businessman kind of way. Manages three gyms in the Lehigh Valley area. Handsome. Ah . . . tall, sort of."

"I see." Blatant lying, apparently, is a Devlin family trait.

"And he's dynamite in bed."

Nope. Not gonna go there. "So what's the problem?" I say, directing us back on course.

"It's my family."

Shit. Now I know I'm about to hear something I shouldn't. I keep silent.

"They hate him. Especially my sister."

I say nothing. What can I say? She's right. Well, perhaps not *hate*. Hate's such a nasty word. Dislike very intensely, yes. The way one dislikes, um, terriers.

"Promise me you won't say anything to Nola."

"Of course not." Never.

"But between you and me . . . I think she's jealous."

I grip the side of my seat and focus on being Britishly reserved—Emma Thompson, Julie Andrews—because otherwise I am afraid I will blurt, *Are you out of your fucking mind? Jim foams at the mouth. Why would I be jealous that you're dating a rabid mutt?*

"Jealous, you say?" I fake serene.

"Extremely. I mean, have you ever actually *seen* my sister?"

Oh, brother. This is going to be bad, isn't it? "No, but from what everyone tells me, she's very stylish, extremely pretty." Hah! Take that, baby sister.

"She could be."

"*Could* be?"

"If she took care of herself. Listen, Belinda, my sister is over two hundred pounds. Jim, who's a weight-loss professional, can guess people's weight to the ounce. The only person he's never been honest with is Nola. If he told her the truth, she'd faint."

"What do you mean, 'the truth'?" I accuse, my British accent totally out the window.

"That she's pushing two-fifty."

My lower jaw involuntarily drops. "Am not!"

"Huh?"

Suddenly I see I've stepped out of line. "I'm sorry. We appear to have been cut off. I said I *am not* surprised."

"Gee. You are good. You knew that about Nola without meeting her?"

"Funny, really. Suppose that's why I'm in the business of dispensing advice, isn't it?"

"Anyway," Eileen continues, unsure what I mean by that, "I'm afraid that when we announce we are getting married . . ."

"Married!" I scream before I can help myself.

"Yes, married. Why? Is there something wrong?"

"It's so . . ." I search for rational reasons why a British advice columnist would even care that Eileen is getting married. "Why, you're so young."

"I'm thirty-three. As of today. That's not young. By this age my mother had both her daughters."

"But in today's world women are putting off marriage for years and years."

"I don't see the point of waiting. I love him. He

loves me. What's the big deal?"

Everything, I think, closing my eyes, envisioning little Jims and Eileens flexing their barbells and making personal comments about ninety-eight-pound weaklings, lifting their legs and peeing on Mom and Dad's furniture.

No, hold on. That's not fair. Eileen's right. She's past thirty. If she wants to marry the vicious terrier, she should. It should be a splendid union . . . provided she's had her shots.

"Brilliant," I am able to squeak out. "Just as long as you two are really, really sure."

"We're sure, all right. Jim's been married twice already. He wouldn't jump from the frying pan into the fire, as he says, if the fire weren't so damn hot." She giggles.

Someone yank that man off the stage. "Let's recap," I say. "You love each other. You want to get married, despite Nola's so-called jealousy, so why are you two having problems?"

"I'm afraid that when we make the big announcement today, Nola will flip. Nana Snyder says it's wrong for a younger sister to marry before the older one. But how long will that take? I mean, Nola doesn't even have a boyfriend. I'm not sure she dates or goes out, even. She's like a . . . a bookworm or something. A permanent spinster."

I could reach through this phone and . . . *Patience, Nola. Steady, girl. Remember who you are supposed to be. Remember that Eileen would not want you to hear what she's confiding to Belinda.*

"And it's not like we haven't offered to, you know, help make her more attractive to men. Jim's tried everything he can to get Nola to slim down, even gave her a diet and exercise program. For free! He charges big bucks for that kind of counseling at the gym and Nola acts like she is insulted every time he brings it up."

"Hmm." Fuming here. Positively fuming. My hands are gripping the rental's steering wheel so tightly, they're leaving permanent imprints. I'll probably be charged extra for that.

To hear these words from my own sister's lips is so dizzying that no matter how much I am trying to be Belinda, the truth is that my lungs have ceased to function. I seem to be slipping into a tunnel. The corner of my vision is all black. Is this how my sister sees me? As a nerdy jealous spinster obstructing her way toward marital bliss? Is this how everyone views me? The big, unmarriageable Nola Devlin?

I bet Nana, Mom, Dad, and Eileen have been sitting around the kitchen table discussing the "Nola problem." I can see my mother wiping off some invisible crumbs and shaking her head, saying, "There's no way to help her unless she wants to help herself," and my father, one eye on the TV, adding, "Aww, let her be," and Nana throwing in a "Well, I think it's disgraceful, a younger sister marrying first."

"Belinda? Belinda are you there? Did we get cut off again?"

I clear my throat and wipe away my tears with the

back of my hand. "For a bit there, yes."

"So what am I supposed to do?"

"I think," I begin, slowly. "I think it would be best . . ."

"Yes?"

"It would be best if you didn't make a big deal of it. Just announce your engagement and I'm sure you'll find that Nola is not nearly as desperate or jealous as you believe."

"Really?"

"Really."

"That's exactly what Dad said."

Good ol' Dad. I must remember to give him a secret kiss on the cheek.

"OK, I've gotta go. I'm gonna tell Jim so we can make the announcement today. I've been keeping the ring hidden for, like, weeks." Eileen squeals again. "Thank you, thank you, thank you. I just knew you'd take my side."

"I usually do."

Eileen misses that.

"If I could have gone to Nola right off, without worrying about offending her or hurting her feelings, this wouldn't have been such an issue. She's just so sensitive, you know, you can't bring up clothes or shopping or guys or anything else sisters talk about. You're like the older sister I never had, Belinda. You've made this the best birthday ever."

After she hangs up, I hold the phone in my hand, staring zombielike out the window at the good parishioners of St. Nicholas's, the dark-haired fathers, mothers, and skipping children in all sizes leaving the church in packs of big Greek families. Here are slim women and large women and grandmothers all in black. Yet they are loved. They are with men. Some are married. Others not. Yet, they are laughing and complete. Why not me?

Somehow the sight of them contrasted with Eileen's pronouncement that I'm destined to be a spinster has a strange effect. I am unable to start the car. I can't stop crying and hating myself for it. I am not sensitive. I am just like any other woman in the world—only slightly larger and with a heart that at this moment is swelling in pain.

Chapter Fifteen

I had been doing so well. Salads. High-protein, low-fat main meals. Water, water, water. Every food I ate was weighed and measured. I was even walking before work.

Then came yesterday. Though, honestly, I can't really be blamed for falling off the wagon, can I? I mean, if your sister had just called you an introverted spinster destined for a life of loneliness, would you resist a bag of chips? No. I'm not talking about a snack bag. I'm talking the whole bag. Ruffles with ridges. Super size. With ranch dip.

I tried to hold off. I really did. After my phony Belinda call, I doused my eyes with Visine, returned to my sister's party, and pretended to act as surprised and thrilled as all of Eileen's shrieking girlfriends when she flashed her Sears diamond-chip ring and trilled, "Guess, what, Nola! Jim and I are getting married. You can be a bridesmaid!"

I stoically kept in mind Dr. Anne Renée Krugenheim's advice from *Who Moved My Fat?*

Learn to recognize your overeating triggers. Remember that the journey to being thin starts with taking a road not traveled. Instead of relying on old, destructive eating habits to get you over a bad patch, try doing the opposite. Take a different path.

And I did just that. In the beginning.

I was very proud of the restraint I showed, even though there was food everywhere. Cheeseburgers. Hot dogs with chili. My mother's omnipresent potato salad. Birthday cake. I didn't even eat one potato chip. As for the cake, just a teensy weensie slice. Rather, two. Two teensy weensie slices followed by nothing more than a dollop of ice cream. Nothing, really.

Yes, it's true that at the New Jersey border I did stop off and get a Subway turkey sandwich, but those things are good for you. Look at that guy on TV who lost all the weight, though I read once that he never ate a sandwich with cheese or mayo. Well, that's just impossible. What's the point of having a sandwich if there's no cheese or mayo?

Then when I got to Princeton to pick up cat food at Wegman's, I might have grabbed a bottle of Dr Pepper. Listen, I was thirsty. Do you know how salty those Subway sandwiches are? While there I noticed a two-for-one sale on Droste 80 percent dark chocolate, which as we all know now, prevents heart disease and cancer and so many life-threatening illnesses. Being very health conscious I bought two and ate both for the sake of cancer prevention.

That I just happened to find the bag of potato chips in the part of my pantry I hadn't cleaned out yet wasn't my fault. After my conversation with Eileen I was vulnerable. So vulnerable that I dug into the ranch dip in the back of my fridge, cleaning off a thin line of green mold at the edge, of course.

And here I am, Monday morning at six thirty, lying in a heap of tangled sheets and self-loathing and suffering from what can only be a salt and sugar hangover. I don't even want to think about the Cinderella Pact.

To tell you the truth, I'm beginning to despise the Cinderella Pact.

I should call it the Cinderella *Packed* because if I hadn't been part of it, I wouldn't have binged like I just did. I would be feeling normal, getting out of bed, taking a shower, making coffee. The usual routine. Instead, I plain hate myself.

I can't do it. I just can't lose a bunch of weight just like that. I'm so tired of it all. I've been on too many diets for too long. I can't stand the constant feeling of being restricted at work, for example, while around me Joel—not exactly light on his toes—is downing grilled pastrami sandwiches and Lisa is helping herself to office birthday cake.

Not me. I've got my Ziploc bag of carrot sticks and have to politely stand aside while everyone helps themselves to either the vanilla or chocolate side of the cake. (In my heyday, I could craftily cut both right down the middle.)

Forget it. I'm done. I didn't want to be in the stupid pact to begin with.

I'm phoning Nancy and dropping out. In fact, I can't wait. I get my cell and dial her before I change my mind.

"Yeah?" Nancy sounds rushed as usual.

"Sorry," I mumble. "I bet you're going off to work."

"Running kind of late, but that's OK, Nola. Is this important? No, wait. What a stupid question. Of course it's important if you're calling me before seven. What's up?"

I take a cleansing sigh. "I'm dropping out."

"Dropping out? Of what?"

"The Cinderella Pact."

Nancy says nothing. A lawyer trick, I bet.

I speak fast before I lose my resolve. "I can't do it, Nancy. I tried. I really did. I drank tons of water and didn't eat any office birthday cake. Last Friday, when the Food department tested a recipe for Southwestern Chicken Fingers I didn't have one. But last night . . ."

"You went overboard at Eileen's party."

144

"Afterward."

"Why?"

This is the hard part. I can't tell her the whole story about my conversation with Eileen because Nancy doesn't know my secret identity as Belinda. Therefore I say the worst thing possible. "She got engaged."

"Oh, for heaven's sake. Don't be ridiculous." Her cell phone starts ringing in the background.

"Listen. If you have to go, I—"

"I do. But I want to talk to you later. In the meantime, do me one favor."

It's never good when friends ask for favors. "Sure."

"Find a Weight Watchers meeting."

"Weight Watchers! I've tried that already."

"And you've lost weight, remember? You do well on Weight Watchers, Nola, because there's support, which is exactly what you need. Unfortunately I can't give you that at the moment because I have an eight a.m. status conference in Judge Willbanks's chambers, and I'll be cited if I spend one more minute talking to you."

"Well . . ." I don't know. I've been to Weight Watchers so often my name must be red flagged in their computer system.

"I bet there's a meeting somewhere. One meeting, that's all I ask. Call me again if you decide to really quit. Don't let one night of binging throw you off track. You've been on enough diets to know that. Remember, set your sights to five months from now." And Nancy's off.

I hang up and think about what she said. I try to time travel to this December when Deb, fully recovered from weight-loss surgery, is strutting around in tight clothes instead of her usual floral tents and Nancy is back to her old zaftig self while I am the same frumpy, overweight me. Too weak-willed to survive a month in the Cinderella Pact.

Weight Watchers. The last refuge of the yo-yo dieter. Why the heck not.

I drag my laptop out and do a Web search for local Weight Watchers meetings, another way WW is like AA. There's always a meeting somewhere, and I've been to all of them. I bet my file is in every one of the sixty three New Jersey locations.

Except the Weight Watchers at *Sass!*

I shudder. I have never been able to bring myself to attend one of the Weight Watchers meetings at work. It's too . . . personal.

Lisa went when she needed to lose a wimpy ten pounds and swore by it since the meetings were held during lunchtime and were right down the hall. It did sound intriguing, I have to admit, especially the part about discovering who at *Sass!* was a closet Weight Watcher.

Afterward, Lisa would come back from the meetings and say things like, "You should go, Nola. You wouldn't *believe* who's in Weight Watchers." She'd drop big hints about "people in management" who are "so thin now you'd never imagine they once couldn't fit in their chairs."

146

As tempting as that was, I still couldn't do it. Not then. Not now.

Fortunately there is a Weight Watchers meeting at nine a.m. in Somerville, fairly close to work. I know that one. It's filled with housewives and senior citizens. There will be much discussion about cooking food in batches and freezing it in Tupperware. They will use the adjective "my" with reckless abandon as in "I make *my* Zero Point Soup on Sunday and divide it into *my* Tupperware so I can defrost it in *my* microwave for *my* lunch."

That's OK. But if they bring up gelatin, I'm outta there.

I arrive in the lightest clothes possible. A pair of khaki rayon pants and a flimsy black top. Every other woman is dressed in similar fashion and as they line up for the "weigh in" they are busily removing shoes, earrings, watches, dentures, anything that could add unnecessary ounces.

"And your name is?" my Weight Watchers weigher asks as I step up to—but not on—the scale.

"Nola Devlin. I haven't been to this group in a while."

She flips through a set of cards. "Devlin. Devlin." Then, not seeing it, she yells to someone to bring her the "dropout" file.

"Have a dropout who's back," she hollers, loud enough for them to hear in Bayonne.

I smile brightly, though I can feel the looks of pity and criticism from my fellow participants. I am a dropout, an egotist who decided she was above

Weight Watchers, that she didn't need to follow Points—and look at her now. The prodigal daughter. A walking morality tale of hubris.

"Here it is," my weigher says cheerfully holding up my card. "You'll have to renew."

I hand her the check already made out. I should have a rubber stamp that says WEIGHT WATCHERS.

"If you don't mind, I don't want to know my weight," I say.

"You sure? It's always good to have a number to look back on."

"I'm sure."

"OK," she says hesitantly, "though it's the heaviest you'll ever be."

"That's what you think."

I step on and watch her face, which she expertly keeps neutral. Then she hands me a tiny folder in which is written the number of points I may use that week. Mine are like 150 a day, which means I am seriously in trouble. Though, really, they are 28—with 35 extra points to goof around with all week long.

I can do this, I think. Sixty-three points is a lot. Until I remember that one of those big muffins you buy at Costco is like 20 points in one shot.

The meeting is already under way when I sit next to an old lady in purple. Exactly as I expected. Housewives, senior citizens, and . . . is that a nun? Why would a nun have to go to Weight Watchers? I mean, nuns are married to God. What does He care if you're packing on the pounds?

148

I feel a nudge from the woman in purple. The leader in black pantyhose is pointing to me.

"It's new member intro," the purple lady says.

I want to explain that I am about as new as the yellowed linoleum under our feet when the leader says, "Please stand, uh, Nola, and tell us your story."

I really don't want to do this, but the leader is beckoning me and now the old lady is pushing me out of my seat. "Come on," she's urging. "It's part of the program."

I stand and smooth down my pants. If I make it quick, maybe I can get through this without blubbering, like I usually do.

"My name is Nola and this is my probably fifth"—try sixteenth—"pass at Weight Watchers. But this time I'm going to stick with it. I know that this is not a diet, but a lifestyle change."

"Good for you!" my seatmate says, as everyone claps tepidly.

"Thank you," I say, and start to sit.

"Wait," says the leader. "You haven't told us your goals."

"Oh, my goals. Um, my goal is to lose weight. Thank you." And I start to sit again.

The leader is laughing and taking my hand. "Don't be so shy. We're all here to lose weight. You're among friends, Nola." She gives me a squeeze. I'm now in the front of the room flanked by a blackboard on which is written the word RESOLVE. "Tell us about your journey."

149

Again with the journey.

"In other words, what brought you here."

"What brought me here was . . ." I can't say my sister called me an unmarriageable cow. "What brought me here were my two friends. We've made a pact to lose weight. We call it"—I pause, wondering if this is going to sound goofy—"the Cinderella Pact."

No applause. Just stares.

"I won't let my daughters read or watch *Cinderella*," one mother in the front row says to her partner. "I spent three years on the couch because of that sexist fairy tale."

"Are your friends going through Weight Watchers?" the leader asks gently.

"No. One has a personal trainer and nutritionist. She's rich. The other is going through"—I instinctively drop my voice—"gastric bypass surgery."

There is an audible hiss.

"Now, now," says the leader. "Every person is unique. Many of us have friends and loved ones who've chosen the gastric bypass route for their own health."

"It's nuts," barks an old woman in row three.

"Actually, it's not," I find myself saying. "It's a tool, and my friend Deb has been through everything to lose weight. She just can't do it without surgery."

"Did Deb do her Zero Point Soup?"

This elicits a round of applause.

"Yeah," says another old lady in the back. "How about some good old-fashioned discipline for once. How about pushing the plate away?"

Clap. Clap. Clap.

"This is a hot-button issue," the leader whispers in my ear. "It might be a generational thing."

Or an asshole thing.

"Please." The nun rises and everyone shuts up. She's not in full nun regalia, just a simple black-and-white headdress, or whatever it is they call it. Wimple, I think. The rest of her is normal. "I come to Weight Watchers for the support and fellowship. Because of all of you, I have lost eighty-two pounds."

Automatic clapping.

"We need to embrace our fellow journeymen and women. Positive thoughts, hugs, and prayers are so much more helpful than blind judgmental criticism."

Have I mentioned that I love this woman? We all applaud heartily and I'm allowed to go back to my seat, though I'm not paying one whit of attention to the testimony of my fellow journeyers. That is because I am having a revelation.

I should become a nun. Meeting this nun at Weight Watchers, it's a sign!

Actually I have thought of being a nun before. In fourth grade, but only because I'd just seen *The Sound of Music* and found the idea of wearing a long white dress and throwing myself in front of the altar as a novitiate somehow alluring. My mother used to say I'd grow up to be the nun in the family. And didn't large Irish families always designate one daughter to be a nun and one son to be a priest? Yes!

OK, our family's not large, but we are Irish

Catholic. At least half. And in being a nun I could do so much good. Why, I could travel to India and model my life after Mother Teresa by caring for castaways with leprosy and children with AIDS. I could eschew the physical and submit to the supernatural. Let's face it, I never had much use for the physical anyway.

No one would care if I was fat or so-called unmarriageable. I would be married to God, and God loves *all* women no matter what our size. He really does. He thinks we're great. He loves us no matter our skin color or double chins or cellulite or love handles. We're His creatures. God doesn't care if I'm putting on a few pounds or getting a bit wide in the caboose. God doesn't hint that I should get my breasts done or my ass lifted. That's what makes God the perfect husband; He loves me for who I am.

It's settled then, I think, as I drift out of the meeting on a cloud. I will become a nun.

Although, now that I'm becoming a nun I'll have to swear off men entirely. Too bad, as I just met Chip and he's the first man in a long time, maybe ever, to have potential.

Still, sacrifices must be made in the name of a higher calling. Therefore, I will call over to Technical Assistance as soon as I get to *Sass!* and cancel tonight's date—if you can call it a date. I'm sure he'll understand when I explain that I've decided to take a vow of chastity.

I arrive at work with a calm and benevolent countenance that, for once, has nothing to do with the tall,

French roast double café latte in my hand. Joel, in his usual cheery Monday uniform of brown shirt, brown pants, and brown shoes, grunts as I put down my coffee and newspaper.

"What're you so happy about?" he asks, shaking out the sports section of the *Star-Ledger.*

"I've found my calling."

"What is it this week?"

"I'm going to be a nun."

"Fucking Steinbrenner," he says, shaking his head. "Someone ought to buy out *his* contract."

I wouldn't expect more than this kind of response from Joel. Honestly, I don't think he listens to me half the time.

Chapter Sixteen

Eager to leave work early and meet Deb in recovery from her surgery, I zoom through the morning's assignments, calling up Belinda's column that I wrote over the weekend, writing headlines, and laying out three pages. Then I move on to "Beauty Tips Only Models Know," which requires me to suffer through another hyperbole-filled rave about the new mascaras that "incorporate exciting new technology that makes even the puniest lashes fuller, thicker, sexier."

I'm too lazy to do the necessary research, but I swear I've been hearing that exact same line since I started reading *Seventeen* magazine twenty years ago.

At eleven I make two calls. The first is to Chip in Technical Assistance. The computerized message on his machine apologizes for being "on the other line," so I leave a message that I cannot make dinner on account of me entering a holy order.

Then I call Lori and ask if I can leave at noon to visit a friend recovering from surgery, noting that I have all my pages done plus some. Lori doesn't say yes or no. Instead, she commands me to step into her office, immediately.

"And I mean hustle, Devlin. You are capable of hustling, aren't you?"

Lori has on her mad face when I find her behind her glass desk. Things must not be going well with Old Mr. Stanton, as there is no evidence of red thongs or push-up bras today. Instead, she is in a rather masculine taupe business suit. Perhaps the Anna Nicole Smith road to riches is not Lori's destiny after all. Or maybe Monday morning is an Anna Nicole Smith day off.

"Mr. Stanton forwarded this to me. Take a look." She tosses me a white printout.

I pretend to study it, though of course I don't need to as I wrote it. It is Belinda's response to Mr. Stanton's questions about what to do concerning the employee who seems to have falsified her records. Interestingly, the e-mail does not include Mr. Stanton's question—simply my response.

"Isn't that incredible?" Lori asks.

"Uh, yeah."

"I mean, the nerve. It's as if she's challenging us to investigate her. Plus, I called up the *New York Intelligentsia* reporter who did that story on our elusive Ms. Apple. As far as he can tell, there was no truth to Belinda's claim that she had been abused by her father and went on the run. And now this . . . Rosie O'Grady? Please."

There was something wrong with Rosie O'Grady?

"I mean, she might as well have put down that she was the daughter of Scarlett O'Hara and Rhett Butler, sister to Lorna Doone."

"I *know*," I say, clucking my tongue reprovingly, still completely clueless. What was wrong with Rosie O'Grady?

"I want to be apprised of any more responses like these. Remember. You're the one who recommended Belinda as our new women's ethicist. It's your fault if she turns out to be a reporter for *People* or *Parade* or one of our other competitors."

"I'm sure she won't."

"OK," she says, turning back to her paperwork. "You can go."

"But . . ."

"But what?" Lori flips her hair and taps her pencil on her glass desk.

"What about me leaving early to visit my friend who's coming out of surgery?"

"Was it a car accident?"

I really, really don't want to tell her, but I have no choice. "Gastric bypass."

"Oh." Lori presses her lips tightly together in disapproval. "It's that kind of thing, is it?"

"I guess."

"How many personal hours do you have left?"

I try to calculate the latest figures. "I believe two hundred forty."

"Impossible! No one has thirty personal days."

"I do. And over a thousand hours of vacation time."

"Don't you ever go anywhere?"

You don't let me, I want to say. "No place to go."

"Hmm. I certainly can't stop you if you have two hundred forty hours of personal leave. Just make sure the piece on which lipsticks to wear for fall are on my desk."

"Will do." Even though the freelancer doing the piece turned it in with all sorts of errors and wrong prices. It will take me hours just to fact-check it.

My holy beneficence has taken a definite hit after my encounter with Lori, and I am in a much grumpier mood when I return and find my phone ringing off the hook.

"Devlin," I grunt into the receiver.

"Is this a bad time, luv?"

Holy shit. It's Nigel. "Uh, no," I say, quickly shifting gears. "To whom am I speaking?"

"Why, Nigel."

"Nigel?" I ask doubtfully.

"Nigel Barnes. You know . . . the rock critic."

"Yes," I say vaguely. "You were talking to me in the hall the other day."

"Or, rather, we were talking to each other."

"Hmm." I make a big production out of shuffling papers. Joel raises an eyebrow.

"You sound busy."

"I'm swamped." I start tapping nonsense on the keyboard.

"Well, I just called to see if you were available this week. I really did enjoy our brief chat several weeks ago. I've been thinking quite a lot about you ever since. I think we should continue our conversation, especially that part about Belinda at Balmoral."

He fell for it. I can't believe he fell for it. This guy is so desperate to get his mitts on Camilla's roast venison that he called me asking for a date, despite his acknowledged loathing of "big-boned women."

Oh, the glory of e-mail and deception.

"That sounds wonderful," I say. "You know, I was just talking to Belinda about you."

"Were you?" His tone brightens.

"Yes. She said something about you being a 'near miss.' Now what do you suppose that means?"

Nigel begins sputtering some sort of awkward answer when Lisa peers over my cubicle, her face red and her hair a mess. "Get off," she mouths.

"Sorry, Nigel," I say. "There seems to be some sort of emergency. Call me and I'll see if I can pencil you in." Then I hang up, gloating. A sin, I know.

"Were you talking to Nigel Barnes?" she says.

"How many other Nigels are there?"

"I had no idea you were hanging out with celebrities

these days. What did he want?"

"I have no idea. You made me get off!"

"Geesh. No need to yell. Are you feeling OK?"

I have no idea what she's talking about. Unfortunately, right at that moment the phone on my desk rings. Probably Nigel calling back to scold me for hanging up.

I give Lisa the "wait a minute" finger and pick up.

"Hi, uh, Nola? This is Chip."

He says this loudly enough that Lisa can hear and now she is jumping up and down like a hyperactive kid coming off a bowl of Lucky Charms. "Get off, get off!" She's mouthing

"Can you hold for a moment, Chip?" I press the hold button.

"What is it, you dingaling? Am I not allowed to take one phone call in your presence?"

"Is that Chip?" She gestures impatiently to my phone.

"Yeah."

"Computer Chip?"

"Yeah."

"I need to talk to you before you talk to him. Tell him you'll call him back. Trust me. It's important."

I get on and ask Chip if I can call him in five. Chip doesn't even say good-bye. He just hangs up.

"OK, so what's the big deal?" I am trying to hide my growing peevish feelings, which won't hold me in good stead as a nun.

Lisa leans over the cubicle wall and lowers her

voice. "Did you leave a message on Chip's machine saying that you couldn't go out with him tonight because you were thinking of entering a holy order?"

"Not thinking of. Committed to."

"Nola." Lisa grips my shoulder. "Chip came to me right after getting that message. He wanted to know if you were insane. He says he never met you and has no idea who the heck you are."

"But . . ." But that's impossible, I want to say, feeling thoroughly confused. Didn't Chip and I hang out all night Saturday night? Didn't he drive me home the other day? Wasn't he my coach at the gym? "He came to my apartment Saturday night," I babble. "I rescued him at the Annex. He cleaned my stove."

"What do you mean you rescued him at the Annex?"

"From this girl who was attacking him."

"Oh my God." She covers her mouth. "Maybe Chip's right. Maybe you are insane. What's that genetic mental disorder that runs in your family?"

"Stupidity?"

Behind me I can sense Joel nodding his head vigorously. "I think you're right, Lisa. She is nuts. She has a special phone that rings 'Rule Britannia.' "

I flip him the bird. "Listen, I'm not mad. Chip drove me home when my car broke down. You were the one who asked him, remember?"

Lisa steps back. "Chip didn't drive you home. I tried to find him, but he'd taken the day off. When I came back to the parking lot you were gone. How did you get home anyway?"

My first response is to accuse Lisa of playing a joke. "No, really, Lisa. If this is one of your . . ."

"I'm serious. You can go to Tech Assistance and meet Chip for yourself if you don't believe me. He's thoroughly creeped out, too."

She is serious. I don't have to go upstairs to Tech Ass to see for myself. Joel and Lisa are staring at me, speechless, while I . . . I don't know what to say either, except nonsense.

"If Chip is not Chip," I say, now confused and feeling slightly chilly, "then who is Chip?"

"Maybe he's that serial killer you've been expecting," Joel offers helpfully.

I run my hand up my neck, which is thankfully intact. OK. Don't panic, Nola.

"Just one more thing," I say, my voice shaking. "Does Chip have a Toyota pickup, blond hair, a slow drawl, and the laid-back demeanor of a surfer?" That would be my essential Chip summary.

"Are you kidding? I don't know if he surfs, but I do know one thing," Lisa says.

"What?"

"He's five-foot-two with jet-black hair and a thick Scottish brogue."

Chapter Seventeen

As a general rule I am not a big fan of hospitals, though I used to be when I was a kid.

160

Hospitals are cool to kids. There's lots of action and ominous signage: WARNING: RADIATION. WARNING: BIO-HAZARDOUS MATERIALS. There are shiny metal carts with wheels and room upon room of beds that can be raised or lowered with a remote, plus televisions galore! Jell-O. Ice cream. Popsicles. At first glance, a hospital is kid heaven.

Not so at age thirty-five. Now when I enter a hospital I'm seeing people closer to my age, and they're not necessarily the doctors or nurses. They're in the beds. Then there's the omnipresent hospital aroma of warm chicken soup or warm urine, I'm never quite sure which. Whatever it is, it makes me sick.

Carrying a bouquet of pink roses for Deb, I enter the medical center, head to the bariatric surgery floor, and hope they don't try to recruit me.

The first familiar face I run into, surprisingly, is Ron. Nancy's Ron, who is leaning against the wall outside of a closed patient recovery room. It is good to see his freakishly tall, Herman Munster–like body in its usual ill-fitting dark suit and the wide, dopey grin on his face. He has kept himself in prime physical shape (for the young trophy wife to be?) but even keeping in mind his Latin Jezebel on the side, there's just no way I can be mad at him. My instincts tell me to hug and hug hard.

"Never expected that," he says, grinning down even more broadly. "To tell you the truth, you were the one I feared most. I thought you'd kick me in the knee or try to sucker punch me in the gut."

"I'm a lover, not a fighter. What are you doing here, anyway?"

Ron straightens his tie awkwardly. "To see Deb. After all, she's a friend too. I'm concerned."

I think about this, about how bad a liar Ron is. As an expert in crafting the big fib, I'm pretty good at assessing the various nuances of a bad lie. "You might very well like Deb. You might even be somewhat concerned. But I know why you're really here."

Ron keeps his face granitelike, as though he has no idea what I'm implying.

"You're here hoping to run into Nancy."

He opens his mouth to object, but I don't give him an inch. "She won't see you outside of her lawyer's office, and so you thought this would be the best way to corner her. What are you after? If you've got annulment papers in your briefcase for her to sign, you should walk out that door right now."

"Nola." Suddenly Ron is super serious. "I have no papers, annulment or otherwise, for Nancy to sign. You don't understand . . . ."

"I think I do."

"I love Nancy."

The statement hangs between us. I don't know what to make of it. Then I remember a February *Sass!* article about how guys who cheat on their wives often say corny stuff like this to ease their guilty feelings.

"As in," I clarify, "you love her and always will but you're not *in* love with her? That's why you're running off with Carmen Miranda."

162

"Carmen Miranda?"

"You know what I mean. Whatever her name is. The Guatemalan clerk."

"My affair—if you can call it that, though I think it's a stretch—is over. It's been over for months."

I'm speechless. This makes no sense. The way Nancy put it at the Princeton Arms, Ron was ready to make his girlfriend a child bride.

"You mean you're not getting remarried?"

"No. Who told you that?"

I don't want to say Nancy because, knowing her, she wouldn't want Ron to know that we'd been talking about him. Though, really, how could we not?

"Have you told Nancy this?"

"Of course. That's why I'm dragging my feet in the divorce proceedings. I've apologized and offered to go to counseling and thrown myself at her feet. But she just won't listen. Even now she walked right past me into Deb's room. Didn't say a word."

I eye Deb's room.

"I'll put in a good word for you," I say, moving to the door.

"Tell her I've ordered a recliner for Deb. From everything I've read, you can't sleep a wink after this surgery without one. It should be at her house in an hour."

I give him an encouraging thumbs-up and go in.

Deb's room is filled with so many whirring and blinking machines that I'm rather shocked. I don't know what I'd expected, but not all this technology.

Deb is in the bed closest to the door and she is knocked out. Nancy is by the window, flipping through a magazine.

There is a pulse monitor on Deb's finger and a tube up her nose. An IV. A catheter bag and other tubes that are mysteries. A machine above her tracks her heartbeat and her oxygen level. And there are these strange stockings on her legs pumping and releasing. Somewhere along the way Deb went in for stomach stapling and came out as Frankenstein's monster.

"Nancy," I whisper.

Nancy looks up from her magazine. I can tell by her expression that she might have overheard my conversation with Ron. "I don't want to discuss him. Not now."

OK . . . I change the subject. "How's Deb doing?"

Nancy the former nurse gets up and gives Deb a professional assessment. Nancy's looking thinner in the face, I notice. Either that or it's the dim lighting working to her advantage.

"She was moaning for Paul a little while ago."

I try to think positive. "Tell me he just ran out to get lunch."

"Nope. He hasn't been here all day. Not even this morning. I asked the nurses."

What is wrong with him? Paul and Deb have been married since the day after graduation from high school. Before that they were boyfriend and girlfriend since fourth grade and king and queen of our high school prom in Manville. It's rare for people to refer

164

to one or the other alone. It's always Deb-and-Paul something.

So it doesn't make sense that he wouldn't be here for this, the most significant medical event in Deb's life aside from her appendectomy two years ago and the birthing of their two kids.

"I tried calling him," Nancy says, "but all I got on the phone was Anna. Naturally, she was worried about her mother and said her dad has promised to take them to the hospital later. Though she had no idea what later meant."

Deb stirs and opens her eyes with fluttering lids. Seeing us, she smiles and then winces. Nancy efficiently takes charge, dabbing Deb's lips with a wet washcloth and applying a thin coat of Vaseline to them.

"Thanks," Deb says, trying to sit up but failing. "I had no idea this would be so painful."

"Won't be painful for long. The sooner you get up and walk around, the better." Nancy fluffs the pillow behind Deb's head. "The good news is that you did really, really well. The surgery went off without a hitch."

Deb beams. I open the shade to let some light in, which is when she sees the large bouquet by her bed.

Instantly I realize my mistake. Nancy shoots me a worried glance as Deb leans over and eagerly reads the tag. "From . . . Ron? Who's Ron?"

Nancy and I say nothing.

"You mean Nancy's Ron?" Deb blinks in the light.

"Isn't that nice of him?" I chirp. "He's ordered you a reclining chair, too, so you'll be more comfortable."

Her face falls five stories. Turning to Nancy she says, "And you're getting me a live-in nurse for a week."

Nancy pretends to be busy checking this and that. Meanwhile I surreptitiously dump my own roses in the metal garbage can under the sink.

"But my husband of seventeen years does nothing. Doesn't even kiss me good-bye this morning." Deb shuts her eyes. I hope she won't cry again. She may be the queen of the waterworks, but she's been crying way too much lately.

Fortunately the bariatric nurse comes in and makes it clear that she wants us to vamoose.

"Do you mind, Nola?" Nancy asks, as we tiptoe to the door. "Could you tell Ron that I really don't want to see him? Not now."

My heart sinks. Nancy can be so stubborn. Just once I wish she could learn to go with the flow.

"OK," I say reluctantly.

As if having second thoughts, she touches my back. "Though make sure you tell him that his generosity hasn't gone unnoticed. I really appreciate it."

Thin comfort, if you ask me.

Ron is still waiting, scrolling through his Black-Berry, when I step out. I don't have to say a word. He gets it right away, smart boy that he is.

"She does say thank-you, though. And that your generosity hasn't gone unnoticed. She really appreciates it."

He nods and shrugs on his coat. "I keep telling myself I deserve this cold shoulder. I guess it's a question of how much is too much."

I have to agree. It's a damn good question. Only, I'm not sure it has an answer.

On the way home from the hospital, I prepare myself for my date/confrontation with "Mystery Chip" by making a pit stop at the Army-Navy Store on Witherspoon—where I pick up a handy, if lethal, Leatherman knife set—and then St. Anne's Roman Catholic Church, a couple blocks from my house. It all makes sense, really.

At church I light a candle for Deb. I practice kneeling for a long time, debating whether this suits me. I don't really like the idea of waking up at four to do sunrise masses or sleeping on a straw tick mattress. Perhaps there is a booklet around here on whether straw tick mattresses are must-haves for today's woman in the holy order.

Luckily, I discover that straw tick mattresses and hair suits are out! That's according to a pamphlet called, *So . . . You Want to Be a Nun?* I found under a bunch of miter boxes. It is written in vocabulary an eight-year-old could understand—which raises serious questions about the recruitment policies of the Church, if you ask me.

It is fascinating reading that answers most of my concerns such as: Who Can Be a Nun? Can You Be a Nun? Can I Be a Nun If I've Been Married? Can I Be a Nun If I'm a Widow? Can I Be a Nun If I've Had Premarital Sex?

Boy. These nun wannabes really get around.

Good news. I *can* be a nun. I have never been married and though I have had premarital sex, albeit bad premarital sex, I am not disqualified. Better yet, I don't have to take a vow of poverty!

Vows of poverty are only for certain orders. Certain orders (would that be the Botox Order of Beverly Hills?) believe that material possessions do not interfere with a nun's relationship with her divine husband, God. (That is until He gets a peek at this month's Mastercard bill.)

The Sisters of Mercy, who are associated with St. Anne's, are made of tougher stock than I am. They take public vows of poverty, chastity, and obedience and dedicate themselves to serving the poor in the community, especially women and children.

Lord. That's asking a lot, isn't it? I mean it's bad enough you've got to be poor yourself, not to mention chaste and obedient. Then you've got to dedicate yourself to helping other poor people. Where's the "me" time?

I fold the *So . . . You want to Be a Nun?* pamphlet and tuck it into my purse next to the Leatherman and head home. The showers stopped hours ago and turned the grass a bit greener, the air somewhat sweeter smelling. It is humid, like Caribbean humid, and once again I am amazed by Princeton's summer students who will exercise in any conditions, their shirts soaked in sweat as they bike past me.

Now that I'm back on Weight Watchers and can eat only 28 points worth of food and drink a day, I forfeit my afternoon pick me up of a cappuccino (4 points) and chocolate-chip cookie (2) for a crisp gala apple (1 point) and a bottle of water (0).

This is followed by the familiar feeling of denial that plagues me whenever I have to give up a treat. I don't mind eating Special K for breakfast, for example, instead of a cheese omelet with home fries and rye toast because breakfast does not fall into the treat category. But my four p.m. chocolate-chip cookie and cappuccino I look forward to all day and I can't help but feel as though I'm being somehow punished by having to be satisfied with a gala apple.

I try to remember what I've learned over the years, that hunger is good. Hunger means the diet is working. Fat cells are being burned! After all, I didn't put on this weight overnight. It's not going to come off overnight, either.

With a couple of hours until Chip arrives, I move into phase two of my plan. The Walk. This, I know, will be something I'll have to do every day, probably before work. I don't mind the Walk. It's the Jog I can't stand. But the Jog will take the weight off faster than the Walk, no matter what the modern media claims. You know it. I know it. We all know it. We might as well stop lying to ourselves that walking is just as good. Therefore, I will slowly, gradually ease myself into a run.

Besides, when I think of the alternative—the gym with hulking Rider—a spell of brisk jogging isn't so bad.

I pull on my freshly washed sweats and sneakers, clip a leash on Otis, and head out. For five blocks I make it look like a stroll with no intention of formal exercise. I dread the possibility of my neighbors seeing me and my wiggling ass as I lumber along, breathing heavily and stopping every twenty paces. That's what I distrust about jogging—too many parts of me jiggle.

At the cemetery where it is cooler and shadier, I unclip Otis and let him practice pouncing on the squirrels and birds. Then, looking around to make sure there are no svelte runners nearby, I move into a slow, heaving jog. I like cemeteries for this type of physical humiliation because there are many paved walkways—and dead people. Dead people cannot point and laugh. Or maybe they can, but no one can see them.

The cemetery is a pleasant place. It smells fresh and, ironically, renewing. The trees are old and spread their green branches protectively. The taller tombstones hide me from other runners, plus they're good for collapsing against when I'm out of breath, which is frequently. I decide after fifteen minutes of this torture in sweltering heat that tomorrow I will bring an iPod—as though that will help.

When I get home I shower and put on my standard going-out outfit—a pair of black pants and a white blouse with mid-length sleeves, accessorized with various pieces of clunky jewelry. My hair is blown out and brushed so it's full and shiny. I expend all my creative effort on the facial area—foundation, taupe eyeliner, brown eye shadow, blush, and the high-tech expensive mascara to make my puny lashes look fuller and longer. I pause and ponder how and why having hairy eyeballs became sexually desirable.

I would outline my lips except that on the dot of six thirty "Rule Britannia" rings from my purse in the living room. Charlotte Dawson has the absolute worst timing.

"Ello!" I say, somewhat testily.

"Oh!" gasps the familiar girly voice. "I forgot. It's probably like eleven thirty your time, isn't it?"

I hold out my phone and inspect the screen. This isn't Charlotte. . . . It's Eileen, my sister! What's she doing calling me, I mean Belinda?

"Belinda?" she's saying. "Did I wake you? The time difference totally slipped my mind."

"No, no," I mumble, trying to sound groggy. "Not asleep. Not quite."

"It's just that I'm soooo excited."

"Er. How did you get my number exactly?" I regret the question immediately as I hear a car door slam and Otis meow from his perch on the windowsill. Must be Chip. Otherwise Otis would be hissing and sharpening his claws on the slate.

"It's in the memory of my phone. I figure that if you were, like, really uptight about that kind of thing

171

you'd have the phone company block your number."

Note to self: Get Belinda's number blocked.

I hear the doorbell ring downstairs and Bitsy clicking across the foyer to answer it. She's laughing and so is Chip. There's a bit of muffled conversation. Good.

"So, anyway, I have something very important to ask," Eileen says.

I close my eyes in horrified anticipation.

"I was thinking of asking Nola to be my maid of honor."

Whew. Easy street. "That seems traditional. Excellent idea. Well, if that's all . . ."

"That's what I *should* do. That's what my mom says I should do, but like you said, it's not her wedding, it's mine, and I should do what's in my heart."

I said that?

"And so, I just want to know if it's OK for me not to ask Nola. I mean, she'd be a bridesmaid and everything, just not the maid of honor."

Relief. Yes! Yes! Yes! I want to holler from the rooftops. Make someone else the maid of honor so I, the unmarriageable hulking jealous sister, don't have to stand next to you, the slim princess in white.

"The thing is," Eileen continues, "she's already been other people's maid of honor lots of times."

Twelve.

"And I'd think she'd be sick of it."

You have no idea.

"So is it OK if I ask another girl instead?"

"Absolutely." I hope we're almost done since there is now a definite stomping up the stairs. A male stomping, not a Bitsy stomping. *Stomp. Stomp. Stomp.*

"Really? That's OK?"

"Positive."

Knock. "Nola! It's me, Chip."

Cripes. What if Eileen hears that? "Come in, the door's open," I call, praying that he's not equipped with a rope and knife right off. What to do? What to do? I have to hide, at least my voice.

Eileen is still babbling as I'm running down the hall, half listening to her ". . . and you're sure my sister will be OK with that?"

"Yes, yes, yes," I say, slipping into the bathroom and locking the door.

"That's sooo great." Eileen trills. "Thank you, thank you, Belinda. I never thought you'd say yes. Don't forget—it's the week between Christmas and New Year's. I'll send you a photo of the dresses as soon as I pick them. You are such a star to come all the way from England, just for little ol' me. Oh, and bring Nigel if you want. That would be awesome." She clicks off.

I don't know what I've done. I'm not sure, but I believe I may have just agreed to be my sister's maid of honor. As Belinda.

Which is when I think that this Belinda stuff, at some point, is going to have to stop.

Chapter Eighteen

I unlock the bathroom door and step out in slow motion, my head in a fog as I try to picture me, as Eileen's bridesmaid (probably last in the lineup) and me, as Eileen's maid of honor.

"I cannot be two places at once."

"Funny thing. Me neither."

I blink and come back to reality. Chip—or the man formerly known as Chip—is before me in a loose gray T-shirt that hangs off his shoulders and those faded jeans again. Does he wear anything else?

"Hey," he says, standing back to take a look. "Don't you look nice. Turn around."

"Uh, sorry." I click Belinda's phone shut. "I'm not really a turning around kind of gal."

"Boy. You are a hard case, aren't you?"

And you're not Chip, I want to say.

"So, ready to go?" He is rubbing his hands, possibly itching to wrap them around my neck.

"Actually . . ."

"Actually, I have a big surprise. I went through a lot of trouble for this, so don't start making excuses that you have laundry to do or it's the night you change Otis's litter."

"Does it involve a box cutter and dark green garbage bag?"

"What?" He is thoroughly confused.

"Just wondering."

"Come on. They won't stay open much longer." He tries to take my hand, but I am too fast for him.

I study the man formerly known as Chip standing there with his messy blond hair and baby blue eyes and notice that they are accentuated by tiny laugh lines. His nose is a bit too large and somewhat hooked, as though it had been broken once or twice, ruining what would otherwise be classic good looks. Yet, these imperfections make him seem innocent and endearing.

Now you take a picture of Ted Bundy and study it as I have, often, and you'll notice his features were neatly divided and perfect—a sure sign of a psychopath. This man formerly known as Chip doesn't have it in him to murder thirty to a hundred women. You can tell by his nose.

"What's the holdup?" Chip is saying.

"Listen. I gotta know. You're not a serial killer, are you?"

He doesn't flinch. "Would you like me to be?"

That catches me off guard. "Not exactly."

"OK, then, no. Being a serial killer is not one of my life goals."

"Thank God." It is flabbergasting how much consolation I take from that statement.

"What else?"

"Why are you being so nice to me?"

Chip makes a face. "Are you serious? Are you implying that the only reason I might want to be nice to you is because I'm a serial killer and you're a potential victim?"

I shrug. That pretty much cuts to the chase. "Kind of."

"Man. You've got to get out more. Now stop screwing around and hurry up. We've got about ten more minutes."

I don't know where I expected Chip to take me. Dinner. Or maybe bowling. A movie. The thing is, I never thought we'd really end up going out because after we got the serial-killer status squared away, I had planned to confront him about his true identity while holding the Leatherman to his neck.

Why I didn't say, "Hey, you're not Computer Chip who works in Tech Ass" is a mystery. If I bothered to undergo some deep analysis, I'd probably conclude that I was afraid of pissing him off.

As for the nun thing, well, I hadn't given myself over to God yet, had I? And, let's be honest. Chip is cute. He's fun. He listens. He's kind of sexy. He's got a groovy nose.

"Do you like sushi?" We're speeding to Lord knows where in his Toyota pickup, down Route 1. "'Cause I'm addicted to sushi."

Sushi? That's what the big rush is for? Excuse me. A four-course meal at the Nassau Inn is worth a speeding ticket. Bait on rice is not. Besides, sushi's not as great on the Weight Watchers points as you would think for something made out of itty-bitty fish and seaweed. One homemade chocolate-chip cookie equals four tuna rolls. I ask you, where are the priorities?

"Sure," I say unenthusiastically. "But I only like California rolls and eel. Sea urchin, I can't even look at. It's too wobbly and gross."

"Uni? I *love* that stuff. When I lived in Japan, I ate so much I had to go to the hospital for food poisoning."

Japan. Ah, so. Another clue to the puzzle that is Chip. "When did you live over there?"

"Years ago. I used to teach English. Man, was that a blast." He smiles to himself, recalling fondly the hours his stomach was pumped in Tokyo General.

"Where do you live now?" A reasonable question.

"I'm kind of bi."

This could have so many implications.

"Bicoastal bi?" I ask. "Or Vince Lombardi Rest Area bi?"

Chip laughs. "I spend most of my time in L.A., though I spent part of my childhood here so it's kind of like home. Either way, it's complicated. Hey. We're almost there."

We can't be almost anywhere, though, because we're nowhere. Where we are is on the bleak, ugly auto strip. I am keeping an eye out for sushi restaurants when Chip swings into Princeton Mercedes Benz.

"Surprised?" he asks, his eyes twinkling.

"Uh, kind of. Are you buying a car?"

"No." He pulls right up to the showroom and kills the engine. "You are. We're here to get that car you wanted, the Mercedes convertible."

In a second, he's out the door, leaving me awestruck, staring at the feast of luscious Mercedes posed behind the plate glass like a line of Amsterdam hookers. I can't go in there. I can't go into this gleaming showroom where cars cost more than my parents' house. I have no business being here.

Chip flings open the door. "Geesh, you're slow to move."

"Chip," I hesitate, choosing my words carefully. "Whoever you are. I have the feeling you're a pretty rich guy."

"Born rich. Didn't earn it," he says honestly.

"But, I'm not. I'm an editor at a tabloid. I can't afford . . . a Mercedes."

"Sure you can. I've got it all worked out." He holds out his hand and his expression is as eager as a little boy's. There's no way I can say no to that.

Together we walk into the showroom, where a tiny, ancient man in a dark, somber suit—looking more like an estate lawyer than the car salesman I'm more accustomed to—is waiting clearly just for us. "Good evening. So glad you could make it," he says, nodding to Chip. "Nice to see you again, sir."

"Ditto." Chip throws his arm around me. "Maurice, this is the woman I was telling you about. Nola Devlin. Nola, this is Maurice. Maurice will set you up just fine."

Maurice extends a tiny, wrinkled hand that I shake in my stupor. "Hi," I say weakly.

"I understand you are interested in an SLK65 in Capri blue?"

178

"Was I?" I say, flushing. "I don't know about *interested*. Fantasizing, maybe."

"Of course." Maurice bows his head with the grace of a kung-fu master. "An SLK65 is a beautiful automobile, though very expensive."

"One hundred eighty-five thousand dollars," I blurt.

Maurice turns to Chip, who is grinning like an idiot. "Your friend has done her research."

"I told you she was smart," Chip says. "And you should see her dead lift."

I give him a playful punch.

"Fortunately, Miss Devlin, I may have another model in stock that might fulfill your wishes, at least for now."

My heart misses a beat as we follow Maurice out the door to the parking lot. How am I going to get out of this? I can't afford a Mercedes. What will my dad say? Or my mom, for that matter? They'll demand to see my checkbook and bank statements. They'll think I've gone on a spending spree, that I'm in desperate need of lithium or a stern lecture. And what about the insurance? That's got to be deadly.

"Right this way." Maurice is taking us around the corner, his suit coat flapping in the warm summer breeze.

"Isn't this a gas?" Chip says, giving my hand a squeeze.

As soon as we turn the corner, I stop dead in my tracks. There it is. My dream car. Not an SLK65, but damn close. It is a Mercedes Roadster, model

179

SLK230. In black with beige leather. The top is down and it is polished and sparkling and begging to be driven.

"Couldn't find you a blue one," Chip says. "Believe me, Maurice and I tried."

"They're very popular," agrees Maurice, opening the driver-side door. "But this one is in top condition." He motions for me to get in.

"I can't . . ."

"You *have* to." Suddenly, Chip throws himself over the door into the passenger side. "I love doing that."

"Yes," says Maurice.

"Come on, Nola. Maurice wants to go home. Let's take it for a spin."

There is Maurice, dangling the keys in front of me.

"It's used?" I ask. "I'll feel better about it if it's used."

"Pre-owned. Nine thousand miles, roughly. It was a lease."

Nine thousand miles is not going to put this car into my budget, that's for sure. I thank Maurice, take the keys anyway, get in, and sit for a few minutes, admiring the chestnut trim, the feel of the German-engineered stick shift, the smooth buttery leather. "They used to come only in automatic until 1999," I say.

"So you know this car." Chip slides an arm along the back of my seat.

My posture instinctively straightens as I feel the hard muscles of his forearm behind my neck. "They

180

call it the, the Kom—Kompressor," I stutter. "Reminded me of Arnold Schwarzenegger."

Tentatively, I insert the key in the ignition, step on the clutch, and shift to neutral. Men always leave a car in gear. It's like a law. Then I close my eyes and turn the key. It starts up smoothly.

"Boy. Do you take this much time with everything? Leaving the apartment. Getting out of the car . . . Put on your safety belt, sweetheart, and put your foot to the accelerator."

A few minutes later, we are on Route 1, which is a pain because there are lots of lights and it's mostly stop and go. "Hook a right there." Chip points to a side road. "I know this road. It goes forever."

We take the turn and I'm in bliss. The wind is blowing my hair and Chip's, too. He's leaning back and smiling in the sun as I push it to seventy, hugging the corners of the two-lane country road. Out of the corner of my eye, I see him stealing glances at me.

"You know, this is the first time since I've met you that I've seen you so happy," he shouts.

"Are you kidding? I'm in heaven." I downshift as we climb a hill, appreciating the power, the tightness of the wheels to the curves.

"Take this left coming up."

"Where are we going?"

"A park I picked out."

A serial-killer park? No. No. Stop that, Nola. Besides, Maurice could nail him, easy. Unless Chip went back and did him in too. There's always that.

The park is on the right and down a slight embankment. There's a babbling brook, willow trees, green grass, and one bench. I stop the car and raise the top, which snaps shut with a satisfied click. For a minute, Chip and I sit in the darkness as my body tries to absorb the rush of adrenaline.

"You like it, don't you, even though it's not exactly what you wanted?"

"I love it." I run my hand over the dashboard. "It's as close to my dream as I've ever come."

"Is this your only dream, a Mercedes?"

"No. I happen to have lots of dreams."

Chip is staring at me again. Thoughtful. "OK, let's have a nosh." He rolls out of the car as I raise the windows and lock it. Only after I've stood there, admiring its sleek black body for a while does the question pop into my mind.

Nosh?

Ahead of me, Chip is running down the embankment toward the river with a basket in his hand. Where it came from, I have no idea. Somehow he slipped it into the Mercedes from his Toyota. Or maybe he planned it all along.

Hmm.

"Don't tell me Maurice offers a picnic with every test drive," I say as Chip shakes out a red-and-white cloth under a willow tree.

"No, I do. Took the chance that you liked sushi. Lucky choice that I erred on the side of California rolls." He opens the basket to reveal four black plastic containers and a bottle of white wine. A French Bordeaux. Producing a corkscrew, he puts the bottle between his legs and uncorks it. "Sorry. I only have plastic cups."

"I can't drink. I'm driving." Besides. A glass of white wine, 4 oz., is 2 points. Unless it's white wine vinegar. That's 0.

"You don't have to guzzle the whole bottle." He pours out a glass and hands it to me. Then he lifts his to make a toast. "To your new car."

"Chip, listen . . ." I sit down, put aside the wine, and he sits next to me, very close. So close I can feel the warmth rising from those great thighs. This is no way to tempt a future nun—with a man like Chip and a Mercedes convertible.

"That car . . ."

"Had a sticker price of twenty-nine thousand. I found a ding in the rear and talked Maurice down to twenty-three. Maurice is a savvy businessman; he knows better than to screw up the relationship he has with me and my family." Chip hands me a container of California rolls. His are much more exotic—eel, roe, yellowtail, and, yup, uni.

"With monthly payments that's about two hundred thirty-eight bucks. Insurance is another two hundred a month, but you'd pay that anyway, seeing that you're living in Jersey and insurance here is out of control. It may be a few more bucks than you'd pay for a Honda, but there comes a time in a person's life when you have to stop pushing aside your dreams and start living them."

He pops the entire yellowtail into his mouth. Chews. Savors. Swallows. "And, Nola, you have reached that time."

"Who are you?" I couldn't stand it anymore. I had to ask.

"Me?" He winks, wiping his fingers on his jeans. "Who do you think I am?"

"I don't know." I mix wasabi into soy sauce (0 points both) and dip in a California roll (1 point).

"Sure you don't want to give the uni a another try?" He holds it out to me and I nearly turn green.

"No, thanks."

"Your loss." He bites into it and I am forced to look away.

"OK, I think that we've arrived at the stage, Chip, where we need to be honest with each other."

"Yes. Honesty. Always good." Though he says this halfheartedly and seems more interested in what to eat next.

"I know you don't work at *Sass!*"

"How do you know that?"

"Because I called down to Chip in Technical Assistance, the guy who was supposed to pick me up Friday, and totally embarrassed myself. He'd never heard of me."

Fake Chip misses the point of this vignette. "How come you were calling the guy you thought was me?"

"To cancel the date."

"Why?"

"Because I'm giving up men."

184

"Really? Huh. How come?"

I chew the slightly tough California roll and, as my nose and eyes tear with the pain of intense horse-radish, decide I could drink or eat anything made out of wasabi and soy sauce. "I've decided to become a nun."

"That'll be interesting. I don't think of nuns driving Mercedes SLKs." He points at me with his chopsticks. "Though, now that I think of it, maybe you could give the little orphan kids rides. There's a movie where Mary Tyler Moore's a nun and Elvis is a—"

"Chip! You're not paying attention. The point of the story is not *why* I wanted to cancel, but that you weren't Chip in Tech Ass."

"Oh." He frowns and sips some wine. "Go on."

"And clearly your name is not really Chip. I noticed with my keen journalistic skills that Maurice was careful to not refer to you directly."

"That's Maurice for you. Discreet. It's his middle name. Really. Maurice Discreet Smith. MDS. It's monogrammed on his briefcase. Swear to God. Check it out when we go back."

Does he take anything seriously? Unlikely. But I am determined and so I press onward. "I gather you're rich. Maybe a trust-fund baby, probably loaded to the gills, which is why someone like Angie is all over you."

"Not because of my baby blues?" He blinks.

"Well, maybe because of your baby blues, but more because of your stock portfolio. So my question is, who are you?"

185

"I'm Chip and I work at *Sass!* You can take it to the bank."

This is so frustrating that I break down and slug back some wine, which turns out to be dry and excellent and worth each of the two points. What else would you expect from a guy who's on a first-name basis with the owner of a Mercedes dealership?

"You know, this is really cosmic." He puts down his sushi—finally!—wipes his mouth, and faces me. "It must have been fate that you were waiting for a guy named Chip. I had no knowledge of that, by the way. I just saw you standing there and thought you looked forlorn and cute."

Forlorn and cute? Me?

"So I gave you a ride. And you were pretty funny. Started talking about how much hot water you were in at work and, you know, my interest was piqued, especially when I ran into you in the gym and found you had bet the toughest guy there into a weightlifting contest."

Yes, that would be me. Petite and delicate.

"Most women I meet come on to me. I'm not bragging, it's just a fact. Anyway, you're right. Their interest probably has more to do with my money than my baby blues, sadly." He picks at some grass, thinking about this. "Then again, maybe you would have been more like them if you hadn't assumed I worked in computers."

You know, he might be right. I am, admittedly, a geek snob, though I have nothing against computer geeks, personally. What they do with their spare time is their business.

Still, I must stay on track. "What I don't get," I say, with such blatant hypocrisy it is shameful, "is why you don't just come out and tell me your full name, rank, and serial number."

He leans back on his elbows, squinting into the setting sun. It is several minutes before he says, "No, I don't think I will."

"What? Why?" I scream, eying his pocket and debating whether to make a go for his wallet to check his driver's license.

"Because, I really enjoy you, Nola. I like your neat uppercut. I like how you keep setting things on fire and how you're apparently in big trouble at work. Very intriguing. I like the way you've formed a pact with your friends to lose weight. That's very cool. And I especially like your killer cat. If I come out and give you my name, rank, and serial number—as you put it—we might not have a chance. And I'd never see Otis again."

I keep my face straight as I mull these words over. *We might not have a chance. We might not have a chance.* This is like music that is so rarely heard by my ears that I have trouble hearing it. Perhaps I am akin to one of those brain-damaged people who can still read, technically, though sentences have no meaning.

How is it, I want to ask him, that you are sitting next to me, sipping a superb Bordeaux on a glorious

187

summer evening under a willow tree? Why would you, who women such as Angie apparently adore, want to be with me, a hulking jealous spinster? At least, according to Eileen.

But those questions are the kinds of questions fat girls ask themselves, and I catch myself. Changes in the body start with the mind, and I'm taking a new path, remember? So I deflect my wonder to the new Mercedes convertible SLK230 perched above us. "Thanks for finding my dream car. I can't tell you how much it means. Makes me feel a little bit like Cinderella."

Chip frowns. "I don't get that at all."

"But I do." And for now, that's all that's important.

Chapter Nineteen

That was six weeks ago.

Nearly two months and the only words from Chip since then have been those he wrote on a note slipped into my mailbox a few days after our Mercedes date.

Dear Nola:
I had a blast with you the other night. Thanks for being such a good sport while I was in town. That car was made for you. Enjoy. Look forward to seeing you again. I'll call you when I'm back.

Love, "Chip"
P.S. Say hi to Otis.

"Love." I've analyzed, calculated, accepted, and rejected every nuance of that word in this context and still I don't know what to make of it.

Worse, every day I wait for him to call. I check my messages with the degree of vigilance more akin to a nuclear monitoring facility than a girl who enjoyed one and a half dates with a guy. I even swung by the Mercedes dealership and casually engaged Maurice in conversation in an effort to extract more information about my mystery man. But Chip was right. Maurice's middle name really is Discreet. MDS. I saw it on his briefcase too.

During my early morning walk/runs around the cemetery I have taken to hashing and rehashing what could have gone wrong in the Chip department. The best-case scenario is this: Shortly after our parting at the park, Chip—actually an agent for the CIA—was kidnapped by terrorists and taken to a remote desert area where he is being held in a cave with no access to a cell phone.

Reasonable.

Worst-case scenario is that he was so repulsed by the way I chewed my sushi that he whipped out his Sharpie and ran a black line through my name in his address book.

Or was it something—possibly someone—else?

Angie comes to mind, along with all the women who know who Chip really is and who are desperate to have him while I continue to labor in ignorance. Me, a mere experiment. A whim, if you will. Could it

189

be that Chip was curious to see what it was like to date a "big-boned woman," as Nigel would say?

Then again, there's the basic societal problem. Simply that good, honest, funny, decent, *single* men in my age group are hard to find and keep. It's true! Consider these *Sass!* headlines we've run in just the past six months:

SO, YOU'VE FOUND MR. RIGHT: IS HE HERE TO STAY?
TEN TIPS TO KEEP HIM BEGGING FOR MORE
ARE YOU SEXUALLY SATISFYING HIM?
SIGNS THAT HE'S "JUST NOT THAT INTO YOU"
IS HE GONE FOR GOOD? OR CAN YOU GET HIM BACK?
   TAKE OUR QUIZ
FIND YOUR NEXT MR. RIGHT. HINT—IT'S EASIER THAN
   YOU THINK!

Or maybe, just maybe, there was no romantic intent to begin with. I helped Chip out of a sticky situation at the Annex; he returned the favor by arranging for the Mercedes. Done and done. That he plied me with French wine, took me to a secluded park, put his arm around me in the car as the sun set—these were nothing but niceties. Courtly love mannerisms of which he gave little thought, being that he is a worldly, wealthy heir from free-love California.

And what am I? I am a pedantic Jersey girl with an out-of-control imagination that consistently gets me into trouble. Like my third-grade teacher warned me, daydreaming would do me no good. Especially when

190

I daydream about being in love.

What I've decided is that now is certainly not the time to be entering into a serious relationship anyway. I mean, I need to focus all my energy on sticking with this Cinderella Pact and losing weight. I can't be going out on dates—beer, hamburgers, movie popcorn—when there are pounds to be shed.

And the good news. Scratch that. The *terrific* news is that I am losing weight. In two months I have lost fifteen and a half pounds. I know this because I summoned my courage and asked the weigher at Weight Watchers to tell me the truth. I was so thrilled when she showed me my stats. I burst into tears when our leader gave me the coveted fifteen-pound gold star.

Actually, it took me a while to start losing weight. After dropping five pounds the first week, I stalled. The numbers on the scale wouldn't move. I even gained a pound or two. The leader at our meetings told me to find the "golden spot"—eating enough points to keep my metabolism stoked, yet not eating too many that my body isn't dipping into fat reserves. Turned out I wasn't eating enough and I needed to eat more fruits and vegetables. One Friday—my weigh-in day—I stepped on the scale and found that four pounds were gone.

Are there days when I'm hungry? You bet. There are days when I long for a grilled ham-and-cheese sandwich or a Reuben with sauerkraut, fatty corned beef, and Russian dressing. Black-forest cake. Unlimited numbers of chocolate-chip cookies. Onion dip and a bag of Ruffles. There are days when I long to just not give a damn.

But then I think of Nancy with her expensive, ruthless personal trainer and nutritionist and Deb slicing her body open, and I am filled with resolve.

We are going to do this. Once and for all. What started out as a whim is now my mission.

Deb now takes a walk with me every Saturday, our *long* day when we try to hit seven miles. I can't describe the change in her. She says she feels as though the fat's just melting off, and I think she's right. She can weigh one thing in the morning and a pound less by that night. Already she's dropped the maternal jumpers and is wearing skirts and tops. OK, they came from Goodwill, but still.

There have been some downsides, like losing her hair. Not all of it, just some. Then she upped her vitamin intake and it all grew back, though straighter.

Deb eats teeny tiny portions. Doll portions. At first it was Jell-O—don't get me started—and then she moved to smoothies. After that it was pureed food. That was gross. Then soft food—scrambled eggs, chicken noodle soup, sweet potatoes, and cottage cheese—and now she's moving on to regular food, albeit tentatively. Peas that might have gone down fine on Tuesday can make you barf on Wednesday, she tells me.

More information than I need to know.

Going out to dinner with Deb is a joke. It's not even worth it. She'll order chicken breast and barely nibble it. Then she'll try some salad, three grains of rice, and that's it. Two points total in Weight Watchers currency. I can remember when that was what Deb mindlessly ate while waiting for the waiter to take away her plate. For her the best part of going out to dinner is knowing that she won't have to do the dishes. It's no longer the Snickers pie at the end.

Of course learning to eat this way hasn't been a snap. In the beginning, Deb got very depressed and Paul was no help at all. Her complaint that she had lost her "best friend," i.e. food, had no meaning to him.

One day he said to me, "I thought you and Nancy were her best friends. Now Deb tells me it's food."

I tried to explain about how food is there even at two a.m., how it triggers comfort responses in our brains, a holdover from infancy. But he just shook his head and said something about football.

Nancy, as usual, has approached weight loss like a trial lawyer gearing up for the big case. In other words, she's gone into overdrive.

Her trainer is at her doorstep by five a.m., six days a week, and they work out for an hour and a half. In addition, she bought an elliptical machine and measures everything. Uh, did I mention that Ron bought her a used treadmill that seems to need an awful lot of repairs? Just Nancy's luck, Ron happens to have the right tools.

Ahem.

Last week we were at the Alchemist and Barrister restaurant and Nancy kept eyeing the table next to us.

"What's wrong with you?" I asked. "You're being rude."

"It's just so disgusting. I can't imagine that I ever ate that much."

At first glance I didn't know what she was talking about. A large cheeseburger on a Kaiser roll and fries. Then, comparing that to what we had just eaten—half a filet of fish and salad—I could understand. For the first time I saw the restaurant portions for what they are, which is to say, obscene.

That's when I knew we'd leaped a major hurdle. Maybe we really were going to make it this time. We were going to lose the weight and keep it off. We are transforming ourselves into healthy creatures— stronger, more energetic, and more beautiful than we'd ever imagined.

At least that's what I keep telling myself. Because if there's anything I've learned as Belinda, it's that lies are like magic. What you believe, most often becomes true.

Chapter Twenty

"Belinda! You are sooo hard to get a hold of. Between the time difference, which is sooo terribly inconvenient, and that simpleton you have for an editor, it's amazing we can connect at all."

"Excuse me?" I am driving in my Mercedes, top down in the September sun, talking in a faux British accent to Belinda's high-powered agent, Charlotte, on a cell phone. I should feel glamorous. I should have a silk Chanel scarf around my head and big Jackie O sunglasses. Instead, my thighs are spreading like quicksand over the hot leather, my hair is beating my face, and I keep accidentally getting pieces of it in my mouth. "Which editor are you talking about?"

"Nora."

"Do you mean Nola?"

"Whatever. They're all the same. A dime a dozen. I've been in the business soooo long, I can't be expected to keep these paper pushers straight."

My hands clutch the wheel as I nearly rear-end a plumber's van in front of me. For the record I, as Nola the paper pusher, do not remember receiving one phone call from Charlotte Dawson, which raises questions about what other lies she's been spreading.

Chip. Eileen. Jim. Lori. Me. Now Charlotte. We all lie. I'm beginning to wonder if anyone tells the truth these days.

"Here I've been in Italy all summer, and I come back to find that you are under some sort of investigation at work. It's the most absurd thing I've ever heard of."

I could think of a few more absurd things, if she's interested.

"I told them it can't be true that you're an imposter. Tell me I'm right."

"Of course you're right." The lie rolls easily from my lips as I find the first quiet street and pull into it. This conversation is too nerve-wracking to conduct while shifting lanes. "I'm absolutely real."

"Good!" She lets out a sigh. "That's exactly what I'll tell your managing editor, then."

"Excellent," I say, happy that Charlotte will finally put Lori in her place.

"When I meet her today for lunch."

Hold on. "For lunch?"

"Yes. In Jersey, of all horrible spots. You don't think I'd let something this serious wait, do you? I demanded an immediate, face-to-face meeting."

"But . . . today?"

"We need to get this issue resolved, Belinda. That producer in L.A. is dying to meet you. Sweet Dream Productions is really eager to get started on this project, but rumors that your publisher has doubts about your authenticity might put a damper on that. Studios have to be very careful these days, especially after that whole Jim Frey and Oprah mess. If he gets one whiff that you're a fraud, it could kill our film deal."

The movie deal. I'd completely forgotten about it. "I didn't know there's a deal."

"Well there might not be. Not if *Sass!* fires you. But don't worry. I'll handle everything. I'm sure this DiGrigio person is on your side. After all, you're their bestselling columnist."

Ha! Bestselling columnist or not, Lori DiGrigio will never be on my side, unless she's pushing me into an early grave.

I hang up and rapidly assess the situation. This is the worst ever. I don't even know what street I'm on, I'm so panicked. Whatever happens, I must not let Charlotte meet with Lori. That would be the end of everything. I'd kept my fingers crossed that silence from management meant that they'd backed off the investigation, but I was wrong. They were just waiting for more evidence.

Damn. I bite a nail (0 points) and mull over my options. There's only one. I must intercept the lunch meeting.

I call up Charlotte right away—on my cell phone, not Belinda's.

"Yes!" Charlotte always answers sounding ultra-impatient.

"This is Nola Devlin. I'm Belinda's editor at *Sass!*"

"Nola!" Charlotte exclaims. "Your ears must be burning. Belinda and I were just discussing what a fabulous editor you are and how lucky Belinda is to have you."

Yeah, right, paper pusher.

"I'm calling because Miss DiGrigio won't be able to make your lunch meeting."

"Oh?"

"Though I'll be taking her place."

Silence. Charlotte is not pleased. She is not accustomed to dealing with management as far down the totem pole as I.

"I'm afraid there's no other choice. Miss DiGrigio's awfully sorry but she"—I think of something that would assure Charlotte there was no disrespect—"she broke her leg."

"My! Is she OK?"

"She's fine. It was a thong injury, I'm afraid. Apparently her foot got caught in one of the straps and, well, you know how elastic those things are."

"Yes, yes of course. Well then. Lunch with you it is."

"Great. Shall we meet at one? How about at the Rainforest Café?"

"I've never heard of it," says Charlotte, who lives in the bubble that is called Manhattan. "Why don't you talk to my driver and give him directions. As long as this Rainforest Café is quiet and child-free, it should be fine. I'm afraid I can't stand children. My doctor says I'm allergic."

The Rainforest Café in the Menlo Park Mall offers a superb dining experience, along with recorded and real parrots squawking constantly and plastic volcanoes erupting every fifteen minutes between ear-splitting outbursts of rain-foresty lightning and thunder.

Children love it.

So do I.

"Has a woman arrived looking stricken and confused?" I ask the hostess, who is wearing a safari outfit, natch. "Oh, and she'll be in all black."

"Is she stick thin with big, big glasses?" Momsai, the hostess, holds up her index finger.

"I'm guessing."

"Right this way," she grabs a plastic menu. "I already got her a martini. I guess the macaws make her nervous or something."

198

Something, I think, following Momsai through the jungle of tables and palm trees and paper kid-menus with crayons, hunting, as we are, for the elusive New York agent, trapped outside of her concrete and power-laden natural habitat of Manhattan.

Charlotte stands out among the young mothers and shouting toddlers like a British soldier surrounded by spear-wielding Zulu warriors. Her hand is shaking as she carefully sips her martini, eyeing her surroundings in horror.

She is white, very white, though being in her fifties, maybe mid-sixties, not really old. Her bleached hair is pulled back severely from her forehead and clasped in place by a thick black hairband. It is the only color on her face besides the sloppy smear of bright pink on her lips. Her eyes are hidden behind the largest pair of black-framed glasses I've ever seen. It's a mystery how the sales clerk sold them to her. What could have been the pitch?

"Charlotte?" I say as fake lightning flashes over us.

Charlotte looks up and flinches at the sight of me. Or was it the thunder followed by the sound of torrential rain? "Yes?"

"I'm Nola. Nola Devlin. Belinda's editor."

Her mouth makes an *O,* but no sound comes out.

"Do you want something to drink too?" Momsai asks.

"Coffee," I say. "Skim milk on the side, please." (1 point.)

When Momsai leaves, I sit across from Charlotte,

whose eyes are grotesquely magnified by the coke-bottle lenses in front of them. "This is quite a place," she says. "Though not a *quiet* place."

"I chose it for a reason," I say. "I have something to tell you about Belinda."

"Oh?" She carefully puts down her martini glass.

"Yes." I smile confidently, take a deep breath, and let 'er rip. "You're looking at her."

It is the first time that I have confessed my secret identity and I can barely sit still, I'm so nervous.

Charlotte blinks her big magnified eyes. "I'm afraid I don't understand."

"I'm Belinda Apple," I try again, wishing she'd just get it so this ordeal would be over with. "I've always been Belinda Apple."

"But you're not British."

"That's true. But one doesn't *arf* to be *veddy* British, does one, to fake it?"

Charlotte cringes. "That's an awful impersonation. You sound like Maggie Smith."

"No, Maggie Smith sounds more Scottish: 'Gurrls. We willl not be trrraipsing about.' Believe me, I know. I've become an authority on faking British accents."

Charlotte takes a long sip of the martini. "So you *are* a fraud, exactly like that DiGrigio person claimed."

"Not exactly." I pinch the skin on my arm, a crude acupuncture technique to keep me from panicking. "I'm very real. I'm just not very British or, for that matter, very thin."

"I'm glad you said it. I didn't want to sound rude."

Momsai comes by and brings me coffee. As she's about to leave, Charlotte clutches her sleeve and asks—no, begs—for a second martini (3 points).

When Momsai's gone, I tell Charlotte the whole story, starting from the application Lori DiGrigio tossed to how I applied merely as a test and then took the job. Charlotte says nothing, though she does manage to drink down to her olives.

"If you want to stop representing me . . . ." I say.

"Don't be daft. This is the best thing that could have happened. I love this." She removes her cell phone, punches in her numbers, and winks at me. "B.J. Martin, please. This is Charlotte Dawson."

She bites an olive and waits while B.J. gets on. "B.J., I am sitting here with Belinda Apple. She's just informed me that she is leading a double life, that she is under investigation by *Sass!* magazine, and may be in jeopardy of running afoul with the IRS."

"What?" I say. It hadn't occurred to me that I might be in trouble with the IRS. I'd paid all my taxes, hadn't I?

Charlotte puts a finger in her ear to block out a screaming baby at the next table. "You either put a figure on the table now, or I'm going over to Board-walk Productions."

I can't help but be fascinated by Charlotte's wheeling and dealing.

"I'll give you five minutes," she says.

She clicks the phone shut and casually picks up the plastic menu. "This is awful," she says.

201

"Awful?" It sounded pretty good to me. It sounds like I'm about to get a movie deal.

"There's nothing to eat. I'm on a diet, of course."

The phone rings. Charlotte picks it up, says, "That's great," and hangs up.

"Well?" I say, so excited I could erupt like the volcano behind me.

"There's no choice but the chicken Caesar salad."

"No!" I screech. "What about the film deal?"

"Oh, that." Charlotte blinks her heavy lashes. "A tentative offer of a hundred-fifty-thousand-dollar signing and five hundred thousand if they make the movie of the week, with five percent royalties. It's not bad."

"Not bad? It's fantastic."

"There is a caveat, however. They want to make sure you are as exciting in person as I've made you to be. That's why they're planning to fly you to L.A. soon. If I were you, I'd brush up on that hideous British accent. I have no intention of telling them that you're really Nola Devlin from New Jersey."

Chapter Twenty-One

The three-foot-high pile of red-skinned potatoes on my parents' kitchen counter should be the first clue that Eileen's wedding preparations have sent my mother over the edge.

"Looks like your mother's cornered the spud

market," my father says, the morning's paper shoved under his arm as he strolls through the kitchen to pour himself another cup of coffee.

My father used to work for Johns Manville until the asbestos company was sued so often for scarring people's lungs that it declared bankruptcy, pulled up roots, and moved west and made paper products. This sent my father into early retirement and my mother to work full-time down at the muni clerk's office in Princeton. Part of his grand scheme, as he likes to say, to get the house to himself.

Dad was born to retire. He spends his uneventful days joyfully fishing, reading, and puttering around, contributing little to the world besides carbon dioxide. Every day he wears a flannel shirt and a gray pair of Dockers. It could be 102 degrees in the desert, and he'd be in a long-sleeve flannel shirt and Dockers. He is a man of few wants and needs.

"All this for a family Labor Day picnic?" I say, eyeing the two pots bubbling madly on the stove and the one waiting on the counter for its turn. "This'll make way too much potato salad. I'll be boiling and peeling for hours."

Dad sits down at the kitchen table with a groan. "Guess you haven't heard. It's not just the Labor Day family picnic anymore. It's Eileen's 'impromptu' engagement party. For fifty."

"What?" He must be mistaken. No one told me about an engagement party. I haven't even bought a gift and I have nothing to wear.

"Bubbles, that hairdressing friend of Eileen's, heard a rumor that Jim's mother was planning a big fancy shindig. Well, you know your mother. She couldn't stand to be beaten to the punch. Or rather, the punch bowl."

I can see Mom now, calling all our relatives, summoning them to our house for Labor Day. No way would she allow Jim's mother the first crack at an engagement party. The wedding is her domain.

"Eileen doesn't know. It's a surprise. Come to think of it, you're not supposed to know either. Whoops," he deadpans, "maybe I said too much."

If my mother is keeping the party a secret from me, then she must be feeling guilty about something. "What's going on now?"

"Everyone, meaning your mother, is worried that you're J-E-A-L-O-U-S."

There is an uncomfortable silence as the letters form into the word I have learned to despise. "You don't have to spell stuff anymore, Dad. I'm not a kid."

"Then you're the only one. These days I feel like I'm living in a kindergarten, what with all the pettiness going on. Your mother and your sister are on the phone at the crack of dawn and they don't get off until the eleven o'clock news. I'm going to live in my camper if this keeps up. And I'm taking the TV with me." He opens up the paper and buries his head.

"OK, I want to hear exactly why Mom and Eileen think I'm jealous."

Dad pretends to be fascinated by the article in front

of him, though peering over his shoulder I find it's nothing but an advertisement of a Labor Day sale—for lingerie.

"If you don't spill," I threaten, "I'll tell all the guys down at Frank's Chicken House that you spent Saturday morning checking out the prices on C-cups."

He lets out a resigned sigh. "Your mother thinks you're jealous because you left Eileen's birthday party early after Jim popped the question and then your sister stupidly chose that Jolinda—"

"Belinda."

"Yeah, her, to be maid of honor. I dunno what the big hullabaloo's about, but your mother is convinced you're on the verge of suicide. And that if you knew tomorrow's picnic was an engagement party for Eileen you wouldn't come—that is, if you hadn't thrown yourself off the Raritan Bridge."

This is so insulting that I don't know how to respond without sounding like one more whining Devlin girl. "That's such a lie. Does Mom actually take me for being that petty, that I wouldn't go to my own sister's engagement party because she's getting married before me?"

"That's what I told her. She told me to shut up and mind my own business. Said I couldn't know because I'm not a girl. So from now on, I'm staying out of it."

"That's so not true." I pound the cutting board, sending a stack of potatoes rolling to the floor.

"You mean I *am* a girl?" he asks, lifting his head from the paper.

Mom walks in with her arms filled with cut flowers from the garden and nearly trips over one of the potatoes on the floor.

"Jeez Louise," she exclaims, falling against the counter. "You guys have a potato fight, or what?" Then, seeing how Dad is studying the two-for-one bra ad and how I'm fussing and fuming, she says, "Oh, no, Pete. You told her."

He puts down the paper. "You can't expect an intelligent girl like Nola to walk in, see two hundred pounds of potatoes, and not guess something's up."

"Mom." I pitch a potato into the sink. "I am *not* jealous of Eileen."

"Is that what you told her, Pete?"

My father knows better than to answer.

Mom turns off the stove and spreads the flowers across what space is left on the counter, maniacally picking out weeds from the red bee balm and black-eyed daisies and blue bachelor buttons.

"I don't blame you for being jealous, Nola."

"I'm *not* jealous."

"OK, angry, call it. Especially after that married man bought you that car and wined and dined you and God knows what else and then never called you again."

This is my mother's new theory, that Mystery Chip—as our family has come to call him—is married. It's not a bad theory, actually. In fact, it's probably true. Truer than I would like to admit. But I wish she wouldn't bring him up in every conversation.

206

"I am over Mystery Chip, Mom. And nothing happened anyway. I'm not angry."

"Not about Mystery Chip, maybe, but certainly about Eileen. It's a disgrace, her picking a woman she doesn't know instead of her only sister to be her maid of honor, just because she's a celebrity. It's so upsetting, I've spoken to Father Mike about it."

"Not Father Mike!" Lord. Does she keep anything secret from that man?

"He had a lot of insight, Nola, not only into Eileen's motives but also what you're going through out there. You know, he's young. He's . . ."

"Good with the youth," Dad and I singsong together.

"Anyway"—Mom flicks a slug off a blade of grass—"he explained that there's a tremendous amount of pressure on a single woman these days. It's as though a girl's personality, her virtue, and spiritual qualities don't count one hoot if she's not putting out in bed. Sex, sex, sex—that's all men these days want."

"And you had to go to a celibate priest to find that out?"

There is a snicker from behind the Sports section.

Mom ignores us. "Society's not fair to you, honey. Here you are a good Catholic girl—unlike your sister, I might add—saving yourself for a man who will respect your commitment to God, and what happens? Some married, free-loving liberal from Californication—"

"Sorry to interrupt your sermon," Dad says, "but this is Nola you're talking about, right?"

Mom flips him the bird.

"OK. Just checking."

"Father Mike and I also talked about the"—Mom's standard throat-clearing here—"the weight issue."

In an instant I bristle. That's all it takes—the throat-clearing followed by a mention of "the weight issue"—for the old triggers to fire. Dad is dead silent as Mom stuffs the flowers into a vase and I stare at the floor.

Then she wipes off her hands, opens her purse, and pulls out a folded piece of paper, laying it on the counter and patting out the wrinkles. Seeing it, I know why my mother sought the help of a priest. Heck, seeing it I think I'll go light a few candles myself.

The paper is a torn-out advertisement from *Bride* magazine or its ilk, and it features a tall blond model in a deep Christmas-green satin gown that grips her perfectly slim form tighter than a kid's fist on Pixie Stix. As though that weren't bad enough, the dress is sleeveless—another designer conspiracy bent on humiliating women everywhere—and in a mermaid cut. Perhaps the most unflattering cut ever known to ass.

Even if by miracle of miracles I get down to a weight that would please my insurance adjuster, I would still look strangely distorted in a sheath like this, like a fat, green Morticia Addams. And one wonders if this was superskinny Eileen's plan all along.

"Eileen's bridesmaid dress," I say, picturing my upper arms wobbling for all to see.

208

"It's obscene. The Church won't allow bare shoulders. You'll have to wear shawls."

I say a silent prayer of gratitude to the Catholic church for sparing plus-size girls everywhere.

Mom bites her lip. "I can't talk her out of it. Eileen has her heart set on this design. Five hundred dollars each—too expensive for your cousins and I'm sure for you, too. Like I told her, you're only a low-level editor. You can't afford a five-hundred-dollar dress."

"Not *that* low-level, Mom." I fight the temptation to brag that, actually, I have $100,000 and change set away thanks to Belinda. That I *might* have a half-a-million-dollar movie deal in the works.

Mom is in her own world. "The wedding dress is just as indecent—so low cut. Seed pearls. Embroidery. All silk. Something a Donald Trump wife would wear. I'm not kidding. It costs six thousand dollars."

"Then Eileen should stop expecting her parents to be millionaires and pick a different dress," Dad suddenly declares. "I sure as hell'd like to own a six-thousand-dollar car, let alone a dress you wear for one day. She's spoiled is what she is, Betty, and it's your fault." He stomps off to their postage-stamp backyard, gets on his knees, and starts yanking carrots from the garden. Mom and I stand at the back door watching him.

"Things a bit tense around the homestead, huh?"

"Eileen's demanding too much. We always planned on paying for her wedding—yours, too, Nola—but not a wedding like this. Horse-drawn carriages. Caviar

209

and real champagne during hors d'oeuvres. Yesterday she asked if I could get the mayor to use his connections at the Princeton Country Club to let her hold the reception there. I can't even conceive of what *that* bill would be like."

Unreal. My family is not caviar-and-country-club material. The Manville Knights of Columbus is about as clubby as we get.

"It's as though she's suddenly out to impress, and I know who."

Here it comes. I've been waiting for this, the moment when Mom turns her wrath on Belinda.

"Between her giving Eileen the green light to marry Jim ahead of you and now her flying in from England to be maid of honor, you'd think Belinda Apple was the focus of attention and not the couple getting married. Like Father Mike said, only a woman of self-centered and egotistical makeup would behave this way. I wouldn't mind, frankly, if she disappeared off the face of the Earth. So help me God."

Chapter Twenty-Two

I have to do something, but what? I can't let my parents drain their retirement savings to pay for Eileen's wedding. They're already hard up, ironing used Christmas wrapping paper, rinsing out Glad bags and saving them for leftovers. The next thing I know, Mom's going to be making baskets out of laundry lint.

The only choice is for Belinda to call and cancel.

On the other hand, Eileen will not put up with a "Manville Deluxe" wedding. If she is relegated to a standard Saturday afternoon deal at Sacred Heart followed by a cocktail reception at The K of C and a honeymoon in the Poconos, we'll all pay in years of spiteful Thanksgivings and sniping Christmases. We'll never have a family gathering in peace again.

I know what my sister craves: a candlelit winter evening service, an ermine stole, and a horse-drawn carriage whisking her through a sparkling snowfall to a grand and glorious hall decorated with wreaths and mistletoe, where fires burn in huge fireplaces and everyone is in satin gowns of green and red.

This is why Eileen is so mad for Belinda, because Belinda offers the magical touch of celebrity. This is also why I'm loath to tell her that Belinda can't come and why I am parked outside Nancy's house on a lovely September evening, unable to punch in Eileen's phone number on Belinda's cell.

Nancy has invited Deb and me to her spectacular house for an end-of-summer party to mark how far we've come since we formed the Cinderella Pact in June. Nearly three months into it, and I've lost a total of twenty pounds. I've also toned my arms and even my abs substantially thanks to an excruciating Carmen Diva Tae-Bo DVD, though if I am ever fortunate enough to meet Ms. Diva on the street, I feel it is only fair to hurt her as she has hurt me. The way I see it, she owes me a new set of deltoids.

"What're you doing sitting in the car, Grandma?" A blond woman I've never met before in a black swimsuit and white coverup is on Nancy's stone doorstep, waving me in. It's not until I squint harder that I realize this is no strange woman—this is Deb.

"Oh . . . my . . . God." It is all I can say, getting out of the car and taking in her thinner legs, thinner waist and, especially, thinner face. I haven't seen her in three weeks, and wow! It's as if the fat's been sucked out of her. Granted, she won't be taking home the swimsuit medal from the Miss America Pageant this year, but compared to how she used to look, the new Deb is a completely different person.

"I can't believe you," I gush, noting her straightened hair and professionally tweezed brows. When was the last time Deb donned a swimsuit? Years. All those summers missed at the Shore, because she was disgusted with herself for having to swim in shorts and a T-shirt, claiming she didn't want to go into the water because of sharks. "You're almost . . . thin!"

Deb smooths down her cover-up. "Nancy said the same thing, but I don't see it. I look in the mirror and see the same old me."

"That's a crock and you know it." Then I hesitate before asking the next question. "What's Paul say?"

"I have no idea," she says, shrugging. "He hasn't said one word, except for last week when he made some crack about me getting awfully flat chested."

Somehow I maintain a smile so Deb won't know that what I'd really like to do at the moment is go over to her house and slap Paul to his senses.

"So maybe I should get a breast job. That might get his attention."

"Well, I think you look amazing and so does everyone else." I give her a tight, tight hug. "He probably is in awe and dumbstruck and doesn't know what to say."

"It's the funniest thing," she says, clinging to me. "We fell in love in high school when I was fat. We married when I was fat. We were happy when I was fat. I'm thinking maybe Paul likes me fat. It's a real bummer."

Or, I am tempted to suggest, maybe you liked him when *you* were fat. And now? Now you're not so sure.

"He'll come around." This has now become the Cinderella Pact mantra: Paul Will Come Around. We must say it to Deb at least once a day. "All right. Let's get this party started."

Nancy lives in an absolutely spectacular gray clapboard colonial she and Ron bought three years ago in Hopewell Township. Four bedrooms. Rumpus room. Designer kitchen with a commercial-grade stove and granite countertops. Plenty of space for the children she never could pencil into her schedule. It's puzzling why she keeps this monstrosity, now that she and Ron are supposedly split and children are fast becoming out of the question.

Nancy is on a lounge chair by the pool, completely covered up and wearing a big straw hat. "Well, well, well," she says, squinting in the sun. "You finally made it."

"Show her, Nancy," Deb exclaims, clapping. "Come on."

"Show me what?" Maybe it's a brand-new engagement ring from Ron, or some other symbol of their reunion. That would be the best surprise of all.

Nancy waves Deb away. "I feel silly."

"If you don't show her, I will." Deb reaches down to snatch Nancy's robe, but Nancy's too fast for her. Hopping out of her lounge chair, she turns her back to us and then, almost seductively, drops her robe to her feet.

I can only stare at the shocking display. Two pieces. This is unheard of in our group. But my eyes are not deceiving me. Yup. It's no mirage. Two pieces. "You daredevil, you!" I holler. "You really went for the whole enchilada."

"Now show the front," Deb says.

Shyly, Nancy spins around. All I see is cleavage, long legs, and not too much cellulite. The suit must have cost a fortune—and worth every penny. There is plenty of elastic in the hips of her modest, high-cut bikini bottom to rein in the fat, and whoever designed the top should be given an architectural award for creative support. She is not Cindy Crawford, but she would not send sunbathers screaming for the surf either.

"You win," I say.

Nancy winks. "We all win. And the best part is that the worst part is over. Now it gets fun."

I'm not so sure about that. According to my dieting

history, I'm due for another plateau right about now, which will mean I'll get frustrated and go back to my former careless eating ways. But seeing how the Cinderella Pact began with a lie—Belinda's lie—I once again heartily concur with false enthusiasm.

When I come back from changing in one of the house's five bathrooms, both women are sitting at the edge of the halcyon blue pool, dangling their feet in the water. The air is heady with the late-summer-afternoon perfume of freshly mowed grass, coconut oil, and chlorine. The season's last cicadas twang in the high green hedges that afford us privacy and shade.

Like Nancy's and Deb's, my swimsuit is built around the revered color black and reinforced with enough elastic to seriously interfere with proper lung function. However, unlike Nancy's, it's an old-lady suit with a little skirt to hide the tops of my thighs. In light of her stunning two piece, I feel like a grandmother.

"You look good too, Nola," Nancy says, shielding the hot sun with her hand. "How much have you lost?"

"I'm not getting on the scale. I figure when I get thinner, I'll be thinner." I can't bear to tell them the truth. I'm clearly last in the running here, what with Deb's bypass surgery and the professional trainer attention lavished on Nancy.

"Not stepping on the scale," Deb says. "I couldn't do that in a million years. I'm getting on the scale every hour."

"Tony"—that's Nancy's personal trainer—"keeps

215

telling me to pay no attention to the scale. And I hope he's right, because I've only lost seventeen pounds."

A bubble of happiness rises within me. Three pounds. I've lost three more pounds than Nancy, and yet she's stunning.

"Why are you smiling?" Nancy says. "Oh, hold on. You *have* been stepping on the scale, haven't you? And you've lost more than I have."

I blush. I can't stand it when Nancy catches me in a lie, which she almost always does. *Almost* always.

"Twenty," I say. "I didn't want to tell you, because you look so good I assumed you were closer to forty."

Nancy opens her eyes wide. "Forty. Those are Deb's kind of numbers. No. Not forty. Heck. I don't know how much I'll lose. As muscle replaces fat it gets denser, Tony says, which means the scale is no indicator of anything."

"Yes," I say, holding up a white wine spritzer. "Chuck the scale."

"Chuck the scale," Nancy toasts.

"I don't know," Deb says, frowning. "I'm beginning to like the scale."

We pelt her with ice cubes and push her into the pool to make her take back her scale-loving ways.

Nancy helps Deb out of the pool and hands her a towel. "Though there is one thing Tony said that made me think of you, Nola."

"Oh?"

"I was telling him about how we got started on the Cinderella Pact. Do you remember? There was that scene at the Willoughby, and then I had that article from Belinda I'd been carrying around."

A funny chill comes over me. Goosebumps rise on my arm.

"And Tony said that no way could you lose a ton of weight just by walking five miles a day and cutting two hundred fifty calories. He said your body would adjust to the exercise and you would have to decrease your calorie consumption accordingly and increase the exercise, just like Brian that waiter said."

"Uh-huh." I nod as if this makes sense. "Good for you, Deb."

Deb has just wrapped the towel around her. No big deal to civilians. Big deal to fat girls. Even so, she is not diverted by my compliment. "Do you think Belinda made it up about losing weight?"

"If she did," Nancy says, "then she should be fired."

I swallow, hard.

"That's what made me think of you, Nola. You should ask her outright."

"Absolutely. I completely agree. I'll call her Tuesday. You know what?" I am forced to resort to an old standby. "I'm starved."

"Now that you mention it," Nancy says, much to my relief, "me too."

Food. The final distraction.

The party fare is not our usual. Gone are the margaritas and nachos with sour cream, the chocolate-tipped strawberries and cookies. Nancy has carefully selected stuff Deb can eat in moderation. A lowfat yogurt dip. Grapes. Raw vegetables for us. Crystal Light for Deb, who says she chews every bite thirty times. I'm not sure how you chew a grape thirty times. I find my self watching her and counting.

We remind one another that it's not about the food anymore. It's the fellowship.

"So, what's up with Chip? You ever hear from him again?" Nancy asks, getting back on her lounge chair.

I've been dreading this question and try to answer as casually as possible. "Uh, no. I guess he went back to California to stay. Mom still thinks he's married."

Nancy raises an eyebrow.

Deb says, "I asked John if he knew a guy named Chip who fit the description you gave us and he could name six right off. John grew up in Princeton, went to Princeton Day in fact. He knows that whole snooty society down there, John does."

I nudge Nancy. "Who's John?"

"Paul's business partner." Nancy says. "He's taken quite an interest in Deb lately. He's been over at the house every day."

"It's perfectly platonic. All he's doing is teaching me yoga," Deb says defensively. "He calls me his support team."

"As opposed to Paul, who's trying to sabotage her," Nancy adds under her breath.

I look over to Deb, who isn't denying this. "How is Paul sabotaging you?"

"He's not, really."

"Bull," Nancy jumps in. "He's insisting Deb cook

218

four-course dinners even though the smell of meat makes her nauseous. And what was that incident the other day with the banana cream pie?"

Deb pulls her cover-up around her self-consciously. "He was only kidding around."

"He was not. He tried to make you eat a spoonful, didn't he? Even though he knew it could make you sick."

Even though he knew it is—was—Deb's favorite, I add silently.

Deb and Nancy regard each other like two hurt dogs. "Why are you doing this to me?" Deb says finally. "What do you have against Paul?"

"I don't have anything against Paul. What bothers me is how he's been treating you ever since you decided to do this weight-loss surgery. You need to preserve your dignity, Deb. Isn't that what you learned in pre-surgery counseling? That the first step toward rejecting the label of 'fat woman with no value' is learning to stand up for yourself. I'm trying to learn that lesson every day."

"Since when do you have to learn to stand up for yourself, Nancy?" I say. "I don't know anyone who stands up for herself more than you. You're in court every day fighting for scumbags most of us would rather ignore and lock in jail."

"I didn't say I haven't stood up for other people," she snaps back so fast I wish I'd kept my mouth shut. "What I said is that I haven't stood up for myself in the past. If I had, I wouldn't have gotten so huge."

"What does that mean?" Deb asks.

"I blame my job." Nancy studies her toes, which are painted bright red. I wonder if she has done them herself—a first for a woman who has struggled to touch her tootsies in years. "When I started out at Barlow, Cafferty and Kline, there was a senior partner, Ted Kline, who kept coming on to me. If I came to work wearing a tight sweater, for example, he'd come into my office, close the door, point right at my chest, and ask if it was too cold or was I just glad to see him."

"Did you smack him?" Deb asks.

"Forget that," I say. "Did you sue him?"

"Are you kidding? Back then I was so thrilled to be in the state's most powerful law firm, I didn't dare drop a complaint about my parking spot. By the way, he wasn't the only one, though he was the worst. It was as though no man there could view me as a lawyer first, woman second. To them I was tits, ass, and, oh yeah, Temple Law Review."

"Whew." Deb takes a swig from the water bottle that is permanently affixed to her side.

"I got so messed up that I convinced myself the harassment was my fault for being full-figured in a man's world. Here I was, taking on clients who were suing their employers for sexual harassment and I couldn't recognize it in my own backyard." Nancy shakes her head. "That's when I really started packing on the pounds. The weight was like insulation against sexual predators and, sure enough, once my figure disappeared, the personal comments stopped and the men

220

started taking me seriously."

We are silent, watching the faint breeze tickle up slight waves on the pool's surface. Nancy's story—the first I'd heard of this spin on her weight gain—goes far to explain what happened to the bubbly girl on Ron's arm back in college, the one who wanted to be a nurse and have a house full of kids. She got lost years ago under layers of fat and anger.

"Does Ron know about this?" I ask.

"We've been talking about it," she says, pushing a pool toy with her painted red toe. "Though between us girls, we haven't been talking much."

"Is that a good kind of not talking or a bad kind of not talking," I ask slyly.

"The good kind. The *verrry* good kind. The long, slow, over and over kind."

"Whoa!" Deb yells as we high-five each other.

This is a stunning twist in the Ron and Nancy saga. I make a mental note to bet Deb that he moves back in before Christmas. "How long has this been going on?"

"A few weeks. I don't know how it happened. He came over to fix the treadmill again and, well, I guess one screw led to another."

That must be some treadmill.

"At least one of us is getting some action," Deb says.

Nancy and I exchange looks. "Don't worry, Deb," Nancy says. "Paul will come around."

From my black beach bag my cell phone rings. I grab the phone and take it to Nancy's kitchen. Probably

Mom reminding me to pick up another bag of charcoal for her Labor Day/Eileen's Engagement party.

"I haven't forgot, Mom," I say.

"That's nice," says Charlotte Dawson. "Because I've just purchased at great cost a ticket on a Continental flight to L.A. You don't have much time, Nola. Your flight leaves at eight a.m. tomorrow."

Chapter Twenty-Three

To: belinda.apple@sassmag.com
From: David.A.Stanton@stantoninc.com
Re: Making arrangements to meet

Dear Ms. Apple:

It just so happens that I will be stopping off in London next week on my return trip from Paris to New York. I would very much like to meet with you and discuss a serious matter that has come to my attention. As I am in poor health, I do not have much time and my schedule is limited. However, I believe that this issue is of such importance that my secretary has been instructed to carve out a half hour for us to talk.

Would Tuesday at 1 p.m. at the Ritz work for you?

Please get back to me ASAP.

David Stanton

David A. Stanton, publisher and president
Sass! Fit! and *Fix Up!* Magazines
Stanton Media, Inc.
West 57th Street
New York, New York 10019

To: David.A.Stanton@stantoninc.com
From: belinda.apple@sassmag.com
Re: Making Arrangements to Meet

Dear Mr. Stanton:
What an unfortunate bit of luck that I will not able
to accept your lovely offer to meet with you this
week at the Ritz. As fate would have it, I will be in
Los Angeles staying at the O Hotel while you are
in London.
    Perhaps on your next trip across the pond?

Sincerely,
Belinda

To: belinda.apple@sassmag.com
From: David.A.Stanton@stantoninc.com
Re: Re: Making Arrangements to Meet

Dear Miss Apple:
Excellent!
    The manager of our California office of Stanton
Media, which is based in Beverly Hills and a mere
two blocks from the O Hotel, is looking forward to

a quick, private meeting at your convenience.

Thank you for your accommodation in this very serious matter.

Sincerely,
David A. Stanton

"Oh, shit."

"Is there a problem, Miss Devlin?" The stewardess is handing me a cup of fresh-squeezed orange juice, standard treatment in first class.

That's right. FIRST CLASS. All paid for by Sweet Dream Productions, which is so eager to finalize the movie deal about Belinda's life story that they're sparing no expense. They even sent a stretch limousine to my apartment this morning and a fully uniformed chauffeur rang Bitsy's bell, causing her Talbot's hairband to practically spring off her head. And then they arranged for me to cool my heels in Newark Airport's VIP lounge until my flight took off.

"No, no, I'm fine."

"You'll have to turn off your phone, I'm afraid. We've closed the doors." She smiles gently and draws the curtain that separates us from those riffraff in coach where a stewardess is barking orders to put up tray tables, raise seat backs, and face FAA imprisonment should they keep their cells on for one minute longer.

Ah, yes, the civility of first class.

I lean back and try to act as though I always fly in

this style, yawning every now and then, checking my Timex impatiently. Across from me businessmen read their Sunday *New York Times* and sip coffee. They're so used to sitting on $4,000 seats that not even the promise of freshly baked chocolate-chip cookies fazes them.

Actually, I'd hoped to catch sight of a movie star, seeing as how it's a first-class trip to L.A. There's a brown-haired woman in brown pants and a brown shirt curled up in the corner sleeping. Might be Sandra Bullock. And the man with white, white hair three rows in front of me I'm pretty sure is Steve Martin.

Nancy told me she used to fly first class years ago, when she was super heavy, that the smaller seats in coach were either too uncomfortable or required seat belt extenders. She's not the only one. I'd say that a good third of the men up here are flying prime because they, too, can't fit the normal seats.

Explaining to Nancy and Deb why I must impulsively rush off to California for three days took some imagination. I relied on Charlotte's advice to stick as close to the truth as possible—for a change. So I told them that I had a meeting with a Hollywood production company, though I couldn't say more because we're still in negotiations and I didn't want to blow the deal.

This is all true. From what Charlotte explained to me in a subsequent brief, chaotic phone call from the Hamptons where she is visiting one of her more famous authors over the holiday, Sweet Dream is putting me up in L.A. supposedly as a courtship maneuver. In reality, they're checking me out, to see if I could market a movie on my so-called fake life. If they are impressed during the twenty-minute meeting on Monday morning, there's a deal. If not, it's off.

"What they're looking for is a woman who can appear on the *Today* show, tell her story about fooling four million *Sass!* magazine readers into believing she's Belinda Apple, and yet be compassionate enough, endearing enough, so that people will want to see her story on the big screen," Charlotte said.

"This woman . . . you mean me, right?"

"Yes, Nola."

"Will I have to lose weight?"

"Well, television does add fifteen pounds."

I do the math. My hard work all summer essentially ruined by one measly camera.

After a microwaved lunch of first-class vegetable lasagna (6 to 9 points, depending, but as the other choice was baked halibut in a white sauce, I took the risk) and fruit salad (3 points, though I didn't eat the mushy pineapple) served on real white linen, I lower my first-class window shade and stretch out, pulling the soft blanket tightly under my chin, imagining how I will wow Sweet Dream Productions.

I catnap and fantasize about me sitting knee to knee with Mr. Bigshot of Sweet Dream in his spectacular L.A. digs. He is hanging on every word. He's calling up writers in town, he's waving in interns to hear my tale.

You pretended to be thin and British when all along

you were fat and rejected? I LOVE it, I LOVE it, I LOVE it.

And then Brad Pitt comes in, does a double-take upon seeing me, falls on one knee, and asks me where I've been all his life.

Don't laugh. It's Hollywood. Anything can happen.

There is a bump of turbulence that sends us downward for a couple hundred feet and causes me to nearly wet my pants. I am now fully awake for, like, the rest of my life. I don't think of uncurling my toes until the seat belt sign goes off and the woman in brown heads to the bathroom. She is not Sandra Bullock after all. Just another California girl with a pair of inconceivably bony hips to remind me that I am a fool for ever daring to hope.

Eileen's right. I'll be a spinster forever.

Which is when, with a shot of panic worse than the turbulence, I suddenly remember my sister's engagement party that everyone predicted I'd miss because I'm a hulking jealous thing. They have no idea that I'm 36,000 feet in the air on my way to L.A. to meet slick movie producers. They are livid that I am not in my parents' backyard writing down what gifts my sister's receiving and from whom, even though I'm not her maid of honor.

Now I *will* have to become a nun. Immediately. A cloistered nun, because that will be the only way to get back in my family's good graces again.

A man in a black suit in baggage claim at LAX is

holding out a sign that says APPLE. I pass it twice before realizing he is not begging for food, that he is waiting to take me in his Lincoln Town Car to the O. Apparently the O is so chic it can't be bothered with the H, T, E, and L, that other, lesser accommodations, seem to require.

As soon as I climb into the car, I pull out my cell and dial home. Mom answers, sounding tired—and slightly put out.

"Oh, Nola. I'm so disappointed. You said you'd come." There is the sound of running water in the background and the clatter of dishes. That's right. It's three hours later there and the party must be over.

"I really meant to come. I have a gift and everything. It's just that I got called away on business."

"You didn't say anything about that yesterday."

"It's, uh, very last-minute."

"It's Labor Day weekend. Everything's closed tomorrow. Who has business meetings on a bank holiday?"

"People in L.A."

"Where?"

"Los Angeles." It's hard to keep my excitement in check. "I took a flight from Newark late this morning and I just landed. I'm here, Mom, really, really here. People are Rollerblading. It's crowded as all get-out, and I'm in a traffic jam. I can see the Hollywood sign, even."

"That imagination of yours. Even as a little girl you took it too far, though then it was sweet because you were a princess in the land of make believe, riding a unicorn. Now you're in Los Angeles stuck in traffic. Really, Nola, perhaps it's time for you to get some professional help."

I search for some way to prove to her that I'm really on the West Coast and start by declaring landmarks as we crawl into the city. The 405. The Hollywood Hills. Finally I say, "If you don't believe me, call the O in Beverly Hills."

"What do you mean 'call the O'?"

"It's a swanky hotel that goes by one letter, like, um, Prince."

"Prince? What prince?"

My driver's shoulders are heaving in laughter. "Just call, Mom. Then you'll see." I give her the number and hang up.

Two minutes later my cell phone rings. Mom again. "Your father and I agree you should talk to Father Mike. At the very least."

"Didn't you call the O?"

"I did, and they've never heard of you, Nola."

Of course they haven't heard of me because my reservation is under Belinda Apple. Dammit. There's nothing I can do now.

"Really. Jealousy is a deadly vice that destroys the soul, Nola."

"I am *not* jealous of Eileen."

"Just know that your father and I still love you, even if we don't love what you do. Cherish the sinner, condemn the sin, that's our philosophy."

229

I hang up, resigned to the fact that no matter what I do, I am in a hole out of which no human can dig.

Beverly Hills looks exactly like it does in the movies, only somehow smaller. The homes are mini-mansions surrounded by lush ferns, red bougainvillea, and spiky palms. Rodeo Drive is pristine and white and I worry that even window shopping as we drive by will ring up a charge on my Visa bill.

A group of women in white capri pants and sleeveless tops stroll past us down Santa Monica Boulevard, their arms laden with yellow and white shopping bags. Their hair is blond without being brassy. Their tans are tan without appearing burnt or sprayed on. They are all honey and grace and put my Malibu Barbie to shame.

I have definite doubts that we are the same species, me and them.

"You are from where?" asks my driver, Fareeq, who hails from Iran, but don't worry—he assures me several times—he's not a terrorist.

"New Jersey."

"Ahh." He nods knowingly. "Springsteen."

"Yes," I say. "He and I hang out often. Old buddies, the Boss and me."

"Really?" Fareeq raises his eyebrows in the rearview.

"No. It's a joke."

For which I will pay dearly, as Mr. Fareeq, who apparently *has* hung out with Springsteen, tells me in great detail what Bruce Springsteen is like. ("He's real people, you know? Like you and me.")

Meanwhile, I'm being eaten away by this question: Do I tip him? I try, but he acts insulted. He leaves my bags by the receptionist, who appear piqued that I have inconvenienced them by arriving at their counter. Clearly I am not L.A. Grade-A.

They do not look like any hotel receptionists I've ever seen. There are no gold vests or bow ties. Instead, they wear black T-shirts, gray suit coats, and headsets (headsets?). Then I get it. These are *professional* receptionists. Oh, and aspiring actors.

"I have two faxes," says 'Enri, who has lost his *H* much like his hotel. "They came in for you about an hour ago."

I take the faxes, along with my unidentifiable room card and my luggage, across the Art Deco lobby to ride the elevator to floor 15 where my room is. I ignore my mother's oft repeated warning never to stay in a hotel room higher than the seventh floor because fire department ladders can only reach the seventh floor. I decide it is time to live life dangerously—eight floors above the safety zone.

My room is huge and decorated in shades of cream and brown with touches of green. I suspect feng shui. The king-size bed is on a dais and there are all sorts of interesting and expensive organic products made out of green tea in the bathroom. Flinging back the curtains, I find a sliding-glass door to a small patio looking out over L.A., where a faint line of brownish haze hangs over the city like an umbrella of smog.

It's a shame. Just think of what this part of the world with its white, expansive beaches and lush growth looked like when only Native Americans walked it, their eyes on the stars in the sky instead of those in concrete.

It is Sunday at five, though it feels more like eight by my Eastern Daylight Saving time, and after all the excitement that resulted in a very restless sleep last night, I'm "coming down." I can't remember when I've felt so utterly exhausted.

Collapsing on the bed, I sink into the mattress, kick off my shoes, and quickly scan the faxed memo.

To: Belinda Apple
From: David Stanton, Stanton Media Inc.
Re: Meeting

Dear Ms. Apple:
Welcome to LA! Hope your stay here is going well and that you'll be able to see some of the sights.

My secretary, Charlaine, has set up a preliminary meeting at the O for four p.m. If that doesn't work for you, please call my office and she will rearrange. As I think you know by now, the matter we have to discuss is very serious as well as very personal. It can't be put off.

Looking forward to meeting you,
Dave

This memo makes absolutely no sense and the words are blurry. I must be more tired than I thought. David Stanton? Here in Los Angeles? What would he be doing here? He's supposed to be in London, scooting around the Ritz in his wheelchair. And how could he meet me tomorrow afternoon when . . . Oh, I'm too beat to analyze it.

I'll think about it later. Right after I take this quick toes-up.

Chapter Twenty-Four

"She's the most absurd person I've ever met. ASAP, PPI. Puhleeze."

Marge Tuttweiller, Charlotte's California film agent, is monstrously tall in a beige pantsuit, her black hair yanked back tightly and twisted into a severe bun. When I enter the lobby of the O, I find she is standing with her hands clasped behind her back, talking loudly to no one.

"Really? She went downtown on Kraunbaum. Disssgusting."

I check behind me. Is Marge speaking to someone over my shoulder? No. OK . . . so it's true what they say about everyone in California being a bit flaky. Riding in the elevator I was serenaded by a guy with a huge afro reciting line for line the sales pitch from *Glengarry Glen Ross*.

Before that I ran into a would-be starlet named

Gloria in tears, crawling past my door on her hands and knees. I guessed it was some drug-related hysteria until she explained losing her earring and now she risked being late for the audition for a spinoff of a *Friends* spinoff that would single-handedly save her career, or rather, jump-start it. Luckily, I found the pearl-and-diamond number by her room door. Gloria said she must have lost it when the man she brought back from the club last night "bit it off."

Right.

"Belinda Apple?" Marge shouts, pointing at me. "*Love* the dress."

Does she really love the dress? Or is that a kind of L.A. code, untranslatable by dumpy East Coasters?

Perhaps this flowing green-and-blue Indian silk number I'm wearing was a bad choice, not sleek enough for a meeting with L.A. film producers. I bought it last year in a boutique in the Village, partially because the tag said it fell into the "normal size" range and I was so thrilled I didn't even read the price tag (huge) before surrendering my credit cards. It was tight then and is delightfully looser now. Almost hangs off my body.

"Ta, ta. You bet." Marge reaches her hand into her pocket and says, "We better hurry. We're late."

Only when she turns and I see the small earpiece do I understand that Marge has been talking on her hands-free. She is not, in fact, another California nut.

"I don't know how much Charlotte filled you in,"

Marge says, taking her Jaguar on a suicidal left turn onto Sunset Boulevard.

"Not much. It was a two-minute phone call." I involuntarily grip the dashboard as she drifts seemingly sideways through traffic.

"Figures. Charlotte doesn't know boo about the film industry. Listen, you just let me do most of the talking. When they ask for your opinion, try to agree with whatever they say. Whatever you say is meaningless to their ears anyway. Afterward you can tell me what you want or what you didn't like at the meeting and I'll go to the mat for you. OK, Belinda?"

"Nola. There's no such person as Belinda."

Marge frowns and yanks the wheel to the right. "Well, in Sweet Dream's minds you are Belinda so let's pretend, just for today. This is L.A., after all, the land of make believe."

The place I've been looking for since childhood—at last.

Sweet Dream's offices are on the fifth floor of a deserted office building in West L.A. Marge explains that everyone is out for the Labor Day holiday and that Bill Benjamin, the producer I'll be meeting, and the "writer attached," Charles, cut their long weekend short to meet with me because they're heading to Vancouver for a month.

Marge tells me they're shooting a movie for Lifetime called *Intimate Stranger*, about a harried housewife who runs away with a man she just met at the checkout counter of Wal-Mart, though she returns when her husband tracks her down to tell her their baby is in Intensive Care after falling into a vat of Mr. Clean while chasing a pretty yellow butterfly.

I am beginning to feel uneasy. Something about producers with two first names. And then there's the *Intimate Stranger* thing. Wal-Mart. Baby at the bottom of a vat of Mr. Clean. Pretty yellow butterfly. How, exactly, will they be treating the story of an overweight editor who poses as an erudite British ethics columnist?

Bill Benjamin, aka Mr. Bigshot himself, greets us at Sweet Dream's glass double doors. He is an older man, balding with gray hair, yet dressed like a twentysomething in designer jeans, expensive Italian loafers, and a T-shirt that evokes the color of doggy doo. I've seen a lot of doggy doo colors here in L.A. Perhaps doggy doo is all the rage. I will have to go back and spread the word in Princeton.

"Belinda?" He extends his hand and makes superb eye contact.

"Actually . . ."

"That's right." Marge pushes me inside his office, which is done up in various colors of beige, accented by bright orange pillows on his couch, cobalt-blue glass bottles on his bar, and a green fern by his window.

I am directed to a flimsy-looking folding chair, the kind I usually try to avoid after writing the Belinda column that started the Cinderella Pact. As I've said before, lies can turn into reality, if you believe them hard enough.

"*Love* the dress!" he exclaims.

OK . . . what is this dress business about?

Charles the writer, he informs us, is running late. He's catching some waves—the knucklehead surfing addict—and he's on his way. He called from his cell minutes ago.

"So, Belinda," Mr. Bigshot asks, "how was the flight? Is the hotel OK?"

"Great," I say, the chair creaking as I shift weight. "And thank you for putting me up. It was so nice of you to go through all that expense—"

"No problem."

OK, so that's what you'd expect Mr. Bigshot to say. But Mr. Bigshot didn't say "no problem." It was Marge who, having not spoken for .23 seconds, is chomping at the bit to get us started.

"Belinda's story is unique and fantastic. And I think you know me well enough by now, Bill, to know that I am no-bull."

"Absolutely." Mr. Bigshot folds his arms and crosses his legs, which as a professional liar, I can assure you is body language for, *I loathe and distrust you, Marge.*

"So let's not waste your time or my time. Let's grab some of our holiday and just finish this deal."

"Sure, sure." Mr. Bigshot puts a finger to his lip. "Just one thing, Marge. I'm a bit concerned about the whole English angle. You know how we are about foreigners these days. To have a British advice columnist . . . it's not American enough."

American enough? What's he talking about? I stare at Marge mutely, as I've been instructed. But instead of Marge defending me, she says, "I couldn't agree more. Same thing crossed my mind. Minor point."

"Minor point." Mr. Bigshot agrees. "So let's say we make her American. Midwestern or . . . I know, Southern. You know, something like Belinda Apple grew up poor in Mississippi, the daughter of a white, uh, merchant's daughter and black field hand."

Black field hand! I blink several times trying to Morse Code to Marge that This . . . Is . . . Baloney.

"I love it!" Marge exclaims. "And it satisfies the networks' need to air more movies about people of color."

"Don't think I didn't take that into consideration."

They cannot be for real. I try to keep in mind what Marge said, that this can all be changed later, and just smile and nod.

"And then there's the whole tabloid magazine thing. I'm not sure that's going to grab enough people. I'm thinking more visual . . . like Belinda becomes a television personality."

But . . . but that makes no sense. How could Belinda be on TV when she's supposed to be a secret identity? They're going to ruin everything.

Desperate, I casually slide my foot over to Marge's and tap her toe.

Marge casually moves her leopard-print Manolos

(I'm pretty sure they're Manolos), blatantly ignoring me. "And then, her father sees her on TV."

"This would be Devlin the brute."

The brute? My father? My father hesitates before swatting a fly.

"Pete, I think." Marge turns to me with a don't-say-too-much-look. "That's his name. Right, Belinda?"

"Yes, but—"

"And Pete Devlin beat her as a child for years."

Hold on! Now this has gone too far. Marge is getting confused with Belinda's fictitious father from the *New York Intelligentsia* article.

"Or," Mr. Bigshot booms, "how about sexual abuse? That's always good."

"Unless it's been overdone." Marge frowns. "Do you think child sexual abuse has been overdone?"

"Never. It can never be overdone. There's always room for more abuse on cable."

"Alrighty then. Abuse it is. Mr. Devlin abused his daughter for years."

"Wait!" I jump to my feet, sending the chair tumbling over with a crash.

"Belinda," Marge chastises me sternly, "remember what I said about saving your comments for later. We can work out the details afterward, right Bill?"

"Just brainstorming, brainstorming," says Mr. Bigshot.

Marge winks to let me know she's on top of it, that we're in cahoots. Hesitantly, I pick up the chair and sit down again. Carefully.

239

"Now, about her sister, Eileen," Marge says.

"The crack addict/prostitute?"

That's it. "Stop!" I shout. "Stop it. I cannot hear you talking about my family this way. My father would never do such a thing to me and my sister, sure she has her faults, but a crack addict/prostitute she is not."

"Belinda," Marge hisses.

"And it's Nola. Nola Devlin. There is no such person as Belinda Apple. Never is, never was. That's the whole point of the story."

"What's this?" Mr. Bigshot looks at Marge, confused.

"Don't look at *her*. She doesn't know," I say. The anger is getting the better of me, but I can't help it. I wish Charlotte were here. At least she knows me. Er, kind of.

Suddenly, I hear Nancy's voice in my head, urging me to stand up for myself, how if she'd learned that lesson long ago, she wouldn't have become fat and miserable.

"I'll tell you what's what," I say.

For five minutes I tell Mr. Bigshot the truth. I made up my identity because I was fat and they wouldn't give me the column. I really live in New Jersey. My family is very stable. My mother goes to church every Sunday and every Wednesday night for forum. She bakes cookies for taxpayers. We all believe in God. I love my sister even though she picked out Morticia Addams bridesmaids dresses and has a boyfriend who requires kibble. Potato salad is our family signature dish.

With each new fact, Mr. Bigshot's face falls a little more until by the end he is studying his watch.

"Listen, I've got a conference call with Vancouver in a minute. I'm sorry that we'll have to cut this meeting short. Thanks so much for coming in," he says, shaking my hand. "And I'm sure either I or Marge will be getting back to you, Belinda."

"Nola," I say weakly.

He shoots me his finger. "Right."

"It's over," I ask, "isn't it? I've screwed everything up."

"No, no," he coos. "It's all good."

Chapter Twenty-Five

There is much to be said for the calming effects of Southern California sunshine, a light Southern California breeze, and a rooftop pool. Several hours go by as I lie facedown on the chaise longue underneath a pink-and-white umbrella, napping and thinking, a hotel towel draped over my ass. There is just no way you can wear a swimsuit with a skirt in L.A. if you are under the age of, like, ninety.

What gets me about my meeting at Sweet Dream was how it all ended in a snap. Once I stood up for myself and told the real story, Mr. Bigshot lost all interest. There wasn't even a follow-up question. And then, to make matters worse, in the car Marge Tuttweiller said nothing except, "You might have held off. I would have handled everything. I know you're naive, but I would have expected that even you could have understood how negotiations work."

Perhaps Nancy was wrong. Maybe standing up for yourself should only be done in limited circumstances, like when they're about to kick you off an overcrowded plane even though you bought your ticket six months before. Or when a pushy mother butts ahead of you in the deli line.

"I'll call you," Marge said. "Though I wouldn't hold my breath."

This means that every two minutes I open one eye and check the porter, who is standing by the towels, staring into space. I haven't eaten a thing all day. A first since I had the Great Stomach Flu of 1999, and what's even weirder is that I'm not even hungry.

"Having a nice sunbath?"

I turn my head away from the porter. In front of me are two long, long legs rising to a teeny white bikini bottom and a bellybutton ring in a slim waist rising to a bust that's so huge it blocks off the sun like a solar eclipse.

Gloria of the bit-off earring.

"I'm recovering from my day," I tell her.

"Yeah. Me too." She sits across from me on the other chaise. I want to advise her to put on a shirt, as her plastic breasts are conspiring to break out of their bikini-top prison. "I didn't get the part."

"I'm sorry. Are you sure?"

"Yup. After all these years I think I know a pass.

242

They didn't have to say it but I'm"—she glances at me wearily—"too fat."

"You?" I wish Nancy and Deb had been here to hear that gem. "You're tiny."

"Not tiny enough. Not L.A. tiny. This morning I woke up and looked at myself in the mirror, saw my pouch of a tummy, and said, 'Gloria. You are going to have to do something. You are out of control.'"

I wrap more of the towel around me and sit up fully, trying not to surreptitiously inspect whether she does or does not have a pouch of a tummy. "You can't be serious. How much do you weigh?"

"Around one-nineteen. Maybe even one-twenty. That's like one-thirty, one-thirty-five with the camera, you know."

Cinderella numbers. Even the 130. Of course if she drained the saline out of her breasts that'd be three pounds right there, but what woman wants that kind of advice after spending all that money on implants?

Gloria sighs and tells me her tale of woe. "It's a rough business. Do you know that the producer on the last show I was in sent a certified letter—a certified letter!—to my agent warning me that I was gaining weight and if I didn't drop ten pounds, I'd be cut? And here I thought I was really knocking off my character. You should have read my fan mail. Not one letter said, 'Hey, Gloria, you're getting chubby.'"

I think about what I would do if I were in her shoes. "I couldn't live in a world like that. I mean, weight can be an issue where I work too, but not to that degree."

"I'd give anything to be like . . . you."

"You mean fat?"

Gloria lies back and adjusts her sunglasses. "I mean more like being myself instead of having to fit this certain mold of maximum and minimum measurements. You don't have to worry about every bump of cellulite or if the fried calamari you ate the week before is going to get you canned."

Fried calamari, I think, 11 points. "I never thought of it that way."

"You should. You're lucky. I mean it."

"Gloria"—I lean toward her, bent as I am on a new mission to set her straight—"You're the one who's lucky. I know you work hard to keep your weight down, and that's admirable. On the flip side, I don't have men biting off my earring in the hallway of the O."

She raises her glasses and squints. "You could if you wanted to, Nola."

"No, I couldn't. Look at me. I'm one hundred and"—I check myself—"I'm several more pounds than you are. What man wants me?"

"Think about what man wants *me*. A guy who's just interested in big tits and a firm butt and long legs and nothing more. The guy who bit off my earring, by the way, got my name wrong twice. Kept calling me Gigi."

She doesn't understand. No woman who's been thin all her life can understand. If you tell them you need to lose weight, they say in a perky little voice, "Well, lose it then!"

Gloria touches my dimpled knee. "This is going to sound very L.A., Nola, but sometimes the fat that does us the most harm is the fat between our ears."

"Miss Apple?" It's the porter in his white jacket. No phone. "The front desk called. There's someone in the lobby to see you. They say they have a four p.m. appointment."

Marge? I didn't have an appointment with Marge, did I? "Did they give a name?"

"It was a Mr. Stanton. A Mr. David Stanton of Stanton Media."

That's when I remembered the fax.

Quickly saying good-bye to Gloria, I rush to my hotel room to shower off the sunblock and change out of my old-lady swimsuit, my brain buzzing. The fax. The fax. There was something on the fax that 'Enri of the errant H handed me when I checked in about a meeting being arranged with Stanton Media.

Except . . .

David Stanton couldn't be meeting me. He's in London. He wanted me to meet him at the Ritz there today. What is he, an eighty-eight-year-old Superman? Able to leap continents in a single bound? There must be more to that Ensure stuff than I knew.

I get out of the shower and, on a whim, approach the hotel scale. They don't have scales in hotels on the East Coast. In California, though, they're every-where—in the hotel gym, by the pool . . . It must be a state law, like not smoking.

I cannot believe my eyes. Is this for real? Back at

home the scale wouldn't budge from that one number. It gives me hope that I'll reach my goal by Christmas. I *love* the Cinderella Pact.

Now, what have I been doing right? I haven't had a bowl of Special K since I've set foot in this state. Then again, I really haven't had much to eat of anything. I fell asleep last night after getting off the plane, made a cup of tea in my hotel room . . .

Brrring. Shoot. I almost forgot. David Stanton. I snatch up the phone without waiting to hear who it is. "I'll be right there."

"Where?" It's the unmistakable nasal twang of Marge Tuttweiller, agent to the stars.

My heart stops. "Marge?"

"You asked me to call you, right?"

She doesn't have to say any more. If it were good news she'd jump right in with how much they loved the proposal, how much money they were paying me. "It's bad, isn't it?"

"That depends." She pauses dramatically. "Sweet Dream does want to pass, for now . . ."

"I knew it." My shoulders slump as I throw myself on the bed.

"I said *for now*. They may reexamine the option later."

"What does that mean?" Is this more California agent double-talk or sincere encouragement?

"They love your story, Nola. I have to admit, I was wrong."

"Wrong?"

"When you gave that speech about your real life in New Jersey and being too fat. Bill Benjamin ate it up."

"I thought he hated it. He suddenly had a conference call."

"He really did have a conference call. No, he was impressed. He's so used to people telling him what he wants to hear that it's startling when someone tells him the truth. To use his words, he was very impressed."

"So what's the problem?"

"Two things." Marge clears her throat, just like my mother. "The first and most important is your, um, visual projection."

"Pardon?"

"Your presence as a larger woman, Nola. I'm sorry. I think it's because Bill had an image of you as Belinda Apple. You know, thin and British and trendy."

Oh, God, is this humiliating. "And I am anything but."

"It's just that you didn't match his mental image. You know how that is. For example, let's say you eagerly go on vacation, like, to a Caribbean resort, anticipating palm trees and white beaches with no one on them and instead you find it's crowded with families and trash. It's somewhat disappointing."

Thanks, Marge. Thanks for calling me trash.

"I was talking to Charlotte and we had this brilliant brainstorm. Why don't you go ahead and write the script and we'll bring it back to Bill."

"Script? Written by whom? I thought the deal was dead."

"It was Bill's suggestion, actually. It'll save him money and it'll be in your own voice. I think it's a terrific concept."

I've never written a movie script before. The only person I know who has is Nigel Barnes.

"Of course, you'll start off with a treatment. Though a treatment *and* a script would be ideal." It's as though Marge is having a one-way conversation with herself and I'm just here to keep her company.

Line two is blinking. David Stanton. I feel awful that I've kept him waiting so long. "Gotta go, Marge. Thanks for everything."

It is now four thirty and I have no clue as to how long I've let Mr. Stanton wait. Nor do I know what I'll say to him in my utter embarrassment. It'll come to me, I think. Inspiration from on high. Yes, that's it. God will whisper in my ear.

OK. I check myself out in the elevator mirror and approve. My hair is done up. My lips are a nice light pink, and I am thinner than I was yesterday. Yes!

I trip over the sill as I run out of the elevator into the lobby, a million apologies on my lips.

But there is no eighty-eight-year-old man waiting for me anywhere. Clearly he got fed up and left.

'Enri is at check-in scrolling through his Black-Berry. Even in a suit coat his muscles bulge. "Uhhh. A Mr. Stanton was to see me," I say. "I'm so sorry I'm late. I got a phone call. He didn't leave, did he?"

'Enri doesn't even look up. He just points over my shoulder. "That's him right over there."

I spin around and face a tall man who has his back to me, his hands in his suit pockets, studying an aerial map of Los Angeles. This is not what I expected at all. "Mr. Stanton?"

He turns and for a moment looks confused. "Don't tell me you're here with Belinda."

But there's no way I can answer because Mr. Stanton isn't Mr. Stanton.

He's Chip.

Chapter Twenty-Six

Of course, what I do is lie.

"Actually, I'm trying to sell a screenplay." I blush easily, red running all over my body faster than fire because I am sooo mortified. Absolutely mortified. Computer Chip is actually David Stanton. He must be the publisher's son, which would explain everything, the chip off the old block, the California/Princeton connection. The fact that Old Mr. Stanton maintained a "country home" in Princeton . . .

"A screenplay? That's awesome." He strolls over and looks down at me with admiration. It's so weird to see him out of context or, rather, in his natural environment. He's blonder. Taller. Better than my imagination.

"Gosh, it's good to see you. You look awesome,"

he's saying. "I'm sorry we never got together again. I had to rush out of town, back to L.A. right away. How's the car?"

I still can't believe I'm talking to the man formerly known as Chip. Here. In L.A. His chest a mere five inches from my own. "The car's great," I manage. "It was so incredible of you to arrange all that. I'll never forget it."

He shrugs. "It was a gas." Then, as if remembering why he's here, he asks, "Listen, you haven't seen Belinda Apple around, have you? We were supposed to meet an hour ago. I think she stood me up."

"Funny thing about that," I improvise. "Uh, Belinda had to leave suddenly to go back to home."

"Really?" He wrinkles his misshapen nose.

"Yes. I ran into her on the street and she mentioned that she had this hotel room all paid for and would I like to stay in it. You see, I was staying at the uh . . ." Wait. I don't know any hotels in Los Angeles. "The Holiday Inn."

"The Holiday Inn on Sunset or Brentwood?"

"Uh, Brentwood, I think it was."

Chip nods. "Uh-huh. Go on."

"And it's not nearly as nice as the O."

"Not nearly."

"Sooo, I said sure. Apparently, Belinda had to fly back to"—can't say London because Old Stanton's there—"Ireland. Family emergency. You know, one of those Irish deathbed scenes."

"Mother?"

"No, she's dead." Ha! Didn't fall for that trap, did I? "This time it's her father."

"Oh, that's too bad."

"But Belinda did remind me to tell you to pass on her regrets. She was really looking forward to meeting you."

"Was she? Interesting." Wheels are clicking in his head. I catch sight of 'Enri, who is shaking his head in definite disapproval.

"Well, that's too bad. I was really looking forward to meeting her." Chip doesn't take his eyes off me. There's a funny twist to his lips, a kind of kissable twist that I can't even contemplate since Chip is a married man, or so my mother claims. If only I could check out his hand for a wedding ring but, darnit, it's in his pocket.

"I've got a crazy idea," he says brightly. "If you're not doing anything this evening, how about I show you L.A.? You know, I even made reservations at Gladstone's."

"Me?" I blink innocently.

"I know, I know. It's touristy, but it's got a very fun atmosphere and they do have great seafood and it's a beautiful evening. There's a deck so you can watch the sun set. We can take a walk up the beach in Malibu, just you and me."

Let me get this straight. Dinner with Chip at Gladstone's overlooking the Pacific Ocean. A beach in Malibu to walk on. Stars of all kinds. I am feeling lightheaded.

This is my chance to make a stellar impression, and I'm not going to blow it. I will be witty and gracious and flirtatious and so delightful that Chip will fall madly in love with me and end up begging to spend the night.

I'm sure of it.

There are a million questions I want to ask Chip, starting with his real name and ending with a delicate inquiry into his relationship status. But for a while he does all the talking as we pull onto Sunset Boulevard in his gorgeous olive green BMW Z4 Roadster. It is a far cry from the Toyota truck, and even though this may be very shallow of me to say, he looks far sexier in this deal.

I know as a liberated woman I'm not supposed be swayed by men with fast foreign cars, but have you ever ridden in a BMW Z4 Roadster? Better yet, have you ever ridden down the Pacific Coast Highway on a warm and sultry September evening in a BMW Z4 Roadster?

I didn't think so. Judge not lest ye be judged, missy.

Chip gives me a quick tour of the area, zipping me through the canyons and magnificent neighborhoods of Beverly Hills. The breeze is blowing back my hair, and Chip's hand frequently brushes my knee as he shifts. I am feeling sexy and daring. This is what it's like to fall in love. I must tread cautiously.

At one moment, while we are stopped outside some pink mansion that used to be owned by Fred Astaire, a helpful Beverly Hills cop strolls up and demands ever so politely to see Chip's license.

"Oh," he says, giving the license a once-over, "it's you, Mr. Stanton. I should have recognized the plate." Then he tips his hat and wishes him a lovely evening.

Chip tells him no problem. He even asks the cop how his wife is doing.

"I guess you live around here," I say, trying not to pry. (Who am I kidding? Of course I'm trying to pry. All I wish is that I'd shot him up with sodium pentothal before our drive.)

"My mother lives around the corner. She moved there thirty years ago, after the divorce." Chip starts up the Z4 again and heads back to the main strip. "I spent every summer with my dad in Princeton—that is, when I wasn't at camp. And during the school year I lived in Beverly Hills."

"Sounds rough."

"I suppose I could drop a fortune on a psychiatrist," he says, taking me seriously. "But I'm not that kind of person."

"Uh, I was being sarcastic."

He grins. "Should have known. See, if you'd been from L.A., we would have gone off on psychiatrists for half an hour."

"I'm from Manville, New Jersey. We don't have psychiatrists. Bowling alleys. Strip joints. Churches. Those are our therapies."

"Now that's interesting. Strip joints and churches. How does that work?"

"Actually, very well. You stay out at the strip joints until they close at two. Then you go to the private clubs—you know, the Polish Club, for example—until dawn and then, stumbling on your way home you stop off at Holy Ghost for sunrise Mass and ask for forgiveness of all your sins." I am sounding like a blue-collar hick, aren't I? Oh well. "Manville is your place for one-stop sinning and repentance."

"Brilliant. You've got to take me to Manville sometime. I'd love to do the whole routine, right down to the Hail Marys at dawn."

All right. What does that mean? Does that mean Chip and I will have a bicoastal L.A. to Manville romance? Or is that some kind of polite, you must take me to meet your crazy relatives when I visit in the next millennium line?

"Listen, Chip. I have to know something," I say. "Why didn't you tell me sooner you're David Stanton's son?"

Chip stops the car in a parking lot by the Pacific Ocean. "Why do you think I didn't tell you?"

"Because you're married." (OK, this has *nothing* to do with his name, but it was a way for me to ask without appearing too girly.)

"Because I'm married?" He smiles, letting me know full well that I'm not fooling him. "I'm not married."

Score!

I go "hmph," as though this amazing revelation is a mildly interesting fun fact, like learning that spiders have fifty-two eyes. "So, then, it goes back to what you said the night I got the Mercedes—that you didn't want me to treat you differently."

"Exactly." He touches me on the nose and says, "Shall we go? Or are you going to sit in the car some more? I know you're slow to move, but there's a whole beach to walk and a fantastic sunset to watch."

Getting out of the car, I am breathless and not just because Chip is single. (It's tempting to sneak away and call Mom in victory, very tempting. Though, on second thought, she'd probably just claim I was fantasizing again.)

No, I'm breathless because I'm in one of the most beautiful spots in the world.

Behind us is the Pacific Coast Highway, a winding strip of asphalt that hugs the rocky California coast. To the north of us Malibu's dramatic cliffs fall to the ocean while in front of us looms a white beach and the magnificent Pacific, the reflection of the evening sun glistening on the water. I've seen all this in so many movies, it feels familiar. Even so, I'm all tingly realizing I am actually here.

"Wow."

"You don't get that in Jersey, a setting sun on an ocean, do you?" Chip reaches out and takes my hand. It's strong and in control.

I have no idea what's going on here. Is this a business meeting like he arranged for Belinda? Or is this more? There are so many conflicting signals—letting his knuckles brush my knee, reaching out for my hand, taking me to the beach. Yet, he hasn't made one move.

Then again, he might just be a friendly California guy showing a girl from out of town the sights every tourist wants to see. Aggh. It's driving me insane. I have to know.

"I mean, Jersey's beaches are fine," I hear myself saying. "I love Jersey, especially the southern part around Stone Harbor down to Cape May. But this. This is . . . awesome."

"You wanna take a walk up the beach? I don't know if you're a celebrity watcher or anything. I guess working for *Sass!* it's part of your job description. Anyway, if you stay below the high-tide mark you can do the entire length without Demi Moore's security guard going ballistic. It's cool sometimes who you run into. Last time I was out here, Dustin Hoffman ran smack into me."

As we stroll up the beach, my only regret is that there is not a mist and I am not wearing a dorky white turban like Barbra Streisand in *The Way We Were*. Don't get me started on Katie and Hubble. Just thinking about them makes me cry. Why oh why couldn't he love her for who she was? It was the McCarthy era, for heaven's sake. She *had* to protest blacklisting.

"You're lost in thought," Chip says.

"Just thinking about the McCarthy era."

"Hey, whaddya know? Me too." And he bumps against me playfully.

It's like we're teenagers. It's odd how thrilling it is to be awkward, making small talk about the rise of a celebrity culture. As we pick up shells and duck incoming Frisbees, I update him on Deb and Nancy, about how Nancy was sexually harassed at her law firm and how Deb's husband won't compliment her on her weight loss. Which means Chip has to compliment me on *my* weight loss and so I change the subject.

Somehow we get onto Eileen and her wedding to the Jack Russell terrier, a nickname that Chip finds extremely amusing and that I assure him he wouldn't if he knew in three months Jim Russell was to become his brother-in-law.

All the while I am conscious of Chip, of how much taller he is than I am, how he turns his head to smile, the crookedness of his broken nose or the way he shakes his hair back from his forehead.

Intimacy steels these observations. If Chip and I are together—Lord, what am I saying? I'm like a girl with a crush. Anyway, if—big if—Chip somehow decided that a bicoastal relationship was the way to go, and if we got to know each other *verrry* well (and I think we all know what that means), I promise that I will try to remember the tension, how embarrassed I was stumbling over a piece of driftwood and then being hit in the head with a volleyball.

How come Barbra Streisand wasn't hit in the head with a volleyball? That's what I wanna know.

We head into Gladstone's and find that there's been a mix-up. Chip's reservation for seven thirty was put down for eight thirty. This is bad news because the place is packed, especially the deck which is where we really want to be, though the sun is setting and I'm getting chilly.

"We could go someplace else," he suggests.

Overhearing this, the hostess begs him off with offers of a drink for each of us on the house. I think she likes him because she keeps bending over to pick stuff up that I swear is not on the floor.

"Let's stay," I say. Besides, I am starved! And watching the huge helpings of crab cakes (4 points), coconut shrimp (16—forget it) and even an iced seafood tower (? points) pass by, I'll be damned if I'll be denied. I haven't eaten all day.

This is a fact that I should have been paying attention to, that I haven't eaten in, oh, thirty-six hours, when a waiter comes out to the deck to bring us our drinks—the "usual" (whatever that is) for Chip and a humongous margarita for me. It has been sooo long since I've had a margarita and even though it is 5 points, possibly more, I take a good long sip.

And nearly swoon.

"You OK?" Chip asks.

"Fine." I smile, steady myself, and enjoy the waves crashing in the twilight beneath us. "I love the salt air. It's so refreshing."

"I thought you'd like this place. That's why I wanted to bring you here."

I eye him slyly. "I thought you were going to take Belinda here."

"Actually, my intention was to take Belinda out to the cleaners."

Silence. Cripes. He knows about the Belinda brouhaha. Better take another sip for fortification. "How so?" I ask bravely.

"I guess it's OK if I talk to you about this. From what Lori DiGrigio and my father said, they've made you aware of the general problem."

"Oh, sure."

"I think their concerns are well founded. I had my staff . . ."

Staff? He has a staff?

". . . research this and . . . I better explain." He leans back, looks out to the ocean, and slides his arm along the back of my chair, exactly like he did in the Mercedes. It is warm and strong. Would it be a crime to wrap it around my body?

"In my father's opinion, a revelation that the ethics columnist violated the basic ethics of, for example, not lying on her résumé, could be a big scandal for *Sass!*"

"Absolutely." Oh, God do I need this drink.

Chip takes a modest sip of his own and goes on. "Since Lori hired her, he felt there'd be a conflict of interest if she did the investigation. So he put me in charge."

This is cause to down half the glass.

"I'm the one who has the unpleasant task of outing her. Maybe even firing her."

I can see the bottom, and it is not pretty. I cannot get over the odds that I have fallen for the one guy who could single-handedly institute my career ruin. The fates, I decide in my tequila daze, are mocking me. Plus, they are thin. I know it.

"And tonight?" I manage to get out two words.

"Tonight, I was going to . . ." He picks up my glass. "I'm sorry. I haven't been paying attention. Waiter?"

Like magic a waiter appears at our side. "Another?" he asks.

"I really shouldn't," I say.

"Oh, come on," Chip urges. "I'm driving this time."

"Well . . . OK," I agree begrudgingly. "But only if you make it a double."

Chip raises an eyebrow.

"I'm thirsty." *And you're cute,* I want to add. *So cute I could pinch your cheek.*

Get a hold of yourself, Nola. It is my inner voice that sounds suspiciously like my mother's. The same one that advised me against the fifteenth floor of the hotel. *You don't want to blow it by making a fool of yourself.*

"I won't," I answer.

"Pardon?" Chip is handing me my drink.

"Uhh . . ." I think fast which is not easy right now. "I won't tell anyone about Belinda."

"That's good because as it turns out, I think she's ducking me."

"Really?" I stir my drink and look around, soaking up the love. Yes, I think dreamily, California is where I'm meant to be. It's so laid back. So forever young. And isn't that who I am? Laid back and forever young? "Forever Young." Boy that was a bad song.

"How did that go again?" I ask.

"What?" For some silly reason Chip seems confused by this question.

" 'Forever Young.' "

"By Dylan?"

"No, no, no. Not by Dylan." Dylan. Sheesh.

"Billie Holiday?"

"What are you, a 'Forever Young' expert? I'm talking about the really bad version. And not the Mel Gibson movie, either." That's when it hits me. "Rod Stewart." And just to prove how bad it is, I sing my own rendition of "Forever Young," artfully incorporating Rod's scratchy voice and dramatic hand gestures.

When I'm done and the couple next to us moves to another bench, Chip abruptly gets up and announces that we apparently need to eat right away, though I'm perfectly happy drinking margaritas. What's the big rush? Who needs all those unnecessary food points anyway?

"I'm going to ask the hostess what's going on," he says.

"Okey dokey." I watch him walk off in his strut that I'm pretty sure is unconscious and decide then and there that he's mine. Oh, yes, he will be mine.

I take another sip of my double margarita—no salt. It seems weaker than what I would expect from a double margarita no salt. I must speak to the waiter, though he seems to have disappeared. *Poof!*

And then I see her. Oh . . . my . . . God. Harley Jane Kozak one table away. I just knew I'd see a movie star sooner or later. I just knew it.

I *love* Harley Jane Kozak. I am like her biggest fan. I loved her as Steve Martin's sister in *Parenthood*. I loved her when she played a virginal nun in *Santa Barbara*. Come to think if it I have vague plans of becoming a nun, which means she is my *role model*. And I need to tell her that *right now*. Even if she was crushed by the letter "C" from a hotel marquee.

I stand and find that the deck wobbles a bit. It must be built on faulty pilings. I congratulate myself on remembering the word "pilings."

"Harley Jane Kozak." I wave to her. "Over here!"

Harley Jane Kozak looks up from her salad. She's blonder than I remember. Skinnier, too. But she's dressed down like a real person. Jeans and clogs. "She's one of us," Fareeq the limo driver would say if he were here. I'm sure she won't mind if I ask her for an autograph.

"I'm so, so sorry to bother you," I say, teetering over to her table. "But I *loved* you in *Guiding Light* and *Santa Barbara*. You are like the best!"

"Thank you." Harley Jane Kozak has perfect teeth.

Boy these people in California are nice. I *love* California. Have I said that already?

"And I wonder if you could sign your autograph."

"Sure." She looks at me expectantly.

Am I supposed to be doing something? Maybe she wants money? But why would Harley Jane Kozak need money?

"Do you have a piece of paper or something?" she prods.

"Oh, right. For the autograph."

"It would help."

Hmmm. No paper. I don't even have a pen. I know! My bra! It's white just like paper.

"How about this napkin?" she says, grabbing a Gladstone's napkin as I begin to fiddle with my bra strap.

I remember that I might be a bit tipsy and that I tend to lose things when I'm a bit tipsy. "No . . . that won't do. I'll just accidentally blow my nose on it or something. I have an idea." I attempt to snap my fingers and miss. "How about my arm?" I push up my sleeve and stick out my arm.

"All right." Harley reaches in her purse, pulls out her pen, and signs my forearm, even putting a little smiling face on it.

"It's beautiful," I gush, admiring her pretty signature. "So what are you starring in these days?"

"I'm not doing movies anymore."

"Oh." I frown in sympathy as I try to stand straight. It's really, really hard. "That's too bad. I was talking to this girl, uh, Gloria, about how hard it is to be an aging actress in Hollywood. I'm really sorry."

"I'm not sorry. I write books. Mysteries. *Dating Dead Men. Dating Is Murder.*"

"Hold on, hold on. You write too?"

"In fact I've won several awards."

"Pretty and smart. Listen. Write those titles down for me." I thrust out my arm again.

"Nola?"

I feel a hand on my shoulder and turn. Chip. And

from the look on his face I can tell he's not here to join in the Harley Jane Kozak lovefest.

"I have a great idea," he says. "It's gonna take too long for us to get a table. How about I drive you back to the hotel and we get dinner there?"

"Room service," I declare, my evil brain cooking up an evil plan of Caesar salad and seduction.

"Yes, room service."

Excellent. He fell right into my trap.

Chip leads me back to my chair, away from my new best friend Harley Jane Kozak, and hands me my purse, telling me—as though I were a child!—to wait for a few minutes while he says good-bye to Harley Jane Kozak. I'm not exactly sure what he's saying, but I overhear the words "I'm sorry" and "the margaritas were too strong."

The margaritas were, like, so not too strong.

When Chip appears again he reveals that he's brought the car around out front. How he managed to do that I have no idea. He's a miracle boy.

"You're a miracle boy!" I declare for everyone to hear.

"Yes," he says, trying not to smile.

The drive back to the O is a blur. So is the part where Chip puts me to bed and turns out the light and arranges for a cab to pick me up the next morning to take me to the airport.

It's not until I'm on the plane home the next day, queasy and filled with regrets, occasionally wincing at the LOVE, HARLEY ☺ fading on my arm, that the memories come back to me in bits and pieces.

They're not exactly clear, but of the following I am certain:

I have told him my weight. My *real* weight.

I have confessed that I am emerald-green jealous of my superthin sister, Eileen. (Why did I do that? Why would he care?)

I have revealed that I am, in fact, madly in love with him, Dave "Chip" Stanton and that should he be up for it, I would gladly bear his child. (Yes. That was a nice touch, I thought.)

What I'm not so sure of is whether I've said anything about Belinda Apple, and that is worse than all of those drunken confessions put together. Except for the having his baby part. That was really bad.

Chapter Twenty-Seven

"Your Chip is David Stanton's son?!"

Lisa shouts this so loudly I have to kick her to shut up. "Shhh. I don't want anyone to know. Plus, he's not *my* Chip. I blew it by getting plastered in L.A."

This was the wrong thing to say. Lisa whips around to my side of the cubicle. "Did you get drunk and sleep with him?"

"No!" I pretend to focus on the new Holiday Energy Pick Me Uppers column written by a freelancer who can't spell either "and" or "the" not to mention "energy."

"Then, what did you do?"

I close my eyes and summon what's left of my dignity. "I did an arresting impersonation of Rod Stewart singing 'Forever Young.'"

"Get out!"

"Hey, you two," Joel says, "keep it down. Lori's in Fashion, and she keeps looking over here."

"What do we care? Nola's sleeping with the publisher's son. She's got clout."

"What?" Joel raises a bushy eyebrow.

"Don't listen to her," I say. "She's got it all wrong. You know how book people are. Fiction, fiction, fiction."

"Devlin!" Lori barks, causing Lisa to scamper off like a scared squirrel. "Stanton wanted you to have a copy of this."

She tosses me a white paper. It is too much to ask that the Stanton to whom she is referring is "my" Chip. If Chip is as bright as I think he is, he'll have nothing more to do with a weight-lifting, jaw-punching, Rod Stewart–impersonating, overweight souse like me.

And, indeed, I realize with disappointment, the letter she has handed me is a memo from his father.

To: belinda.apple@sassmag.com
From: David.A.Stanton@stantoninc.com
Re: Investigation of your résumé

Dear Miss Apple:
This is the seventh attempt at contacting you in as many days and you have not responded once. As

of course you are well aware by now, *Sass!* has determined that you are not whom you portray, that there was no such magazine as *Go Fab!* in London for which you supposedly worked, and that, in fact, your entire résumé is a sham.

In order to uphold our commitment to our readers and our contractual obligation—such as it is—to you, we will continue to run your columns under your name until we can definitively prove your fraudulency. However, they will actually be written by your editor, Nola Devlin, while you will be put on extended unpaid leave.

My son, David, who heads our West Coast offices, has conducted a thorough investigation into this matter and is prepared to deliver a full report to the board within weeks. I suggest strongly that you hire a qualified attorney well versed in labor fraud, that is if you have not done so already.

Sincerely,
David A. Stanton

David A. Stanton, publisher and president
Sass! Fit! and *Fix Up!* Magazines
Stanton Media, Inc.
West 57th Street
New York, New York 10019
CC: Arthur Krauss of Krauss, Krauss and Krauss
Lori DiGrigio

David A. Stanton III
Nola Devlin

I have already read the memo, of course. And this was the reply I sent.

To: David.A.Stanton@stantoninc.com
From: belinda.apple@sassmag.com
Re: re: Investigation of your resume

(The following is an automated reply sent by belinda.apple@sassmag.com)

Thank you for your e-mail. Unfortunately, I will be out of my office on a remote island off the Irish coast until next year and will not be able to access a computer. If this is an urgent matter, please contact my editor, Nola Devlin, at nola.devlin@sassmag.com.

I look forward to replying to your e-mail in the future.

Belinda Apple

"I want you to put together a report as well, Devlin," Lori says. "David Stanton has requested one from you in particular."

"The hot David Stanton?" Joel asks. "Or the old?"

"The young one. Dave." Lori smiles. "As a matter of fact, he and I were talking about this issue only last night. And I thoroughly agreed with his conclusion that as Belinda's editor, Nola, you were the person who had the most direct contact with her and should have been aware she was a fraud."

Shoot me now. Please, someone, put me out of my misery. This constant mortification, I think, is why I haven't shown my face at work in a week.

When I got home from L.A., I made the mistake of stopping off at my parents' house on my way back from the airport to pick up where I left off on the explanations and apologies for missing Eileen's engagement party.

Mom took one look at my thinner, paler self, at the LOVE, HARLEY ☺ scrawled on my forearm, and ordered me to undergo an emergency infusion of Rosemary Baked Chicken. Rosemary Baked Chicken is my mother's Prozac and penicillin wrapped in one. She is convinced that the drug industry would be decimated and the divorce rate would fall if more people turned to chicken in times of crisis.

Of course you can't just have Rosemary Baked Chicken alone. There must also be stuffing with walnuts, mashed potatoes with sour cream and chives, butter-slathered broccoli, and cherry cobbler with ice cream. I am ashamed to say I wolfed it all down. Including second helpings on the cobbler.

"Good. Good. Your body needs it, Nola," Mom said, topping the warm cobbler with an extra touch of whipped cream. "And don't bother going back to your place tonight. I've got your old room ready. New sheets and everything. Take a bath after dinner, watch some TV, and go to bed. I even bought a new bottle of Mr. Bubbles."

That night, squeaky clean, drowsy with Mom's cooking and tucked tightly among crisp cotton sheets in my old white-framed single bed, I looked around my familiar pink room with its sloping eaves and flowered wallpaper border and my Duran Duran poster from high school, and felt a comforting peace. Yes, my tiny childhood home in Manville was about as far away from the sophisticated feng shui at the O hotel in L.A. as you could get, and thank heaven. I decided then and there never to leave and couldn't fathom why I'd been so eager to flee when I was eighteen.

The next morning I awoke to the fresh homemade cinnamon rolls Mom was pulling out of the oven.

"Cinnamon sets everyone right. It's been scientifically proven." Mom put one on a plate, refilled my coffee, and handed me another cut grapefruit. I silently reaffirmed my vow from the night before.

Bitsy took care of Otis and I called in my personal days as I "decompressed" at my parents' house. The days of three-course meals and soup and sandwiches for lunch, chocolate-chip cookies for snacks, and soap operas from noon to four passed by in one blur. One very pleasant, satisfying blur. I didn't step on the scale once for the simple reason that my parents don't own a scale. Like my father says, once every other year at the doctor's office is often enough, thank you.

Probably a wise thing, as when it comes to fattening

comfort food, no one can beat my mom, who was determined to comfort me until I exploded. We feasted on baked macaroni and cheese with real cheese and buttery breadcrumb topping. Meatloaf with a ketchup sauce. Thick bean soup with sausage and homemade bread. Pineapple upside-down cake. Baked Alaska. And, of course, rice pudding with raisins and extra cinnamon.

The more I ate, the more whole I felt. This was so familiar. I knew *this*. Why had I put up the fight with all that water drinking, exercising, and portion control? Better that I accept who I am. Isn't that what maturity is all about? Accepting ourselves? Therefore, I accepted that I was a closeted, spinster bookworm like Eileen said. It wasn't as though Chip was ever going to call me again anyway.

Chip. Every time I thought of him, of embarrassing myself in front of Harley Jane Kozak, of ordering a double margarita and tottering around Gladstone's, I changed the channel or helped myself to another butterscotch brownie. And as my independence eroded, as the sugar in my blood spiked, Mom inched in for the kill.

"There's my favorite girl back again," she said, smoothing my hair as I sat like a lump on her brown tweed couch feeling particularly sated and warm. "Why don't you tell me what's going on, hon? Let it all out."

But I couldn't. Frankly, I'd eaten so much in the past few days that my capability of putting words in coherent order had diminished. All I could blurt was, "I think I might like to be a nun."

Mom quickly crossed herself. Then she took my hand again and said, "Let me call Father Mike. I'll arrange everything."

Which is how I have arrived in Father Mike's study, staring at the embroidered, multicolored LOVE tapestry one of the church ladies must have framed for him, thinking not of Christ's message, but of how much I missed Chip and so very much wanted to hop his bones.

"So, Nola, what's this your mother said about you wanting to become a nun?"

Father Mike has nice brown eyes and a beard. He's about my age, which is kind of amazing when you think of what normal guy in my generation would voluntarily choose to give up sex in exchange for being on call 24/7 to all those old ladies in the altar guild who think nothing of calling him when their tomato soup goes cold. I am pretty sure he is not one of those molesting priests. He plays baseball and runs in marathons. Not exactly molesting-priest hobbies.

"I think," I begin, looking away from the smiling Madonna in the painting behind Father Mike's desk, "I think I have a calling."

"A calling."

"Yes."

A calling sounds so much better than explaining that I want to be a nun because the garments are loose and because God as a husband doesn't mind if I have a fat ass and, anyway, there's not much point of me forging onward in life as a practicing heterosexual woman after embarrassing myself in front of the one man I could truly see myself spending a loving lifetime with.

"That's right," I reaffirm. "A calling."

"I see." Father Mike leans back in his swivel chair and looks up at the ceiling. I can't tell if he's amused or taking me seriously. It's so hard to discern with that beard. "And how, may I ask if it's not too personal, did that calling manifest itself to you?"

I'm a bit confused by what he means here, but I give it my best shot. "In a Weight Watchers meeting."

"In a Weight Watchers meeting."

"While I was arguing with a couple of old ladies about Zero Point Soup," I add.

"I see," he says again. It could get annoying if he keeps up this repetition.

"So," I say, getting to the point, "are there any nun orders that aren't, you know, too bad?"

"Too bad? I'm not sure I'm following you."

"Well, I read this book I found in church called *So . . . You Want to Be a Nun?* And it said that with some orders you didn't have to wake up before dawn or take a vow of poverty."

"Or wear a habit," Father Mike suggests.

"Actually, I like the habit. They're black. They're loose. They hide figure flaws. I think habits could be a marketing campaign for the church if it ever started recruiting for more nuns. You know, 'Make it a habit!

273

Become a nun!'" That's pretty clever if I do say so myself.

Father Mike laughs and gets up to pour us two coffees. "The church recruits all right. But I don't think telling women to join so they can wear a heavy, shapeless cloak is exactly a wise move. I mean, being a nun means giving yourself over one hundred percent to others. It's the most selfless act a woman can perform in the Catholic Church."

"I was afraid of that."

He hands me a cup, not bothering to ask me if I want milk or sugar because he knows and I know that I would never drink the sludge he lets condense every day in the bottom of his pot. "I hear what you're saying, Nola, and what I'm not picking up is the spiritual component of your calling. Correct me if I'm wrong or if you've been going to another church, but I haven't seen you at St. Anne's in weeks."

"Months."

He makes a face and pulls up a chair next to me so that we are eye to eye. Father Mike is not one for patriarchy. He's all about being one with the congregation. "What I am hearing, Nola, is pain." His voice is soft and sincere. "Would you like to talk about that pain?"

Something inside me stiffens protectively. "No."

"It wouldn't have anything to do with your sister's upcoming wedding, would it?"

"Absolutely not. If Mom's been telling you that, ignore it. It's a lie."

He reaches out and touches my knee in a non-sexually-harassing way. "Please, Nola. How about we lower the fence for a moment. It's me, Mike. We went through catechism together every Monday night. You used to babysit my little brothers."

(For the record there are 115 kids in the Salabski family, of whom Mike is like number twelve.)

"You can tell me what's in your heart. Trust me. Your word here is safe."

I'm still not sure.

"We all want to be loved, Nola. You especially. I've always thought you'd make a great wife and mother. You're warm and generous. And I'll let you in on a little secret."

Ick. I'm not sure I want to hear a priest's secret. It's supposed to be the other way around. He hears ours.

"If I hadn't had my own calling, I might have considered asking you out."

"Oh, come on." I mean, really, does he go around telling this to the altar guild?

"Well, to be honest, I had the calling at a pretty young age. Like ten. I guess what I'm trying to tell you is that as a child of God you are worthy, Nola, of being loved for who you are."

It's too much. That did it, the child-of-God-worthy-of-being-loved thing. From some deep well within me rise a fountain of tears I never knew was there. Between sobs and sips of Mike's truly shitty coffee, I let it all out. Everything.

I tell him about how I hate being fat, that I just want

to wake up thin and have it done with. I explain about the Cinderella Pact and how Deb and Nancy are threatening to outpace me in the weight-loss race. Then I really let loose and confide that I have fallen madly in love with Chip, a man who seems to really enjoy being with me, only to find that he is investigating my alter ego about labor fraud and that he is my boss's son.

That's right, I even blab that I am Belinda Apple. Interestingly enough, Father Mike had no idea who Belinda Apple is, though he cottoned on that she was thin and British and some sort of celebrity in a materialistic culture he abhors.

When I am through, my body is weaker than if I'd just suffered through a twenty-four-hour bug. My shoulders ache and my joints hurt. I have the sense that my face is puffy and bloated. There is an empty tissue box discarded on the oriental carpet beneath our feet and another one in my lap.

All I want to do is go home and take a nice long nap. Father Mike, meanwhile, says nothing as he cleans out the pot, refills it with water, and spoons out more coffee. An antique wall clock ticks out the minutes. I like it here in his office, which he has decorated in standard priest décor. I like the faded oil paintings of Jesus with children, the Bibles on the shelves along with books about teaching the Gospels and each of us experiencing our "personal Calvary." I even like the smell of must and dust. Church smells.

Maybe I wouldn't be such a bad nun after all.

"John 10:10," Father Mike says from his shadowy corner near the coffee pot. "Do you know it, Nola? It's one of my favorites."

If this is some kind of nun quiz, then I am definitely going to flunk. "Um, kind of."

"'The thief comes only to steal and kill and destroy,' Jesus says. And then he adds, 'I came that they may have life and have it abundantly.'"

"Oh." I squirm in my chair. It makes me very uncomfortable when priests get all religious.

"God wants us to live life abundantly. But it is impossible for us to have an abundant life if we follow the thief instead of the Lord. And I am afraid, Nola, that you have been misled into following the thief."

Oh, brother. I am definitely beginning to regret this visit.

The coffee pot spits out its last and Father Mike gets two fresh cups. This could be Father Mike's fifteenth cup of the day. Priests must develop serious prostate problems, is all I have to say.

He hands me a warm cup and goes to the window, his back to me. "Think about what that means. *The thief comes only to steal and kill and destroy.* According to what you've just described to me, you have lied to your employer and to the readers of your magazine. The thief strikes."

I drop my head and study the floor. He's right, of course.

"And then you express jealousy, the most destructive emotion we have, toward your own sister. The thief again."

OK, now I'm really in pain. I eye the door with longing. Get . . . me . . . out.

"But worst of all, you hate yourself. You have let the thief convince you that you are unlovable, invaluable, worthless. You have let him rob you of the wonder of being alive. He has stolen the preciousness God has imbued in each of us from birth.

"Think of a baby, how she smiles and coos and reaches for the sun. Does she care if her little legs are chubby or if her belly is round? Of course not. All she knows is the joy of love. And my question to you today is why did you let the thief steal that joy from you?"

Goddammit. There go those tears again, and I'm back to the tissue box, though this round I'm only crying and not speaking. Yes, what did happen to the joy? I think back to when Eileen and I played dress-up, her as the ever-marching bride, me as Cinderella. We didn't care who was fat or who was thin, who had a boyfriend and who didn't.

I am miserable. I never knew how miserable I was.

Father Mike is behind me, patting me on the shoulder. "I don't mean to get down on you. That's not my intent. I just wanted you to see what was what."

"I know." I dab my cheeks and notice that my tissues are black. Next visit to a priest for a soul purging and I'm going to remember to wear waterproof mascara. "So, what do I do now?"

"Not enter the nunnery, that's for sure. That's not your calling. You actually flinched when I quoted from the Book of John."

Thank heavens. "So, what can I do?"

"Give and forgive. My two favorite words. Magic words." He returns to the chair across from me. "First, in the way that Jesus instructs us to love God, with all your heart, with all your soul, with all your mind, and with all your strength, to paraphrase Mark, so should you forgive.

"Forgive your sister for not asking you to be maid of honor, for all the cruel comments she's made to you. Forgive your mother for coddling her like a spoiled child and always taking her side. Forgive the boss who discriminated against you because of your weight."

"OK, but you don't know Lori DiGrigio. She's evil incarnate. I'm telling you, if you're looking for Satan, she's right up the road at the Princeton Corporate North Office Park."

"Ah, ah, ah." He's wagging his finger like Nana Snyder. "Absolute forgiveness is absolute freedom. When I say it's magic, I mean it. Magical things happen when you forgive completely, Nola, especially if you practice forgiveness every day and every minute of every day until it sticks. And no holding on to a grudge here and there. That's not forgiveness, that's rationalization."

This is a tall order, especially the Lori DiGrigio part. Despising Lori is a company pastime at *Sass!*, like Thursday night happy hour or the pickup basketball game on Saturday afternoons. If I stop hating Lori, I might as well throw in the towel on my office social life.

"As for giving, I'd like to see you give as much as you possibly can."

Figures. That's the deal with church, always hitting you up for money.

I open my purse and reach for the checkbook, but Father Mike puts out his hand. "No, not like this— though I'm never one to turn down a contribution. What I suggest is that you go home and search your soul about to whom you want to give and as well as how much. Look for those who aren't expecting your gifts—a rival, a stranger, a family member. And don't boast. Enjoy giving secretly."

Suddenly, for no obvious reason, I'm smiling like a fool. Father Mike tosses me another tissue, but I don't need it. I've heard about people experiencing spiritual transformations, and perhaps this is my turn. Because something, something has changed within me.

I feel hopeful.

"It's good to see a smile on your face. Now, one more thing before you go." He pulls his chair closer. "How am I going to get Ron and Nancy back together forever?"

"Don't worry, Father," I tell him. "God invented a handy sin for just this occasion. It's called animal lust."

Chapter Twenty-Eight

The trepidation that Eileen and Jim show walking slowly from Jim's muscle truck to my front porch is almost too good to be true. Eileen is wearing a clinging sweater in her favorite lime green (better to show off her lustrous—i.e., dyed—bronze locks) and brown pants that are smaller than most of my underwear. Jim has his arm around her protectively, like he's leading her to the executioner's block. It is all I can do to hold myself back from letting out a whoop as I watch them from my second-floor window.

I feel like Scrooge on Christmas Day. I do, and it's wonderful.

The conversation I had with Eileen on the phone the week before was very simple. I asked her and Jim to stop by my house after visiting our parents on Sunday so that we could have a "long overdue heart-to-heart about this wedding."

"Ooookay," Eileen said. "Mind giving me a hint what this is about?"

"I think you know very well what it's about," I snapped. And then hung up.

Perfect.

I let Mom do the rest after I explained to her and Dad as gently as possible that they would not be paying for Eileen's wedding. At first my dad put up a stink. There was a lot of getting up from the kitchen table and shouting about the two of them being quite able to pay for their daughter's wedding, blah, blah, blah. But in the end he couldn't deny me, or rather, Belinda.

Mom says Eileen's been calling every day, sniffing for clues. And Mom has been playing her best frazzled mother—a role she has honed for thirty-five years—by replying with, "I don't want to get involved. This business is between you and your sister. Don't drag me into your soap opera."

I *love* that.

So now is the big day. Sunday. It is October and delightfully colorful outside. The air smells of wood smoke and rotting leaves. Children are getting ready for Halloween, and Bitsy has hired workers to reinsulate the attic.

It is several weeks after my meeting with Father Mike. I have left my parents' house, returned home, and resolved to get my life in order despite my dieting setback. I can feel the weight around my middle, the tightness in my jeans and in my face. Still, something's changed.

Instead of throwing in the towel as I have after previous binges, I have simply shrugged off my week of comfort food, accepted my whatever-pound weight gain, and gotten back on track. Exercise. Water. Points.

For breakfast I routinely have an egg-substitute omelet made with mushrooms, peppers—any vegetables around— and the hottest salsa I can find. Zero points. Sometimes for lunch I have a three-point cheeseburger: "light" English muffin, veggie burger, one slice of low-fat cheese, and the works. Tomatoes. Lettuce. Mustard. And, of course, hot sauce. Hot sauce raises your metabolism. I am thinking of designing a hot-sauce diet.

Vegetables have taken a starring role in my life. My salads are huge, though the dressing is small. Mustard and balsamic vinegar combined can make anything palatable, including sautéed chicken breast. And if I want something sweet, nonfat whipped topping sandwiched between two low-fat cinnamon graham crackers and frozen for ten minutes. Yum!

I no longer need to look up points. Eating this way has become instinctive. For the first time in my life, I don't hate a diet because—I know this sounds corny—they're right. It's not a diet, it's a lifestyle change accomplished in small increments.

Meanwhile, Nancy has gotten down to where she feels comfortable and has announced that she has stopped dieting. From now on, she's just working out and watching what she eats. But basically she's just working out. Tony's even talking her into training for a mini-marathon—an inconceivable thought last spring.

Tony's own magic is working wonders. Nancy's old-fashioned big blue eyes are bigger and bluer. Her cheekbones have reemerged, as have her shoulders and hips. She is so strong, too. You should see her biceps and feel her calves. Like, don't ever get into a leg-wrestling match with her.

That said . . . there is one problem. Actually two.

"I've lost both of them," she told me the other day while we were jogging—yes, jogging, you read correctly—around the cemetery.

"Who?"

"Betty and Veronica." She cupped her chest. "That's what Ron named them."

I stop running to bend over laughing. "You're kidding. He named your tits?"

"They were more like *our* tits. I loved our tits. They were my best asset. Do you know I was once a 54-G?"

Where did she find bras?

"I'm thinking of getting implants, but then I worry that I'll be back where I started. You know, that's how I got fat because crusty old Ted Kline kept making comments about my chest. It seems stupid to enhance my bust now. It's like inviting trouble from Ted."

"Then maybe it's time you stood up to him. That way you can get your big bust back *and* still go to work."

She frowned. "You know, you're right. It's about time I told him to stuff it. I should threaten to sue and get him kicked out of the firm or, better yet, get him to pay for the plastic surgery to beef up my chest."

"Now you're talking."

Meanwhile, Nancy and her measly chest were too busy with Ron on Friday to accept Deb's invite to shoot pool with Paul, her, and me at the Tiger Tail. I was glad to hear that she and Paul were going out and was all too happy to join them. Frankly, I'd been a bit worried about their marriage from the stories about Paul sabotaging Deb's weight-loss efforts. It would be nice to support them.

I wore my standard outfit—the black pants, white button-down top, big jewelry, and high-heeled boots. It was a toss-up what Deb would wear. She doesn't go out much.

The Tiger Tail was crowded and smelled of stale beer and popcorn, and if cigarettes were still allowed, it'd be smoky. All in all, not my favorite kind of place. But I wasn't here for me, was I? I was here for Deb. It wasn't so long ago that she was a house bound, shy matron sequestered at home with her knitting and tatting.

But there was no Deb at the Tiger Tail. No Paul either.

I waited five minutes, walked around, and deciding I must have gotten the night wrong, was about to leave when a distinctive peal of laughter broke out from the far corner where a bunch of men in dirty jeans and work books were huddled around a table.

Then, upon further inspection . . . Was that Deb?

Sure enough, it was her—pushing the limits on fat fashion in a low-slung top and *tighhhhht* jeans. She was half dressed in a black V-cut strappy tank top more often seen on teenage girls than on mature mothers of two. OK, so she'd lost weight. But not *that* much weight. She still had a gut that spilled over the top of her jeans like a muffin top.

"Hi, Nola!" Deb's hand shot straight up. "Come on. We're over here."

I pasted on an oh-there-you-are smile as I trotted on over, one eye out for Paul who had either left or wasn't invited to begin with. The men didn't seem nearly as thrilled to see me as they were to be gathered around Deb. A construction crew, clearly. Mud still on their boots, beer in their guts, lust in their eyes. Eeek!

"Let me see if I can get this straight." Deb squeezed her eyes shut in concentration. "Kevin. Josh. Tyler. Steve."

Tyler and Steve gestured to each other. "Vice versa."

Deb giggled. "This is my closest friend in the whole wide word, Nola. Have a seat, Nola."

I sat next to Kevin (who smelled kind of like running shoes) and zeroed in on Deb's drink, which was pink, noncarbonated, and in a martini glass. I knew from our Saturday morning with Suze the nurse/nutritionist that Deb was not supposed to drink martinis or Cosmoplitans or anything alcoholic for at least a year after surgery—if ever.

Then again, I wasn't sure Deb was supposed to be throwing a leg over the laps of strange, sweaty men either, though I don't think Suze addressed that particular issue.

Now, if my mother had been here, she'd have had no problem bringing Deb in line. Would have enjoyed it, in fact. In a very loud voice she'd have asked where Paul was and then probably would have noted that Deb shouldn't be drinking alcohol after weight-loss surgery and what about those two adorable kids of hers? Weren't they recovering from the stomach flu?

I highly doubted that Deb had mentioned her

maternal status to the construction crew and from the searing glare she was shooting me from across the table, I had better not bring it up either.

I ordered a Diet Coke and engaged in small talk with Steve (who didn't smell half as bad as Kevin) about the mechanics of building a stone wall—a fairly interesting topic involving ancient Celtic lore. I also tried to keep an eye on Deb, who had begun flinging herself onto the pool table, flashing lots of cleavage, and asking for "hands-on instruction."

"What's she doing with the cue now?" I asked Steve as Deb began gyrating in a circle.

"Looks like a pole dance." Steve crooked his head upside down. "I've never seen anybody suck a pool cue before."

Right. When they're sucking on pool cues, it's my cue to go. "I think I better get her."

"I'll be here as backup."

I was glad for the offer as Deb was more than recalcitrant, stomping her foot and shouting movie clichés like, "Back me up here, boys."

"I don't think she should drive," Tyler said, leaning over her protectively. "I'll take her home."

Deb folded her arms and pouted, her lips still blue from pool-cue chalk.

"Come on, Deb," I said, taking her hand.

"No. I wanna stay." She yanked her hand back. "Besides, I've only had one drink."

"Yeah," chimed in the shortest player, Josh. "Leave her alone."

Most scientists do not believe in ESP, but I have never been good at science, thankfully. Which is why I mentally radioed to Deb that if she did not come with me at that very moment I would have no choice but to announce that waiting for her back at home were two children, a dog, a cat, a pile of tatting, and a husband with a serious temper problem.

"Forget it, guys. We'll do it another night." Deb stepped away from them, one strap of her tank top sliding over her shoulder—very classy.

"Aww," they chorused in regret.

Even though it was a chilly fall night, I put the top down in an effort to rouse Deb to her senses. There was none of the foot dragging she displayed at the Tiger Tail. Au contraire. She was bubbling with excitement.

"You mind telling me what the hell's going on with you?" I asked her point blank. "What were you after back there?"

"Just some fun. Is that a crime?" She sounded exactly like she did in high school when her mother found us hanging out in the parking lot with Paul, smoking cigarettes. "I've been cooped up in that house for years, Nola. Years. Me. The kitchen. The washer and dryer and the TV. That was my world and now that I have been freed, I never want to spend another minute in that prison. Isn't that why I went through all the hassle of surgery?"

"I thought you went through all the hassle of surgery so you could go to your son's graduation without embarrassing him."

Deb bit her lip, thinking about this. "OK. That's what pushed me over the edge, but . . ." She threw up her arms. "Look at me. I haven't looked like this ever. At least Nancy was popular in high school and thin."

"Not that thin."

"But I've never been thin. Not until now."

I hated to inform her that crossing the 200 barrier did not on the catwalk put her.

"Relatively thin," she said, reading my mind. "And it's not stopping. The weight's falling off. It's falling off so fast, I'm scared. It takes my breath away. I can't believe this is happening."

It was infectious, this enthusiasm of hers. Once again the green goblin of jealousy tiptoed out of hiding and whispered in my ear how I wasn't losing weight that fast. I tamped it down by remembering Father Mike's advice to concentrate on the positive.

"I'm happy for you, Deb," I managed. "Really."

"My only regret is I waited too long. I'm in my thirties and I feel like my life is half over. I wished to hell I'd done this sooner so I could have enjoyed my youth as a thin person. Then I wouldn't have ended up with a drip like Paul. I only married him because I was scared no one else would have me."

As far as major confessions go, this one's a biggie. Even Deb must have realized this, because she was struck dumb by what she'd just confessed.

"Are you thinking of . . . divorce?"

Deb heaved her shoulders with resolve. "If I could find a way to earn some money, I'd do it tomorrow."

We didn't speak again until we pulled up in front of her house and Deb refused to get out of the car.

"He's asleep." She stared up at her bedroom window where Paul was snoozing. "When I come in, he won't say anything. He won't even ask where I've been. He doesn't give a damn."

"Is that why you aren't wearing your wedding ring?"

She glanced at her hand as if it were simply an oversight. "I took it off when I got too fat to wear it. So how come you just noticed?"

"Because back then not wearing the ring meant you were too fat. Now it means you're not in love with your husband."

"Yeah," she said squarely. "You're right about that."

With tears in her eyes, Deb leaned over, gave me a quick hug, and told me not to worry. Then she got out, set her shoulders, and marched up the stairs that a few months ago she labored to climb.

That's when I understood what it really means to lose weight. It's as though fat is a cloud that's around your mountain of problems. Not until you drop the weight and clear the fog, will you know how high you've got to climb to get on top of them.

Chapter Twenty-Nine

So I really got off subject there, thinking about last Friday with Deb. Right. Back to the task at hand. Setting things straight with Jim and Eileen who are slowly, slowly treading up the stairs to my apartment.

I practice standing in nasty poses, one hand on hip, arms crossed, brows furrowed, and settle on answering the door with a frown.

"You're late," I accuse.

"I'm sorry." Eileen gingerly steps into my peachy apartment. "Mom and I had a knockdown drag-out about my wedding dress again. I swear, when she's through planning this event, my wedding is going to be Palookaville. I keep trying to tell her this isn't any old wedding. This is mine."

"That's right," I agree.

"I mean, Belinda Apple's going to be standing right next to me. What's she going to think when she sees me in an off-the-rack from Loehmann's."

Oh, for a moment there I forgot. This wedding wasn't about saying vows to love and cherish each other before your family and friends in a church of God. This event was to impress Belinda the celebrity.

Steady, Nola. Keep it positive.

"Don't tell me. Let me guess." Jim is in his standard navy Adidas tracksuit, scrutinizing me with an expert eye. "One . . . seventy—"

"Jim!" Eileen barks. "I thought I told you to stop guessing people's weight. It's so embarrassing."

"What? What? She should be happy. Last I saw her on your birthday she was at two hundred—"

Eileen shakes her head ever so slightly. Jim, fortunately, takes the hint.

"Why don't we sit?" I suggest, leading them over to

my "living area," where I have arranged a pitcher of iced tea and homemade lemon cookies. Otis growls at Jim. He knows a reincarnated Jack Russell terrier when he sees one.

Eileen throws herself down, reaches for a cookie, and then, meeting Jim's stern gaze, drops it. "If this is about the bridesmaids dresses, I want you to know that Mom has totally nixed those."

"So what are the plans?" I ask.

"The usual. It is really boring."

She doesn't have to tell me. I know the drill by heart.

"Wedding at two in the afternoon. Absolutely no evening wedding allowed. No rice. No confetti. Not even birdseed to be thrown. After that, a reception at the Union Club. Beer. Wine. Soda. Coffee. And buffet hors d'oeuvres to cut down on the cost of waitstaff. Which means"—she holds up her well-manicured hand and ticks off her fingers—"No band. No deejay. No champagne. No sit-down dinner. Not even a big cake. It's all going to be over by seven."

Jim clears his throat. "I'd contribute more, 'cept that I'm trying to gather as much capital together as I can."

"Don't tell Mom and Dad, but Jim's breaking out of Valley Fitness. He wants to start his own gym and he's looking for business partners. He's even drawn up a business plan."

"Really?" I say. It's the first interesting thing I've heard Jim do. "And how will your gym be better than Valley Fitness?"

"Better located," he says, straightening. "I got in on an old commercial property in Hellertown, right off I-78 near the waste haul. Perfect site for a gym 'cause you can get the commuters going back and forth from Jersey, coming into the Valley to work. My motto's going to be 'No Excuses!' 'cause we're gonna be open really early and really late."

"Jim's got the septic and zoning approvals already. It's going to be—"

"Jim's Gym!" I exclaim.

"Hey!" Eileen claps. "I like that."

Jim nods in approval. "You know, I hadn't thought of Jim's Gym but I have to say, that's not bad. Not bad at all."

It boggles the mind how he hadn't thought of Jim's Gym. Never mind.

"Anyway, the reason I asked you guys to meet me here was to discuss the wedding."

Eileen sinks into the couch, dreading the inevitable lecture.

"It turns out, Eileen, that you won't have to worry about your wedding being, as you say, set in Palookaville."

"Huh?"

"I've gone ahead and made arrangements for you to have a seven p.m. candlelight ceremony right here in Princeton at St. Anne's, followed by a full sit-down dinner for two hundred in Barnard Hall."

Eileen seems confused. "*The* Barnard Hall in the university?"

"That's the one. Decorated to the hilt, any way you like it."

"What?!" Eileen pushes Jim aside and pops up, rigid. "Are you for real?"

I suppress a smile of absolute joy. "Completely."

"Mom and Dad are paying for that?"

"Noooo." I grab an iced tea and take a sip. "Belinda is. She has offered to pay for the entire wedding, or at least up to a hundred thousand dollars."

She slaps her hand across her mouth in shock.

"Good going, girlie." Jim hi-fives the air. "I knew that British chick would go all out for you. You were smart to make a celebrity your maid of honor. Probably got wind of the Manville thing and said to herself, uh, no way."

"She did no such thing," I correct, monitoring Eileen, who is this close to fainting. "Belinda would have been perfectly fine in Manville. She did this because she knew a winter candlelight wedding was what Eileen's always dreamed of."

"But . . ." Eileen runs her hands over her tiny hips, trying to comprehend it all, not letting herself get too excited until she knows it's for real. "But . . . Mom and Dad."

"I've already cleared it with them. When I told them why Belinda wanted to pay full boat, they couldn't argue."

Eileen regards me with caution. "Why? Why would Belinda want to do this for me? We've had two phone calls at most."

"Because she works for your sister, dingbrain!" Jim shouts. "She's trying to suck up to the management at *Sass!* Geesh. Don't you know anything about business?"

This gift would be so much more pleasurable if Eileen were marrying someone who didn't need regular rabies shots. "Actually, Jim, there's a sad twist to this story."

I stroll over to the window with my hands behind my back so I won't have to keep a straight face. "You see, Belinda doesn't want anyone to know this but she has"—I pause for dramatic effect—"only months to live."

Eileen lets out a gasp and again slaps her hand across her mouth. "Does Nigel know?"

Nigel? What a bizarre first question. Why would . . . Then I remember how Nigel and Belinda were supposed to be an item. "Uh, yes. In fact it was Nigel who reserved Barnard Hall." A relatively easy task, considering the school would be closed during Christmas break anyway.

There is an awful choking sound. When I turn from the window, my heart clenches to see Eileen in full sob. She has her head on Jim's shoulder and he's patting her soothingly, his mind obviously calculating the expenses Belinda has just saved him.

"What's wrong?"

"It's just that . . . it's so nice of her," Eileen gulps. "No one's ever done anything so nice like that for me, ever." Eileen lifts her head and dabs her eyes with a napkin from the lemon cookies, getting powdered sugar all over her cheeks. "It's as though Belinda somehow knows me, knows me deep down inside."

I am touched. I am also tempted to scream, *I do know you deep down inside! You're my sister and I love you, Eileen.* But I remember what Father Mike said, to give generously and to give anonymously.

"Yes, well." I sniff back my own tears.

And then an awful thing happens. Eileen plunges her hand into her purse. "I should call Belinda right away to thank her."

Panic. This could be bad. My Belinda phone is in my bedroom and turned on. "Not a great idea. She's in the hospital for a few days and can't be reached."

"Oh." Eileen's face falls. "Is she going to be all right for the wedding?"

"I should hope so. Meanwhile, you have no time to waste, Eileen. Call this woman," I say, handing her a sheet of paper with a name and number written on it. "She's your wedding planner, Helen Whittingham."

Eileen delicately takes the paper as though it were gold leaf. "I've heard of her. She's awesome."

"She's expecting you to call this afternoon. We're getting started on this late, you know. You and Jim are going to have to attend accelerated sessions with Father Mike, and then there's the dress you want . . ."

"You mean the Christos? The ivory, strapless—"

"That's the one. You're supposed to order it at least six months in advance for fittings so I went ahead and just bought it, with Belinda's permission, that is."

"Ayyyee!" Eileen is back to being ecstatic as she leaps off the couch and throws her arms around my neck, squealing so loudly that my eardrums are about to burst. "Belinda might be paying for all this, but I just knew you had some input." She cups my face in her hands. "Thank you, thank you, thank you . . . thank you so much for introducing me to Belinda."

Slam! Sucker punched. Mustn't let it get to me. Giving for giving's sake and all that.

Jim snorts after Eileen races out for a quick introductory meeting with Helen. "So what am I supposed to do while she's busy with all that? I'm not spending my Sunday afternoon flipping through cake books."

"No," I say, smiling sweetly. "Why don't you relax. Read the newspaper or something."

"Forget that. I'm going to show you how to drop that extra weight once and for all."

"Here's your problem." Jim plunks down an innocent looking can of diced tomatoes with basil and garlic. "Read the ingredients. Out loud."

I read the ingredients. "Tomatoes. Water. High fructose corn syrup—"

"Aha! Stop right there. High fructose corn syrup."

"Oh, no. Not this with the 1980 corn lobby again."

"You can laugh all you want. In the end, I'm speaking the truth." He drops the can in a bag that we will schlep down to the local food shelf.

Where I'd assumed that I'd purged all junk food by cleaning out my cupboard of nachos, Hershey's syrup,

297

movie butter popcorn, and Snickers bars, I apparently couldn't have been more wrong. Who knew that in almost every "healthy food" I'd been eating lurked high fructose corn syrup and added fat?

Take for example the multigrain bread I'd chosen as a "complex carbohydrate," far preferable to Wonder. Guess what? It has more calories and the same amount of fiber as two chocolate-chip cookies. Let me tell you, I would have far preferred the cookies.

Or the "diet" granola bar I've been grabbing for breakfast. Jim had a total fit about that. Turns out the granola bar has fewer nutrients and as much sugar as a Pop-Tart.

Cruel, cruel world. Why do you mock me with chocolate-chip cookies and Pop-Tarts?

"Processed sugar." Jim flicks out a finger. "And unnecessary fat." He flicks out another finger. "These are the two enemies hidden everywhere that are making Americans huge and are keeping you from getting below—"

"Watch it," I warn him. "Keep your weightstimates to yourself."

"Knowledge is power, Nola."

"Yeah, yeah. Why don't you tell me what I'm supposed to do."

This is the moment Jim's been waiting for, the opportunity to stand on his soapbox and preach to the fat girl. "You're going to learn to eat like nature intended you to eat—as an omnivorous mammal."

Such big words for a Cro-Magnon. "Which means?"

"A diet made up mostly of raw, organic vegetables followed by a little lean protein—chicken, some beef—and the occasional fruit."

Yummy.

"You're going to eat according to when you're hungry, not by a clock, and you will not overeat. Until you have trained your brain to tell you when to stop, we'll be limiting your portions so you can develop instinctive portion control."

"This does sound like fun. What about the four most important food groups—bread, cheese, cookies, and margaritas?"

Jim rolls his eyes, his Cro-Magnon brain not quite able yet to grasp the concept of a joke. "All those things you mentioned are processed or unnatural."

"Margaritas are so not unnatural. They're made from limes and tequila, which I happen to know is a derivative of a very natural cactus plant."

"*Processed* from a cactus plant. Plus, they contain alcohol, a sugar in a certain chemical form that your body will work to metabolize first, thereby neglecting other more important duties. You don't see mammals in the wild drinking alcohol, do you? Nor are they downing four cups of coffee every day."

"They would if they could. Remember that bear with the cocaine—"

"Don't get distracted." Jim goes over to the tiny cabinet above my refrigerator, removes my one item of alcohol—a bottle of tequila—and an unopened bottle of margarita mix. "Look at the high fructose corn syrup level in this. If the tequila doesn't kill you, that damn corn syrup will."

I stand by his side solemnly as he dumps both down my sink. I fight back memories of my margarita-fueled disaster with Chip.

"As for bread, that's processed food too, I don't care how whole the grain is. Hey, you want to eat some quinoa or tabouli, more power to you. But don't even think about steamed white rice."

I vow not to think about steamed white rice.

"Brazil nuts are good," he continues. "High in selenium. So are sunflower seeds for magnesium and Vitamin E. Both must be consumed raw and unsalted."

No salt? Why bother?

Jim's only exception on "processed" food is yogurt, but I will have to make it myself, using bacteria purchased from the local co-op and organic milk.

Already his diet is working. I am beginning to feel ill.

"I'm telling you, Nola, six weeks on my whole-food, no-sugar, no-fat, no-alcohol, no-caffeine eating plan . . ."

Jim does not like the word "diet."

". . . and your body will begin to settle, as I like to call it, to its natural weight. That might not be super thin, but it'll be healthy and you will live longer and live better because of it. Better yet, you can skip all this low-fat, low-carb marketing hype and all the chemicals that come with those stupid so-called foods. You can stop counting your stupid points. You're going to have more energy, more happiness, more vitality."

"Like you?"

Jim disregards this and draws up the plan.

For breakfast he suggests I have a small bowl of either oats or brown rice topped by blueberries and a half an orange. Lunch is either a homemade soup, perhaps miso with tofu or tomato vegetable with a little diced chicken, or a piece of broiled chicken and an artichoke (no butter). Jim is big on artichokes, though, honestly, who packs an artichoke to take to work?

Dinner is a large salad made up of at least five different vegetables including, but not limited to, spinach, carrots, red cabbage, broccoli, sprouts, avocado (though high in fat, it's a good fat), minced raw garlic (yipes!), and perhaps some black beans—the highest anti-oxidant legume around. For dessert there's a couple of dried prunes, a couple of dried apricots.

Apparently, crème brûlée is right out. Go figure.

Beef should be limited to no more than four ounces a week—if that. Fish, though desirable, should be eaten in moderation due to high mercury content. Farm-raised salmon is not acceptable.

Ideally, I should outlaw all cooked foods forever, he says, which rules out meat. Gnawing at uncooked flesh, he tells me, is not an option. Fortunately this also rules out gelatin, which is a check in Jim's column.

For beverages, I may drink herbal tea until I sprout

301

chamomile buds. Like Weight Watchers and every other diet plan I've been on, it is mandatory that I consume at least five glasses of water a day. He swears that I can avoid all sorts of problems, cancer, heart disease, bad skin, an unpleasant personality, by drinking tons of water.

Finally, all the food must be organic.

"People claim you spend more on higher quality food, but lookit"—he holds up a bunch of broccoli—"ain't no label on this sucker. No marketing bud get. No packaging. If you stick to this eating plan, you'll end up paying a smaller grocery bill because you won't be paying the man to return dividends to his fat-cat shareholders who don't give a hoot about your health because they want you to get sick so you'll by the pharmaceuticals they've invested in."

I know he's right. I also know that Weight Watchers is right when they harp on reducing *how much* you eat as well as *what* you eat. And that Atkins probably had a point too with all that protein or South Beach with the protein and vegetables. Jane Brody, on the other hand, hit the nail on the head by noting we humans were meant to be gatherers, not hunters, and that nuts, berries, and whole grains are the way to go.

Low-carb. Low-fat. High-protein. No-fat. No-meat. All-meat. Everyone's right. We lifelong dieters know that intellectually. That's not the problem.

The problem is that until they find a healthy substitute for ice cream or a non fattening pan of brownies that can be consumed while reading a Daphne du

Maurier novel, I will have to deny my upbringing, which taught me the most natural cure for life's disappointments is not to exercise or have another glass of water, but to sit down to a roast chicken dinner with all the trimmings.

Chapter Thirty

To: belinda.apple@sassmag.com
From: lennonlives@princeton.edu
Re: Where are you, darling?

Belinda:
It's been ages and I've heard nothing from you. Not a peep. Not a moan. Not even a shot heard 'round the world fired from Balmoral. (How is dear Prince Charlie and his lovely wife, What's-Her-Horse?)

Evil rumors are swirling at *Sass!* that you have gone AWOL or that, perhaps, you never existed to begin with. But of course you exist, darling, as you and I have been in correspondence, though, true, not lately.

You should know that I have been extending myself above and beyond for your editor/friend Nola Devlin, racking up as many frequent lover points as I can in order to see you.

First I helped her secure Barnard Hall for her sister's wedding, then I introduced her to Final

Draft, a software program used to write screen-plays. Now I've been giving her screenplay tips during her early morning exercises. She's become quite a fanatic and is not nearly the cow she used to be. Unfortunately, the strict Miss Devlin insists I join her, though running definitely cuts into my coffee and ciggy time. Quite unpleasant.

I hope these tales of my devotion have stirred some feelings in your desired heart and that you will be able to persuade the Windsors that the MacLeods are actually a fine clan.

By the way, your columns just keep getting better and better. I absolutely adored your answer to ITCHY IN KENTUCKY—"seven years is long enough to put up with a pig. Dump his ass and join the living!"

Give me a ring, luv. Must I admit that I am a tad worried?

Cheers, Nigel

To: lennonlives@princeton.edu
From: belinda.apple@sassmag.com
Re: re: Where are you, darling?

(The following is an automated reply sent by belinda.apple@sassmag.com)

Thank you for your e-mail. Unfortunately, I will be out of my office on a remote island off the Irish coast until next year and will not be able to access a computer. If this is an urgent matter, please contact my editor, Nola Devlin, at nola.devlin@sassmag.com.

I look forward to replying to your e-mail in the future.

Belinda Apple

"OK, what the devil is up with Belinda? A remote island off the Irish coast? One might assume she's become a monk."

Nigel Barnes stands over me, holding his cigarette to the side so the smoke won't blow into my face while I lace up my Saucony running shoes, which Nancy has insisted that I must own. I am in old black sweats and a purple ADWOFF T-shirt. Nigel, on the other hand, is completely kitted out in Spandex running tights and a matching top, which do absolutely nothing to enhance his skinny body that I've just noticed is remarkably devoid of muscles.

"What's your obsession with Belinda, anyway?" I bend down and touch my toes.

"It's obvious, isn't it? We're meant to be together. She's British, I'm British. She's witty, I'm witty— though a bit more erudite, if I do say so. And of course there's the physical thing. Clearly she's attracted to me. How can she not be?"

"How can she not?" I wince as I stretch a somewhat sore hamstring.

"I mean, I've paid my dues. I've been patient and attentive. I don't quite understand why she's treating me rather brusquely. I thoroughly expected to be tromping the moors around Balmoral by now."

I give him a look. "Am I to infer that you've been so quote unquote attentive to me so that you can curry favor with Belinda?"

"Heavens no. Though . . . is it working? Has she said anything?"

"Nigel!"

"Drat it all." He takes one last drag on his cigarette and gives it a loving glance before tossing it toward the tombstone of Henry J. Wallingford 1923 to 2000.

I point to the butt and he picks it up dutifully, pinching it between his fingers until we reach a garbage can. "You are such a Puritan, aren't you? God, Americans can be so tiresome."

How Nigel is able to smoke before running, then run faster than I can, in fact, is a physical accomplishment I can't even begin to fathom. It makes me think of those little air sacs in his lungs, straining with each intake of oxygen, the poor dears.

"So," I say, when I am past the initial I-hate-this-my-chest-hurts part of the run, "let's go back to the screenplay. I've gone over a hundred and fifteen pages. Is that too much?"

"I should say so." Nigel waves to a couple of students passing us in the early morning fog. " 'Ello." They seemed shocked to see him doing anything besides inhaling tobacco or listening to music. "You've got to get that page count to under a hundred, luv."

"But it's hard. How am I supposed to condense my life story into one hundred pages, double spaced with margins so wide they would have made us giddy in high school English?"

"Your life story? I thought this was fiction."

"It is . . . kind of." Stark horror. I've slipped and given away too much.

"I mean, isn't this about a fat girl who disguises herself as a thin girl à la Cyrano de Bergerac? How, exactly, is that you?"

I launch into a sprint—one of Jim's commandments is that for every quarter mile I run, I must sprint until I count to sixty—hoping to avoid Nigel's enquiring mind. *You nincompoop. You have to be more careful. You totally let the cat out of the bag.* Speaking of which, where is Otis? He must have sauntered off when I was stretching.

Nigel catches up to me as I am bent over, panting, exhorting myself to go on because stopping decreases all the benefits of a heart-healthy workout.

"A terrific thought just occurred to me. One wonders if the rumors are true. That perhaps Belinda Apple never existed. That she is . . . you."

I pop up. "What?"

"It makes sense, really. Here you are, her editor, the only one who seems to have any contact with the bird."

"There's her agent. Charlotte Dawson," I trill, thereby sounding even more guilty. "Charlotte's where I get all my news about Belinda."

"What news?" Nigel steps closer to me. He really is extremely attractive in that British twit kind of way, the long, angular face and constant half-smile. Straight out of the eighteenth-century drawing room.

"You know." I turn and begin a slow run away. "The news about her taking a break."

"A break? Where?"

"To the remote island off the Irish Coast."

"Would that be the Kilkenny Island or the Tooraloora Island?"

I think fast. Tooraloora. I've heard of that. "Tooraloora, I believe."

"Aha!" He grabs me by the elbow, yanking me back. "There is no such island as the Tooraloora Island. I knew you were fibbing."

"I was not. I just forgot."

"All right. Then if Belinda does exist, as you say, I want to set a time and a place where I'll meet her. One on one, in the flesh. Otherwise, I just might have to blow your secret. I don't care if I have to fly to bloody Galway and take a bloody boat to the Arans . . ."

Arans. Damn. I should have thought of those.

"I want to meet this mythical goddess."

"OK. Deal." I stick out my hand. "I hereby invite you to my sister's wedding here in Princeton on December twenty-seventh, which is being entirely planned by Belinda, who also happens to be the maid of honor."

"You mean she'll be there?" Nigel's eyes gleam.

"In a green satin mermaid-cut dress. You won't want to miss it."

"Never fear, I won't. Even if that means skipping Boxing Day with my great Aunt Docia. A potential million-pound inheritance is nothing compared to meeting Belinda Apple in her creamy white flesh."

Chapter Thirty-One

It is dawning on me that slowly, gradually, I am merging Belinda Apple's perfect existence with my imperfect one. It is true: Believe it; be it.

By November it is no secret at *Sass!* that I am now writing Belinda's column. I figured the response would be, "Who's writing it? Nola? That frump? You've got to be kidding."

I never expected so many editors and writers to stop by my desk to tell me what a great job I was doing, how I was so much better than Belinda and, by the way, was I losing weight or was I doing something different with my hair, because I was really looking good.

"Honestly?" Lisa told me the other day over lunch (ginger tofu and sweet potatoes—8 points). "I was getting sick of Belinda. She was so flip, especially the way she'd end sentences with *really?* You're much more down to earth. Like your advice to Debbie Does Debt. I never knew you had the guts. That was great!"

Actually, I don't know how great it was to tell a mother of two who owed Discover $6,578 that it was perfectly ethical of her to call the credit card company's executives at home and sob pitifully about her children going to school with holes in their shoes thanks to their company's brutal late fees. I just felt so bad for her. I mean, five years ago she bought a new mattress, some groceries, and paid for repairs on her car and—*wham!*—suddenly she's slapped with a huge bill.

OK. So maybe publishing the names of the executives and their home numbers was a bit over the top. Still, don't these credit card companies call *us* at home? And besides, that's what the magazine's lawyers are for, right?

A few months ago I never would have had the courage to do such a thing. I was such a worrywart back then, constantly afraid of getting in trouble. And now, having weathered the Belinda investigation, having stood up to Mr. Bigshot in Hollywood, and having taken responsibility for my health, I'm finding that worry is the world's most useless, unhelpful emotion. It accomplishes nothing besides spiking your blood pressure and increasing your stress. Better to relax and Be Fab in true Belinda Apple style.

Like Joel says, we're all going to be dead in sixty years, so why fret?

Or maybe it's the whole-food diet that I'm on (kind of . . . . I could take only so many days without Drost dark chocolate or the occasional slice of cheddar). Or the daily exercise that my body now craves.

Don't get me wrong. I despise running when I start and even after more than four months of regular jogs I still cannot run for four miles without stopping or slowing down. I'm not sure I ever will. I have to mix it up between running and walking. (Or pausing to suddenly examine that fascinating leaf on the ground.)

But once I'm in the cemetery by myself, away from my neighbors, once my legs have absorbed the shock that they will be expected to exert themselves for the next forty minutes, I am able to breathe deeply and enjoy my body moving simply for moving's sake. It's late fall, almost winter. My feet are shuffling through brown leaves. The air is crisp with the promise of new possibilities, and I am now much lighter and healthier than I used to be.

Except that . . . nothing else has changed. Absolutely nothing.

I guess I'd always fantasized that when I lost weight, my world would magically transform. That I'd be trim and blond. Birds would alight on my fingers and handsome, amusing, and kind princes would show up at my door carrying very impractical shoes.

Do you see any princes on my doorstep? Believe me. Bitsy would be all over them like white on rice. That girl is one serious social climber.

In fact it is stunning how unexciting my life is now that I'm thinner.

This is my glamorous routine: I get up in the mornings. I drink a glass of water. I do ten brutal pushups per Jim's instructions, twenty-five crunches, and a bunch of stretches before clipping the leash on Otis and making my way to the cemetery.

I've also bought a couple of five-pound barbells that

I lift while watching taped episodes of *General Hospital*, stepping into the bathroom to check my technique in the mirror. It's a heck of a lot better than torturing myself on a treadmill and staring dumbly at CNN, or, worse, battling Rider in the gym weight room.

After the morning exercise thing, I take a shower, eat some All Bran or brown rice with blueberries or a cut up dried apricot, count up my Weight Watchers points, pack a lunch of soup in a Thermos and an apple, and go to work. Then I come home, make a salad with some chicken or hardboiled egg, clean up, maybe do some laundry or a crossword puzzle, work on Belinda's column, read, watch TV, and go to sleep. The next day I do it again.

Thrilling, huh?

There are moments when I feel particularly sorry for myself. Sorry that my days are flowing seamlessly one into the other, sorry that I can't help shake the perception that everyone else is doing better than I am. Nancy's in shape and back with Ron, at least sexually. Deb is thinner than I ever imagined. Eileen is getting married. Lisa's dating the real Chip in Tech Ass. While I'm treading water, coming home to my peach apartment and my cat and wondering just how long this loneliness is going to last. Dreading that the answer might be forever.

These are the days when I'm tempted to chuck it all and call Domino's for a large pizza with extra cheese and pepperoni. Or when I'm strolling past Olive's

Deli and Bakery on Witherspoon and whiff the heady aroma of warm yeast and baking bread. Why can other people go into Olive's and order what they want, but not me? Why must I be punished? Why must I never have the plea sure of a sweet almond bear claw on my lips again?

Give in a voice whispers. *Sweet rich crushed almonds in a buttery, flaky croissant. Just this once. What's the worst an almond bear claw can do? Don't you deserve some fun for once, a bit of luxury?*

Then I look down and see what all the bits of luxury have done to my thighs and think no, not today. Change requires change. I can't suddenly be slim with the same old habits. If I could, I'd stock up on bear claws and chocolate tortes with whipped cream and raspberry sauce. (I think my heart just trembled.)

To get me through these trials, I rely on the Cinderella Pact and my fellow "journeyers," Nancy and Deb. Nancy reminds me that an almond bear claw's not going to kill me, though it could set me back psychologically so why take the risk? Anyway, think of Chester Markham, the nasty owner of the Willoughby. We have to wait only one month to shame him. And as soon as I think of outing Chester as a fat phobe, my dreams of bear claws disappear.

And that's what makes the Cinderella Pact so special.

Sometimes in our efforts to remain on course, Deb or Nancy will meet me at the Quakerbridge Mall after dinner and we'll motivate ourselves by "doing Lane

Bryant." Doing Lane Bryant involves us searching for the smallest size pants, trying them on and discovering—oops!—they're *too big*! Nancy will call from the dressing room for a smaller size. I'll bring it to her and she'll yell that it's much too large and both of us will squeal. Sick. I know. But something's got to get us past the food court.

Nancy and I don't dare go into the "normal" end of Lord & Taylor or any major department store, however, for fear that we won't fit into the sizes they have, that we are without size. We picture the sales clerks pursing their lips as we exit the dressing room filled with pants that couldn't make it past our knees and the sales clerks politely but firmly directing us to "women's," one floor up.

Deb assures us this is impossible, that we would probably fit into even the fourteens easily. Already she is squeezing herself into size sixteen Kate Hill brown velveteen pants and green beaded camisoles. Deb is distancing herself as far as possible from the decades of her mother's hand-sewn flowered jumpers. Her sweaters are low-cut and tight, in bright colors like tangerine and lime and lemon. Nothing she owns is in pink, not even her new love—black lace thongs.

Nancy says Deb is regressing to her twenties which she misspent as a fat young mama cooped up in a house with young kids. She has taken to lecturing Deb that shooting darts three night a week down at the Tiger Tail with assorted construction crews is flirting with danger.

"No, it's not. It's flirting with men," Deb says.

"Have you forgotten that you're married?" Nancy retorts.

"So what? Flirting isn't violating any vows." Deb flashes her new professionally whitened teeth. "I predict you will be worse than I am once you give in to the sexy women inside each of you."

I'm afraid she's right.

Not a night goes by when I spend much of my time trying to avoid thinking about Chip, aka Dave Stanton. I don't need a psych degree on my wall to realize that perhaps I am engaged in some over-compensating. I'd rather do another lap around the cemetery on a ninety-degree day than relive our sunset beach walk in Malibu or, worse, my disastrous margarita-fueled Rod Stewart impersonation. I get red just thinking about it.

Chip raises all sorts of disturbing questions. If I had been thinner in California, would he have fallen for me? Would he have joined me in bed instead of leaving me with a six a.m. cab call? Would he have called since I got home?

"Don't torture yourself," Nancy says as we cautiously peek in the window of Abercrombie & Fitch, Mecca of the young and thin. "It is what it is. Over. Look back on Chip as your moot court. A warmup for the real thing. And be grateful he was such a nice guy."

"But I don't want him to be a warmup. I'm warmed up enough. I'm ready for the real thing."

There's another, far less romantic reason why I try not to think of Chip, and that is the investigation into

Belinda Apple. The powers that be at *Sass!* have been strangely silent on that front. Too silent. There've been no e-mails from David Stanton, no missives from Lori DiGrigio. Charlotte Dawson, Belinda's agent with whom I've spoken for all of five minutes since the Sweet Dream production fiasco, says no one from *Sass!* has contacted her either.

And then, just when I'm adjusting to the fact that everything is returning to normal, that Chip will not be a part of my life, I open Belinda's e-mail the Monday after Thanksgiving and find this:

To: belinda.apple@sassmag.com
From: hankstamper@hotmail.com
Re: Private and confidential

Dear Belinda:
I've been a fan of yours for years and never thought I'd be writing. However, I have a problem that is so personal, I can't discuss it with anyone I know. So I'm coming to you, albeit reluctantly.

For many years I've been involved with a woman named Olivia who was, I thought, everything I wanted in a wife. She had style, wit, beauty. She was gorgeous. But lately I've realized something was missing, something that makes me feel alive and happy.

This change of feelings started when I went home on business and met a woman who, even in writing this e-mail about her, makes me smile. I met her in a gym weight room, of all places, where she was challenging the biggest man to a dead-lift contest. Later, I witnessed her deliver a swift right hook to a woman who'd insulted her. I know the way I'm describing her makes her sound like a bar hall queen. However, she is anything but.

During a recent visit to my area, I realized this woman—Nola—was someone I wanted to get to know further. The problem is Olivia, whom I've been living with for over a year. She is under the impression, one that I'll admit I gave her before meeting Nola, that we will be together forever. And part of me feels I owe her that after so many years of a relationship.

To that end, I tried to forget Nola. I purposely did not call or write her, I did not come home for Thanksgiving. And yet it's been to no avail. I think of her constantly, wonder how she's doing, if she's seeing anyone.

In short, I think I have fallen in love.

My question is this: Is it ethical to tell a woman like Olivia who has been with me for so long that I want to separate for a while to consider whether my feelings for Nola are genuine?

Or should I just "grow up" as my mother says and "do the right thing"?

I'd appreciate any insight you can offer. Thank you.

CONFUSED IN CALIFORNIA

For an hour, I sit in my guest bedroom with Otis on my lap contemplating all the many ramifications of this note. I cry. I shout. I pace. And then, finally, I sit down and write a private reply from my heart.

Chapter Thirty-Two

"Devlin!"

Lori DiGrigio is rushing over to me, her face flushed. She is all a-titter, tugging at a new white cashmere sweater over an incredibly short black knitted skirt, which also must be new since it is completely lint-free. Her jet-black hair is glossy and angled. She's practically sparkling.

"How do I look?" She says this like a horse so as not to smudge her shiny red lip gloss.

Lori has never asked me for my fashion opinion before, so something must be up. "You look—uh—good, Lori. What's the big occasion?"

"The meeting."

"What meeting?"

"The meeting with David Stanton."

"Oh. *That* meeting."

I do a quick check. Sure enough, there are the telltale straps of her red thong, and would that be a brand new Victoria's Secret push-up bra? I believe it is. If I were her, I'd hold off on that until after the wedding, though.

"Well, have fun," I say, flipping through a fresh pile

of "On Being Fab!" letters I've just printed out. Lori doesn't do real work, so she has the luxury of heading to Stanton's mansion for coffee and chitchat with the publisher.

Meanwhile, the rest of us staffers are killing ourselves for the double Christmas issue. This year management wants expanded editorial copy so *Sass!* isn't 250 pages of just glossy watch, makeup, and underwear ads (though no one's complaining about that). Unfortunately, double the copy means double the editing for me and twice as much writing too, since Belinda's column is being stretched from one to two pages.

I came in all weekend to get a handle on the work and barely made a dent. Now, on Monday, I'm beat. I didn't even bother to dress in office clothes because what's the point? Not like I'm going anywhere. I'll be chained to this desk until our deadline on Wednesday.

"Aren't you going?" Lori asks, loitering by my desk for no reason.

"I can't. I've got too much work." I pick up a letter from Sex Slave in Suburbia that I haven't read, but will definitely put on my "in" pile based on that signature alone.

"You have to go." Lori pouts. "The meeting's mandatory."

"It's also forty minutes away."

For a nanosecond, panic crosses Lori's pale, severe face before her old confidence snaps back like a whip. "No, it's not. It's here. Eleven a.m. on Monday in the conference room. Didn't you get the memo?"

Actually I did get the memo and I promptly round-filed it, as I do with any letter that begins: From: Lori DiGrigio, Managing Editor.

"Uh, I glanced at it," I lied.

"I didn't get the memo," says Joel, who's been eavesdropping while pretending to lay out the women's holiday fiction supplement.

"You didn't get the memo because you're not invited," Lori retorts. "This is a personnel matter involving David Stanton, me, and Nola. It's strictly confidential."

Joel nods. "Oh, so it's about Belinda Apple then."

That catches my attention enough for me to tear myself away from Had-It-Up-to-Here-Mother-in-Law. "The meeting's about Belinda?"

"Hello? Where have you been for four months? Of course it's about Belinda. You didn't think David Stanton's simply swept that mess under the rug, did you? And if you'd actually read my memo, you'd know that you're supposed to bring in that report I requested outlining what you've found out about her. David's putting it together for his own final report to the board in New York this week."

Do you know those moments where you get incredible news, maybe even news you've been waiting for—like winning a lottery, or dreading, like notification of an IRS audit—and you can't quite comprehend the reality of it? You might see the words in front of you. Hear them in your ears. And, yet, it all seems so unreal. As though it's happening on TV or to someone else.

I reassess Lori's red underwear. "You mean *young* David Stanton?"

"Yes, I mean young David Stanton. Though I can call him Dave, since I'm management." Lori checks her impeccably manicured nails. "It might be better if you keep it to Mr. Stanton, though, seeing as you're staff."

I sit there stupidly gazing at the pile of letters in my lap. He's here. Chip. Or, rather, Mr. Stanton. Here in this very building where I am to meet him in a matter of minutes. And I'm dressed like a freaking bag lady.

My hair, unwashed, is pulled into a tight ponytail. I'm in a baggy pair of Levi's and a black turtleneck sweater covered by cat hair. Plus, in my grogginess I might have forgotten to wear deodorant, though I haven't been able to find a secluded moment to sniff my armpit to make sure.

Super. The last time Chip saw me I was loopy on tequila and now I'm outfitted for Dumpster diving. Plus, I've just noticed a spreading red Sharpie blotch on my jeans. It's all so pathetic, so loser-me, that I could very well sit here and cry.

So many silly fantasies I've entertained of running into Chip on the streets of Princeton. Naturally, I'm slim and beautiful and decked to the hilt in a beautiful, flowing dress and Chip has to do a double take before he recognizes me. "Nola? Nola Devlin!" he exclaims. "My God, you're gorgeous!" And then he can't help himself. He takes me in his arms and bends down, bringing his lips to mine as he confesses the passion he has tried to deny all these months in California.

"Is everything OK, Nola?" Joel's avuncular voice breaks through my daydream.

"Sure." I see the Sharpie stain again and wince. "It's just that I wish I were dressed better."

"I'll say," Lori agrees. "For someone who's lost as much weight as you have, Devlin, I'd have expected you to improve your wardrobe. Especially in the office and especially on the day you get to meet the future publisher of *Sass!* Though it's too late now. You'll just have to go like you are." And she stomps off ahead, her knit skirt hugging her well-toned thighs perfectly.

Future publisher of *Sass!* What did Lori mean by that?

"Hey, Cinderella," Joel says softly. "Don't forget the moral of the story."

"Mice make lousy footmen?"

Joel smiles beneath his graying beard. "True beauty needs no adornment."

"That's a bass-ackward philosophy for an editor of a magazine that makes most its profits from cosmetic ads."

"I know. Don't tell anyone. Now, quit stalling and go get him."

I stop by the ladies' room and attempt to adorn my beauty nevertheless with a touch-up of pink lip gloss and a pair of faux gold hoop earrings I found in my desk drawer.

Resigned, I carry my trusty yellow legal pad and pen into the conference room where Lori has positioned herself in front of the door, her legs crossed, the straps of her red thong peeking ever so slightly above her black knit skirt. Alicia, her evil debutante/henchwoman Valley Girl secretary is smirking behind her.

"Dress-down day?" Alicia asks as I quickly sit farthest from the door, where I feel safest. "Or is this like a grunge thing you've got going?"

"It's called meeting a deadline, Alicia. I've been working fourteen, fourteen-hour days straight."

Alicia smirks. "Ohmigod. Like, I could never do that. Eight hours is definitely my limit."

Lori clears her throat to get our attention. "Before Mr. Stanton arrives, there are a couple of things you should know about him, Nola," she says, checking the door to make sure Chip's not within earshot. "First of all, he's used to dealing with L.A. types. I know that you, being an inveterate East Coaster, haven't a clue what that means, so I'll explain."

"Thanks," I say, trying to keep a straight face.

"Mr. Stanton is extremely high-powered, a weekend warrior. He's used to and expects from his employees enthusiasm and energy. He likes to be surrounded by young, bright staff who can rapid-fire ideas just as fast as he can fire them back. There's even a certain rhythm to his process."

"Like at Starbucks?" Alicia asks. "You know, where I come in and order a triple caf skim latte and the girl at the cash register grabs a cup, marks it, and hands it to the girl at the latte machine, yelling, 'Triple caf skim lat?' I love that rhythm."

Lori is aghast. "Just take notes, OK, Alicia?"

"OK."

The prison camp overseer swings back to me. "Listen, Nola, I don't want to see you sitting there like a bump on a log, which is what you normally do at our meetings. Mr. Stanton won't approve at all. If you knew him as I do, you'd be dressed more L.A., for one thing, and you'd be sharp and energetic. This is your career we're talking about. Not to mention that one staff member reflects on all the staff."

"How well do you know Mr. Stanton?" I ask. I can't help it.

Lori could kiss me, she's clearly so grateful for that question. "Very well," she begins coyly. "When he was here this summer, he sat across from me at this table, three chairs down. That's how close I was to him. Within touching distance."

"Wow." I try to look suitably impressed.

"And don't forget that phone call this week," Alicia points out. "Remember? He asked if you'd found Belinda's personnel file or if it was still misplaced."

Lori frowns.

I pull in my chair conspiratorially. "So what's he like. You know, in the flesh?"

"Between us? Unbelievable." Lori flashes another

324

wary glance at the door. "The most gorgeous, intelligent man I've ever met."

Also rich. Get your priorities straight.

"Think of Owen Wilson with an Ivy League education and a five-billion-dollar trust fund."

"Really?"

"Haven't you read the articles about him in *Esquire*?" Lori says.

Heavens, no. I fall asleep just looking at the cover. "I'm afraid not."

"Two years ago he made their America's Ten Top Bachelors list. They had him standing on a beach, leaning against his surfboard. You know, he could have been in Armani at his desk, but he's so secure with himself that he chose to be on the beach. And talk about abs."

Alicia holds up her pencil. "Didn't you tell me once that you thought he really liked you and that he was pretty much coming on to you at that meeting."

If Alicia keeps this up, she's going to be out of a job like Lori's former assistant, Dawn. At least Dawn knew when to keep her mouth shut. Also knew which end of a pencil goes to the paper, I think, watching Alicia mindlessly scribble a note using her eraser tip.

"I am so sorry I'm late."

Like hens scattering upon hearing the rooster, we three women push back our chairs and attempt to look professional. I can't help but steal a glance at Lori, who is practically salivating as first *Sass!* lawyer Arthur Krauss from Krauss, Krauss and Krauss enters and then His Majesty, His Royal Highness Lord "Chip" Stanton.

Chapter Thirty-Three

Chip smiles politely at Lori and Alicia, who are both gawking worse than teenage groupies meeting Green Day. Arthur Krauss the lawyer, gruff as usual, begrudgingly shakes my hand and then slaps his briefcase onto the table, clicks open the brass lock, and begins removing file upon file that no doubt concern the misdeeds of one Belinda Apple—aka, me.

Watching him, I begin to feel slightly ill. So ill that I don't notice Chip smiling at me from the other end of the table.

"Good to see you again, Miss Devlin," he says crisply, his lips twitching ever so slightly as he sits and opens his own file.

"Oh!" Lori peeps, her eyes shifting from me to Chip. "So you've met. I was about to introduce you."

"No introductions necessary. Miss Devlin and I have, um, worked together before."

In your face! I want to shout to Lori.

"I see." Lori's eyes shift once more to Alicia, who is busily erasing the eraser marks she's made on the page.

I have never seen Chip in a suit before and I have to say it beats a T-shirt any day. It looks like Armani. (Though maybe the T-shirts were too.) His hair, still longish, is tucked neatly behind his ears so that he is more commanding and respectable. I think about what Lisa said when I showed her a picture of Chip, how sex with a man like him must be like the Imax version of lovemaking.

"OK. Let's get to why we're here. Belinda Apple." There's a new authority to Chip's voice. "My goal is to put this matter to rest before I officially take over as publisher of *Sass!* next month."

So it's true! I accidentally let out a gasp of excitement and then cough to hide it. Chip raises his eyes briefly to me and then continues.

"Miss DiGrigio. Have you found out anything more since we last spoke?"

Lori licks her bottom lip. "Please. Call me Lori."

"OK, Lori. Since you hired the legendary Belinda Apple, I assume you have the most insight of all of us."

I slide down slightly in my seat, hoping somehow this will make me less noticeable.

"My conclusion is that we, meaning Nola Devlin and I," Lori points to me in case Chip's not sure, "especially Nola, who has been editing Miss Apple for a year, have been, for lack of a better word, shystered."

"How do you spell that?" Alicia asks.

"Shystered, huh?" Chip reclines as though he were getting ready to watch a double feature. "What do you mean, exactly?"

"I mean that clearly Belinda Apple does not exist. Having been hired by your father . . ."

Chip sets his jaw. It's obvious he does not appreciate this ass-saving zinger.

". . . this fraudulent personage proceeded to take advantage of a somewhat naive and gullible editor."

"You are referring to Miss Devlin."

Did he just wink at me?

"Yes. Nola, uh, Miss Devlin has edited this so-called Belinda Apple for a year, e-mailing and speaking to her directly at least once a week and despite that, never managed to detect that this person was a phony. I don't know what this says about Miss Devlin's editing ability or her judgment—"

"Which I'm sure is excellent." Chip cuts her off. "Miss Devlin? What's your take on this matter? Do you think Belinda Apple is a fraud, perhaps a writer from another magazine?"

"No." I sit up and flip officiously through my yellow tablet on which I have very competently written a very thorough itemization for Eileen's wedding—*shoes, flowers, chicken or fish? White wine or champagne?* Names of potential bands, caterers, florists, and cake designers. "I feel confident that Belinda Apple, who-ever she is, does not work for another magazine. Nor has she engaged in plagiarism, which I guess is your biggest concern."

"It is." Krauss speaks for the first time. "How can you be sure she's not a plagiarist? After all, if Jayson Blair can rip off the *New York Times* for over a year, if James Frey can dupe Oprah, I'm sure this woman, or man, can fool you."

Krauss wears a bow tie that I'm tempted to give a swift, sharp tug. "Considering Belinda wasn't assigned to report on a news story, unlike Blair, she could have been writing in her bathtub"—*and in fact she has*—"and it wouldn't have mattered. I keep up on other magazines, and I haven't seen any columns that come close to Belinda's despite my, um, naiveté."

I don't dare look at Chip after this last line.

"Hmmph." Krauss returns to his files, disappointed.

"And what about you Art? What's your opinion?" Chip asks.

Krauss pauses, thinking. Nancy once told me that law firms teach their new associates to do this in the courtroom, as silence motivates the juries to listen. Nancy pulls the same stunt when disputing a restaurant tab and I swear, she's always gotten her way. Nancy will argue anything: Wasn't that chocolate mousse on the menu for $4.25? Then why is it listed as $4.00? Was it defective? Did the chef spit on it? Or can't you add? And if so, let's go over the whole bill and see what else you can't do.

"Without all the evidence I'd like in this situation, my best educated guess is that Belinda Apple is"—he turns to me—"one of your own employees."

He and I regard one another levelly. I don't give an inch.

"Impossible!" Lori declares.

"Is it?" asks Krauss. "Why?"

"Because, because," Lori sputters, "because I would have known. I've interviewed her myself. I certainly would have recognized her voice if she'd been on my staff. Belinda had a very authentic British accent."

"And an American cell phone number," Krauss points out.

"It saves her money!"

Krauss laughs an evil lawyer laugh, which is more reminiscent of a hiss. "That should have been the first clue you were being, as you said, shystered. There is no such thing as an American cell phone working in the UK—at least not one that would save the user money. Do you know how expensive it is to use an American cell in a foreign country?"

"I do," pipes up Alicia. "I was in Paris in my junior year abroad? And my purse got stolen in the Louvre? And when they found it the phone was gone? But you should have seen the charges for the first hour before I reported it stolen. Ohmigod. I could have bought, like, a fur coat for that, if I was into fur, which I'm most definitely not. Except fake. Good fake is cool."

Lori slumps, seething.

"OK," Chip says. "We're getting somewhere. Belinda Apple is most likely an employee at *Sass!* Goddammit, that really irks me. Bad enough to have someone from the outside lying, but one of our own employees . . . It's so disloyal, so cheap. I can't stand liars, especially liars who are so cowardly they have to hide behind a made-up persona."

I sink down even lower. It is more than I can bear to hear him go off this way on someone he hates, namely me. There is no hope, I realize at that moment. Even if by some wild Disney-like chance he admitted his love for me, there would be that awful secret hanging over us and the moment where I would have to confess and that would be it. The end.

"If we paid her, and of course we did, then all we have to do is check her IRS identification number against the current employee's," Krauss suggests brightly.

A hot new burst of panic sweeps through me. I hadn't thought of that. I grip the side of my tablet to keep myself steady and try to think whether *Sass!* has my social down as Belinda's. Let's see, Charlotte sends me all my checks. She's the only one who had Belinda's social . . . Wait. No. There was that form . . .

"Wouldn't this person have expected that, or were they too stupid?" Lori asks.

Too stupid, I answer for her.

"Whoever they are, they better have used their own social security or taxpayer ID, because if they didn't they're going to be in a lot more trouble than just with us. They'll have the IRS to answer to as well."

The IRS!

"Right, Miss Devlin?" Krauss asks me.

"Huh?" I say. "Oh, yeah. I don't know. I don't really pay attention to taxes."

Krauss shakes his head ever so slightly.

"I'm not sure I have the authority to make that kind of inquiry," Lori says nervously, looking to Krauss for guidance.

Krauss is about to reply, probably about to say damn

straight you have that kind of authority, when Chip jumps in. "Perhaps you're right, Lori. This is a job best left up to the publisher. I'll ask personnel to cross-check the socials. Maybe the computer can do it in minutes."

Devastation. That's it. I'm sunk. I didn't have a spouse with a number I could use. It's mine all right. The computer will take one second to announce NOLA DEVLIN IS YOUR WOMAN!

"Gee," Alicia says. "What'll happen when you find the person?"

Krauss hisses again.

Chip shrugs. "I'll cross that bridge when I get to it. For now, my main interest is outing a skunk from the staff."

Brilliant. Now I'm a skunk. Me with the $150 worth of Chanel I sprayed on in the bathroom.

"I totally agree," says Lori. "By the way, now that you're back in Jersey and in control of *Sass!*, David, are you going to continue the tradition your father and mother started years ago?"

"What tradition was that?"

Lori giggles as though how could he possibly not know. "Why, the annual holiday open house. Anybody who was anybody was invited. Your mother did such a fantastic job of decorating that gorgeous mansion. I swear, I haven't seen a Christmas tree that big outside of Rockefeller Center."

Chip shuffles his papers and shuts his file quietly. "That was my stepmother who did the decorating, not my mother. I was with her in California for the holidays. And now that my father is moving permanently to Manhattan, I don't think he'd care."

"Oh." Lori, mortified for the umpteenth time, brushes invisible lint off her cashmere.

"On the other hand, it does sound like a good idea," he adds, graciously. "Sure. Why not? And since you remember what it was like, Lori, I'll put you in charge of drawing up the guest list and organizing the whole shebang. Unless . . . you have too much work with the double issue."

"I don't have any work at all," she blurts, so thrilled to be picked as head of the prom committee she has no idea what she just admitted. "I'd love to. How many can I invite?"

"Well, if I'm going to do this, I'm going to do it right. How about . . . four hundred?"

Four hundred! Is he nuts?

"But," he adds, thoughtfully, "let's change it from a Christmas party to a winter solstice gala or something to make it more inclusive."

Yes, I'm sure the three pagans in Princeton will appreciate that.

Lori's eyes are gleaming. "Winter solstice. That's perfect because December twentieth falls on a Saturday this year."

"I know," says Chip.

"I'll have to work very closely with you on this so that I don't mess up any of the details," Lori says. "I hope you won't mind me contacting you at night on your off hours."

"Better than at work."

Lori flashes me a smile of victory.

This is just great. Wait until I tell Joel. Lori will probably be signing the invitations herself as Mrs. David Stanton III*—(*in future).

Chip gets up to go and stops at the door. "Just be sure you send an invite to Belinda Apple. You never know, she might just show." And then, as if putting Lori in her place, he says, "And I'd like to see you in my office Miss Devlin, ASAP."

I feel Lori and Alicia's stares burning through me as I take a left toward the publisher's office instead of a right toward mine. Lori obviously wants to ask me what's going on, but she doesn't dare. She hasn't yet calibrated my relationship with Chip.

Chip is standing at the window of his huge paneled office when I enter, knocking hesitantly on the door. He turns and smiles, motioning for me to close the door so we can be alone.

My heart is racing. I have no idea what to expect. I keep wishing I looked better. Oh, brother. Why did I have to wear pants with a Sharpie blotch today?

"It is so good to see you," he says, still standing, his hand in his pocket like a Ralph Lauren ad.

"I only wish you saw me in a decent outfit," I say. "I'm so sorry. I've been working overtime and I—"

"Nola," he says softly. "You look fine. In fact, you look more than fine."

I exhale. Then I go for it. "And while I'm apologizing, I should say I'm sorry for getting so plastered on margaritas. I hadn't eaten all day and—"

"My fault. They were very strong. You didn't know I made the first a double."

"You didn't!" I cover my mouth to laugh.

"I felt you needed some loosening up and took the liberty."

"OK. Then I'm sending the bill for a bar of soap to you. Do you know how long it took me to scrub off Harley Jane Kozak's autograph?"

Chip smiles. "Probably about as long as it took me to get your godawful rendition of 'Forever Young' out of my head."

"It's gone? Hold on." I open my mouth to sing when Chip rushes over and covers it with his hand.

Suddenly we are inches apart. His hand is on the small of my back and he is bending toward me. It feels so good to be held by him, so close that I think he just might kiss me.

"Nola," he whispers, "I, uh . . ."

There is a sound outside his door and we break away. Lori DiGrigio is enough of a fink to rat us out if she caught us. Which could be very bad if Chip is trying to establish himself as the publisher.

Worse, if he has decided to stay with Olivia.

"I think I should go," I say, tucking a strand of hair behind my ear. "Holiday issue and all that."

"Right." Chip steps back. "See you around, then."

"Sure."

I put my hand on the doorknob and it's then that

Chip says, "I wonder if you've been reading the e-mail that comes to Belinda's box, I mean now that you've taken over her position while she's on leave."

But all I do is smile and open the door. I know better than to give him the satisfaction of an answer.

Chapter Thirty-Four

"I still don't understand how we're supposed to size a dress for Belinda. I mean, can't we ship it to her in England and she can get it fitted and then she can bring it with her?"

Eileen is chattering a mile a minute, proving indeed that nonstop talking can provide a strenuous workout. Perhaps I should take up incessant gossip.

This is her fifth fitting at Weddings by Chloe, and Chloe herself is wrestling with the size 5, soon to be size 4, Christos that really is an elegant dress. The embroidered bodice perfectly hugs Eileen's torso so that she is a perfect princess rising out of a swirl of satin and tulle, its faint cream color highlighting the warmth of her red hair.

"Eileen, you're stunning," I have to say as Chloe and I both stand back to admire Eileen on the dais in front of the many mirrors.

My mother runs out of the dressing room in a bilious pale green mother-of-the-bride chiffon special screaming, "Let me see! Let me see!" Then, pulling out one of the disposable cameras she seems to carry at all times these days, clicks maniacally. "You and Jim are going to have so much fun looking at these years from now. Trust me, it's the impromptu photos that are the best."

Eileen twists and turns. "Do I really look good?"

"Like my Cinderella," Mom says, adding under a breath, "though a bit anorexic, if you ask me."

My heart does a hiccup.

"So how are the bridesmaids dresses coming along?" I ask Chloe.

Chloe removes a pin from her mouth. "Such a disaster. Still no deliveries."

"No deliveries?" Eileen whips around. "But it's been four months."

"There's nothing we can do. It is completely out of my hands. Labor dispute, you know. Something about overtime for sewing sequins." Chloe attempts to toss back her sprayed stiff blond-white hair. It doesn't move.

"Such a shame," I say with faux concern. "They were beautiful."

Eileen stamps her tiny foot. "I have to have them. The wedding will be ruined otherwise." My mother trips over the dais to comfort her, an act she performs several times a day lately. I don't know what's up with Eileen, but she certainly is acting like a brat, stamping her feet, throwing dishes, hanging up the phone on people. I wonder if all brides are like this or just my spoiled sister.

"Wait. I might have a solution." Chloe disappears

into her back office and returns holding a gown in a white garment bag. "One of my brides canceled last week, leaving me with a number of these. They are absolutely lovely. Georgio Hermano all satin with a handsome square neck and V back with satin covered buttons in an A-line. It is unusual to find a maids dress that so flatters nearly everyone's figure as this one does."

"What do you think, Nola?" Eileen asks.

I do my best disapproving frown. "I dunno, Eileen. Is this really what you had in mind?"

"It's black!" my mother screeches. "You can't have bridesmaids in black! It'll look more like a funeral than a wedding."

"I beg to differ," Chloe says. "Black is a very au-courant color right now. Especially for an evening winter wedding. So glamorous, don't you think? I mean, black really is the new white in weddings. And with Eileen's radiant red hair, she'll be stunning."

Eileen gives the dress a second-chance glance.

Mom sticks out her lower lip. "Well, it's still maudlin, if you ask me."

"And you agree, Nola?" Eileen checks to make sure.

"I'm sorry," I say pitifully. "I worry that black will make the bridesmaids awfully pale and deathly."

That was the clincher. "I have to say it's growing on me. And black was my second choice," Eileen says.

"It was?" Mom says. "You never told me that."

"I told Belinda."

Lie. One-hundred-percent lie.

338

"And she approved," Eileen concludes. "So it must be au courant."

"Belinda Apple is a slut," Mom says. "I've said it before, I'll say it again."

"Please! She's my maid of honor."

"Belinda Apple?" Chloe chimes, well experienced as she is in diffusing tension between mothers and daughters. "Personally, I love her. She's an absolute gas. Though I understand she's not writing her column anymore, at least not really, that she has a ghostwriter or something."

I examine the toes of my boots and think about something boring, like this past Thanksgiving when Jim handed me a smiley-face sticker for eating only turkey, green beans, and a spoonful of pumpkin pie. (Oh, had he only known about my midnight trip to the leftovers in my refrigerator!)

"Mom, I don't care what you say. I'm going with the black dress. After all, Belinda is famous. She knows. Chloe, can you get six by the wedding in the right sizes?"

Chloe flashes me a subtle smile. "Absolutely. As a matter of fact, the bride who canceled had six bridesmaids too."

"Excellent!" Eileen claps like a little girl.

A-line. Square neck. Black. Every zaftig girl's dream of a bridesmaid's dress.

I couldn't have chosen better myself, which, in fact, I did.

Chapter Thirty-Five

"This is the last one. I don't know how you're going to get it to Belinda but, hey, I've done my part. I nearly forgot about it, having sent out the others weeks ago. I hope that's not a problem."

Lori DiGrigio hands me a slim white envelope on which *Miss Belinda Apple* is scrawled in calligraphy.

I don't have to open it to know what the letter is and, more importantly, know that I didn't get one as well.

Lori stands by my desk waiting for this question: *What about me? Did I get an invitation to David Stanton's holiday open house?* But I refuse to give her the satisfaction.

"I'll see what I can do," I say, slipping the envelope into my purse. "Though I haven't spoken to Belinda in months. I don't even know how to contact her."

"I don't really care, frankly. I'm too exhausted, and it's only the beginning. I've been sooo busy lining up the caterers and the party planners. Do you know how many fresh pine garlands I've had to order? Forty-two. That's how many doorways and mantel pieces and staircases we'll have to adorn."

It is positively killing her that I am not begging for details. Who's invited? Who's accepted? What's the dress code?

Next to me, Joel tugs at his familiar brown cardigan and bends his head over a set of layout sheets. Then plugs his ears as Lori goes on and on about the guest list: the governor, U.S. Senator Frank Lautenberg, Christie Todd Whitman (whom Chip apparently used to call Aunt Chrissy as a child), even the Boss himself along with his wife, Mrs. Bruce Springsteen, a name I happen to write expertly, having scrawled it on most of my eighth-grade notebooks a zillion times.

There will also be no fewer than four Christmas trees, New Jersey homegrown, each at least twelve feet tall and trimmed with the famous Stanton heirloom ornaments dating back several centuries from when the family still lived in England. There will be a string quartet in one room and a brass quartet in another belting out "Joy to the World" as guests mingle over champagne and hot cider wearing their diamond necklaces and those omnipresent Manolos.

"How come you're so glum?" Lori pesters Joel.

"I hate Christmas."

"Why?"

"Because every grown-up Jewish kid hates Christmas, do you mind? Isn't it enough that as soon as I step outside, I'll be blasted with Christmas lights all the drive home while I'm forced to listen to Christmas music on the radio and walk past stores with that fucking Santa Claus? Do I have to be subjected to it at work, too?"

"Well, if that's your way of finding out if you've been invited, you're not," Lori says, though clearly Joel had no desire, interest, or even an inkling of curiosity about whether he was invited.

"And, I'm sorry, Nola . . ." Lori makes a pity face.

Here it comes. She just couldn't resist, could she?

"But as much as *we* wanted to invite you, *we* just couldn't find a way without having to invite the rest of the staff."

"We?" I can't help it. I take the bait.

"Yes. Dave and I. We've been working *verrry* closely. In fact, I'm having dinner with him at his house tonight, to go over plans."

It hurts. It does, to think of the two of them acting like a married couple decorating "their" home, inviting "their" guests—one of whom is pointedly not me.

Keep it professional, Nola. Remember what Nancy says—that he's the warm-up for the real thing.

Still, I have to ask. "Isn't Olivia helping out?"

Lori wrinkles her nose. "Olivia? What would she have to do with the party planning?"

OK. Now I'm confused. Unfortunately, Joel steps in so I can't pry.

"Better Stanton should work late and focus on mollifying advertisers than eat pizza with you," Joel says. "Have you seen the circulation numbers for the holiday issue? The pits."

This, I know, is a total lie as (a) circulation numbers are highly guarded secrets known only to our advertising department and Interpol and (b) the holiday issue isn't even out yet. Still, it's enough to shake up Lori so that she must go tottering off on her high heels to check.

"Why do you let her do that to you?" Joel says after Lori's out of earshot.

"Do what?"

"Treat you like such a schlub. That woman thrives on making you a doormat and look at you. You're gorgeous, thin like a willow, and you're knocking off that column like an old pro."

I smile placidly. "It's not as hard as I thought it would be," I lie.

Joel dismisses this. "Nah. You're a natural. What I want to know is, why don't you spruce yourself up some? You know, treat yourself to a new wardrobe. Show off your new figure. Then maybe Mr. Bigshot Publisher will take notice."

That's the thing about Joel. He's flattery, flattery, flattery right up to the last line until he slams with the zinger. He should learn to edit himself.

Plus, I am not as thin as a willow. I am still a hefty girl, though I prefer the word zaftig. Zaftig connotes Mae West—my secret personal role model. All bosom, hips, and attitude. Yes, I'd do all right in life if I could get by as Mae West.

My phone rings. It's Nancy sounding breathless. I eye my watch. Four p.m. Odd.

"How soon can you get to Trenton in this traffic?" she asks.

"Why? What's wrong?"

"Everything, but that's not why I'm calling. I'm about to do something very drastic and I either need to be talked out of it or be supported. Are you game?"

"Give me an hour."

I find Nancy packing up her grand office. Pictures are down and leaning against the walls along with her framed diplomas and citations from various bar associations. Cardboard boxes are out and filled with folders. The fire in her gas fireplace (yes, it's that fancy a law firm) is roaring full strength. Nancy herself is flushed red.

In our friendship that spans two decades, I have never seen Nancy so striking. Her auburn hair is long so that it falls to her shoulders with Pantene-like shine and bounce. Her jet black suit is tailored, making the most of her new waist and slimmer hips. A Diane Von Furstenberg scarf hides her post-fat wrinkles at her neck and her ears are decorated with stunning pearls. She looks years younger—a far, far cry from the harried woman in dusters—and I wish desperately that Ron were here to see her.

"My God, you scared me," she says, putting her hand to her chest. "You completely creeped me out standing in the doorway, staring. What are you doing?"

"Uh, nothing." I step in and close the door. The office is bizarrely quiet for five in the afternoon. The receptionist said everyone was in a meeting. "I think the question of the moment is what are *you* doing?"

"Leaving." She flips through another file and tosses it in the trash. "Probably."

"What does that mean?"

"That I'd rather pack up my office and be good to go

before I get fired than have everyone trotting back and forth, whispering as I pack up my desk."

"Oh." I have no idea what's going on.

"I never could have done this without you, Nola. I hope you know that."

"Get fired?"

"I don't mean that. I mean, tell off Ted Kline in front of the firm."

Now I'm the one with my hand to my chest. Ted Kline is the most powerful lawyer in New Jersey. Taking him aside and delivering a few choice words is one thing, but the whole firm?

"Listen, Nancy . . ."

She pushes me back. "Don't talk me out of it. For months, ever since I told you guys that the reason I let myself blow up was so Kline would lose interest in me, I've been thinking about what it means to stand up for yourself. It's been my little project, shrinking my body while building my self-esteem."

Finished packing, Nancy goes over to the fire and warms her hands, though it is perfectly warm in here and the fire's not really that hot. "I kept telling myself that maybe Kline wasn't so bad and maybe I made the situation worse than it was because I was under a lot of pressure as a young associate or because Ron and I were having financial difficulties."

Financial difficulties—that's a new twist.

"Then, this morning, he did it again. We were standing in the elevator and I noticed him ever so slightly pat the ass of Tanya Williamson, a kid who's

345

so fresh out of law school she still has the bar tapes memorized."

I know "bar tapes" has something to do with the law, but hearing the words made me think of some Paris Hilton Internet spam.

"That's when I realized that even if I'm not on his radar anymore, this guy is constantly on the prowl for fresh meat. He's not going to quit until someone steps forward and slaps him down. You following me, kiddo?"

"Uh, yeah."

"OK." She goes over to her drawer, pulls out a compact and lipstick, and does her lips so they are an affirmative brownish red. Goes very nice with the hair, actually. "I'm ready."

"I'll be right here waiting for you when you get back."

"No way." She takes my hand. "You're going with me. You don't think I'd jump into that shark pool without a witness, do you? How're you at raising your right hand and swearing to the truth, the whole truth, and nothing but the truth?"

If she knew about Belinda, she'd know better than to ask a ridiculous question like that.

"Gentlemen, ladies." Nancy marches in ahead of me, smart and efficient in her suit, a heavy file folder tucked under her arm. I can tell by the way everyone snaps to attention that she is a commanding force here.

Me, on the other hand, not so commanding. The serious faces gathered around the oval table can't help but glance at me questioningly, I'm so out of place in my black elastic-waist skirt, tan ribbed turtleneck sweater, and scuffed boots. Clearly they have concluded I am one of Nancy's lowlife clients, the kind who sue candy bar companies for getting their dentures stuck on caramel.

"This meeting's almost over, Nancy. I thought you were too busy on the Boardman case to attend." A white-haired man with a flushed face and a loud pink-and-navy striped tie that you see on the cover of catalogs but you can't imagine some real man wearing is standing by a chart with all sorts of zigs and zags on it. CLIENTS CONVICTED? BILLABLE HOURS? It's a mystery.

"Maybe someone here can bring her up to speed."

"I don't need to be brought up to speed, and I don't give a tinker's damn about this firm's third quarterly report."

There is a shocked gasp, the kind of shock one might express, say, if it were revealed that the Reverend Pat Robertson had conducted a longtime affair with a hooker—a gay hooker, at that. I suppose this is what passes for scandal at the Barlow, Cafferty and Kline law firm, not giving a "tinker's damn" about quarterly reports.

"Nancy," Kline is saying, his tone instantly patronizing. "If it's outside the scope of the firm's fiscal health, then at least wait until the end."

"Oh, it's within the scope of the firm's fiscal health, all right." Nancy slams the file onto the table and opens it, pulling out a stack of copies that she distributes. When I get mine, I see it is a sworn affidavit of some sort. A "quick, sleazy" read (the kind we do best at *Sass!*) tells me it's from one of Kline's clients swearing that he sexually harassed her during a divorce case.

If Mr. Kline hadn't gotten me more alimony than I asked for as well as full custody of the children and our primary and vacation home, I would have walked, Ms. Suzanne Cantos of Cranbury, New Jersey, writes.

Hmm. Now what would Belinda say about something like that?

"Before we go any further, I think that for obvious reasons this meeting should not be open to non-members."

I look up to see Kline glaring at me.

"Right." I put down the affidavit. (Too bad, because I was just getting to the part where Kline suggests after taking the poor, well not poor exactly, former Mrs. Cantos out to dinner, that she and her fantastic body go back to his place to celebrate.)

Nancy starts to protest but stops, since Kline's obviously got a point.

As I walk toward the door, glad, really, to get out of there, I whisper to Nancy some Belinda-ish words of advice: "If you only stick up for Mrs. Cantos and Tanya Williamson, you're not sticking up for your-

348

self. Keep that in mind."

"I will," she whispers back. "Thanks." She gives my arm a squeeze.

For the next hour, I make small talk with the receptionist who, it turns out, is a complete Bon Jovi groupie like Eileen and, by the way, occasionally sleeps with Kline to keep her job. I hope Nancy in her wisdom had the foresight to interview her, too, because this woman makes Ms. Cantos's story look like Kline wanted to hold hands.

"For the record, he's got a super-small dick. You can barely see it," the receptionist informs me. "Then again, those kinds of guys always do."

Now that's the kind of news you can use.

It's not until six thirty, long after the receptionist has pushed in her chair and gone for the day, that Nancy emerges, ominously alone. Her expression is taut, defiant, and I know immediately who's won.

"Give me your keys, and I'll bring your car around," I say. "And I'll take a box while I'm at it."

Which is when Nancy bends over and dashes for the ladies room where she promptly throws up in a Barlow, Cafferty and Kline private loo for the very last time.

Chapter Thirty-Six

To: belinda.apple@sassmag.com
From: david.stanton@sassmag.com
Re: Holiday Party

Dear Belinda:
After learning that you would be in town for Eileen Devlin's wedding, I made sure that Lori DiGrigio, who is eagerly handling this nightmare of a holiday party I'm throwing, would see to it that you received an invitation. The one she sent to your Deeside address in Scotland was returned with a somewhat puzzling note claiming that you do not live at that address, that you have never lived there and would *Sass!* magazine please "cease and desist" from sending further correspondence to Balmoral Castle. (?)

Anyway, I do hope you've received my invite and that you will come. I promise there will be no talk of whether you have or have not been writing your column.

However, I should confess that I am CONFUSED IN CALIFORNIA, who wrote you about being torn between a woman I have known for many years and a woman I have met recently. That's one of my reasons for inviting you to this party, my selfish need to speak to you, alone.

As an update, there is a tremendous amount of

pressure on me from all sides to allow Olivia to permanently move in with me in Princeton, though she hates the East Coast and has been complaining constantly about the rain and snow since she arrived. She much prefers sunny Southern California.

I tried to talk her out of the move on the premise that time and distance apart would allow us an opportunity to "reevaluate" our relationship. She countered that I was commitment-phobic and that the only way for me to "cure myself" would be for her to show just how committed she was on her end by hiring a moving company to deliver all her belongings to my doorstep last Friday as a surprise!

Talk about an ethical dilemma.

Nor has it helped matters that my father's health continues to decline, and he is not expected to live throughout the upcoming year. Or that my mother back in L.A. is so in love with Olivia that she has sent her own mother's platinum and diamond Medici ring to a jewelry store in Princeton so that it may be reset and presented to Olivia at the party in front of four hundred people.

Help!

I know that in the past you've advised me to really consider whether my feelings for Nola are merely a distraction and that many "commitment jerks," as you so quaintly phrased it, often decide they're in love with women

351

they've just met right when they're about make a big commitment. I've thought about this and I can honestly say that I'm past that phase in my life and that what I feel for Nola goes beyond diversion.

It is hard for me to describe my feelings since, being male, I apparently am biologically incapable of doing so. But in a nutshell, without getting sappy, Nola does it for me. That's all I have to say. When I look at her, when she laughs or smiles and rambles in that endearing way of hers, all I know is that she is the person I want by my side for the rest of my life. I've never felt that way before.

And yet . . . there's Olivia already taking over my house, a beautiful, understanding woman I've known since I was a teenager, a woman who's stuck by me through my moments of supreme pigheadedness. Is it right to simply say thanks, but no thanks for our years together? To say, uh, there's this woman who works at the magazine who seems kind of kooky whom I'd like to get to know first?

I can hear Olivia now, accusing me of being an incurable adolescent, and maybe she's right.

So perhaps you see why I have to meet you— before it's too late.

Please come.

David

I have read and reread this letter so frequently that I recite whole passages by heart as I lie awake at night, unable to sleep because I am thinking about what could be and what never will be with Chip.

Nola *does it for me*. Ditto and double ditto, as Eileen and I would say when were kids. Maybe I'm biologically challenged too on this front, because while in the past I've called other guys cute or drop-dead gorgeous hunks, I am at a loss for words when it comes to David A. Stanton III.

He does it for me. Yup. That's about it.

So what to do? Do I arrive on his doorstep like Olivia's moving men and present myself? I can't. I can't because every word of love Chip has uttered has been to Belinda. Aside from the occasional smile or his playful kiss as my boyfriend in the Annex (which was before he was even interested in me), Chip has said nothing directly to me besides, "How's that car working out?" or "We're looking for an extra feature this spring on the lipstick line. We just nailed the Elan makeup account."

Sometimes I wonder if in these e-mails he is talking about the same Nola. I have to beat back those old insecurities that he can't possibly be referring to me, the frumpy editor in Lane Bryant Venezia Supremes. And then I remind myself of what I've learned during my "exciting weight-loss journey that is guaranteed to change my life forever."

I am and have always been worthy of great love, no

matter how many extra inches of denim around my thighs.

Fortunately, I have our much-awaited shopping spree to look forward to. Our promise to meet six months later at the Willoughby Café and celebrate the Cinderella Pact is here. Nancy has even reserved the table under a different name as part of a grand scheme. I only hope Chester Markham is in the building.

It is weird to think of how we were back then. Nancy was looking at a divorce. Deb was attached to her husband like a lamprey eel. And now Nancy's looking to get back with her husband and it's Deb who's considering divorce.

OK, so our shopping spree and Willoughby Café date is also on the day of the famous Stanton Winter Solstice Gala. You don't think I know that? I know that. Look, I need some kind of celebration to keep my mind off the fact that every other woman in Princeton is having her hair done and her nails lacquered in preparation for the big event.

Apparently, all the salons are booked starting at six a.m. and all the decent eveningwear is sold out. My landlady, Bitsy—who has been invited because she heads the Princeton Historic Revitalization Committee—has been whining that she had to order her dress online. The horrors! At least Nancy and Deb don't know Chip, so I won't be subjected to hearing how they blew the bank on a Carmen Marc Valvo cocktail dress.

It is snowing lightly on December 20, the shortest

day of the year and what I dread will turn out to be the longest night of my life. Nassau Street is so sparkling white and festive, it might as well be the movie set for *It's a Wonderful Life* (the colorized version), what with shoppers bustling by with bags of gifts and carolers singing on the sidewalks. The quaint eighteenth-century street is decorated with pine furs and tasteful little lights that practically scream high-end retail.

Deb and Nancy look fantastic when we rendezvous outside the Willoughby. Deb is in her favorite skinny jeans, high-heeled faux leather boots, and a Calvin Klein peacoat. Her blond hair is no longer bright and frowzy. It is a rich honey color, pulled back straight from her head in a casual, though sophisticated, ponytail, and her makeup is sleek and tasteful. She bears no resemblance to the shy dumpling in the pink jumper back in June.

In her Burberry trenchcoat, Nancy is equally stunning—though a bit paler than usual. She still hasn't been able to find a firm willing to bring her on as a senior partner, and so she's been rambling around her big house, depressed and fretting.

Word on the street is that Ted Kline has smeared her reputation, accusing her of being one of those women who imagine sexual harassment and is out to ruin the careers of all white males. Gee, who would have expected such nasty behavior from the most ruthless attorney in New Jersey?

As for me? I am wearing a clinging cashmere twinset and black velveteen pants—the product of our fabulous shopping spree. At Nancy and Deb's insistence, I went whole hog. In Ann Taylor alone I bought a three-quarter length plush wool coat, a fine knit cashmere turtleneck in gray, and three pairs of flare pants, including this pair in velveteen.

Nancy also convinced me to splurge on the bone-colored cashmere twinset I'm wearing and a pencil skirt. Don't even talk to me about the suede slingbacks ($108!!) I bought to go with these outfits. I was so out of control, my saleswoman wrote her home phone number on her business card—in case I needed her in an emergency!

Figuring it was too late to turn back now, at Talbot's I picked up a wrap dress, several camis and tank tops, not to mention an entire suit. Then there was the shimmering velvet skirt and belts (I never buy belts!) made out of brass and glass stones I threw in at Chico's, where I also snagged a green ribbed turtleneck that clung to every inch of me and thigh-high black boots in leather. The pièce d' résistance? A set of Dolce & Gabbana stretch silk string bikini underwear. (That's when Visa wanted to talk to me personally to make sure my card hadn't been stolen.)

By the end I was giddy and possibly delusional, as I could hear my mother's voice chastising me for spending so much on myself at Christmas when children are hungry and homeless. So I wrote out a check for $500 and slipped it into the bucket of the Salvation Army Santa Claus. He handed me a candy cane in thanks, which I bent down and gave to a kid who was hanging around for the rejects. When I looked up, I saw *It* in the window of Ann Taylor.

It is the most beautiful dress in champagne silk with adorable satin ribbon ties at the waist. It is strapless, though there is a matching silk shawl. My body literally aches to wear such a thing, which I immediately realize is a ridiculous extravagance.

I mean, where would I wear a strapless, dupioni silk dress in champagne? This isn't something you can throw on for running out to the grocery store or even wear to work. It wouldn't be appropriate for Eileen's rehearsal dinner, for which I bought the wrap dress at Talbot's today. No, this is the kind of glorious item that would hang in my closet for years like some pathetic reminder of my fleeting youth, haunting me, reminding me of the dances and balls I never attended and the kisses I never received.

Eventually, when I turn eighty, I will have to resign myself to my spinsterhood, pack the Dress up in its original garment bag, and take it down to the church auxiliary, where I will say in a shaky old lady's voice, "Here. When you sell it, make sure you note that it was never worn." Did I mention the tears welling up in my faded old-lady eyes?

"OK," Nancy announces, shaking me out of my dress lust. "Are we ready to go in?"

Deb opens the door to the Willoughby. "I think I've got my lines down. How about you, Nola?"

"No problem." We've only gone over the script seven times.

The Willoughby is packed with shoppers, even though it's late in the afternoon. We arrive right on time and, sure enough, there is Chester Markham, buzzing about, making small talk with his chic clientele.

"Greene," Nancy says to the maître d'. "Table for three."

The maître d' grabs three menus and directs us to a booth.

"Actually," I say on cue, "could we have the table by the window?"

He frowns. "I'm sorry. It's reserved."

Of course it's reserved. We reserved it ourselves, under the name Cindy Packer.

"Oh, that's too bad." Deb pulls her best pout. "That would have been so nice, to watch everyone passing by on the street, shopping. And look! There are carolers. How sweet."

He assesses Nancy in her elegant Burberry. "Let me talk to the manager. The reservation is twenty minutes late."

This is the moment we've been waiting six months for. Nancy, Deb, and I don't know where to look as the maître d' approaches Chester, points to the table, and then to us. For a minute it seems as though Chester doesn't care. And then he starts walking toward us, his lips set sternly.

"Shit," Deb whispers, "maybe we shouldn't have done this."

Nancy pokes her. "Knock it off. This is what we spent six months dieting for."

"I understand you are interested in the table by the window," Chester says.

"Yes," says Nancy. "It's our favorite."

His squirrel-like eyes take me in, then Deb, and finally, Nancy. There seems to be a moment of recognition, but I must be wrong because he says, "Your favorite spot? But I've never seen you here before, and surely I would have remembered three beautiful women such as yourselves."

Brilliant. Deb giggles and I have to step on her toe to shut her up.

"Really?" Nancy says, the long lost color rising in her cheeks. "Are you sure?"

"I am certain." Chester takes her hand and kisses it gallantly. "And I see no reason why you cannot have the window table."

"But it's reserved."

Still holding on to her hand, Chester confides. "That is nothing. I will take care of everything if the party arrives. Please." He points her to the table but now it is Nancy gripping his hand with an ironlike force.

"On second thought," she says, "I don't think so. I understand there are other places in town to eat. What was the restaurant that you recommended last June? Oh, that's right . . . Hoagie Haven, I believe it was."

She drops Chester's hand dramatically. The moment of victory has been claimed.

He reassesses us, squinting. "Ah, yes," he says. "I thought you were familiar."

"But you said you'd never forget three women as beautiful as us," Deb blurts.

To his credit, Chester throws up his hands. "What can I say? I made a mistake. I've often thought how poorly I handled the situation. I was rude. I apologize. My only excuse was that I'd just entered the business and I didn't know squat about running a restaurant. Had I to do it all over again, I surely would have given you the table . . . as I did just now."

For some reason, this strikes me as extremely funny, and I can't help but burst out laughing. Here we'd made so much out of Chester's bumbling snubbing that we'd put ourselves on a six-month regimen of diet, exercise, and, in Deb's case, major surgery. When all along it was Chester's inexperience to blame.

"What's wrong with you?" Nancy asks me. "It's not that funny."

"It is. It is." I have to hold my nose to stop. "Can we just sit down?"

Chester seems relieved, especially since once again we've drawn the attention of his other patrons. "Yes. And how about a champagne for each of you—on me."

"Actually," says Deb, "a coffee would be fine."

"Me too," says Nancy. "Decaf, please.

To me the champagne sounded pretty good, but I go along with their choices and vote for coffee.

"No cakes to go with your coffee?" Chester asks. "We have a triple-layer chocolate raspberry torte, a bouche de nöelle, an almond tart, and, the specialty of the Willoughby, a lemon poppyseed cake with orange glaze. All on the house, of course."

It is tempting, and we've *so* earned it. Then again, we've learned to reward ourselves in other ways besides food, right? I should hope so, because I just plunked a ton of dough rewarding myself at Ann Taylor. "No thanks," we say in a unison that is so earnest, we break into a fresh round of laughter.

After Chester leaves, I say, "We should have ordered something. I mean, wasn't that the plan?"

"I think we got our message across. We're done," Nancy says. "Besides, dessert didn't really appeal to me. Like the saying goes, nothing tastes as good as thin feels."

Deb adds. "And it's getting late. I can only stay five minutes if I'm going to make my four p.m. hair appointment."

"You're getting your hair done today? It'll be a zoo." I check my bags to make sure I still have the thongs.

"Not like I have any choice. What am I supposed to do, go to the Stanton party with my hair like this? Nancy's lucky, getting her stylist to come to her house."

Suddenly, everything goes silent—except for the *thud* of Nancy's Ferragamo boot kicking Deb under the table.

"You're going to David's party?" I ask, odd prickles running up my back.

"Oh, Deb," Nancy says with a sigh. "You are such a Sagittarius."

"I thought she knew," Deb says.

"Knew what?" Though I don't have to ask, because I am well aware of how stingy and nasty Lori DiGrigio is. She purposely invited my two best friends and not me to rub salt in my wounds, though when I rant about this, I sound like some crazed conspiracy theorist. "It's all Lori's doing, isn't it? She hates me."

"You had nothing to do with it. Lori probably doesn't even know we're coming," Deb calmly explains. "Paul got invited because he heads Princeton's largest software design firm. So he's taking me and Nancy's going with Ron."

"It's an ACLU thing," Nancy says. "Ron's the president, and I guess civil rights is a big Stanton cause."

"In fact"—Deb glances at her watch—"I have to go—now. I've got to pick up Dylan from his friend's house and get the kids' stuff together before I drop them off at Paul's mother's and get to my appointment."

"Me too," Nancy adds, pulling at a strand of hair. "Sheila's coming to my house, and with this traffic I don't want to be late. Could you imagine if I stood her up?" She pushes back her chair. "Sorry, Nola."

"That's OK," I chirp. "Fine. No, really. I've got to go too."

"You do?" Deb asks incredulously.

"Yes. Absolutely. Oh, dear." I make a big production out of checking my watch as well. Then, out of nowhere, I stupidly say, "Belinda's arriving at JFK this evening, and I've got to drive up there and get her."

Deb smiles eagerly. "That'll be exciting. Have you ever met her before?"

This is getting worse and worse, the lying. "Uh . . . not actually."

"She's coming to David Stanton's party, right?" Deb says. "That's the rumor."

"I don't know. . . ."

But Deb is too excited to pay attention. "Because I'd love to thank her in person, for that column she wrote that got us started on the Cinderella Pact. I've been thinking about her all day."

"She knows," I say.

"I hope so," says Nancy, kissing me on the cheek. "Have fun with her, OK?"

"OK."

My friends leave just when Chester arrives with the coffee. "I've reconsidered," I tell him. "I'd like a slice of lemon cake, please. And this time, you can hold the other two forks. I want it all to myself."

Turning off Nassau Street, I pull my coat tighter against the damp December breeze as I trudge home in the dark to my apartment where I will spend the rest of the night alone. It might be my imagination, but it seems as though every one of my neighbors is getting ready to go out for a holiday party.

Cars are warming up in driveways and a husband is

barking to his wife to get ready. One mother is giving firm instructions to a babysitter at the front door, the sound of shouting kids echoing behind her. There is a woman silhouetted in a bedroom window, brushing her hair and another is shrugging into a fur coat.

And me? Well, I've got Otis, who is perched on the windowsill of my bathroom, meowing to me as I climb the front steps.

I tiptoe quietly, but my stealth abilities are no match for Bitsy's CIA-trained ears. "I'm glad I caught you!" she says, opening the front door. She is dressed in a full-length black sequined dress. "A man stopped by to see you. He was carrying a big package. He looked trustworthy, so I let him in."

A strange man. What could a strange man be doing in my apartment, and why would Bitsy, who suspects the mailman of thirty years, have let him in?

"Who was it?"

"Never seen him before. He said he was dropping off another gift for Eileen's wedding. You know, your apartment is getting crammed with her junk."

"Oh." My heart sinks. Just when I thought a surprise was waiting for me, I find it is but another silver plate or wine goblet or Irish linen tablecloth for my sister, who will be married one week from today. Mom doesn't want the stuff filling up her house, not with all the wedding preparations going on, and since Eileen is in the middle of a move to the new condo that she and Jim bought, the obvious option is to stash her wedding presents in my apartment.

After all, it's not like I've got a life.

I thank Bitsy, who tells me she's going out to dinner at the Nassau Inn with a man she's had her hooks into from the historical society before they head over to the Stanton gala.

"Aren't you going?"

"As a matter of fact, no. I've got other obligations."

"That's too bad," says Bitsy with pity. "I can't imagine what could be more important than a party being thrown by your own publisher."

Somehow I can't bear to tell her that I haven't been invited.

Thankfully her phone rings and Bitsy rushes off. I climb the stairs and contemplate moving myself—maybe to Timbuktu, where they've never heard of David Stanton III or Belinda Apple. I could start over, edit a small newspaper perhaps or raise man-eating house cats. Yes, it wouldn't be so bad. I'm still young, right?

Meanwhile, all I will have to do is get through this night. I will find those earplugs I bought when they were doing construction outside my apartment so I won't have to listen to Bitsy coming home late, laughing and singing. I have a good book to read. Some hot chocolate. A movie on TV. Yes, I'll make it just fine.

But I'm not just fine when I slip the key into the door. Something about the sound of metal against metal feels so lonely, especially knowing that on the other side no one is waiting for me.

A big teardrop lands on my wrist. I quickly wipe it off. Then another takes its place.

Just get inside, and you can cry all you want, my inner voice scolds.

Pushing open the door, I am in full sob, tossing my bags ahead of me and running to the couch, where I bury my head into a pillow. Otis, immediately sensing distress, leaps in from the window and lands on me. Hissing.

Hissing? Otis never hisses at me.

"Nola?" A man's voice is soft above me. It must be God, I think. Who knew God had a British accent?

"C'mon, luv, enough of that."

I look up, my tears and the darkness of my apartment blurring the vision in front of me. In the glow of the streetlight outside, I can faintly make out a shimmering sight. Is it satin or is it silk? A ghost?

Then my table light flicks on, and I see it is Nigel Barnes.

"Cheer up. We can't have tears on the night of your coming-out party, can we Belinda?"

"What?!" He called me Belinda. Perhaps I'm dreaming. "What do you mean, 'Belinda'? And what are you doing in my apartment, Nigel?"

"Come off it." He's still grinning as he perches himself on the arm of my couch. "I couldn't let this charade go on much longer, not with you locked up alone while your alter ego is in so much of a demand. You're coming to Stanton's tonight, and you're going to be my date. Didn't I tell you I'd do anything to walk through the door with Belinda Apple on my arm?"

I am too awed to speak or even breathe. Nigel Barnes knows. And from the looks of his devilish grin, he has known for quite some time.

"But . . . how . . . ?"

"We can discuss that later. Right now we have too much to do to get ready. Look at you! Your hair is completely the wrong color, and I've been through your closet. You haven't a thing to wear. Which is why I took the liberty."

I watch stupidly as Nigel enters my bedroom and returns holding a long, shimmering champagne-colored evening gown. The exact same gown I'd been admiring in the window of Ann Taylor less than an hour before. It can't be, but it is.

"Like it?" he asks

"Yes . . . I—I saw it and . . ."

"I know. The saleslady told me you were salivating over it. Quite a mate you've got there, by the way. Now, get up. Gordon is waiting at Salon Salon to spice up that mousy-brown mane of yours, and we have to hurry. We're already late."

I am giddy. This can't be happening. I am actually going to the gala with Nigel Barnes. I am going in a floor-length Ann Taylor silk gown after being made over by none other than the most famous stylist in Princeton.

I can't help but think that this wouldn't have happened six months ago. Never would I have been able to fit into an Ann Taylor gown. Nor would a man be able to waltz in, talk to a clerk who knew me, and buy it off the rack as a gift—as though I were Audrey Hepburn or something.

It was worth it. The months of dieting. The exercise. It was all worth it just so I didn't have to say to Nigel, "I'm sorry. But there's no way I can squeeze into that. Perhaps a pair of black pants . . ."

"It's like I really am Cinderella," I say dreamily as Nigel leads me out the door.

"Yes. But if you call me your fairy godmother once, just once, then I turn you into a pumpkin and I never turn you back."

Chapter Thirty-Seven

My dreams of being Cinderella cannot compare to the real thing. I know it's supposed to be the opposite, that no reality can match our sweet imagination, to paraphrase Paul Simon, but honestly, this evening is sparkling and surreal.

Though it didn't start out that way. I mean, we arrive at Salon Salon, my dress and makeup in tow, and find it is dark. Closed down for the night.

"Oh, no," I wail. "We're too late."

"Never fear," Nigel says, pulling out his cell. He engages in a brief conversation while I rub my hands together, trying to keep warm. The clock on Nassau Street says it's quarter past eight, and the party is already underway.

Like magic, the door opens and there is Gordon in a black T-shirt and white jeans. I'm ushered in, Gordon looks around, shuts the door, locks it, and pulls down the shades.

"If they know I'm in business, they'll be demanding to be let in," he says. "Now, where's that photo you showed me earlier."

I say nothing as Nigel pulls out Belinda's photo from *Sass!* and the two men consult. Gordon is tall, fit in a kind of—oh, I might as well just say it—gay-revue kind of way. It crosses my mind that, hey, maybe Nigel is gay, and that this is why he so easily agreed to be attached to Belinda in the tabloids. But I'm not about to ask. I am none too eager to be turned into a pumpkin.

"All right. I've got just the color. Come on, sweet-heart. Where are you going with your coat on, already?" Gordon helps me off with my coat and leads me over to his chair. In a few minutes he comes back, stirring chemicals in a bowl "You know, I never would have agreed to this if it hadn't been for Nigel. I've had a crush on him for years!"

I laugh as Nigel rolls his eyes, though he can't help but smile, too. Meanwhile, Gordon is rapidly painting my hair with pinkish goo and wrapping the hair sections in foil.

"Gordon lives next door to me, and that's it," Nigel whispers. "Just in case you're wondering."

"Listen, don't let his stiff British demeanor fool you. Nigel can really let it all hang out when he wants to."

369

I raise an inquiring eyebrow at Nigel, who tells me to ignore everything Gordon says, that he is an incurable flirt.

"OK. I'm putting you under the dryer for five and then I'll check on you. You want me to get you something, hon? Coffee? Tea? Tequila?"

"Tequila," says Nigel.

"Oh, you." Gordon slaps him playfully and takes me to the dryer.

They are the fastest highlights I've ever had, and the most luxurious. In an hour's time I have been transformed into a stunning, sultry redhead. Auburn with deep red tones. Exactly like Belinda. Gordon then lifts my hair and wraps it into a glamorous French twist, tacking down the ends with petite rhinestone clips.

"Now, let me see what I can do. Makeup's not really my bag." But that is a total lie. Studying the photo, Gordon arches my brows with pencil, darkens my lids, and makes my eyes sparkle. My skin is flawless. My lips are full and russet. Extremely kissable, if I do say so myself.

"You've done it. You're a master," Nigel says. "Now, my ersatz Belinda, if you just step into the dress, I'll bring the car around."

"Wait!" Gordon screams. "What about her shoes? Cinderella needs her glass slippers."

"Don't worry. Got 'em covered."

When I step out of Gordon's back office, I catch sight of myself in the mirror and gasp. I have never seen this woman before except, maybe, between the covers of *Sass!* My upper arms are more toned than my bathroom mirror had led me to believe, the every-other-day weightlifting regimen finally paying off. I am actually not embarrassed to be in a strapless dress. In fact, I—I can't believe I'm saying this—I like it!

The bodice hugs my chest and fits perfectly at the waist, which is flattered by the satin bows. And with my newly red hair, the cream silk makes me luminescent. It's a dream. A dream I've treasured since childhood—to become a princess. It makes up for all the proms and dances and society balls I've never been invited to.

"Well, look at you," Gordon says. "Miss All Dressed Up and Ready to Party. No. No. Don't cry. That mascara's not waterproof, honey."

I blink to keep from crying until Nigel walks in with a blast of cold. He is in a tux, a real tux, with a white silk scarf. I've never seen a man so handsome.

"Nigel!" I exclaim. "You can really clean up."

"Can't he? Ohmigod." Gordon feigns a heart attack. "Hold me back."

"And for the final touch? I do believe these are Belinda's slippers."

He is holding up a pair of very famous, rhinestone-studded pink cowboy boots, which of course, fit like a dream.

The Stanton mansion is so lit up with candles and lights that the glow from its windows extends down the long driveway lined by dark, bare oaks.

"How did you know I was Belinda?" I ask Nigel as we wait in his car until other partiers have stepped inside. Nigel has sent word ahead that Belinda Apple is arriving, to build buzz.

"Your columns. They were written by someone pretending to be a Brit. I mean, what kind of colloquial dictionary were you using? It was as though you were going out of your way to write things like 'bangers' instead of 'sausages' and 'motorway' instead of 'freeway.' "

"There is a book, actually."

"Burn it. It's terrible. Then, when I met you, I saw the similarities. I heard about the scandal, did my own snooping around, and had pretty much resolved it was you. Of course, when you told me about your idea for a movie script about a fat girl posing as a thin British girl well . . . it was obvious, wasn't it?"

I smile in the dark. I've become very fond of Nigel, whom I once considered a pompous braggart and a fattie biggot. "So, why are you doing all this for me?"

"Mostly because I like you. You are funny and bright and too good for that rag you work for. Also because I feel tremendously guilty about what I wrote Belinda—a note you must have read."

"That said I was big-boned and you couldn't stand fatties."

"That's the one. But let me ask you, did you ever analyze what made me so afraid to be near fat people?"

I mull this over. "Because you had a big British

372

nanny who threatened to sit on you?"

Nigel laughs. "Oh, come on, Belinda. You can do better than that. Who hates fat people the most?"

And then it hits me. "Because you were once fat yourself."

"Huuuge," Nigel says, holding out his arms to show how big.

"But you're so thin!"

"Not always. I spent most of my youth holed up in my room, listening to music and hiding from the world. Don't you know that about rock critics? We were all once upon a time loser teenagers."

"No. I didn't know."

"Then I went to university and started to slim down. Of course, you spend your nights going to the Palladium, snorting coke and smoking cigarettes until three, and you'll find your weight drops."

"Nigel," I say in a reproving tone.

"The coke is gone, and I'm cutting down on the fags, promise." He peers out the window. "It's been fifteen minutes. By now you'll have quite a crowd gathered. Ready?"

"Wait." I put a hand on my arm to stop him. "You've been so wonderful to me. I have to know. Are you looking for something between us?"

Smiling gently, Nigel leans over and kisses me sweetly on the cheek. "I am madly, deeply in love with you, my dear Nola. But I'm afraid there already is something between us. And he's right in there."

I give his arm a firm squeeze and, mindful of

Gordon's mascara warning, resolve not to cry as Nigel pulls up to the valet and we get out, ready to meet whatever awaits us as Nigel Barnes and Belinda Apple—the party's celebrity couple.

Nigel's right. There is a small crowd gathered as we enter the grand marble foyer. The air is filled with the sound of a string quartet playing Bach, along with merry conversation and glasses clinking as waiters and waitresses spin by carrying large silver platters of hors d'ouevres. I drink in the deep, Christmasy aromas of freshly cut pine boughs and woodsmoke.

It's not until the brass quartet switches to a rousing rendition of "Rule Britannia" that I realize all eyes are on us. I falter, and Nigel grips my arm tighter.

As we pass by, I nod to Governor Christy Todd Whitman, who points me out to Governor Thomas Keane, a large, affable fellow with a plaid cummerbund. I may be wrong, but I think that was former Governor Jim McGreevy in the corner. Is he trying to pick up Bruce Springsteen?

"You're doing fine," Nigel assures me quietly. "Keep your head up, your lips in a smile, and don't forget the emperor who had no clothes."

"The emperor who had no clothes," I reply, spying Lori's black coif bobbing up and down, trying to get a closer, better glimpse of Belinda. "What do you mean?"

"If they believe you are Belinda and you believe you are Belinda then, voilà, you're Belinda," he says. "Just hope and pray there's no snotty kid to rat you out."

Around us I catch faint whispers of: "Belinda Apple! . . . She's gorgeous. . . . So much taller than I thought she'd be. . . . They make such a lovely couple. . . . Don't you just love the British? . . . Is it true that they're engaged?"

Yet there's just one person I'm looking for. One man I desperately want to see. Where is he?

"Hey, Belinda!" I turn to find myself face-to-face with none other than Alicia, Lori's evil—but fortunately daft—assistant. She is wearing a slinky red dress, the straps of which keep sliding off her slumped shoulders, and she shakes my hand limply, not recognizing me one bit. "I just want to tell you that I so like your columns. Also, thanks writing back to Works for the Worst Boss Ever." She winks. "I've got my résumés out now, thanks to you."

Excellent. It is the best news I've heard all week.

I'm about to tell her so when I see Nancy and Ron by a baby grand piano. Ron looks at me and does a double-take.

"Uh-oh," I say to Nigel. "I think I've just been spotted by the snotty kid."

"Not to worry, my dear. I will execute Plan B. In here." With apologies to Alicia, Nigel yanks me into a room of glass walls, illuminated only by tiny lights around its edges. "The conservatory. Every nouveau riche house has one."

"It's not nouveau riche. It goes back to the nineteenth century."

"Exactly." He glances behind his shoulder. "You wait here. Stare out at the falling snow or something. Look diaphanous."

"Where are you going?"

"To get your host . . ." He holds up a finger. "Don't say it. I'm not kidding about that pumpkin threat."

He leaves and I stand with my hands behind my back, trying to act like an unapproachable celebrity who very much wants to be left alone. I can sense people milling around behind me.

"Miss Apple?" A woman who, thankfully, I've never met comes up to me holding a cocktail napkin and a pen. "Would you mind signing this? I am such a fan of your column."

"No problem," I say, completely forgetting my British accent.

"I thought your answer to Split My Pants in Bayonne was hysterical. I split my pants once in public and nearly died. Scotch tape is a great idea."

I'd like to tell her this is based on a true story. My own true story, but I don't dare. Instead I sign *Belinda Apple* with a flourish, say thank you, and go back to the window.

"I think she doesn't want to be bothered," my fan informs the rest of the group.

They leave, and it is getting cold and I worry that before Nigel can snare Chip, Alicia will remember who I am or Deb will rush to thank me and that'll be the end of my night. All I want is two minutes, a minute maybe, alone with him so I can hear him say

376

the words that he's written only to Belinda.

That he is falling in love with me.

"Belinda?"

There is a light touch at my shoulder, and I turn cautiously.

I have to keep myself from saying his name, though I want to desperately. To think that this was once the truck-driving guy I passed off as a computer geek. In his own tux he is even more handsome than Nigel, and the white bow tie at his throat makes him sexier too, if indeed that is possible. He smells faintly of a subtle cologne that Olivia probably purchased for him.

Olivia. She must be here somewhere. Does she know I've arrived? Will I have to meet her? I don't want to. I just want him for one minute like this in the darkened conservatory under the tiny twinkling white lights. Just us and no one else. My miniature fairy tale to hold in my heart, to take out and read when I'm alone years from now.

"Belinda," he says again. "I'm so glad you came. We finally meet."

"David?" I pretend. "Thank you for inviting me." I don't even try to fake the British accent.

"You look stunning."

"As do you."

"My God," he says, seemingly speechless. "I had no idea you were so . . . beautiful."

We're silent suddenly. And then the string quartet in the next room, launches into "Baby It's Cold Outside," the sultriest Christmas song ever.

"Care to dance?" he says, taking my hand.

"I'd love to."

Which is when he brings me to him and we sway together drifting as if on air, spinning around the conservatory, the tiny white lights like little stars, blinking on the winter's eve.

"I'm afraid we don't have much privacy," he whispers. "Everyone's watching us."

"Including . . . Olivia?"

"I would assume. Listen, I need to see you alone. Not like this. How about—"

"I can't."

"Then later."

"No. . . . It won't work."

"Are you going away?"

"Yes."

"For how long?"

"Maybe forever."

"But there's the wedding. . . ."

"I may have to miss it," I say. "Nola will take my place. She should be the maid of honor anyway."

"Ah," he says. "Nola."

"I came here to help you," I say as he leads me dangerously to the brightly lit room where other couples, including Nancy and Ron, are dancing. "Tell me what you've decided. Is it Olivia or Nola? And please be honest."

He pauses and I don't dare look at him. If I do, I know it'll be I who will have to be honest with him and I cannot risk that right now.

"Interesting choice of words," he says. "*I,* for one, am always honest."

"I mean about"—I bite my lip, scared to say the words—"whom you love."

"I can only love a woman who is honest with me, and that is not Nola. How can I truly love a woman who doesn't trust me enough to confide her deepest secret?"

Hesitantly I meet his gaze, which, in the warm light of the party, is piercing and yet full of longing. Desire surges through me. It's almost a force as strong as the fear that is gripping me at the same time. I had never known it was possible to so love another person.

Chip reaches out and strokes my cheek with tender affection. "It's OK."

"You don't understand." My heart is fluttering.

"I do. Better than you think."

"I need to go."

"Don't. I have to talk to you. I have to be with you."

There is a murmur behind us as a group of women marches in, led by a large maid. One of the women I've never seen before, though I surmise that this regal brunette in a multicolored, body-hugging sequined gown must be Olivia. The other two I know all too well. Alicia and . . .

Oh, God. Lori DiGrigio.

"Where is she?" Lori is shouting.

"Don't worry about her," Chip says. "She won't try anything as long as I'm here."

"It's not Lori I'm worried about," I say earnestly. "It's Olivia."

"Olivia?" Chip stops dancing. "Do you really want to meet her?"

"I, uh . . . I." No, I'd like to say. Not exactly. I'd like to do anything but.

"Then you will." Turning to the three women he says, "Olivia? There's someone I'd like to introduce you to."

Cautiously I allow my gaze to meet Lori's. Her mouth is gaping so wide her lips have disappeared and her body is swaying slightly. Her eyes seem to be swimming. The tall woman bends down to inquire if there is something the matter. The tall woman who is Olivia.

Except . . . why is the maid coming forward?

Chip reaches out and takes her hand. "Olivia. This is the woman I was telling you about. Um, she calls herself Belinda Apple."

"Pleased to meet you," Olivia says, her large moon-face breaking into a broad grin. "I read you every week."

Thickly, I understand and feel both relieved, extraordinarily happy, and downright pissed.

"Olivia has been with our family since I was sixteen. Apparently she won't hear of leaving me, even though she hates Jersey. Now, that's true love, don't you think?"

I've been played.

I look up to see Chip laughing so hard that the wrinkles at the corners of his eyes are practically ruts. He's known all along. He knew from the get-go that I was

Nola and Nola was Belinda, and he turned the tables on me. Here I fell for his scam and thought he was in love with Olivia.

Then it crosses my mind. What if he never loved me? What if he just wanted to out me as Belinda? And this was how he did it. For all I know this whole party was one elaborate ruse too. Did Lori know?

Suddenly, I am drowning in confusion. Everyone is staring at me. Chip is asking me something but I can't hear what he's saying.

Over by the stairs, I see Nigel waving his keys in rescue.

Flee, a voice in my head urges. *Run. Run as fast as you can!*

No. Not yet. First I have to know once and for all if Chip's declarations of love were real. Or if, like his game with Olivia, it was all a tease.

Summoning all my courage, I boldly throw my arms around his neck and plant on his lips the most fantastic kiss I can imagine. For eternity, the craziness around us disappears as he puts his arms around me and pulls me tight, not willing to let me go. I swear that if no man ever kisses me ever again, I will never care because I have been kissed like this.

"Don't go," he says when we finally break apart. "Stay."

"I can't," I say, pushing back. "Not until you decide whether you can live with the truth, that I've been lying to you all this time. And if you can find it in your heart to love me, still."

381

And then, not waiting for an answer, I run as fast as I can to the safety of Nigel.

Chapter Thirty-Eight

Don't even ask me what happened next, because I don't remember. Well, not everything. Nigel kindly took me home, but when we pulled up to my apartment it occurred to me that Bitsy might be the type to lead a group back to my house where she would tell everyone that she knew all along that I was the real Belinda Apple and did they want to go upstairs and have a look for themselves?

"I have an idea," Nigel suggested when he saw me staring at my house in utter terror. "How about we go back to my place? We'll order in Chinese and you can, you know, hang out as you Americans say. It so happens that I have wonderful tranquilizers at my fingertips."

In case you are getting the idea that martinis and Chinese food in Nigel's artfully decorated loft led to something more, then you should know that for most of the evening I vented while Nigel drank and ate sparingly of his kung pao chicken.

Finally, tired and worn from listening to me recite for the seventeenth time, " 'Oh what a tangled web we weave when first we practice to deceive,' " and arguing over whether that was Shakespeare or Sir Walter Scott, Nigel popped me one of his Valiums, and I promptly passed out.

The next morning I slipped back home before dawn (still in my Ann Taylor, no less) and composed my resignation letter.

To:david.stanton@sassmag.com
From:nola.devlin@sassmag.com
Re: My resignation

Dear Mr. Stanton:
I hope you will consider this e-mail to be my notice of resignation, to spare you the task of outing the "skunk" you now know is me.

In addition, for reasons that are obvious to you, I am happy to say that Belinda Apple is entering retirement. I'm sure you'll have no problem finding a suitable replacement, since it appears that everyone has a much better grip on ethics than I.

It is with a heavy and sad heart that I am resigning. I wish everyone at *Sass!* the best success ever and thank them truly for the wonderful years we worked together.

Sadly,
Nola

cc:lori.digrigio@sassmag.com (prison camp overseer)

With a flourish, I pressed Send and shut down my

computer, resolving not to check it again until the new year. Then I wrapped my Christmas gifts, threw my new clothes into a suitcase and Otis into a cat carrier, grabbed my bridesmaid's dress, and headed to my parents'—the haven of comfort food and uncomplicated living.

I was halfway there when I pulled a U-turn, came home, and yanked the line on my answering machine to spare myself Lori's angry calls.

Christmas passed without merit, as though Christ's birthday was insignificant compared to whether enough poinsettias had been ordered for the reception and whether the organist knew how to play "Whiter Shade of Pale" (a prank my cousins and I were planning to play on Eileen).

Throughout it all, I ate too many cookies and drank too much wine, sure signs that I was a nervous wreck. On Christmas Day, a day I'm normally up at first light, I slept in until my mother woke me at nine, insisting I go to church, where I sang "O Come All Ye Faithful" tepidly.

As each day progressed with no word from Chip, I felt more and more numb, as though I was going through the motions of living. For the most part it was an out-of-body experience. It was as though I was looking down on myself. There I was, trimming the tree. There I was, cooking roast beef for Christmas dinner. There was Eileen, opening her stocking and Mom opening her present (a bread maker) from Dad.

And there I was, smiling, raising toasts, dressing in

384

my fantastic new wardrobe, and kissing people on the cheek, pretending everything was normal when inside I was certain that my soul had shriveled and died.

People complimented me on my new figure and said rather obnoxious things like how now that I've lost weight, maybe I might find a man like Eileen. I smiled and delivered my standard reply: "Hey, you never know!"

Fake it, I told myself. *Fake it until it feels real.*

My parents had no idea about the Belinda Apple debacle at the big Stanton holiday gala, much to my relief. The only people around me who knew were Nancy and Deb, who called me the day after to ask what had happened, since there were so many rumors flying around the party that no one could tell what was what. I begged off, explaining that I knew as much as they did.

And then today, the day before Eileen's wedding, when I am hanging up pine boughs in Barnard Hall, a miracle happens. Eileen's wedding planner, Helen Whittingham, engages me in a bit of gossip.

"Did you happen to hear about the big scene at the Stanton holiday ball?" Helen asks as she fastens a big red bow on a wreath over the fireplace.

"Uh, not much." I pick up another bough and try to act preoccupied as though tying up boughs is one step down from neurosurgery.

"I was certain you would, seeing as how you're Belinda's closest friend here."

"No. I'm afraid not."

"Well, it was the most romantic thing ever."

I give the string around the bough a good hard tug.

"Belinda Apple arrived at the party with Nigel Barnes and ended up in the arms of David Stanton."

"Really?" Another hard tug. My heart is beating fast. I'm dying to hear more.

"Apparently it was love at first sight. David's mad for her. Isn't that a riot? A grown man in his thirties falling head over heels after one kiss."

I grip the banister and catch my breath.

"Are you OK? I know, tying up those boughs is harder than people think."

"No," I squeak. "I'm fine. Just tired, from the holidays."

"Yes," says Helen, standing back to admire her work.

"So," I manage, "what happened between the two of them?"

"Well, that's the mystery, isn't it? Belinda ran off and David can't find her. He even called me up this morning and asked if I'd seen her, but I told him that she'd dropped out as maid of honor and flown back to England."

"And what did he say to that?"

"He said what I expected him to say." Helen pulls out a gold ribbon with a flourish. "He's taking the next flight to London to find her."

Our very last fitting is that afternoon. We are doing this at the insistence of Eileen, who is on a mission to wed as a toothpick. Our cousins Angela and Maureen who are, as my mother likes to say, from "the hefty side" of the family, decline this last fitting on the premise that their dresses are just fine, thank you. Jim's sister Grace (as in under pressure) and Hope (as in let's hope Jim gets a real personality) are flying in from St. Louis and Oklahoma City, respectively, which means that the only two members in the wedding party in Chloe's shop are Eileen and me.

Disaster strikes as soon as Eileen steps into her dress and asks me to zip her up. I bring the zipper halfway up and it stops.

"What's wrong?" she asks in a panic. "What's wrong?"

"It's uh, stuck," I say. Though, what I really mean is, "You've put on a few, Eileen."

"Stuck?!"

Chloe, who has a roomful of two brides and a bazillion chattering bridesmaids and mothers next door, is so attuned to this horrified cry that she comes rushing in without being asked. "What do you mean, stuck?"

"Try it." I step back and let Chloe exercise her expertise.

"Oh, my," she says, careful not to force it. "I am glad you tried this on."

"Why? Is it OK? It's not ruined or anything, is it?" Eileen's constant state of normalcy these days is Defcon 5. It's impossible that she is gaining weight.

A strange expression comes over Chloe's face. "May I ask you a delicate question?"

She doesn't even have to ask. I already know, and so does Eileen because she is blushing scarlet.

"Yes," Eileen whispers. "Three months."

I just start laughing. I can't help it. Perfect Eileen who has starved herself to get down to a size 0 for her wedding can't help gaining weight this time. This is why I love life. You come for the love, you stay for the irony.

Eileen whirls around on me. "Don't tell Mom!"

"What? You don't think she won't figure it out?"

"Not until after the wedding."

"I got news for you. How old am I?"

"What's that got to do with anything?"

Think about it.

She lifts her eyes to the ceiling. "Thirty-five."

"And how long have Mom and Dad been married?"

"Thirty-six years."

"Do the math. Mom may have been a hundred and twenty-seven pounds when she got married, but she didn't get fat because of her desserts, as she likes to say. She got fat because of me."

"Oh!" Eileen blinks. "Do you think . . ."

"Do I think you'll become a mother who serves up meatloaf and mashed potatoes every night? No. You don't have to worry. You'll be fine. You'll be your old self by this time next year. Only, you'll be a bit more busy."

With that, Eileen bursts out crying and falls off the dais, hugging me. "You don't know how worried I've been. I've been sick about it." Chloe, the queen of tact, politely backs out of the dressing room to attend to her other clients.

"Why?" I say, patting down her hair. "It's perfectly natural, Eileen. Besides, you're in your thirties. You've got money. And you love him."

But Eileen is sobbing and I understand it all. I understand why she's been so pale and bitchy and out of sorts. "Does Jim know?" I ask gently.

Eileen lifts her blotched face. "No."

"Why not?"

"I wasn't sure how he'd react. You know how weird men can be about pregnancy. You have to ease them into responsibility. Marriage plus a baby is an awful lot at once."

"Jim seems pretty mature. Why don't you tell him right now?"

"I don't know. That's, that's"—Eileen hiccups as she talks—"that's what I was going to ask Belinda. That's why I wanted her to be here. She's the ethical expert. She'd have known what to do."

"Eileen," I say, sitting her on a chair. "*I'm* Belinda."

Eileen wipes away the tears with the back of her hand. "What?"

"I'm Belinda. I've always been. I pretended to be her so I could write a column at *Sass!*"

"You're just saying that so I won't throw one of my tantrums."

"No, I'm not. It's true."

It takes a few seconds for my sister to comprehend this. And it's not until I explain about the accent, the cell phones, and all the rest that she finally catches on. "Does Mom know?"

"No."

"Who else knows?"

"Only a few people."

"And you told me?"

"I thought it was time you knew. Besides, you're my sister and we've been together a very long time."

Eileen pulls herself together and tries to undo the zipper herself. "Then it wasn't Belinda, it was you who I said those awful things to on my birthday, about you not getting a guy . . ."

"Forget about it." I finish undoing the zipper for her. "That was my fault for pretending."

"No, Nola," she says sincerely, though it's kind of funny because the dress is hanging off her hips. "That was my fault for being a jerk. You've done so many nice things for me, not the least of which is springing for this superexpensive wedding and I've never really appreciated everything you've done. And after all my nastiness . . ."

"Stop, Eileen. It's over. Done with."

"Not for me. I'm going to make it up to you. You just watch. I'm going to knock your socks off, Nola. I am so, so glad you're my maid of honor. I could not have asked for a better sister."

Chapter Thirty-Nine

"I guess we're smarter than you think. We figured it all out about a week ago."

Deb drops this bomb as we are cooling our heels in the upstairs lounge—what some people might call a library—of St. Anne's, waiting for Eileen's wedding to get under way. We can hear the muffled organ playing "Greensleeves" in the nave below, as a December rain falls outside on a damp evening. I have chosen this moment amid oriental rugs, heavy maroon velvet curtains, and musty Bibles to confess to Deb and Nancy that I am, indeed, Belinda Apple.

In other words, to do it before Eileen and her big mouth blab it all over hell's half acre.

I don't know what I expected. Shock, I suppose. Or maybe, selfishly, admiration that I could pull off a scheme so well. At worst, anger that I hadn't told them sooner. Somewhere along the way I must have forgotten that these are two women who have known me since public school and that they probably know me better than I know myself.

"How could you think we wouldn't know?" Nancy asks. "When you said you were picking her up at the airport it was clear you were lying. It just confirmed our suspicions."

I am completely befuddled by this. "So why didn't you say anything?"

"We figured it was your business," Deb says. "If you

391

wanted to keep it a secret we weren't going to pry."

"Though I have to say," Nancy adds, "that seeing you at Stanton's gala took my breath away. I mean, I've never seen you so stunning."

"I wish I'd seen you," Deb says. "I missed everything all because of stupid Paul."

Nancy leans toward me. "They were having a fight. A fight to end all fights."

"I hate to tell you this on your sister's wedding day, Nola, but Paul and I are through. He moved out yesterday, after Christmas."

Even though I knew they were having problems, it's always a shock when couples who have been together as long as Deb and Paul finally break up. "I'm so sorry." I reach out and give her a hug. "I guess Paul won't come around, after all."

Deb heaves her shoulders. "Don't be sorry. It is what it is. Like I told you when you rescued me from the Tiger Tail—and thanks for that, by the way—I had to get down to a normal weight to realize I was no longer in love with Paul. I had settled for someone who would accept me instead of looking for someone I wanted to be with for the rest of my life. I had absolutely no faith that someone would find me loveable."

She doesn't have to say another word. Silently we wrap her in a big hug. Deb cries and says she doesn't want to get makeup on my dress. Nancy tells her to put a cork in it and I am backing away because, hey, I really don't want to get makeup on my dress.

"So this probably is not the best timing, but it seems like I ought to come clean about Ron and me," Nancy says. "You and your sister aren't the only ones hiding a secret. In fact, Eileen's kids could be playmates."

I shoot a glance at her stomach, which is still relatively flat.

"What? I say I'm pregnant, and the first thing you do is eye my gut?"

Deb laughs so hard that tears come out her nose. "That's rich. You, the hard-as-nails lawyer, knocked up after hot sex. I knew you'd turn into the tramp you were born to be once you lost the weight."

"Ain't that the truth," Nancy says. "We've been insatiable. In the bathtub. On the kitchen counter. Think of it. Me. On the kitchen counter."

"No, thanks," Deb says.

"A once holy and sacred spot reserved only for the most holy sacrament of food. Who knew that it's the perfect height for eating—"

"Stop, Nancy," I hush. "We're in a church, for God's sake. You're about to become a mother."

"I hate to bring up a touchy subject, but what about Ron's girlfriend on the side?" Deb asks.

"Ancient history. I don't want to get psychoanalytical or anything, but if there was anyone holding on to the adultery, it was me. I was just so mad at Ron, but also so angry for letting myself get out of control."

That's not much beyond college psych 101, but I let it slide.

There is a knock at the door. Nigel pops his head in.

"I've been sent to find you. Your sister's in hysterics that you might have run away."

"She's always in hysterics." Deb insists on fixing my lipstick. We give each other one last hug before they run down the stairs and into the church.

"Ready?" Nigel holds out his hand.

"As I'll ever be."

"You know, I take a dim view of marriage in general and weddings in particular, but I have to say you might be changing my mind, Nola Devlin," he murmurs as he escorts me down the winding stone steps. "You're such a vision of beauty, I can barely take my eyes off you."

"You'll never change, Nigel. You're not in love. You're just a sucker for redheads in black satin."

"Don't I know it. I'm destined to be cursed with a broken heart." He stops me in the foyer. Ahead of us Eileen is waiting in billowing white on the arm of my father while the bridesmaids ahead of her are tittering nervously. Eileen flashes a strange smile at Nigel.

"By the way, my darling, I am not the only one with a broken heart tonight," he whispers.

I wish he would stop talking and let me get in line. Can't he see the whole wedding pro cession is waiting for me to snap into place?

I turn to tell him so and find that Nigel is gone and that in his place is David Stanton. My heart stops. What the heck is he doing here? Isn't he flying to England to search for Belinda? I don't know what to say. It's so unreal. "What . . . ?"

"You know what I love about weddings," he says, completely unconcerned that the sexton is motioning us to the church. "Being with the one you love while two other souls profess their own love for each other until death do they part."

There is the swelling strains of "Ave Maria." People must be standing, because this is the first processional song. And here is Chip telling me about how much he likes weddings.

"Listen, Chip. We can talk after—"

"I love you," he says.

I study his face, searching for truth.

"Holy Mary, Mother of God, Nola." Dad is getting peeved. "What are we waiting for?"

"Shhh!" Eileen says, nudging him. "Give her a few minutes."

"I'm sorry. I didn't quite catch that," I say.

David takes a deep breath. "Nola, I love you. I came here to tell you that."

"You're sure you mean me and not Belinda?"

"I mean you. Not Belinda."

"And you're not too mad about Belinda?"

"Are you kidding? Not after your sister showed up at my doorstep this morning and told me how and why you came up with Belinda, about Lori not giving you the job until you pretended to be Belinda. I'm wondering if maybe Lori should be seriously demoted. Possibly sued. Anyway, Eileen said that if I loved you, I should come tonight because after this"—he pauses—"there was something crazy about you going into the nunnery, though I know that can't be true. I mean, who goes into a nunnery in the twenty-first century?"

I am speechless. Eileen did that for me? My selfish baby sister on the day of her wedding went to the man I love and pleaded my case? I think of Father Mike's mystical advice, that giving a gift from the heart with no expectations is the font of miracles.

"Nola," Eileen says calmly, "it's time."

Dad throws up his hands. "I'll say. Let's go and get this over with."

"No," says Eileen. "Not for me. For you. It's time for *your* fairy tale to come true. Remember when we were little girls?"

Then I see us with our dress-up box playing Cinderella. We have come full circle. She is right. "And you are the bride," I say.

"And you are the princess." Eileen smiles at Chip. "Who has finally, finally found her prince."

"You OK with that?" I ask Chip.

"Your fantasy is my fantasy, Nola," he says gently. "And you don't know how much I've wanted to make your fantasies come true. You might say it'll drive me mad until I do."

And then he bends and kisses me in such a thoroughly iMax sexy way that the bridesmaids break out in applause and my father lets out a groan loud enough to drown the church bells.

Acknowledgments

I have been overweight since adolescence, so I didn't think there was much anyone could teach me about dieting, losing, maintaining, and gaining it all back again. Boy was I wrong.

In the course of researching this book—and that is no joke—I heard many people willingly share their stories and their knowledge. They are Kim Calabrese, Toni McGee Causey, Stephanie Cotterman, Estelle Jowell, Bonny Kirby, Joni Langevoort, Lisa Sweterlitsch, and Alyson Widen, R.N. Thank you, thank you. I'm so sorry that I was not able to do justice to your very moving experiences.

In addition, I relied heavily on my stints as a past, present, and probably future follower of Weight Watchers. Unlike at Nola's weigh-in, I have never known a "weigher" to shout, *"Drop out!"* Weight Watcher leaders have always been courteous, understanding, and, best of all, discreet.

I must also thank those who have joined our online, weight-loss support group, The Cinderella Pact, a wonderful bunch of people from all over the world. Please stop by http://health.groups.yahoo.com/group/cinderellapact/ for a fun crowd of "losers." Or you can find the link at my Web site: http://www.sarah-strohmeyer.com. Paula Farrell, thanks for the photo ideas.

Nor could this book have seen the light without the

supreme help of my wonderful editor, Julie Doughty, at Dutton, who never flipped out as I slipped in revisions long past their due date. My agent, Heather Schroder, at ICM, also remained calm despite other much more pressing—and miraculous!—events in her life. Thank you, Margot, for filling in and providing lots of laughs during Heather's absence.

There are also three women, three fantastic writers, who hold a very special place in my heart. They are: Harley Jane Kozak, Nancy Martin, and Susan McBride. Together we make up the Lipstick Chronicles, a blog about writing, laundry, life, and all that women's stuff. They are my rock, my support and my buddies. I hope you'll stop by http://thelipstickchronicles.typepad.com/ and see what I mean. They are truly a *Cinderella Pact*.

Finally, thank *you* for reading this book. I'm always interested to hear from readers, so please write me at cinderellapact@aol.com. I look forward to hearing from you.

Center Point Publishing
600 Brooks Road • PO Box 1
Thorndike ME 04986-0001 USA

(207) 568-3717

US & Canada:
1 800 929-9108